BY KIT WHITFIELD

*Benighted*
*In Great Waters*

# IN GREAT WATERS

# IN GREAT WATERS

## KIT WHITFIELD

BALLANTINE BOOKS · NEW YORK

2009 Del Rey Trade Paperback Edition

Published in the United States by Del Rey, an imprint of The Random House Publishing Group, a division of Random House, Inc., New York.

DEL REY is a registered trademark and the Del Rey colophon is a trademark of Random House, Inc.

Originally published in hardcover in the United Kingdom by Jonathan Cape, a division of The Random House Group Limited, in 2009.

ISBN 978-0-345-49165-7

Printed in the United States of America

www.delreybooks.com

2 4 6 8 9 7 5 3 1

Text design by Julie Schroeder

*To my parents*

They that go down to the sea in ships,
that do business in great waters;
these see the works of the Lord,
and his wonders in the deep.
—*Psalm 107*


Man's life is warm, glad, sad, 'twixt loves and graves,
Boundless in hope, honoured with pangs austere,
Heaven-gazing; and his angel-wings he craves:—
The fish is swift, small-needing, vague yet clear,
A cold, sweet, silver life, wrapped in round waves,
Quickened with touches of transporting fear.
—*Leigh Hunt,*
*"The Fish, the Man and the Spirit"*

BOOK ONE

# HENRY

# ONE

HENRY COULD REMEMBER the moment of his birth. Crushing pressure, heat, and then the contact with the sea, terrifyingly cold—but at the same time a release from constriction, the instant freedom of the skin. His mother gathered him up in her arms and swam to the surface, cradling him on her slick breast to lift his head above the water for his first breath. Henry never forgot it, the mouthful of icy air, the waves chopping his skin, a woman's arms holding him up in a world suddenly without warmth.

For the first five years of his life, Henry swam with the tribe. His name was not Henry then, it was something else, a sound best rendered by the word "Whistle." The boy was a slow swimmer. His bifurcated tail was weaker than the strong fins of the other children, leaving him unable to keep up at full speed. Nor could he stay under for as long; even his youngest companions could last half an hour without needing to surface, while Whistle was breathless in half that time. Sometimes the other children would mob him, try to pull him down; usually the adults would pull them off and give their ears a sharp twist. Usually, but not always.

One day, the children surrounded him, pulling at his legs and chattering, *Stranger, stranger.* He called out for his mother. She appeared from the depths and viewed the struggle for a moment. Then, with a twirl of her arms, she twisted in the water, presenting her back to him. Small hands were gripping him, hard nails digging into his limbs, ready to drag him down. Whistle was desperate. He looked again at his mother, but she was floating upright, still not turning to help him. His chest was starting to throb in panic, the air in his lungs shrinking, sucking his chest in. He was going to die.

With the last of his strength, he cried out again: *Shark! Shark!* His mother turned, other adults appeared, grabbing for their children to make a break for it, and the clawed little hands tugging at him broke free as the children fled, leaving Whistle to swim as fast as his legs could propel him to the surface to gasp in the air.

At three, Whistle knew that he was a stranger. The others were stronger than him, but they were also stupid. The predator trick worked more than once. His tribe did not think hard about motivations and could not afford to ignore a possible threat. The adults, he realised, were frightened, frightened continually. Even the smallest risk had to be evaded.

Whistle himself lived with fear, but he could not have put a name to it. He could identify shark, killer whale, poison fish, sharp rock— and he knew the feelings that went with them, a pulse in his chest, a shiver against the chill of the water, a speeding up of things that made everything appear brighter. His mother would clutch his hand and tug it away from a stark-spined creature that otherwise looked like a meal; she would grab him by the arm or the hair and drag him away if a shark burst into view. He saw others taken. When such things occurred, he saw eyes widen on the others' faces, and he felt his chest beat, but this sensation was not something he could have explained, even had his mother done more in the aftermath of a chase than examine each of his limbs for cuts, then turn to carry on swimming. His chest was always tight. His hands could relax, his legs could stop churning the water, but the feeling of looseness and rest was not something that ever reached his chest, and he no more thought it could than he considered trying to see with his feet. Tightness was part of his body. But he would not flee from a threat at someone else's call, not without looking around to see it first for himself.

He was growing, becoming too big for his mother to carry in her wake. She cradled him less, left him to fend for himself more. Fish were difficult to catch. It wasn't hard in theory: as the tribe swam their routes, they rehearsed strategies, singing lessons back and forth among themselves, and Whistle learned the chants easily enough. He understood the method, could remember all the tactics, the different kinds of prey and styles of hunt and changes of attack when opportunities flashed by—but he wasn't as quick as the others. He swam and corralled, heading off shoals as well as his legs would drive him, but seldom managed to grab one before some other tribe member got there first. Always his hopes rose as the tribe rallied together, driving up from below to surround and snatch at a swarming shoal, the fish coiling round and round in a sparkling whirl of bodies that whisked themselves out of his grip—only to have his hand knocked aside by a stronger reach, or, in the moments when he did manage to grab a fish of his own, to have only a few seconds of live, grappling food held tight in his fist before nails were digging in and his prize was pulled away to be eaten before his eyes by a bigger child. When his mother was around, she would share with him, splitting her catch between them, but she was not always there; when other predators caught the sound of the hunt, when marlin or dolphin threatened them for the prize, there would be a fight, the stronger men and women rising up to fight them off. On those occasions, the children would be herded together, one or two women keeping watch on all of them. Injured fish might flop their way, and the women would share what they had with their own children, the children of their sisters—but no matter how much he begged, no gifts ever came into Whistle's hands. For the most part, he lived on crustaceans, teaching himself to break open the shells of these slow, rich-fleshed crawlers. Whistle learned to lever and bend, to slip tools into the chinks and twist, releasing white drifts of meat to stuff into his mouth while he hid behind rocks and under weeds, away from the sharp ears of the tribe. Having learned, he knew he should pass the knowledge on, add it to the tribe's greater store, but he didn't dare. Better to hunt for himself and guard his catches: he was still too small, and the older he grew, the less his mother passed him a share of her own food. If others started beating him to the crabs, he might get nothing to eat at all. Secrecy was not an easy thing to maintain, but though it strained his nerves, he kept his discoveries to himself. It was becoming clear that it might be a choice between secrets and starving.

He was also getting old enough to wonder about the great dark shapes that passed overhead, the ones his mother always kept him away from, even as she grew less and less interested in protecting him. They were a recurrent presence; not every day—not as common as a hunt—but still, familiar. The first time it happened, Whistle remembered for the rest of his life.

A sound preceded it, carrying down from above, steady and unfamiliar. Whistle was used to chirruping voices, the crash of wave against rock, but this muffled, regular drumming was strange and alarming. It sounded like something thudding, but the rhythm was weirdly fast: nothing large enough to make that much noise could be wielded under the water. Whatever it was banging away, it must be horrifically strong. Whistle was already anxious by the time the shape, a great long swell of a thing, cruised overhead—and as it came into view, there was a call from one of the women: *Come here, children. Stay down.* Whistle was uncertain as to whether this meant him; *children* meant the children of the tribe, the guided and cherished and admonished young of other mothers, and it was already becoming clear to him that while he was admonished and guided at times, he was not entirely cherished. The shape above was alarming, streamlined like a shark, but it stayed on the surface like a gull, still making that strange noise: as far as he could see, it had no teeth and did not chase, and that was a novelty. No hunting creature would advertise its presence so loudly. Whistle decided to exclude himself from the category of children and started paddling his way up to where the black shape was driving along, splitting the wind-spackled ceiling and leaving it roiling in its wake.

The hand on his arm appeared faster than any grab he'd ever experienced before: it was his mother, holding him hard, her sharp nails digging into his arm. *No,* she said. *Stay down. Not you. No. No. No.* The line of her body emphasised her words, a stiff, upright pose, conveying the force of her meaning. He'd never heard her sound so fierce, and the grip on his arm was painful. Perhaps the shape was something dangerous after all. Her fingers were hurting him, but Whistle didn't struggle: as long as he was near his mother, perhaps he was safe.

But as she and another woman corralled the children, there was another sound: everyone was starting to chant. The noise was deafening: the water around them rang so hard he could feel the sound buzzing in his tightened chest. Surely this was a risk: whales could call so loud, but this was the tribe, smaller than sharks, smaller than dolphins, fierce when attacked but not so grand that they could afford to call such attention to themselves. Any predator could hear them from miles away. And the call wasn't a challenge, wasn't *Stay away, we are strong,* wasn't a bounce of sound to locate a shoal. It sounded, if anything, like a request. There was a word in it he didn't recognise: *Coming up. Don't drop a*—something. The others swam up and after the shape, chanting over and over not to drop this mysterious something, and when he turned to his mother and said, *Something?*, she merely tugged his arm to keep him down. Whatever the something was, it could not be named.

Whistle's chest clamped. They were calling so loud that any shark could hear them, and the world was turning strange. Nobody had ever refused him a definition before. How could he know not to eat a poison fish or grab an urchin if nobody told him? To stay silent about this mysterious something that everyone so feared was horrifying. It went against all reason, and if it made no sense, how could he know if it was safe?

Little spots were shadowing the corners of his eyes, and his ears were starting to buzz. He needed to breathe; his heart was beating against his empty lungs. He turned to his mother, saying as quietly as he could, *Go up, need air.* But she held him down. The something-droppers were overhead, and she would not let him rise. Whistle's head ached, pulsing, as if his very skull was being sucked down towards the vacuum in his chest, and he pulled against his mother's unyielding grip. He could ill afford the energy, but he was struggling, his body was caving in. He began to whimper, little keening sounds he'd never heard himself make before.

His mother did not look pleased, but after a moment she leaned towards him. Her free hand gripped hard around his jaw, and as she leaned in, Whistle flinched back: was she going to bite him, snatch out his whimpering tongue? But her mouth closed around his, and as her fingers dug into his face, he parted his teeth a little, and his mother exhaled. A stream of warm air flowed down into his lungs. It was thin and weak, but it was air, and his head cleared just a little before she withdrew her cold lips and handed him over to the other woman, making a fast, graceful drive for the surface. Whistle stayed down, an untrusting grip holding his arm, as his mother raced to the surface to breathe, and the dark shape moved on above them.

As the weeks and months passed, Whistle grew more used to the shapes. He grew bigger, and better able to conserve his breath. Sometimes tribe youngsters were taken up for a peek, but never Whistle. He would remain below, dizzy with lack of air, with a firm grip on his wrist holding him down. When they returned from the passing shapes—there was a word for them he learned, *ships,* a word that featured frequently in the chants about which route to take in which season—they would bring food, sometimes great handfuls of it, enough to share freely. It was a good day when a ship sailed overhead. The fish would be plentiful, so much of it that there was no need even to fight over it, and Whistle could eat until his stomach was full, a sensation he never knew at other times. The fish tasted odd, a little stale and lukewarm instead of the chilled, chewy flesh that the hunts caught, but it made a change from scavenged crabmeat. The ships had nothing about them that suggested any kind of threat, and the tribe were always quick to follow when they heard one. Nonetheless, the undefined word, the thing they did not want dropped, preyed on Whistle's mind. It was uncanny and dangerous, living with a mystery, and Whistle, new to the uncanny, decided he did not like it.

It was some way into his fifth year that Whistle's mother took him for a swim on their own. She was obliging, slowing her pace to his, sharing fish she caught rather than letting Whistle stop to search for crabs.

The water around them grew brighter, cloudier, the floor rising up and up, pressing them closer to the surface. The lack of space made Whistle nervous; everything seemed to be shrinking. If he chirruped, sound bounced back at him fast: there were no distances to scan. Something was blocking the echoes. He made to turn around, and found his mother's hand on his arm, dragging him on, faster than before. The floor loomed up beneath them, nearer every moment, and there were suddenly barriers on either side of them, walls of rocks, and then a harsh new sound beat in his ears—for a few yards up ahead, the world gave out, the water thinned to a ragged edge, crashing again and again, dying on the bank.

Whistle found the floor was right up against him, the surface breaking over his back. His mother gave him a shove. His feet felt the pressure of the sand: his eyes saw a vast bank of it, terrifyingly dry beyond the waves. He turned, holding out his arms to his mother, saying, *Move on. Bad place.* She pushed him again, raked her nails across his arm. The push took him into the breakers, and he fell on all fours, unbearably heavy without the water to hold him up. Whistle tried to get into a pleading stance, to beg for her kindness in the posture of appeal, but the air would not support him and he stumbled. He turned again, and received a slash across the chest. His mother waited in the shallows, teeth bared, and lifted a rock in her hand.

Whistle, light-headed with the endless amount of air, turned his back and crawled up the beach, sitting on the wet sand where she could not follow. His mother watched him for a moment, then turned. She had to thrash to free herself from the bank, and then she was gone, swimming fast out to sea.

For two days, Whistle sat in the surf, digging for buried molluscs to eat, hungry, dry, utterly alone. On the evening of the second day, he heard a new sound, a rhythm like the waves, only faster, multiple. A creature appeared: finless, square, four narrow legs pounding upon the beach. On its back sat a man, covered in colours like a crab, but with a face almost like the ones he knew, and, like himself, split down the middle, a leg on either side of this beast. Whistle was afraid of the animal, but he also knew, with the clarity of one who has always been close to the edge of survival, that if he stayed here, he would die. He did not look back at the sea. He drew himself a dizzying lungful of air, reached out his arms, and called.

～

The journey was a long one, and unnerving, but Whistle showed nothing on his face. The man had stared at him, paced to and fro on the sand and stared again. His expressions were not unlike the expressions of people from the tribe, but his square teeth and white-rimmed eyes were distracting. In bulk, he wasn't large, but the air was so thin here and gave no support: Whistle was collapsed on his flexible legs, unable to rise, and this long-boned, upright creature towered over him. In the sea, he'd been small, smaller than other boys his age, but this skinny creature made Whistle feel tiny. Most strange of all was the tint of his skin, a pink-red pale colour like you got in the first few feet of water below the surface, before descent into the depths greyed everything out to shades of blue and green and white. The man himself gasped endlessly for air, inhaling again and again, faster than the waves beating on the shore. Whistle watched the straight limbs of the man as he paced, bizarrely inverted with his body upright as if permanently breaking the surface. Salt was drying on Whistle's skin and itchy sand stuck to him instead of falling away in the water; as he rubbed at them, he saw a shade of colour in his own webbed hands, on his own scratched arms, that was pinker than he had thought, pale, but closer to the pacing being's redness than he had ever seen. It was not his own colour, could not be. This sight was worse than that of the gasping, striding creature before him, and Whistle sat frozen, still sick with oxygen, looking fixedly at his own arms as the man eventually lifted him up and set him atop the large creature. The smell of it was appalling: sensation flooded Whistle, new and horrifying, entirely alien to a nose used only to the mild salt of the sea and the beach, a rank, choking, red-coloured rush that jolted him almost as much as the animal's motion as the man climbed up behind him and jerked them forward.

Whistle sat as still as he could, making no move to grasp the juddering animal, no response to the rumblings of the creature behind him, trapped and bewildered as they took him past the yellow-grey beach, on through fields, through lanes, through woods, stretching on for miles, dazzlingly bright, impossibly green.

~

Whistle was brought to a towering rock, stiff-sided and grey, with a dark entrance like that of a cave. The man lifted him down and tucked him against his side. All of Whistle's instincts were to struggle, but this place was unbearable, and if the man were to drop him, he would be lost on the blinding green ground, stuck on his crumpled fins with no molluscs to dig for, and then he would starve. This man must eat, and possibly would give him food if he begged. So Whistle turned his head aside from the reeking red skin and took a breath, and stayed still in the man's arms, muscles rigid, as a smothering dark thing the man wore over his shoulders was draped over him and the man entered this dim, alien cave. Under the edge of the cloth he could see something grotesque, a stack of rocks, all just as straight-sided as this new edifice, and then the man was jolting Whistle again as he began to climb, stepping up and up. With no sea to cushion him, Whistle's head rocked and bounced on his neck, shaking back and forth until it ached in the empty, thin-sounding air. The movement pressed on his bladder as well, and he released it as he would in the ocean, expecting nothing more than a drift of warm water that would dissipate cleanly into the salty sea. Instead he found scalding rivulets running down his limbs, a stinging sensation over his dry, rasped skin, and a loud exclamation from the deep-voiced stranger, who shook him in disgust. Entirely bewildered, Whistle kept his face turned away. He could think of nothing else to do.

More strides and Whistle found himself in a room with narrow windows and stone walls, straight-sided and smooth to the touch, stacked up against each other in unthinkably neat lines. Regular shapes were not a new sight to Whistle, but he knew only the overlapping half-circles of a fish's scales or the rounded hexagons of a sea urchin, and these four-cornered shapes were threatening: an endless profusion of boxes that dazed his focus with their stiff, enclosing order. At the window, a grim-shaped chink of light, were hard, straight objects in a cold substance he had never seen in the sea, barring him in. It was difficult for him to see beyond them: his sight had trained itself underwater, where distance gave way to haze within ten yards and the distortions of the currents and plankton and salt concealed everything in the blue-green blur. Above the water when he surfaced to breathe he had seen further, but focusing on anything more than ten yards away was an effort that made his head ache and his eyes waver, sometimes distorting his vision for minutes at a time.

Whistle was to stay in this room for a long time. He saw no one but the red man who had brought him from the beach. The confinement was maddening; after ranging over wide miles of sea, free to swim off in every direction, the rigid walls and weighty, earth-bound gravity drove the child to rages of impatience. Left on his own he bit at his hands, struck the walls, pulled and tore at the covers that had been left for him on a straw pallet. Sleep was all but impossible: after the yielding embrace of the water, the hard stone floor bruised him into endless wakefulness. It did not occur to him to use the pallet: its smell and colour were strange, and its four-sided angularity was of a piece with the rest of this room, this tense-cornered world. Instead he worried at it, pricking his hands on the straw, feeling nothing but the same enmity he felt for the walls. Once the covers were in rags, he could heap them up into little nests that gave him some relief from the rigid, cold floors, and into these he would crawl, rocking to and fro, amazed at the speed with which his body could move through this new, forceless substance that surrounded him.

The swiftness of the rocking was the only thing that contained him. Unattended, Whistle launched counter-attacks on the room that seemed so hostile to him, hauling himself from place to place across the floor, but when the sound of footsteps came to the door, he froze, sitting where he was, only rocking a little to keep his attention fixed away from the red man who stood tall over him, shaking his head at the devastation.

With him the man brought objects. Whistle had expected to beg for food, and indeed, the first time the red man appeared, there was something in his hands that he held out to Whistle and, getting no response, lifted to Whistle's mouth, tapping it against his lips. Whistle recoiled, for the substance was hot like urine, and its brown, seaweed colour seemed utterly inedible. The boy held his breath, refusing to smell, already too threatened by the appearance of this stuff he was expected to eat, and carried on rocking, turning his face aside every time the meat was proffered. He was afraid of offending the man, whose posture was so permanently upright that he seemed to be emphasising every sound he made, but he was more afraid of this corrupt-smelling substance.

After that, the man tried a fish. Whistle recognised the shape of it, but the flaking, loose-skinned texture convinced him that the fish was rotten, unsafe to eat, especially in this new environment where excrement stayed where it lay instead of washing away on the tides. The man showed it to him again and again, and Whistle rocked, hunger clamping his stomach, paralysed with indecision. It was many minutes before he came to the conclusion: eat or die. A sore stomach was better than an empty one; better to eat and be ill than starve and be dead. The fish was still in the man's hand, and Whistle had no desire to be close to him, but there was no sign that the man would give it up. He leaned over, took two quick bites, swallowed. His empty stomach immediately convulsed, spewing the food onto the floor. Whistle took another bite, then another. Almost none of the food stayed in his stomach, but he kept on biting until the fish was gone and there was no more hope of nourishment in it.

After a while, the red man took to bringing raw fish. Whistle liked this little better, seeing the limp tails and dull eyes and tasting the beginnings of corruption in their flesh, but he bolted them down. His stomach always ached. The red man stared as the boy took food from his hand, but Whistle never met his gaze. He was too wary of the man's white-rimmed eyes.

Along with food, the man brought other things. One was a pair of sticks, brown and straight. Whistle chewed them when left alone, rattled them along the floor, trying to break them. The clash of them against the stone was the loudest thing he had heard since leaving the sea, but the noise reached his hearing thinly, with none of the vivid, intimate echo of sound carried through water. The red man held the sticks in his own hands, tapping them against the floor and leaning his weight against them, walking to and fro, four-limbed with the sticks as supports, but Whistle did not watch.

The other thing quickly introduced to his room was a flat square framed in some oddly bright gold wood, pink and blue and red in the middle. All he saw of it at first was that it was, like the door and the cupboards and the windows with their blurred green light, four-sided. The man presented it to Whistle and turned his head towards it, trying to get his interest, but, though the bright colours and curved lines within the frame were not unpleasant, Whistle, intimidated by the square shape, struggled and twisted his face from side to side, trying to escape from it. The man persisted for some time before giving up and lifting the object to hang on the wall. Safely away, Whistle squinted at it, but now it was too far away for him to distinguish details. Seeing him squint, the man pointed, and said a word so strange Whistle could hardly process it as speech. He could make out syllables, just about, but they meant nothing to him: Angelica.

# Two

I T WAS ONLY when other individuals started to appear in his doorway that Whistle understood the trouble he was in. One red man
and a prison of lines was dismaying enough, but with unfresh fish to
keep him from starving, it was a little better than oblivion. After a few
days and nights, however, another creature appeared in the doorway.
Its voice was higher pitched than the red man's, a bit closer to the
shrills of home, but its body was incomprehensible: bowed out over
the lower half with huge, rustling fabrics, swollen at the chest like a
tribeswoman but black to the wrists and neck, covered in cloth.
Whistle, still naked and shivering against the stone, tentatively considered that the figure might be female, but this was an uncertain comfort, even if her hands held no rocks and her teeth were sheathed by
pink lips. As the figure approached him and bent down, he froze.
Tribeswomen other than his mother had little liking for him if he
came too close; only in the case of some dire outside threat had women
shown much concern for his life. While he was dimly aware that pin-
ing for his mother was something he could ill afford, the idea of her
lingered in a current of hurt and confusion that he could not swim
against.

Such feelings were only vaguely present at the appearance of this
woman. So strange was her aspect that it was unclear to Whistle
whether she could be considered a person at all. As she stepped nearer,
the swinging bulb overlaying her lower half resolved itself as the same

flexible stuff that was providing him with a little padding against the rock floor, and that was a more definite solace than any action on her part. Whistle reached up his sharp-nailed fingers to tear off some strips, hoping to add to his bedding.

A jump, a shriek, and the creature was back against the wall. The movement had revealed, under the layers of cloth, limbs like the red man's. Whistle froze again, retreating his attention back into himself and rocking to and fro. The swathed woman was like the red man, two of a kind, and that was a disaster. There were more of them.

Warfare was something Whistle had understood almost from birth. Marauding dolphins swam in packs through the sea, strong-tailed and sharp-toothed as the tribe; even when rights of way and shoals of prey were not in dispute there was little mercy between them. A single dolphin was always a creature to attack: Whistle had seen the tribe circle and mass on lone swimmers, biting fins and gouging eyes, raking long scratches with their clawed hands and leaving dark billows of blood drifting through the water. Dolphin meat was not good to eat, and the corpse would be left to sink into the depths for scavengers to swarm on, but no dolphin swimming unprotected was ever ignored. A child of the tribe, found by a troop of dolphins, could expect no greater mercy. Its ravaged body would spiral in a slow descent to the ocean floor, only its tongue and jaw chewed away as a trophy. It was when the tribe encountered dolphins in groups that Whistle's chest tightened the most: the tribe would stiffen, the dolphins would poise, the very water would tense around them as the two bands circled each other, weighing up for combat. Whistle and the other children could only swim around the melee as dark shapes thrashed and struck, churning the water, a teeming mass of shadows slashing and grappling in silent, furious killing; stay out of the fray and keep lookout for other predators homing in, calling alarms and scanning the blood-dimmed water for the sight of their own mothers, watching to see whether they would come out of the war alive.

This was what Whistle understood of other peoples. The dolphins were another kind, strong as the tribe but different in form and language. There was a concept for that in his tribe's speech: *enemy.*

Whistle was isolated, away from the group, surrounded by what could only be another tribe, different in form, different in language. So far they had offered him food, but there was no certainty that this wouldn't change. The boy rocked back and forth, waiting with averted head to see whether this new woman would define him as an enemy.

Rather than point and call, however, the woman raised odd, webless hands to cover her face, and began to make a harsh, throbbing sound. Out of the corner of his eye, Whistle saw with puzzlement that droplets were rolling down her face, out of her eyes. From its motion, falling like beads of brine when a tribesman surfaced for breath, it could only be water. Never had the boy seen such a feat before, and curiosity briefly contended with his fear. The keening continued, and Whistle struggled to think about it. The noise was unfamiliar, but her posture and manner suggested defeat. Perhaps she was not a threat.

Earthbound on his curved legs, Whistle pulled his way across the floor. Catching at her skirt, he made an effort and pulled himself closer to upright. The woman covered her face, cowering back, and Whistle gazed in astonishment at this great creature that flinched away from him with such fear. The water fell faster, and he reached up, yanking her down with more confidence. She tensed again, pulling back, but when the red man made some kind of sound across the room, she stopped, not leaning down but ceasing to retreat. This stillness Whistle understood as submission, and with the authority of a dominant tribesman, not sure how he had come by this position but determined not to relinquish it, he tugged her down and touched the tears falling from her eyes.

The taste of them was familiar, not unlike the sea, though with a meaty undertone that unsettled his stomach. As he tracked them across her face, his sharp nail drew a line across her pink skin, and he stopped, poked again, puzzling at its softness, the way it yielded under his callused finger and split, leaving a thin trail of red at the touch of his nails. His clawing touch made her shiver, and the flow of tears increased; interested, Whistle poked at her cheek, giving rise to still more tears.

At this, the red man strode across the room and grabbed his wrist. The gesture was cautious, but Whistle recognised it from years of being pulled out of danger, away from a passing whale or down out of sight of the dark ships overhead, and he froze again, unwilling to provoke the bringer of food. The man spoke to him in a raised voice that made Whistle struggle with an impulse to cower: "No, Henry."

Whistle froze.

The man reached for the sticks lying on the ground, the latest of a series of repeatedly renewed pairs that Whistle had not yet managed to break, and pushed one into each of the boy's hands.

"Up, Henry," he said, lifting the boy high on his bending, sliding legs.

Whistle staggered, paddling at the floor, falling this way and that. The rapid approach of the ground as he swayed almost drove him to panic, but as the man set him again and again on the sticks, Whistle gripped at them as the only way to keep hold of the man's supporting hands. Sticks were not entirely new; his lifetime of levering flesh from crustaceans had given him an interest in anything that could be used to prise, and as the man pushed them down again and again, the boy began to place them against the floor, levering himself up against the threatening stone.

Finally the hot red hands withdrew, and the boy stood there for a few seconds before the sticks wobbled in his hands and he tumbled down with a jarring crash. The pain of the stones against his knocked flesh distracted him, but the man was leaning down and patting him. The boy squirmed: the impact did not hurt, but, unshielded by water, was more forceful than he was used to. The man spoke again. "Henry," he said.

The woman in the corner shivered, but the boy made no move to acknowledge her, uncertain now as to their relative status.

"Henry," the man said. He laid his hand on his own chest, with another word: "Allard." The red hand pointed at the square on the wall that the boy was still avoiding: "Angelica." Then again, indicating the boy with a lighter touch: "Henry. Henry. Henry."

~

This was a new difficulty: the acquisition of a name. By the time a second woman appeared in the doorway, then another man, the boy had begun to grasp the degree to which he was outnumbered. Those four people were all he saw for a good length of time, but he had not survived the tribe and the oceans for nothing: he had always needed to be less stupid than his companions. If there were four, there were others. There were no fathoms of cloudy water for them to swim out of, but they might appear at any moment, from behind any rock. Surrounded on all four sides by walls of stone, the boy could only use his reason to understand the likelihood of an attack. Day after day, it didn't happen, but that did not mean it was impossible. He saw how the land people surrounding him watched the windows and started at noises from outside, and he understood. This hard-sided, hard-ceilinged cave was a shelter. They were all hiding from something.

# THREE

THE WOMAN who had first appeared in the doorway was seen little. The boy was not sorry at her absence. Members of the tribe were sometimes taken by sharks or dolphins before his eyes, and sometimes swam away and did not return; possibly she had been taken by some land creature like the stinking animal he had ridden to this place. In any case, her skittishness had bothered him; fear-frozen creatures sometimes lashed out, and he had found her impossible to predict.

Another woman appeared soon after, guided by the red man. "Nurse," the man said, pointing at her; the boy kept rocking, not meeting the man's eyes. The man seemed to have a habit of staring at him when he made certain sounds, usually shorter ones, saying them over and over. The sounds were too far removed from the language the boy knew to make any sense, but the staring was threatening. Clearly the man wanted something from him when he made these noises, but whether he was demanding a display of submission—but how to perform it in a way the man would understand?—or that the boy give him something—what? he had nothing, no fish or clams or crabs to hand over—the boy could not tell. Until he could work out what the man was demanding, it was safer to rock and hope that, like a tribesman, he was too stupid to work out that the boy had heard him.

So, the woman associated with the command of "nurse" drew little response from him at first. The red man, however, left the two of them alone together. At the sight of her settling down to watch him, claustrophobia gripped the boy: the walls of the room seemed closer than ever, and with someone's eyes upon him, he did not quite dare return to the frenzy of tearing and snapping that released some of the tension oppressing him when he was left alone. Anxiously, he raised his fingers to his mouth to nibble at them; the pain was sharp, but in the absence of salty water stung less than he would have expected. Pain and interest together held his attention for a while, and he continued to take careful nips at his hands, sharp, tiny teeth punching through his tough skin.

At the sight of dark red blood trickling from his hand the woman made a sound and reached to pull it away from his mouth. The boy snatched it free, crawled away as far as he could, only to be frustrated by a flat, hard wall. The woman approached again. The only way to get further away from her would be to crawl into a corner, but the boy was afraid of corners more than of the rest of the room, a horrible nexus of lines that blinded him on all sides; he could not quite shake the notion that if he became trapped in one, he would be unable to surface for air. As her hand, dry and hot, touched down on his arm, he struggled away, lashing out with his sharp nails. Blood sprang easily from her fragile skin, and water gathered in her eyes. The boy stopped to watch, dabbing at his own cut fingers with his tongue, hoping for a repetition of this curious trick that land women could perform, or possibly that it would lead to her moving away from him.

Instead, the woman blinked her white-rimmed eyes and took hold of his arm in a firmer grip. The first impulse he had was to bite her, but fear of the red man overcame him, and he managed to control himself enough to limit his attack to her skirt, ripping and snatching at the swinging fabric. The woman lifted the back of her hand to him, but the gesture meant nothing to a boy used to being chastised with a twisted ear or tugged hair, and he carried on snatching at her dress.

At this, she reached up and pulled another piece of fabric from over her shoulder. The boy had not noticed it against the other garments she had on, but suddenly he found his hand being forced through a tight tunnel of cloth, his head pushed through a hole, his whole body grappled into a prison of fabric. He was so appalled that he could think of nothing to do; urine ran down his legs, and the woman stepped away, lifting aloft the garment he was now trapped in before turning to mop up the mess with some of his precious rags, his nest, the only thing between him and nights on the hard stone floor. He lunged for them, falling hard, and gathered the remains to his chest, rocking to and fro, gripping all that was left of comfort in the world. The stiff, dull-scented fabric gripping him checked and baffled his touch at every movement, as if he was tangled in seaweed; again, the fear of drowning rose in him and he gasped at the air, kicking his legs as if to swim up to the safety of the ceiling and draw breath in some saner world. With his back to the nurse creature, he began tearing at the fabric she had forced on him; with blankets, he had never dared rip until left alone, but the cloth on his limbs was simply unbearable. The woman called, and the red man returned. Together, they took another of his rags and tied his hands together.

Bound hand and skin, the boy rocked to and fro, too inconsolable even to take the fish that the woman proffered. There would be days upon days of fighting against clothing before hunger pressed him to take a bite. Once he had taken his first mouthful, it only took him another day to realise his mistake: they had seen that he could eat clothed. Ever after, food only came once the clothes were donned.

～

Nakedness was, he soon learned, a forbidden thing. Though he was a little warmer dressed than bare, the notion that clothes were for warmth was not one he considered: in the sea it was always cold, and his garments were a blindfold for his body. Shoes were even worse; the day they forced his feet into these flexible traps, he panicked himself into a tantrum that ended up gouging his own face in his struggles. How was he to swim, to get anywhere, with his soles smothered and his webs bound together? The harsh floor of his room had rubbed his feet raw, uncalloused as they were from a lifetime in the water, but he felt no protection in these monstrosities; it was like having a clam clamped around your ankles, and the boy drew breath in fear, struggling to believe that these dreadful things weren't going to hold him down and drown him.

Once he was used to being dressed, though, he managed to grasp that the creatures surrounding him were also dressed; their shape was not clear or easy to see under the concealing garments. Seeing them naked became an urgent priority. The difference in shape between himself and them, or between them and the tribe, could tell him whether they might wage war on him. The legs of the red man, he had seen, were stiff: bifurcated like his own, but single-jointed, upright, too rigid to flex well in the water. This had always been the difference between himself and the tribe, his double tail, and he had taken enough pinches and scratches to learn the cost of it. Two limbs, and a mutation between them: the mollusc shape between his legs was a deformity he had never seen on the smooth-fronted tribesmen. Out of the water, he developed a habit of tugging anxiously at it, but this was a habit he was forced to learn to keep private, as his nurse would grasp or bind his hands if she saw him doing it, or refuse to hand food over. But a second man came to visit the nurse on occasion, and would sometimes pull her into another room. The two rooms were linked by a door, and Henry, disturbed at this half-proximity and concerned that damage might be done to the woman who brought him food—even if she did also bring clothes and bound hands—pressed his eye to it, watching her for safekeeping.

It was in these circumstances that he learned that, like his own hated garments, the clothing of the landsmen was removable, and under it, they were recognisably human. Flat-chested men and swollen-chested women, as with the tribe, but the jellyfish-skirted women concealed under their clothes two plain legs like the men. They were not like him, but neither were they like the tribe; closer to him than to the tribe in appearance. Perhaps close enough. The motions he observed through the chink of the door seemed familiar to him, almost like the ordinary swimming movements he had grown up among; if he ignored the panting, the incredible breathlessness of all who now surrounded him, the sight was a relaxing one. He had enough sense to scamper away when his nurse showed signs of rising upright and returning to him, picking up the sticks he had been left and conspicuously practising pushing himself upright on them, but his chest was a little looser than it had been. Attack was still a possibility, but these creatures were not entirely alien. There was a chance that they might not war upon him.

~

The red man returned repeatedly, addressing the nurse woman and examining him. As he repeated certain words, the boy came to recognise them, but understanding how to react eluded him. He knew he was being addressed; he just didn't know what he was expected to do. The clothes fretted him endlessly; rocking was still possible, but the cloth pinched and folded with every movement. The nurse woman patted him as the red man spoke; the boy disliked the impact, but bore with it: the sight of her dual legs and smooth-swelling chest had reassured him a little. He still had the sense that she might grasp a rock and shove him away at any moment, but there was a certain satisfaction in knowing that he was placating the one who fed him: it was the only means of controlling his fate he could find.

Over and over, the sounds were repeated. Henry. Henry. Henry. It was said to get his attention, but not to get anyone else's, so, like Whistle, it might be applied to him. Given that the man was a stranger, the fact that he kept trying to use a name was bewildering; why he thought Whistle's name was Henry, two odd exhaled syllables, made less sense still. However, the boy was too wary not to look around when the word was said, and often enough, a pat on the shoulder or a small piece of fish would be presented to him when he responded.

Henry, then. If it was the price of food, he could accept it, as long as no other means of survival were at hand—and even as he tried to master the sticks in moments of privacy, learning to lean his weight down and prop his bending legs up, to hunch over two canes and shuffle forward, upright like a land man, he realised this method of getting around was slow, a crustacean's crawl after the darting miles of the ocean. And there seemed to be no other choice. Henry was learning to see a little further, but still, the temptation to swim out of the window was ever-present. Only the dazzling green of the lawn beyond had kept him from it on the first few days; having taken dozens of falls against the painful stone, and learning from experience that the further he fell, the worse it hurt, he could understand, in his head at least, that even if he could slip through the bars, any attempt to launch himself out could only lead to a longer fall, more pain, a crash like the impact of storm-waves hurling you against a cliff wall. Still, his instincts pressed him to it, the more so as the words were repeated endlessly, frustration upon frustration, nerves and boredom wearing him down equally as he plucked at his binding clothes and stared at the bright square that looked so deceptively like an escape. Though an escape into what, he couldn't have said. Whatever they were hiding from, it must be serious enough to make people endure these imprisoning walls.

"Deepsman," the red man said, indicating Henry. "Deepsman." He indicated himself. "Landsman. Deepsman. Landsman."

Henry rocked, head averted. It was a bright day, and light was slanting in. Even the light was straight in this world: fixed and unshifting for hours, never flashing or glimmering off the still surfaces that surrounded him, slicing through the window in clean-sided bars. Under the water, surfacing to breathe, he had seen such shafts of light before, but they had been wavering, moving under the waves like stroking fingers. Here, it was bright in the day and black at night, and even yards down below the window, the light still shone, the depth lending no sheltering darkness.

"No, Henry," the nurse said, pulling his hand from between his legs, where it had strayed to alleviate his boredom.

"Deepsman," the red man said.

Henry rocked, growing tense. Except at night, they never left him alone. These endless sounds wore thinner and thinner on his patience.

"Staff." The red man indicated one of the two sticks that Henry used to walk around. Henry watched out of the corner of his eye; he had learned the purpose of the sticks, but he wasn't going to acknowledge that he knew how to use them if it meant associating them with these endless demands. They were just sounds. Back home, the tribe

had litanies of its own, but they were *about* things, they told you where
to go and what to eat. They recited, and you picked it up as you went
along; no one was stupid enough to say a single, pointless word over
and over. "Staff," the man said again. "Staff."

Henry looked out of the window. The sky reached up above him,
fading into blue like the depths of the ocean, but bright enough to hurt
his eyes. Something flew past, and that caught his attention: a creature
that could swim in the air. He shuffled to the window to watch it.

"Staff," the red man said, proffering the sticks. "Staff, Henry.
Staff."

Henry was not about to beg for the staff if it meant accepting the
sounds. He leaned forwards, pulling himself on his hands until he
reached the window, then grasped the ledge to lever himself up.

"Staff." The man stood over him, holding one in front of him.
Henry pushed it away. "No, Henry. Staff."

All familiar words. *No* usually meant he was about to be stopped
from doing what he wanted, but Henry wasn't going to let on that
he'd grasped that; it would only encourage them to stop him more. He
hoisted, and then he was leaning out of the window, propped on the
hard stone, following with his eyes the white creature swimming
through the sky above him. It was a gull; such creatures were familiar
from home. Henry had seen them floating on the surface, ducking for
fish, sometimes congregating above while the tribe harried a shoal of
fish and diving down to snatch a share of the prize, those white wings
swimming through the water with stretched, forceful strokes. His
vision had never been good enough to see what happened when the
gulls took off into the air, leaping above the water like dolphins: he
had no idea they could go so high. Was it possible that his webbed
hands and feet could beat at the air like that? Could he swim through
the air?

*Gull,* Henry said to himself in the language of the tribe, ignoring
the red man. The man looked at him sharply; the boy had never made
a sound in his presence before. Henry shook his hands in the air,
spreading his fingers out and trying for lift. Nothing. The breeze
cooled his palms, but he was still earthbound, heavy in the air.

"Bird," the man said, pointing. Finding himself observed, Henry abruptly sat down, tearing his eyes away from the gull. He resumed rocking, testing the beat of his webbed fingers against the unresisting air.

The man pointed at the painting on the wall. Henry ignored him.

Finally, the man exhaled heavily, and spoke to the nurse. His voice rumbled; Henry could make out the sounds better than he could have done a few weeks before, but the speech was too rapid for him to pick any familiar syllables out of it. The nurse evidently understood it, though, for she disappeared out of the door. Henry sat on the floor, refusing to turn his head at the red man's attempts to interest him in other words, rocking quietly and thinking about the gull. Maybe he could try to eat one, if he could catch it. Tribesmen had sometimes managed it, swimming with slow stealth up from below, barely stirring the water around them before shooting up their arms in a sudden, violent grab, pulling the birds down into the water in a flurry of feathers. Henry had tried it himself, but he had been too little; it was a skill only the adults seemed to possess. It would be difficult to catch one here, but the sight of it, flying alien through this new sky, quickened his homesickness, filling him with an angry desire to store the bird safe in his stomach where it could change no more of its ways.

While Henry considered thus, the nurse returned. In her hands was a curious object, a bright circle that flashed with light like a fish scale. The shiny surface and round shape caught Henry's attention: sea urchins were round, and fish eyes, and in this boxed-in world, it was a fascinating sight. Desire for something not dull and square overcame Henry's determination to ignore his lesson, and he reached out for it.

"Crown," the red man said, as Henry played with the circle in his lap. "Crown. Crown."

Henry licked at the metal. It had an unfamiliar non-taste, no strong smell. Light glimmered off it like sunlight on waves.

"Crown. Crown, Henry?"

Red hands reached into his lap. Henry bared his teeth, gripping hard onto his shining circle.

The hand descended and patted his shoulder. "Good, Henry. Crown. Crown."

Henry tightened his hold. The man was going to take it away; he could see it from his posture.

*Mine,* Henry said in the language of the tribe. The sound was a high-pitched squeak, and the man did not seem to hear it.

"Crown."

*Mine.*

The red hands closed over Henry's own and lifted the circle up. Henry refused to let go, and his fingers, he knew, small as they were, were too strong for the man to pry apart. However, the man did not attempt to pull his circle loose. Instead, he lifted it up and fixed it on Henry's head.

Henry flinched, pulled away. The touch of a circle around his head was the snap of a shark's mouth, the bite of a killer whale, a predator's fatal grip. He thrashed back, kicking desperately against the hard floor.

The hands persisted, held the circle down over his head. "Crown, Henry. Good, Henry. Crown."

The band pressed down, gripping his head on all sides. Horror overwhelmed Henry, freezing any ability to think. A metal mouth had him in its hold; any moment, there would be teeth.

"Crown," the voice persisted.

Henry shrieked. The word came to him, strange against his tongue, awkward in his mouth, high-pitched like the cry of a bird, but it was all he could say to free himself of the terrifying grasp. "No! No! No!"

The red hands relinquished him at once, the crown clattering to the floor. There was a long moment when two pairs of eyes stared at him.

Henry reached out and retrieved his circle, rocking, staring at its soothing light.

The red man breathed, breathed again. A patting hand hit the boy's shoulder. "Good, Henry," the deep voice said. "Good. Good."

*Mine,* Henry said in his own language, clutching the crown to him in tense little hands. *Mine.*

# FOUR

HENRY HAD BARELY learned enough English to get by before the red man—Allard, Henry eventually gathered, was his name—began telling him stories. These stories made little sense to Henry at first; the names of people and places rattled off were too different from his native tongue to be easily remembered. Allard's tales had no shape to them, no echoes of sound or regular beats, and he tended to say them only once—and if Henry needed a repetition, would tell the story again, but in entirely different words. Used to rhythm and rote, Henry found his attention bent in new, uncomfortable directions. What he did learn quickly was that there were more than four of these red people, these "landsmen," as Allard called them. More than there had been members of his tribe, of "deepsmen." More, if he understood right, than there were fish in a shoal. Places tended not to have names in Henry's language; he understood the concepts of current and surface and rock, of places with good food and empty stretches to be travelled at speed, of summer route and winter route and the migrations his people made as the seasons turned. For a place to have a name like a person, though, was a difficult concept. How would you name a stretch of ocean, when the water flooded to and fro and moved endlessly from one place to another, when things changed and shifted and the miles stretched before you on all sides with nothing to stop you swimming through? A name was something you used to call someone, only useful for getting a person's attention, and when Allard sat in his room and said words like "England" and "France" and "Spain," nothing replied.

What Henry did understand was that these stories told of conflicts, of other peoples. Given the fact that these people were enemies, Henry supposed that the landsmen of France were entirely different from the landsmen of England like Allard. Allard showed him pictures, though, flat images that Henry had to struggle to perceive as anything other than lines on a page, and when he could get his eyes focused for long enough to work out what the lines meant, he could see no signs of difference: two legs, webless hands, red-pink skin, white-rimmed eyes. Henry had seen other tribes in the sea, which must be what Allard was talking about—other tribes, rather than other creatures—but the idea of long-running battles with them seemed bizarre. Some tribes stayed near shallow coasts where the fish were rich and plentiful, others followed the currents, tracing the same paths every year, and one tribe trying to encroach on the hunting waters of another would find itself in a fight fairly quickly—but once those fights were settled, the losers retreated, went back to seeking their food elsewhere. Long-running clashes, when there seemed to be enough to eat in all the countries involved, were a crazy waste of energy. These stories failed to capture his imagination; Henry sat on the floor, tossing his crown from hand to hand and blinking.

Personality was something that Henry understood; he had learned, faster than other children of the tribe, which members—which *deepsmen*—could be trusted to spot a dolphin and which would start at the click of a harmless fish, which would always steal his food and which might leave him alone if he stayed unobtrusive. Allard was difficult for him to understand, though. Sometimes restless, pacing and staring, at other times he would seat himself with a long feather in his hand, dipping and scratching at a thin, tan leaf of something, as if levering at the flesh of an invisible crab. Sometimes he appeared with objects in his hands—*book* was the word he repeated, pointing to them and trying to persuade Henry to pick them up, but their square shape and meaty smell were too nasty for Henry to want any contact with them. These books hinged open and closed neatly like joints, and their insides, which all looked similar to Henry, seemed to puzzle Allard; he would look from Henry to book and back again, and shake his head, scratching at the leaves with his dark-tipped feather. This action irritated Henry, but nothing he did seemed to prevent it; whether he rocked and refused to meet anyone's eye, or obediently sat up for his fish, straining his voice around the syllables of "thank you," whether he cricked his back tottering around on the sticks Allard seemed so insistent on or lay curled on the floor stroking his rags and refusing to move, Allard's feather scratched and scratched. Most gestures meant something in the sea; posture and motion emphasised or softened words or expressed relationship, but Allard was a mess of gestures, all apparently meaning nothing. Had a deepsman spent so long fiddling with a shell or stick, Henry would have assumed he was deranged with nerves, but Allard was quick to pull Henry's limbs into line, to grab him before he could scratch his nurse, and the nurse and the man with her obeyed Allard quickly and without protest, which made the idea that he was nervous all but impossible: such open anxiety would sit ill on a leader. It would be an invitation to any who wished to depose him.

When the stories Allard told were accompanied by a book, Henry quickly took against them. Even as his understanding of English grew, the words Allard used were difficult, and the stories themselves were wearisome and complex, and hard to see the point of. Allard produced a book he kept referring to as a "Bible"; the word was easy to say, two puffs of air that could be made under water without filling a mouth with brine, but with it came a horrible object, two straight lines crisscrossed over each other, an interlocking nest of corners that upset Henry just to look at it. The fact that there was a figure on it, what appeared to be the shape of a tiny landsman with corded muscles like a half-picked corpse, did nothing to improve his liking for it. Allard seemed to take this object seriously, more seriously than the crown he had let Henry grab: when Henry tried to take it away and break it up, Allard lifted it up out of his reach, looking almost alarmed; his grip was light and cautious, as if holding a clam that might be prised open for a meal but would clamp its shell shut at a tap. Allard used words like "Christ" and "cross" and "crucifix" and "Jesus," but Henry had difficulty telling them apart, and the tangle of S-sounds struck awkwardly on his ear. There were stories attached to this object as well, about places that weren't France or England or Spain. When Henry asked about these places, Allard could explain little, except that they were hot and had landsmen ruling them, because they had no sea except a great body called the Mediterranean, which had deepsmen in it but not ones the landsmen cared about, because the landsmen needed deepsmen to fight their enemies, and these landsmen's enemies weren't on the other side of the sea but on land. This Henry could follow, but when Allard tried to explain what this ugly cross had to do with it, he grew confused. Allard said that the figure on it was a king, but he didn't seem to rule anything that Allard could make clear, and as the man looked nothing like Henry it was hard to see the connection. There were words like "sin" too, but that was a difficult idea as well. Henry knew that deepsmen children received a twist on the ear if they strayed off in a dangerous direction or provoked another tribe member, but it was a simple business: they either learned not to repeat such mistakes, or they stayed stupid and generally drowned or fell prey to a shark or a dolphin. Having done his best not to be stupid for as long as he could remember, Henry could not see any reason why a dead landsman who looked nothing like him should be accusing him of doing bad things. The notion obscurely hurt his feelings. He was aware that tribesmen too old for a twisted ear would become unpopular if they regularly snatched food or refused to help in a crisis, and he supposed this might be the kind of bad things Allard meant. But nobody seemed to like Henry, and nobody ever had. He assumed it was because of his queer legs, but those weren't his fault. Try as he might, he could think of no clearer reason why he should be so isolated. A two-legged landsman who looked like so many others, starfished out on an ugly criss-cross, could have little to do with such problems. Henry kept his eyes off the object as much as he could, and shook his head; eventually, he took to curling up whenever Allard brought it into the room. For some reason, Allard was less willing to wrestle him upright when he had the cross around, so Henry grew stubborn, and eventually Allard stopped bringing it in.

The one thing Allard had not done since the first few days was point to the painting up in Henry's room. Henry remembered the word "Angelica" associated with it, so he assumed that was what it was, an angelica. When left alone, Henry still tore blankets, but more for comfort than anything else; the room remained square and straight however he attacked it, and it was too hard to keep bruising himself on the walls for so little reward. But with the loss of tantrums came boredom, worse than before, pressing him down as oppressively as the room itself. With nothing else to do, Henry took to exploring the room, examining its every inch, even occasionally reaching a cautious finger into a corner to touch it at its tightest point, before snatching his hand back quickly, out of harm's way. But aside from scaring himself with corners, there was almost no other occupation: his ruined pallet and fraying rags, his two staffs and the chair Allard sat upon were the only distractions. Apart from the angelica, hanging low enough on the wall that Henry could scrunch up his short-sighted eyes and make out its shape.

It was reddish, like so many things in this world, with swirls of colour and arching lines all over it; within its disagreeably straight edges, it was more like water than anything else he could find. As the image was flat, he could not suppose it served any purpose except, like his clothes, to be a colourful nuisance, but once he had accustomed himself to it, he found its variety pleasant and spent hours of solitude rocking quietly with his eyes on its soothing curves.

Allard waited until he caught Henry staring at it before he tried to interest the boy in its contents. When he finally managed to come upon Henry with his eyes on the picture—by dint of opening the door faster than usual and putting his head in before the boy could retreat to his usual rocking and blank expression—he smiled and patted his charge. Henry retreated from the smile, bared teeth being a threatening sight, but Allard sat down on the floor beside him, dust and threads from Henry's rags covering his fine clothing, and offered the boy some fish.

Henry took it. He was becoming accustomed to the bland, saltless taste of the food, and as the season grew chillier, he knew he should eat as much as possible, laying down fat to keep out the cold—although the supply of fish was not increasing as the days grew darker and the temperature dropped, and the lack of food was worrying him. Allard passed him another piece, and said, "Good boy, Henry. See that?" He pointed. "That is Angelica."

"Angelica," Henry said, and reached out his hand; Allard generally gave him a small bit of fish when he repeated words.

"Good." The fish was produced, and Henry stuffed it into his mouth. "Queen Angelica."

"Queen Angelica." Henry held out an expectant hand, but no fish came.

"Queen, Henry?" Allard gave him a stern look. "What is a queen?"

Henry said nothing; there was no reason to expect him to know what a queen was.

"Do you want to know what a queen is?"

"Fish," Henry said; the sentence was a complicated one.

"Later. A queen has a crown."

"Crown." Henry patted his lap; the crown was his only other plaything, a cheering bright circle in this bleak room.

"A queen is married to a king."

"Fish."

"Talk to me and I will give you fish," Allard said.

"Not know 'married,'" Henry said, frowning with concentration. He needed more food if he was to avoid freezing.

"King and queen are together. Man and woman," Allard said. This made little sense to Henry, but he said nothing. "King is the son of a king and queen."

Henry nodded; he had seen children born in the sea, and the spawning that preceded it; sometimes a deepsman and woman grew attached to each other and stayed together, breeding season after season, if the man wasn't too weak to defend himself. King and queen must mean a breeding couple.

"You have queen?" Henry said.

"No." Allard tapped the ground impatiently. "Only one king and queen in one country."

Henry lowered his head; "country" was another difficult concept. "Fish?"

"Very well." Allard passed him another piece. "King and queen are leaders. King and queen rule. They tell all the subjects—the people who are not king and queen—what they must do. Subjects obey king and queen. Loyal to . . ." He stopped. The glance he gave out of the window made Henry start up in alarm; sudden looks usually meant an approaching predator.

Allard showed no sign of flight, though, so Henry repeated, "Subjet-ss obey king an queen." The consonants were difficult, but the idea was not. He had been used to having a single leader in the tribe.

Then he frowned. "King have crown. Henry have crown." He looked at Allard in consternation. Henry knew only too well how the leader changed: another leader challenged them. The battle would be bloody and frantic. He had only ever seen two such, but he had never forgotten them, the rocks clenched in hard fists, the rising plumes of white bubbles and the cloudy trails of dark blood as the loser sank out of sight, arms limp and adrift on the current.

"Angelica was not born a queen, Henry. Listen."

~

The story of Angelica began in Venice. Henry struggled with the ideas for weeks, but Allard was patient. He repeated the tale over and over, passing the boy titbits, giving him unwelcome pats, seeing no sign in the child's still expression of the idea that possessed him: a ravaged body, head cracked with a rock, falling through the air, not even with the slow inevitability of a slain deepsman, but with a swift crash to the shattering ground below. A vague notion occupied Henry that someone might take his crown away, though, and he was determined not to have that happen. He had lost too many things in his life to relinquish it.

In the ninth century of our Lord, hundreds of years ago, Allard explained, the great city of Venice was finding its strength. "Century" and "our Lord" were lost on Henry, but he gathered that the story happened a long time ago, before living memory, many generations back. "City" meant little either, but Allard described a place of land and sea both, of islands and waterways, where the solid ground was parted and split by the flowing ocean.

"Go there," Henry said at once. He could get around in such a place much better; he could break his sticks and swim.

"Venice is far away, Henry."

"Go there."

"Venice is not in England. We cannot live there, we would not be welcome."

"Far?"

"Many miles. Many weeks to travel."

This did not sound so bad to Henry; the entrapment in a single place worried him as much as the coming winter. How could they continue to eat if they did not move on? Existence in the sea had been an endless search, and weeks of swimming were part of life.

"Go," Henry said. He did not really expect Allard to take him to Venice—unless Henry was asking for food, Allard never granted a request—but he was tired to death of his room.

"Some day, perhaps, Henry. When you are ready."

Henry felt ready; if he could only have had more to eat and knowledge of the way, he would have set out for Venice that moment. Allard was staring at him, though, not giving anything, not troubled by the cold or the confinement, so Henry gave up and asked for another piece of fish.

People had come to Venice, Allard explained, because they were unhappy in other lands. They wanted to rule themselves. But they were still subject to Constantinople, a place Henry could not understand any descriptions of. Venice a strong city, living on fish, harvesting salt, selling it to people who came to buy it. The word "salt" Henry did not recognise, until Allard produced some for him, a little pile of sand, startlingly white in a bowl. Henry made nothing of it until he tasted it, but when he did, he stopped dead, rocking himself to avoid speaking to Allard, his mouth filled with taste of home. The boy refused to listen to any more of Allard's story until he had finished the bowl, licking out its curves with a dark, tough tongue before turning to Allard and saying, "Salt an fish."

"You want salt with your fish?"

"Yes." Henry spoke imperiously; salt was too important to be denied.

"Very well, if you are a good boy, you shall have salt." Allard had added another bribe to Henry's attention, but a punishment too: on the days when Henry did not listen, when he rocked too much or tugged between his legs or showed his teeth to the nurse, fish would arrive without salt, dull grey and tasteless.

The people of Venice were happy there, Allard said. They lived well, even though Constantinople ruled them. Then one day, the people of the sea came.

Down the canals they swam, around the islands, turning and diving in the brown water. The Venetians had never seen such a sight. Some had seen deepsmen before, yes, riding the waves as the prows of ships cleft the water, but for most of the landsmen, the deepsmen were entirely unfamiliar.

"Ship?" said Henry.

"Yes," Allard said, and produced a model. He waved it before the boy's eyes, making it dance as if bobbing on a wave. Seeing the boy's blank face, Allard stopped and handed him the toy. Henry sniffed at it, tasted the edges, but it was still puzzling. Allard had moved it to and fro, but when Henry turned it over in his hands, something tugged at his memory. He lay down on the floor and held the model above his head. There it was, a sight only seen from fathoms below: a dark fin-shape that meant a strong hand on his wrist, the sight of the tribe swimming up to greet it while he remained below, chastened and guarded by his mother.

"Ship," Henry said. "What do ship?"

"Ships are how people travel the seas, Henry. How landsmen go across the water."

Henry frowned; it was difficult to see why they didn't swim, but already he was learning that landsmen had a passion for *things,* for fabrics and chairs and doors and windows, that they stayed to guard these things and tied your hands if you damaged them. Now it seemed that they wanted a thing if they were to go through the water as well. It was no clearer than before why these ships had been forbidden him. He frowned again, and asked Allard for some fish to cover his disappointment.

The people of the sea came to Venice, Allard said. The Venetians were bewitched by these strange newcomers, by the sound of the voices that rang out across the canals. Pale faces flashed through the brown water, dark tails churned foam from the depths, and the deepsmen's song echoed off the clean, damp walls. For a while, all the music of Venice was composed around it, flutes trying to imitate the sonorous groans that the deepsmen called across the waters. Then the Venetians sent people out, ambassadors, in flat-bottomed boats, flutes playing this new sound.

Hearing the weighty notes called across the canals, the deepsmen united in groups of three and five, strongest at the head, in the phalanx formation that was to become familiar over the years. They swam out to greet the ambassadors, and as the flautists strove to imitate the sounds they made, powerful hands reached out and overturned the boats.

Allard explained this with sign language, with words, with sounds and grimaces and gestures. Explaining music took a while, and Henry responded poorly to Allard's awkward attempts to play a flute; singing he understood, but the flute was just sounds without meaning. Just occasionally Allard managed to pipe out a note that sounded a little like a word—the echo of one, blurred and imprecise—which attracted Henry's attention a little more, but either Allard's musicianship or the boy's willingness was too faulty to make much headway. This was all difficult for him to explain, but Allard took a great interest in Henry's wavering enthusiasm for the flute, scratching note after note before carrying on with his explanation. Henry learned how the deepsmen had challenged the flautists, toppling them into the water to fight. Landsmen fare ill in underwater battles, and the deepsmen fought by their own traditions. Water cushions the blow of a striking tail a little, but the great muscles and flexing joints of a sea man's tail are always better able to clash and wrestle than the fragile limbs of an unseated musician. Several of Venice's most promising composers suffered broken legs before the boating attempts were abandoned.

Unfortunately for the city, once the musicians had been subdued, the deepsmen took to refusing entry to the canals where such ambushes had taken place. They swam up and down, rolling over in the water, wide-eyed and thoughtful, tolling out a sweet-voiced chant very similar to the tunes the well-meaning ambassadors had relayed to them. The translation was becoming increasingly obvious to the philosophers of the city: *Ours*.

Venice, independent and strong, found itself with enemies on its banks. The sea people attacked boats, pulled down bridges, until it was all but impossible to travel. Attempts were made to block the canals: the deepsmen broke the dams. Arrows were fired into the water and some casualties followed, but it was hard to take aim on a quarry that could disappear into the opaque depths within a moment. Nets were of little use: the deepsmen spent little time in the Grand Canal, only flashing across it fast enough to do damage. Instead, they prowled the narrower waters, where no boat large enough to haul up the full weight of a deepsman could travel. Citizens waited on the banks grasping harpoons; the deepsmen swam silently under the water, concealed in the cloudy brown tide, only flashing up for long enough to cast rocks, toppling the huntsmen, dragging their bleeding bodies into the canals, never to surface again.

The city fell under siege. But as the Venetians struggled to make it past the deepsmen's barricade into the harbour, Constantinople did nothing to help. Venice was weakening, and the setbacks of a subject people were no hardship to a city with a whole world of cities to command. Let Venice struggle, Constantinople decided. If Venice broke, they would be more obedient to their liege city; the Venetians had struggled hard for self-rule, but if their new-minted independence was no help against the enemy within, so much the better for Constantinople's hold on them.

Venice turned from the East to Charlemagne, Emperor of the West. In the year of our Lord 805, Allard explained, on Christmas Day—a term foreign to Henry, to whom birthdays were a mystery and days were reckoned by season, not by month, even if the story had not involved more of that disagreeable crossed statue—the Venetians did homage to Charlemagne, Charles the Great, newly crowned and formidable. The Doge of Venice, Oberlerio, took to wife a Frankish bride, a woman from across the seas, a woman of the Western race, who became something entirely new: a Dogaressa, queen of Venice.

This, Allard told Henry, was not an easy question for the Venetians. They argued about it, he explained, for five years—an unbelievable lifetime to carry on a quarrel, Henry considered, especially as the quarrel, complicated though Allard made it sound, seemed like a simple one: they had a choice of leaders, there were greater tribes in the world who wanted to rule them and the Venetians didn't want any of them. Allard used words like "strong" and "proud," spoke of freedom to govern oneself, independence from a greater power. The boy flinched a little as Allard's gestures grew larger, wondering why these ideas seemed to drive the man so. But it was clear that Allard did not approve when he spoke of how the Doges, desperate to free themselves from the tyranny of the blockading deepsmen, managed to smuggle a message to the King of Italy: Pepin, son of Charlemagne. The message was clear: come to Venice. The offer was not alliance. It was submission. Pepin was invited to conquer Venice, hold the city against Constantinople, to settle internal divisions and, most importantly, to drive the deepsmen from the canals. The Venetian people might have wanted independence, but with the deepsmen in their canals, their leaders had decided otherwise. They would follow Constantinople, if Constantinople would help them.

To the canals of Venice came Pepin, hastily prepared, unaware of the anger of the Venetians who awaited him. In defiance of their leaders, the citizens gathered, ready to battle the invaders. But as Pepin's ships sailed into the bay, a sight met their eyes that struck them like a wonder. The deepsmen had gathered to fight.

The sea people did not share the landsmen's view of nationhood.

More land people arriving in great ships were simply more people making claim on their canals. The sea people massed, called to each other across the miles of water and swam out to meet the fleet. With sharp rocks and strong hands, they breached hulls within minutes. The massive galleons of the enemy went down. The canals of Venice filled with floating spars, and the air filled with the crash of splitting wood and the shrieks of drowning men. And through the noise, the resonant song of the deepsmen sounded, a deep bass undertow: *Ours*.

Pepin's surviving ships ploughed through. He had come too far to retreat in disgrace. The blood of the deepsmen darkened the waters as sailors lowered themselves on ropes to slash with swords at the lithe figures battering their hulls; as webbed fingers washed up upon the shores and shrieks rang through the water and echoed up the canals, Chioggia fell, then Pellestrina. The lagoon, Venice's safeguard against the world, was giving way.

The Venetians had no love for the deepsmen patrolling their rivers, but they had less love for French princes called in to conquer by their treacherous leaders. And as the sailors' swords flashed and the heads of deepsmen bobbed in the bay, black of eye and slack-jawed, tumbling over and over in the current, the people of Venice united.

It was one man who turned the battle around. Agnello Participazio was a long-established settler, a fierce Venetian who had organised men to block the channels, removing markers and leaving Venice an impassable maze for the invaders to founder in. The citizens followed him, damming their rivers as best they could, preparing to face Pepin with all their strength.

Then a naked woman walked out of the sea. Her legs were supple like a sea woman's, jointed with vertebrae rather than shin bone and thigh bone, and her webbed feet spread like fans on the ground. Men crossed themselves and murmured of Venus, and she stared at them, lifted her head, and spoke to them in their own tongue, saying: "Give me something to wear." Her teeth chattered in the cold wind, and drying salt sparkled on her rough skin.

Agnello looked up from his dam, laid down the spear in his hands, and stepped forward to offer her his cloak. She took it with a swift gesture, and cast it around herself like a queen.

"We must turn back these ships," she said.

And Agnello bowed to her, and she reached out and took him by the hand.

The cloak he had lent her barely covered her body, her twisting unnatural legs and beautiful breasts like a girl's, her whiter than white skin with veins that darkened as the air of the land warmed her water-chilled flesh. But she would not give it up for a dress, not while Pepin was at the shore. She covered herself as she spoke to Agnello, then leaned down into the water, dipping her ragged head and releasing from her slim throat such heavy calls, louder and deeper than a bull's bellow, that the landsmen stared at her, speechless.

At her call, a phalanx of deepsmen swam into view, twenty deep.

The woman turned to Agnello and said, "Where should they go to block them?"

Agnello was a level-headed, strong-willed man. He hesitated only a moment before remembering his plan. His instructions were clear and direct: block the Malamocco channel. And the woman lowered her head again, chattered and clicked and moaned into the water.

The deepsmen turned on the instant; their huge tails raised such a fountain that Agnello's men found themselves soaked to the skin. The woman addressed herself to Agnello: "I will go with them. You must meet me there." She stripped the cloak from her shoulders, standing naked as a fish on half-steady legs before his gaze. "Have this ready for me again," she said, and passed it to him. Then she was gone, lost in the water.

Deepsmen and landsmen worked together. Mighty stakes barricaded the Malamocco channel, impassable to Pepin's fleet, and between them the deepsmen slipped, silent as wolves, under the water. Within Venice, the canals were passable again; only to outsiders was the deepsmen's fury turned. And everywhere, between land and sea, swam the two-tailed, bent-legged woman, white-faced and clear-spoken, turning from Agnello to the deepsmen and back again.

Pepin held out for six months, trying starvation and patience, force and endurance, to no avail. Venice had become something new: a city that could not be taken by sea. Pepin struggled on, but in the end, he turned away.

After he had gone, and the banks of Venice were clear, the city turned within itself, united. Agnello, the hero of the city, was elected, the only possible Doge. And by his side was something utterly new, even to the name given her by the Venetians: Angelica. Dogaressa, lady of Venice, queen of the land and sea.

It was common to speak of a woman's gentleness, but no one said that of Angelica. When an assassin tried to suffocate her in the night, Angelica lasted easily without air under the smothering pillow, wrapped her flexing legs around his hips and broke his spine with a single jerk of her strong, mobile back.

Venice thrived in her salty grip. Icons of the Virgin took on her features when artists decorated the churches. But it was more than that. Angelica and her children spread their tendrils through the royal houses, until the houses of Europe all grew intermixed, the dark-tinged blood of the sea people safely mingled in the veins of its rulers. For what nation with a vulnerable coastline could call itself strong if it could not defend itself from attacks by sea? The first time Angelica's deepsmen struck at the Spanish navy, out on open water, miles away from Venice, not even plundering but dragging the boat down and its sailors with it, was the beginning of the end of landsmen kings. Let the Switzers be ruled by landsmen, let nations with no sea borders keep their old ways if they wished, but there were navies to maintain, and the deepsmen of the sea were no longer neutral, no longer sailors' yarns, but an engaged force with loyalties of their own. Venice had a sword against the throat of the world. For against the wolves of the ocean—that implacable army Angelica could command without warning—there was no defence. Unless there were other deepsmen on other shores.

Angelica's children by Agnello were strong and healthy, fast-growing, cloven infants that could chirrup and shrill their mother's language, reproducing the deepsmen's sounds as no landlocked throat ever could. For years, Venice grew in strength: a great empire, unchallengeable ruler of the waves, the deepsmen riding the trade routes and salvaging lost sailors, protecting their nation, mauling unauthorised ships. The world took notice of the small city, even far-distant continents, Chinese and Arab merchants bartering their wealth for safe passage, Europe in thrall. Venice was growing to a second Rome.

Before Angelica's first daughter was old enough to talk, she was being offered the hands of princes. That first generation, Angelica refused; instead, she favoured noblemen of her choosing, sending them out into the bay to find themselves brides in the water to bear husbands and wives of mixed-blood for her children. Before Angelica was an old woman, the spread across the courts of Europe had begun.

A monument was raised by the Doge's palace after Angelica's death, housing a golden reliquary containing only her right hand. The remains of her corpse were buried at sea, but the hand rested in its glass-fronted, pearl-studded tomb, its webs shrivelling and pulling the fingers tight, until all that could be seen was a corrugated mass, small as an egg, brown and pitted like a bundle of seaweed. Angelica had never acquired the habit of piety, but the Virgin in stone adorned her tomb, and gilt letters announced the sacred legend: Stella Maris. Star of the Sea.

This, Allard explained to his charge. The boy sat, black eyes wide open, his mind filled with the drifting corpses of deposed leaders, the jawless bodies of conquered dolphins and the broken limbs, crooked against the dark, vibrant emptiness of the deep that followed after a struggle for authority; of bodies falling through the empty, unresisting air. That was the lesson Allard had to teach. The words were hard for Henry to understand, but the images were not. There were others like him on the land. Not many, but others like him. Only they were not like his nurse, not like the men who obeyed Allard, nor even like Allard himself. They were kings.

"Henry king?" he asked Allard.

"Not yet, Henry," Allard said.

"Kill king?" Henry said.

Allard looked at him again, fish hanging limp in his stilled hand.

His brow wrinkled, narrowing his white-rimmed eyes, as he stared at his charge. Henry leaned forward out and took the fish out of Allard's grip. His chest was tighter than it had ever been, but his face was immobile. He said nothing as he filled his mouth with meat, readying himself for winter.

# FIVE

Henry never learned to speak Latin, the language of the courts. English was difficult enough for him, accustomed as he was to a simpler mother tongue. But he listened to his keepers' voices, even when they were not addressing him. These people spoke to each other, they spoke and spoke, about things that had nothing to do with the circumstances at hand. Most of the words in his own language had been warnings or commands: *Dangerous tide; Move on; Give me that,* or else they had been lessons, navigation chants and hunting methods that everyone recited together. Discussion was far more limited. But Allard and his nurse—Jane Markeley, a name it took him weeks to understand fell into two parts, not a single one, Janemarkeley or Mistressmarkeley—spoke to each other endlessly. They spoke about him. Even when he was doing as he was told they talked and talked, and Henry strained his ears to understand them, though he kept his back averted and rocked to cover his eavesdropping. Jane Markeley and her king—no, her man, her *husband,* Thomas Markeley—spoke to each other of all sorts of things, people Henry didn't know, ideas he didn't understand, places he couldn't picture. At first he attended mostly to the rhythm of their speech, trying to get the measure of it. Only after growing used to it did he begin to pick up the tone of anxiety in their voices.

He listened to their chatter, even when they were not addressing him. But Latin, he hated. Allard spoke English, Jane Markeley and

Thomas Markeley did, even the missing woman, Allard's wife, who never came to look at him after those early days—could follow those words fine. With Latin came the repetition over and over of a new word, spoken by Allard: "Understand?" It was this word that irritated him beyond endurance. It was hard to say, to begin with: Henry wrestled with the syllables, but they clattered uncomfortably in his mouth. But it was the meaning that bothered him the most, though his grasp of English was still not good enough to explain this to Allard, even had he wished to. It was too hard to separate the two words out. Such a combination, *under* and *stand,* could bode nothing but ill. "Stand" was what Jane Markeley said over and over again as she forced the sticks into his reluctant hands, what Allard said as he hauled him to his feet and forced him to practise, risking so many tumbles against the hard floor. "Under" was bad, too; in the sea, hiding beneath a rock might have brought him some privacy to eat without being robbed, but the intractable ceiling of his room had soured his taste for such things. *Understand,* in Henry's mind, was a word of imprisonment. To Allard, perhaps, it was a natural thing, accustomed as he was to these dark ceilings, and easy as he was on his straight, quick legs. But to Henry, "understand" meant to take up the posture of a landsman: impossible, and unwelcome. He could see the meanings of words Allard said to him, at least in English, but he didn't want to understand.

As a result, he made a recalcitrant pupil. Latin was a language Allard insisted he learn, but he could not tell him who it was spoken by; Henry did not know what a court was, and if it was associated with no living tribe, not even a country, Henry refused to abandon English for it. To understand was to submit, and Henry, though dependent on Allard for food, was coming to think that he had less reason to fear than he had thought. Allard might look strange, but the twisted ear or tugged hair he would have expected from a stern deepsman adult never happened. The others obeyed Allard, but with his odd liking for books and his endless repetition of single words, he was, to Henry, eccentric, possibly even stupid. Henry listened when Allard addressed the others, listened to the tension in his voice, and ignored his attempts to teach Henry anything he did not choose to know.

One day Allard sat down with him once again to teach him Latin. Henry sat hunched on a chair, legs tucked under, angry and restless at being expected once again to struggle with the wretched, useless syllables. There was no need to have two words for everything, and Allard's repeated, "Understand, Henry? Understand?" was almost as maddening as his tight clothes.

Determined to escape, he remembered a well-tried trick from his time in the sea, a quick way of driving off deepsmen when they bothered him too much to bear, when their attacks and harassments threatened to drag him under. Henry looked suddenly at the window, pointed, and shouted a word he had heard spoken with fear: "Soldiers! Soldiers!"

Allard did not flinch. He rose slowly, walked to the window and looked out over the green lawns. Then he turned back to Henry.

"I will not have you lie to me," he said.

Henry looked at him in terror, understanding something new: his tricks for survival would not work, for these dry people were not stupid like his family. He was smaller than all of them. If they wanted to drag him down, they could do it.

Allard beat slowly, and picked up one of Henry's sticks, lying abandoned on the floor. Sitting back down, he grabbed Henry by the collar and hauled him over his knee. The stick whistled impossibly fast through the thin air, and Henry shrieked and thrashed. The chair rocked, and Henry twisted under Allard's hand, flailing his legs. He heard a grunt, and felt the strain in the arm holding him down. With a desperate effort, he pulled himself free and buried his pointed teeth in Allard's hand.

Allard yelled in pain and Henry turned again, shoving them both onto the floor. He pounded his fist twice into Allard's face, then spread his webbed hands and covered the mouth and nose, stanching the flow of shouts and commands. Allard struggled up, but Henry's nails were in his face. Henry gripped.

It was only a few moments before Allard started to weaken. Henry stared, astonished. Hands flapped helplessly around him, losing strength with every second. Henry, who hadn't paused to breathe in the whole struggle, watched as Allard turned scarlet and stopped fighting, letting the stick lie harmless at his side.

Henry released his grip. He sat astride Allard and spoke into his face. "No Latin," he said. "Show me a soldier."

—

It was this fight, the first of Henry's life, that changed his world. Allard did not answer his question right away. But the next day he came to Henry's room and announced some astonishing news: they were going outside. His words were clipped and he stood in the door-way of Henry's room, not seating himself on the chair, lowering him-self to Henry's eye level. Instead, he loomed above the boy, forcing him to crane his neck to see him. Henry considered rocking and ignoring him to protest this inconvenient stance, or else speaking to Allard's knees, but when Allard said the word "outside," he found himself staring at Allard's face before he thought about it, interest crowding out every other feeling.

"Outside," Henry agreed, nodding his head in a gesture he had learned from Jane Markeley.

"Listen to me now, Henry," Allard said. "You will be good when you go outside. You will not shout. You will be very quiet. You will stay by my side."

"Bad place?" Henry said. These were precautions for places where sharks gathered.

"No, Henry. But you will be quiet."

A few days ago Henry might have agreed without further ques-tion rather than risk provoking Allard, but he had lost his fear of this breathless man. "*Why* quiet?" he said.

"You will be quiet, or you will not go outside."

"Will go outside. Why quiet?" Henry refused to lower his eyes. He craned his neck and gave Allard back stare for stare.

Allard looked at him for a long moment. "I do not want anyone to see you."

"Why?"

"Because, Henry, you are not a king yet."

"Sub-jets see king man before he be king," Henry said. The concept would have been very difficult to express in his own language, and his vocabulary was still inadequate to handle such shifts of time, but it was an important point. "King not come from not-know-what-place today, king tomorrow. See king."

Allard, who had turned away, turned back. He studied his charge again, then sat down. "You are right," he said. "But you cannot fight a king now. You are too small. And the—" He stopped, frowned, gave Henry a careful look. "Henry. If you were a king, who would you want to be king after you?"

"No man," Henry said. "Stay king."

"After you died, Henry. If you had to choose another king."

"Stay king, not die." Deepsmen seldom died of old age. Sharks took them, dolphins; they lost fights.

Allard shook his head. "When the king is old, he wants to know who the next king will be." He said it firmly. "Who would you want to be the king after you?"

Henry gave up on death, which he had no intention of succumbing to, and thought about it. "Deepsman," he said. "Deepsman king talk to deepsmen, talk to landsman."

"Yes," Allard said. "The kings on the land want their sons to be kings after them."

Henry said nothing. He had never had a father in the sea. He had seen other children's mothers with the men, taking food from them that they brought to their children, but no man had ever shown much interest in him beyond twisting his ear if he got in the way.

"You are not a king's son. What would the king do if he knew you were here?"

"King not here."

"He must not find out," Allard said. "Or he will send his soldiers." Henry reached for his staffs and raised himself as tall as he could. His head reached just above Allard's waist. "Show me outside."

"You will listen to me first," Allard said.

"*Outside!*" Henry raised his voice; landsmen seemed unable to shout as loud as he could, and he'd noticed before that they tended to flinch when he yelled.

Allard did flinch, but he didn't step away. "You will have another lesson, and then we will go outside," he said. "You need to understand something."

Henry bared his teeth: the prospect of more unreasonable demands, when outside had been so close within his grasp, was infuriating. "Outside," he said.

"You will listen now, or you will not go outside for a month," Allard said.

Henry snarled again, but behind the snarl, he was dismayed. Allard had kept him inside for so long already; months and months, as far as he could understand the term. Exactly how long a month lasted was still unclear—Allard had told him to watch the moon, but his eyesight still hadn't cleared well enough to see much beyond a white blob in the sky—but it sounded much too long, and the prospect of another one trapped inside was sickening. He dropped his sticks and sat on the ground with a thump; his head remained defiantly turned away, but he didn't argue any further.

"There is a word for boys like you," Allard said. "Bastard. Can you say it?"

The idea of there being a word for him, not just a random name but a useful description caught Henry's attention. "Bastard." It wasn't too difficult to say.

"Good," Allard said. He looked into the distance for a moment, seeming to gather himself.

"Bastard," Henry said again, trying to get his attention. He wanted his explanation, and he wanted to go outside.

Allard inhaled, a whistling gulp of air. "Angelica's children became the royal houses of Europe," he said. "She had many children. And she found landsmen she wished to favour, and found them deepsmen brides, to have more children, to marry her own."

"Brides?" That wasn't a word Henry had heard before; it certainly didn't sound like anything the deepswomen did.

"Wives." Two words for one thing was an annoyance Henry was

already used to, but he wasn't pleased to find it applied to his own people. "There have to be children, but brothers and sisters—children with the same mother and father—cannot marry. Their children get ill, come out wrong."

Henry thought about that. The complexities of adult courtship had been beyond him while he lived in the sea; he'd seen the dances, the woman and man spiralling each other, crooning and trying to impress, but how they'd chosen each other in the first place was not something he'd considered. Now Allard mentioned it, he was right: brothers and sisters did not mate. Deepsmen with too many sisters would sometimes leave the tribe, go and join another.

"Angelica's children could not marry each other," Allard said. "She lived a long time. The Venetians did not want her children to be princes in other countries: they did not want princes in other nations who could challenge them. But Angelica made it happen. When Venice would not agree, she went into the sea for two months and would not come back. She said that nations could have her children and grandchildren, that she would see to the breeding of deepsmen kings, if they would submit themselves to the Venetian Empire. That the Empire would be ruled by brothers, and would be strong. But that this was her will, and if her people would not submit to it, she would not protect them. She went away, and when she came back, the Venetians agreed. And she was right. She built a great empire, and while she was alive, it held together. Angelica was an extraordinary queen, there has never been a queen like her. But after she was dead, there were wars."

"No." Henry did not know how to express the feeling, but the idea of Angelica being dead rather upset him. She had sounded strong, victorious. Death, as Henry had witnessed it, was a matter of defeat; strong deepsmen stayed alive.

"There were wars, Henry. Angelica had favoured her most loyal men, chosen them to go out into the canals and—and marry with deepswomen. Their children married her children, those children were kings. But when she was gone, there was no one to choose who would have deepsmen brides and who would not. Men fought for the right, tried to take brides in secret, would not accept children born to the wrong men. There was no order without Angelica, and men killed each other, sent assassins and held battles. Nobles fought for the right to decide who would have deepsmen children and who would not, and they sent soldiers, battles on land, where the deepsmen could not help. The world grew dark, it was a terrible time."

This was harder to follow: landsmen tended to care about strange things, so following why they'd be angry was an uncertain business. It sounded like a power struggle, but back home such fights only happened with children that already existed. A mother might lash out at another tribeswoman who threatened her baby; fighting over children not yet born was bewildering. Possibly Allard was talking about mating fights, but the idea seemed strange: what was the point of landsmen having mating fights over deepswomen, fighting on land where the deepswomen couldn't see them? Such a man was likely to find himself with an unconvinced mate, Henry considered, and would have endangered himself for nothing.

"What bastard?" he said, returning to the important point.

"I am coming to that, Henry," Allard said. "After too many wars, the Venetian Empire started to fall. China went its own way, the Arab princes made treaties with their own tribes of deepsmen to protect their traders and would not have to do with Europe any more. We could not stay allied with pagans, not stay at peace with them. Christendom and the heathens—could not treat together. There were wars, wars between the faiths. We have been apart from them for centuries, we are only enemies now. But they—they do not have as many seas between them and their rivals as we do. We needed deepsmen kings. Christendom did. Europe was alone again. Europe made a law that no landsman could—marry a deepswoman. The kings we have now, they are all the children of that first century, all from Angelica's time. A landsman is not allowed to marry a deepswoman. But those children—they were born hundreds of years ago. They—they married each other. They are too close to all being brothers and sisters now. Their children are not always strong."

"So, Henry fight them, be king." The news seemed good; it was hard to see why Allard appeared so uncomfortable saying it.

"That is the point, Henry. Sometimes—your father must have been a landsman. Nowadays, nobles do not try to take deepswomen brides. The women swim away, take their babies with them. But we have sailors, Henry, men who are on ships, on the sea for many months. Sometimes, they go into the water with the deepswomen. It is not allowed, but sometimes it happens. Then there is a child like you. A bastard. Understand, Henry, you have the body of a king, but not a king's parents."

"So, fight king." Henry still didn't see the problem.

"It is not allowed, Henry. A king wants his own children to be kings after him, not a bastard."

Henry's heart sank. Landsmen were already proving implacable; since he'd been on land, Henry had yet to gain a single thing, beyond salt, that he really wanted. If the king's people were anything to go by, there was no hope. Perhaps he'd spend all his life stuck in this stupid room.

"There have been bastard kings, Henry," Allard said.

Henry perked up.

"But not many. They must fight for the throne. Understand, no king wants a bastard trying to take the throne from his children. But if a bastard can get a throne and keep it, then in five years, everyone will want to marry him, marry his children. He will be healthy, you see."

"Bastard king now?" Henry said. Perhaps if there was one already present, he might be inclined to help them.

"The last one was in France, a hundred years ago. Jean le Bâtard. He was very strong. There was a great war. But now the king of France is healthy, and has three sons. Jean's children married many princes. The queen of England, even, is his great-granddaughter. That is why she is strong."

A hundred years was too long to think about, but Henry gathered that this Jean le Bâtard had gone. The idea that you might vanish even if you were strong was new, and horrifying.

"Do you understand, Henry?"

Henry twitched. That word again. He didn't want to understand. He saw well enough what Allard was talking about. This was a leadership battle. No one welcomed a stranger, but if the stranger proved strong enough to win, everyone would want his protection. It seemed simple enough. He didn't see why Allard was so nervous talking about it. "Henry not fight king till big and strong. King not want bastard. Yes."

Allard took a breath, and nodded. "That is it, Henry. So you must be quiet, and careful."

"Outside." Henry's voice was peremptory. He had listened, and put up with Allard talking about the strong dying. Allard had talked so much that Henry felt sticky, covered in words. He wanted something new, something he could see and touch, to wash them away.

"You will be quiet," Allard said again.

Henry braced himself on his sticks. "Henry heard you."

~

Going outside required a journey Henry had never made before. His room was high up, and to get down, there were steps. Henry remembered the jolts as Allard had carried him up them, and now he stood at the top, facing straight-edged stone after straight-edged grey stone.

"Use your staffs," Allard said.

Henry looked down. The distance would have been a few seconds' worth of swimming, but he had learned to be wary of heights.

Allard reached out and took Henry's hand, placing one of the sticks on the first step down. The movement tugged Henry out of balance; his legs could flex and adjust, but they were still ill-adapted to carrying him upright. Henry snatched his hand away, dropping the stick and leaving it to rattle down the stairs. He fixed Allard with an aggressive glare, then dropped the other stick, leaving it to follow its partner down and sat, slithering one leg after another over the sharp stone ledges. His skin scraped and bruised as he descended, but he did not fall.

The chambers he passed through to get to the door were large, but to Henry they still seemed confining: walls on all sides, ceilings, straight-sided furniture, and no better than the chamber he was used to. It was only when Allard opened the door and dazzling light flooded his eyes that the world changed.

Light was different under the sea: grey shafts wavering at the surface, or a blue haze above that shaded down to nothing beneath. In the few moments of surfacing to breathe, there was nothing more than a quick flash, half-blinding him while he filled his lungs. But here the light had *heat,* the sun shone from above, and where it fell on his pallid skin, it warmed. And the fields of green stretched on and on, further than he could have seen under water, into what Allard described as "forests," a stiff, huge gathering of plants that grew straight up, hardly moving—but then a gust of wind passed, stroking cool air over his skin, and the forest swayed, a great rustling roar unlike anything he had ever heard filling the air. The wind continued, and Henry stood, marvelling at this new thing: a current that parted around you, caressed your flesh and gave way to your solidity, not pulling you along, but whispering by. The air was weak: it carried none of his weight, gave him no help in bearing himself up or transporting himself through it, but neither could it drag him with it. It gave way before him.

~

That first day, Allard stood by while Henry played in the grass. He made no attempt to stop the boy as he pulled off his clothes and rolled naked on the cool, damp ground, pressing his nose to the earth and inhaling the scent, unfamiliar but pleasant, free from the rank red undertone of so many things he encountered inside, unwashed clothes and cooked meat, the flesh of landsmen and the air of closed rooms. Henry said nothing, but tumbled on the earth, happily stretching out his limbs, while Allard stood over him and scanned the horizon with anxious, watchful eyes.

# Six

THE YEAR THAT followed was filled with weapons and movement. Markeley, who had previously been little more than a man who occasionally appeared to draw his wife into a side room, became a constant presence, teaching, pointing, hefting weapons into Henry's hands and goading, goading, goading him on, forcing his tired muscles to greater efforts, his webbed fingers to grasp the heavy hilts of swords almost as long as he was.

Allard watched the practice daily, but not continually. As Henry struggled to subdue a reeking, plunging horse unused to having a deepsman on its back, there was something in Allard's steady stance and folded arms that reminded him of his mother, waiting with her back to him all those years ago.

Once he had the feel of it, Henry wielded a sword without trouble. The heaviness of his body in the air was never again such a burden once he realised how the wind would part for him, and the speed at which he fell was compensated for by the speed with which a blade sliced through the air as he swung it. Markeley was bigger than him and knew tricks with the blade, but he was also slow. Though barely up to Markeley's waist, Henry could already wrestle a weapon from an adult hand. Spears and arrows interested him more than toiling to manage a heavy shield, until Allard took away his horse and insisted he fight on the ground.

Henry's legs were strong when they gripped his mount or churned the water, but they were not designed to hold him upright. A long shield acted as a prop while he struck with his sword over the top of it. After six months of daily training, Henry was introduced to the manor's armoury, and on the wall he saw something that suited him perfectly: two heavy blades mounted on either side of a thick pole, a staff that could prop him up until he needed to lift it and swing, standing alone for the duration of the blow.

"What is the name of that?" he pointed.

"Axe," said Allard. "Not the weapon of a lord, usually."

"It will be mine, give it to me. It must have a longer handle." Even though Henry was learning English rapidly, Allard was accustomed to Henry's lack of interest in such words as "please"; but with the boy standing soldierly and deciding for himself, he made no suggestion of manners, only taking the axe off the wall and handing it to his promising young pupil.

Winter set in, and the grass covered over with frost. Henry still insisted on going out to practice, lying in the frost as often as he could. Markeley, who was a sturdy man of few words with one eye half-closed by an old scar, would shake his head at the sight of the small figure rolling over and over, supple legs twining in the snow and heaping up drifts of white, but would say nothing, clapping his arms against the cold, and occasionally grinning to himself. The snow felt no colder to Henry than a winter sea; a sharp sensation, but not unbearable. As water melted on his skin, he felt it loosen a little; the dry flakes that formed under his clothes would soften, and his flesh would wake up, stimulated and alive. The sight of his breath pluming in the air was an endless fascination—though it was more fun to watch the breath of landsmen. They breathed so often. Markeley had shaken him the first time they had gone out in such cold, apparently worried at the long pauses between exhalations: he had looked into Henry's black eyes with his white ones, felt for a pulse under the boy's ear, examined his hands. Henry's skin was still fairer by far than the pink tint of the landsmen's, especially as Markeley's cheeks turned scarlet in the winter air, but he felt quite well. He never got sick at all.

The only trial that winter brought him was the fires. Great logs, smelling of the clean outdoors, were piled and set alight; the tattered, dazzling flames were a sight that horrified Henry the first time he saw them. Their motion was too quick, the heat they gave singeing; the sight of their bright, flickering forks in an indoor hearth was one that blinded him to all else around him, his eyes unable to adjust to so much light and darkness at once. The landsmen clustered to them, but Henry hung back, alone, as the others reached out their webless hands. The flutter and rush of the air around them, the crack of logs as they broke in the heat, was enough to drive him back, right to the edge of a room. Even a corner was more comfortable than a blaze.

When summer returned, everything changed once again. Allard announced to Henry that he was going to see another man. This man was a friend, he said; Henry had not heard of him before, but according to Allard, he would be there before the day was out.

"You said no one should see me," Henry said.

"This man will tell no one." Allard twisted his hands together. Then stopped as he saw Henry watching.

"Why will he come?"

"He will help us."

"Does he have soldiers?" Henry still wanted to see a soldier. Even if they were just landsmen who could do the things he was learning to do, he had the notion that there would be something unusual about them, something worth seeing. They were always spoken of as a group, like a shoal of fish; Henry imagined they might move together like one, or all look alike.

"He could raise them, yes. And he has a son."

Henry frowned. "Is that not bad?" The fact that the king had children and would object to Henry as a result was something he understood; as deepsmen were not generally friendly to children not their own, he supposed that a son would make this man less inclined to like him, not more.

Allard frowned in his turn. "No, Henry. Good. He will bring his son with him."

Henry could think of reasons why this was not necessarily good, but curiosity to see the son overcame his objections. The son might be near his own age. He felt some caution towards this person— deepsmen children had always been quicker with a pinch or an insult than the adults—but he had learned from sparring with Markeley, as well as grappling Allard on that strange day, that landsmen adults could be overcome. The son must be smaller, and no threat to him. Perhaps he could even threaten the son. It would be good to dominate someone else for a change.

So when Allard rode in with another mounted man by his side, Henry, who had been practising with his axe, was intrigued to see a brown-haired, blue-eyed boy riding on the saddle before him. The boy scrambled off the horse, but the man stayed mounted. Allard got off his horse and walked over to Henry.

"Here is the child," he said.

Henry did not like being talked about as if he could not hear, but there was something curious about the situation: while Allard was clasping his hands, moving from foot to foot, a little more restless than usual, the man on the horse was rigid-backed, looking down on Allard. Henry had seen others act this way towards Allard, but never before had he seen Allard so submissive.

The boy trotted over to Henry, neat legs flashing to and fro faster than an adult's. "Let us see you fight," Allard told them.

Henry was too absorbed studying this pink-cheeked creature to pay much attention. The boy stared at Henry's bent legs and webbed fingers. Henry didn't move.

"Can I see your hands?" the boy said.

"Can I see yours?" Henry said back.

The boy grinned and approached him. "I am John," he said, studying the pale skin that bound Henry's fingers together. "John Claybrook." The grin was not something Henry was quite comfortable with, having won few smiles at his home, most of them close-lipped. A memory of bared fangs troubled him for a second before he gathered himself.

"Your teeth are blunt," he said. Landsmen's generally were, but Henry felt it important to state at the outset that he wasn't going to be intimidated.

"Can I see yours?" The smile didn't fade. Henry shook off the memory and obliged with a grimace, his interest in the white squares in the other boy's mouth taking over.

"Come, let us see you fight," Allard said again.

Henry hefted his axe.

John's eyes widened. "Not with that, you will cut my head off," he said. "Here." Two wooden swords were in his belt; he proffered one.

"These are no use," Henry said.

John didn't answer. Instead, he gave Henry a poke with his own sword, then another, before falling into the formal *en garde* position. He leaned in and prodded Henry again, pushing the other toy weapon into Henry's grip.

Henry reared up on his legs, smashing the sword aside. John fell back and started to parry in earnest, but Henry, with the frantic haste of a boy who knew his legs would only bear him up so long, chased John furiously, slashing and swiping until the wooden sword fell from John's hand. John jumped as it fell, and Henry pounced, taking the weight off his legs and sitting astride John, who struggled to get up until Henry pressed both hands over his face, covering his eyes.

"Enough!" came the voice of Allard. He turned to John's father, who was looking at Henry with an expression the boy had seen once in his early childhood, when a man of his tribe had touched a rock that turned out to be a moray eel.

Henry turned back to John, who was spluttering under his hands. He released the boy's head, but stayed sitting on him while he thought of the word he wanted, trying to phrase the sentence correctly. "Would you like to be my friend?"

BOOK TWO

# ANNE

# SEVEN

A<small>NNE WAS BORN</small> a disappointment, but such was often the fate of royal girls.

King Edward, Anne's grandfather, had held the English crown for forty years. It had been a fine start: two sons born in quick succession. Auguries had predicted that William, perfect first-born Prince William, would have a brother to follow him. But when the courtiers first beheld the child that emerged, slick and silent from his mother's womb, none so much as dared cross himself. The deepsman strain had been preserved in royalty down the generations, prince marrying prince, cousin marrying cousin. And sometimes the salt blood thickened in the veins, cankering the flesh into mutant twists and clots that produced such children as Philip. Philip the Sufferer, second son of King Edward, fused from hip to knee in a single, solid tail, with two stunted and withered limbs branching off beneath. The court declared him a boy, and silently prayed that their guess, their resolute view of this flat-fronted, ungenitured infant, would prove correct.

William was the hope of the crown, as fine as Angelica herself in his mixture of elements. Coming up alongside Philip, who grew deep-voiced and massive, unquestionably male, with a rapidity equalled only by the slow development of his wits, was an endless lesson to him about the dangers of breeding too closely. William travelled the courts of Europe to find a bride. When he returned home with his Magyar princess, Erzebet, the country might have rebelled at the intrusion of such a foreigner into the sacred English palaces—not the daughter of a familiar foreign country like Scotland or Germany, not a child promised to William since birth and raised in an English court, but a distant, harsh-tongued princess—were it not for the news and rumours of Philip's stupidity, his lumbering foolishness, his violent outbursts and clumsy mind, that travelled the country in gossip that could not be stilled, in songs and plays that the common people were careful not to perform in the presence of soldiers. Fierce, steady Erzebet was strange, but she was healthy, she was as deepsman as the English royals, she was not related to William for generations back, and she could be trusted to produce a clean-blooded heir.

Their first child Mary's early birth and fine proportions were enough to counterbalance the girl's sex. Were it not for Philip, Anne, second-born girl though she was, might have been equally welcomed. But as the midwife held her up, a tiny, struggling bag of bones, chirruping in protest at the removal from her mother's arms, the skin on her face betrayed her.

Poets tried to write odes to her beauty, carefully referring to the "light of her countenance." But the phosphorescence of Anne's face was not enlightening. As the skin around her cheeks and eyes glimmered its queer blue light in the shade of indoor rooms, a glow that no amount of candlelight could quite blot out, there was no impression of beauty. The effect was only to cast her eyes into shadow, rendering the sockets hollow like a skull. Sailors told tales of fish in far-off seas that glowed in the dark, even of deepsmen with lit-up faces; most likely, Erzebet told her daughter, some distant ancestor of Angelica glowed just like Anne did. But courtiers only saw the deepsmen in glimpses at the best of times, and the people, whose faces thronged the streets as Anne's litter went by, making her shy with their stares, never saw the deepsmen at all. Anne did not look royal. She looked ghostly, and it made people uncomfortable. Before she could even speak, the girl was a living memento mori, her eyes concealed, her visage a blank page on which any person, well-versed in tales of Philip's idiocy, fearful of the collapse of the throne of England under the weight of corrupted blood, could read any story they cared to.

At least she was not like Philip, her sister Mary told her once in a moment of kindness. At least she had two legs that could walk. There would be plenty of princes who would be happy to marry her.

Anne had been four years in the world before she became aware that she had a sister. She was only five when William, her father, was killed by a soldier's blade in Scotland. She was six when her mother shed her mourning dress and married her uncle Philip.

~

Erzebet's intermittent attention dazzled Anne. From earliest memories, she had been a figure inspiring a kind of strained, yearning awe that Anne called love for want of a better word.

Anne spent most of her babyhood in the arms of nurses. Tight bands swaddled her legs in the hope of instilling some firmness in them, and wet nurses remained at hand to supply milk that flowed thin and tepidly sweet over the princess's hardening gums. Erzebet appeared at intervals. Though her memories stretched back far, her wits ripening early like a deepsman's, Anne remembered little of her first year—but later recollections of her mother were coloured by an unsurprised anxiety that suggested such scenes were already familiar. Nurses would be dismissed with a clap of the hands, deafeningly loud from Erzebet's stretched webs, and then the bands would be loosed, her mother muttering imprecations against them that Anne, too young to understand the precise terms, was never sure were not a criticism of her. Yet there were other sensations too. Anne could still recall an occasion when her mother unlooped her great pearl necklace and opened the bodice of her weighty gown, guiding into her daughter's mouth a tough, cool nipple, faintly salty but producing a thick, buttery nourishment that warmed her baby as the nurses' offerings never had. The familiarity of the feeling led Anne to conclude that it was not the first occasion, that memory as well as appetite might be causing her discontent with the watery secretions of her attendants. Erzebet rocked her daughter and crooned a sound that Anne, still without language, recognised: a reassurance, meaning *my baby, safe, my baby.* It was the last occasion she was to experience the uneasy pleasure of

Erzebet's nursing, rich milk in her mouth and an intense voice overhead. As soon as her sharp teeth appeared, nurses pulled her away with cries of alarm, and Erzebet made no further efforts to feed her. Nurses gave way to tutors as soon as Anne could speak. Latin followed English along with French and Spanish, languages of the great courts that Anne studied with devoted attention, always aware of the slap that would follow a mistake. When she was three, her first nurse was sent out of her life, and on an occasion when Anne encountered the woman walking outside and wobbled up to her hoping for a kiss, the woman curtsied and called her "your Majesty." Anne studied anxiously, absorbing the languages of Europe all at once, translating doctrine and rhetoric she could barely follow from language to language, knowing that at an uncertain interval, her mother would appear to test her. Those intervals could last a long time. Sometimes, Erzebet did not appear for months.

Erzebet insisted that there was nothing wrong with Anne's wits, and courtiers deferred, at least to her face. As only a few tutors had the privilege of teaching her, and all were too frightened of Erzebet's unforgiving temper to speak without her permission, opinions on the blue-faced girl were varied. Undoubtedly her languages were better than Philip's: Philip could speak the deepsmen's language and a few phrases of English, but children of two could construct better sentences than he could. Anne learned English and Latin, French, Spanish and Magyar with equal ease, but to courtiers raised to be equally cosmopolitan of tongue, this skill did not seem exceptional. And up until Erzebet's second marriage, it was only to her mother and tutors that Anne displayed anything else. After six years in the world, she was still a blank to the court, the light of her face shielding her expressions, and her tongue stilled in the presence of so many awesome men. She could have been anything.

It was in the context of lessons that she first became aware of her sister. Later, Anne learned the reason for this: Mary was a prize for any prince seeking a healthy bride, but tales of Philip's idiocy had travelled fast and far. To prove Mary's clean blood, Edward had insisted that she be handed to a royal wet nurse and taken across the courts of Europe to show herself: Mary had spent the first few years of her life away from home, with Erzebet sometimes leaving Anne behind, making diplomatic visits to the courts where her oldest daughter was a temporary guest. Erzebet had never set foot in England before she was crowned there, and she knew the hostility that such queens gathered; a princess from England would be all the more welcome if she had visited her people before her marriage, even if she was only a toddler at the time. Mary had been passed from nurse to nurse, court to court, laying the foundations of a future that remained, as long as they had no brother to ensure England's succession, unclear. By the time Anne was old enough to study, Erzebet had insisted that enough was enough, that it was time for Mary to come home, and anybody who wished to inspect her could visit England. But all of this, she had not mentioned to Anne. Erzebet's appearances had been so wide-spaced, so unpredictable, that Anne had never asked about the outside world, that great, weighty place that fought so hard for her mother's attention. Erzebet, in her turn, had a focus, a blade-straight intensity when she spoke to Anne, which left little room for outsiders. Anne thought it was only the two of them in the world.

Hence, the first time Anne was lined up with this unfamiliar child, waiting for Erzebet's attendance, the two of them stared openly. The fact that this girl's legs were bent and her hands webbed like Anne's was astonishing and, after a second's study, outrageous. Other people were straight and split-handed, but Anne and her mother had shared a bond, and the nerve of this stranger openly laying ownership to this shape, *her* shape, provoked Anne to horrified fury. The girl pointed, raising her unfairly webbed hand, and said to Anne, "What ails your face?"

The question could only be an insult, for Anne had sat quietly through a rough-clothed washing before being ushered in. "Go away," she said.

"Your face is blue, it shines." The girl's face was pretty and pink-skinned; Anne glared at her.

"Nothing ails my face," she said, her voice choked with an anger that sounded frustratingly like tears.

"It shines in the dark." The girl pointed again, and Anne forsook the safety of one of her canes to give a hard shove that toppled the girl to the ground.

It was at this point, while Anne's tutor was pulling her back with a jerk to her ear and setting about her with a series of blows from the abandoned stick, that Erzebet made a slow, steady progress into the room. Anne ceased struggling and looked up wet-eyed, waiting for her mother to save her.

"What happens here?" Erzebet's Latin was perfect, but she reserved it for foreign dignitaries, asserting to all the court in her flawed, accented English her claim to rule the country as well as a woman native born.

"The princess Anne pushed her sister, your Majesty." The tutor, a woman by the name of Margaret, still held Anne by the arm, but the cane she held limp in an uncertain grip.

"Why do you have the cane?" Erzebet's eyes on the woman's hand were cold.

"I—I wished to correct the princess, your Majesty." Margaret's voice had gone dead. She made no effort to move back or even lower her head as Erzebet came towards her, canes tapping on the ground, the rustle of her skirts loud over the whisper of her feet on the floor. She stood before her attendant for a long pause before passing her right stick into her left hand, and with her free palm, giving Margaret a slap across the face that made her stagger.

"You do not touch the cane without a prince's permission," Erzebet said, her voice clear against the woman's muffled whimpers. She turned to Anne. "Did you push your sister?"

Anne looked up at her mother. "The girl said I have a blue face." The word "sister" was starting to hurt, and she reached up for her mother's hand.

"Bad girl," Erzebet said. "Go away." She turned her back, and spoke not another word to Anne as her daughter was carried out of the room.

Anne spent a further week with her tutors, not knowing if she would ever see her mother again. Her inattention to lessons brought punishments that made little impression. It was only when her mother reappeared to find her daughter behind in her studies, and left again, that Anne reapplied herself, struggling to master her letters with a frantic haste that made the words swim on the page.

A week later, Anne found herself once again in a room with this sister, her mother watching over them both. The sight of Erzebet made her heart beat frantically; her mother had called her a bad girl, and Anne was desperate for some sign of forgiveness. Erzebet gave none, neither frowning nor smiling at Anne; she sat watching both daughters, her eyes passing from one to another, the same intense, steady gaze on each little face. Anne answered when addressed, a sharp knot tightening in her throat every time her mother's eyes flicked away to the girl. To Mary. The questions changed from Latin to Spanish, French to Magyar, and the sisters answered, correct and formal.

After some time, Mary was called on to recite an answer in Latin. Anne listened, struggling to find something in the girl that could justify the loss of her mother's attention, when she heard a mistake.

Erzebet stopped Mary's recitation with a raised eyebrow. "No," she said.

Anne raised her courage on a tide of savage satisfaction that the interloper had misstepped. "It should be *benedicta,*" she volunteered.

Erzebet turned her head to Anne's tense face. "Yes," she said, "that is right." She gave the girl a small smile that stayed in Anne's memory as she studied for hours each day, learning anything she could find that might win her more.

Together, they studied. Languages. History, the story of the great houses of Europe and the complex strands of Angelica's line. Geography, the cities and borders and armies of the nations that either of them might one day rule as queens. The first time Erzebet introduced that idea into a lesson, Anne found herself crying, for reasons she was too ashamed to explain: Erzebet had left her own country, her own mother, to be a queen in England. Anne had no desire to do such. She would never see Erzebet again.

"Enough, Anne," Erzebet said. There was a little wrinkle in her forehead, but her tone was firm.

Anne couldn't manage it. "I do not want to go abroad," she said. Her voice was feeble-sounding; to talk this way in front of her rival sister was shaming.

To her surprise, she felt a small hand patting her arm. "Other nations are not bad," Mary said. "They have different fashions and different foods, and they wait on you at banquets."

Anne looked at Erzebet, waiting for her to say something enlightening, but Erzebet was sitting back, watching the two of them.

"I wish to stay home," Anne said in a small voice.

"I have been to France," Mary said. "The Dauphin gave me a ring, and this string of pearls. Would you like it?"

"What?" Mary was such a rival to her mother's affections that Anne had found more or less everything she did offensive, but sending gifts was usually done by courtiers aiming to please people. Anne had nothing to offer Mary, nothing to make Mary wish to keep on her good side, so there was no good reason why Mary should give her anything. The pearls, though, were pretty, not unlike the string she remembered Erzebet wearing in those few moments when she had nursed Anne. Temptation and antagonism warred in Anne's stinging throat.

"They would look well when your face is alight," Mary said. "They would glow."

So there it was: her face again. The girl was just teasing her. "You should go back to France," Anne said.

To her astonishment, Mary's eyes filled with tears. "You are unkind," she said. "I offered you a gift. In France I thought of my sister, that I could bring her back a gift." Mary wiped her face with the back of her wrist. The gesture was so inelegant, so unlike a courtier's delicacy, that it filled Anne with a startled sense of fellow-feeling. She had thought she was the only clumsy one.

Anne didn't want to surrender, didn't want to be the one to climb down, but her mother was still sitting there, watching them both. The idea of Mary thinking of her in France gave Anne a sense of guilt, too: she hadn't thought of Mary in England, hadn't known of her existence, and part of her still heartily wished the girl back in France. But nobody had offered Anne a gift before. Mary was the first person who had ever suggested she'd minded Anne's absence.

Anne cast around. "I have a sapphire bracelet that is too big for me," she said. "I could give you that if you give me the pearls."

Mary looked up with something like interest.

"You cannot give away a gift," Erzebet cut in. "It offends the giver. A princess must not give offence."

Anne sighed. Erzebet hadn't reprimanded Mary, but now she was chiding both of them. Perhaps it was only Anne who caused offence.

"I do not like pearls," Mary said. "Courtiers always give me pearls, and I have too many of them, and they look dull."

"Pearls are royal, from the sea," Erzebet said. Her tone brooked no disagreement.

Mary cast Anne a glance of conspiracy. It was a limited start, but it was the first time Mary had looked like anything but a rival.

At times, Erzebet still visited her younger daughter alone. On these occasions, she would sit beside her and croon in the language Anne had only heard her mother speak. She was growing resignedly aware that such scenes were probably taking place with Mary as well, but she drank them in, taking in every second of her mother's presence. The language itself was easy, a fluid, musical flow of groans and squeaks, whistles and clicks that soothed her even while she knew the moments couldn't last.

From infancy, it had been the language with which her mother called her to safety when they swam together. Anne was long accustomed to the court's journeys from castle to castle, and had as clear an understanding of the lakes and streams of each residence as she had of the rooms within. There were many times when her mother, away from the court, would place Anne before her on a horse and the two of them would ride off—Anne thrilling with the secrecy and closeness of the adventure—and strip off their heavy court gowns to slip naked into the water. Released from the strain of bearing themselves up like landsmen, mother and daughter would dive and whirl, their legs coiling like whips through the water, cold and clean and free.

Once the two sisters had been introduced, there were other trips too. The first time the court gathered up for a journey to the shore, Anne was anxious. She had understood that her mother made such trips, but as she was placed onto a litter with her sister, ready to be carried, Erzebet's litter seemed a long way ahead, carried side by side with William's and Edward's, and there was no one to ask.

Mary, beside her, was wearing the same kind of garment as Anne: a dress surprisingly plain for a formal occasion. Anne's nurse had dressed her that morning, but the gown had only ties at the front, tapes that could be unknotted even by small, webbed hands, and the fabric was light and unjewelled. Both small heads were weighted with silver crowns, but these light dresses were a mystery.

Anne was becoming more and more nervous. She didn't quite want to admit it to Mary, but she wanted someone to explain things. "Have you done this before?" she managed.

Mary shook her head. "No. Have you?"

It was that question that warmed Anne a little. Mary seemed so big, so assured. The idea that she might consider Anne ahead of her in anything at all was a shocking compliment. "No." Anne felt sufficiently better to admit some ignorance of her own. "What will happen, do you know?"

"We will go into the sea with our mother," Mary said. "We are going to see the deepsmen."

Anne blinked. She had heard stories of them since she was old enough to talk, those mighty, essential allies in the water, but Erzebet had always told her that she wouldn't see them until she was big enough. Bobbing along on her litter, she didn't feel very big.

"Do you swim well?" she asked Mary.

Mary nodded. "Yes, very well." She sounded a little more pleased with herself than Anne could like, but before she could feel too annoyed, she noticed one of the litter bearers, a man named John Fisher, of whom Anne had always been shy, watching them out of the corner of his eye.

Anne took a chance. *Is it safe?* she asked. She put the question in her mother tongue, her and Erzebet's private language. If Erzebet spent time with Mary, Mary would understand it, and at least they would be safe from Fisher's ears.

Mary looked at her, a quick, startled look. There was a pause before she slipped her hand into Anne's. *Stay with me,* she said. Mary's head was upright, but as her hand gripped hard around Anne's it trembled a little.

The reason for the gowns became clear at the water's edge: following Erzebet's lead, the two girls found themselves stripping off, unaided, before the court. Anne struggled to keep her mind off the dozens of eyes behind them, to look out to sea, holding herself steady. If she could get through this well, her mother would be pleased with her.

The court musicians were sounding music, playing a march of approach. Anne noticed that Philip was still in his litter. His voice rose, louder and louder, protesting: "Go in! Go in!"

Edward, their grandfather, laid his crown on the sand, and William and Erzebet followed. Anne cast a quick look at Mary, and the two girls imitated the motions of their parents, wobbling a little on their flexible legs; neither of them could manage it as gracefully as Erzebet. Then Edward was wading into the water, a few arthritic steps before the sea grew deeper and he dived forward like a young man. William followed, a great leap that drove the water up in plumes around him. Anne and Mary hesitated, then Erzebet reached back, took one girl by each hand, and led them into the shallows. *Stay with me,* she said. They swam off together, into the cold, salt water, where the tides pulled and the currents ran in icy streams beneath the surface, and they could hear, ringing through the water, cries the musician's march had tried to imitate: *We are coming. We are coming.*

And ringing back, from out in the bay, louder and stronger and richer than the cries of the family, were other voices: *We are here.*

As Erzebet speeded up, her hands slipped free, and she swam ahead, calling back quietly—*Keep up, children.* All around, the water was dark, and if Erzebet swam into the shadows, they'd lose sight of her. Anne kicked as hard as she could, but her legs were small, and she found herself alarmed.

*Don't lose me,* she said. And before Erzebet could answer, Mary called back, *Stay with me.* Anne felt a moment of resentment that her sister was answering when it was her mother's voice that she wanted, needed to hear, but Erzebet was calling, sending her voice after her husband: *I have children with me. Do not threaten them. We are strong. We have children.*

*Stay with me,* came Mary's voice again, definitely a frightened squeak now, and Anne gathered herself. Mary knew no more than she did, and they were wild in the water, and the voices were tolling out all around them, louder than a cathedral organ. Their parents were there. Freedom rushed to Anne's head in a sudden torrent: she was in the dark, away from the court, away from everything, and there were deepsmen out in the bay.

From the sounds of their voices, there were many deepsmen in the court they met that day, thirty, forty, a whole choir. But the water in the bay was muddy and stirred, and though Anne had seen pictures all her life, her first glimpses of the deepsmen were only a few white bodies flashing through the haze. They were massive, larger even than her father, and as they approached, one of them swam out of the dark and stared straight into her face. There were black eyes, tiny sharp teeth, a small, flattened nose, and Anne leaped in the water, too shocked to react: the face that stared at her was almost skull-like. Sharp-nailed fingers reached out, and she heard the deepsman cry out: *Face. Deep face.*

It was her blue face again, Anne realised. But then she saw it: little glimmers of blue shining up from the depths. Not on every deepsman, but glints here and there, glints that told her she was not alone.

Anne pulled all her courage together, and spoke through the water. *I am not a stranger,* she said. *Welcome me.* And the deepsman swam round her, round in a rapid circle, fast as a minnow.

After a moment, Anne heard Mary's voice repeat the call. There were other sounds, noises she recognised as welcome. As the deepsmen circled them—glorious, she saw now, great magnificent beings white as milk and mighty as horses, and circling *her*—Anne smiled into the brine. Mary might know more about the land, but Anne had spoken first, and she had spoken well, and Mary had learned and followed. It was a moment of pure victory.

～

A year later, it was in the water that Erzebet told Anne of the death of William. The tale was quickly told: there had been a war. Anne had been aware of a great army going out, the rattle of weapons and pounding of hooves, and her father had been among them, but the reasons for it had been unclear to her. As Erzebet explained it now, it seemed as if the war had mostly gone well. There were no more kings in Scotland. Like Wales, it was now under the rule of one family: their own. Edward ruled the whole island.

Erzebet did not sound happy. Anne had tried to understand why, if the war troubled her, it had happened at all. All Erzebet could say to make it clear was, "It is not good to have borders on land." Countries divided by seas maintained a reasonable peace. The deepsmen guarded their shores, and few nations ever risked their sailors against a fleet of patriots who could swim up from beneath and smash hulls, pull off rudders, drag men down to a thrashing death. But nothing guarded borders on land except landsmen. Soldiers who feared a dark end in the deep water were not afraid to fight each other. Landlocked countries sparred with their neighbours like cats in a sack, but countries protected by deepsmen on their shores were safe from countries overseas, more or less. This was why the princes were so vital, Erzebet explained. They treated with the deepsmen, and if the deepsmen did not protect the country, it was an unguarded feast, ready for any flock of ships to swoop upon. Deepsmen must be loyal, or nations would be as unstable as if they were landlocked.

Now the island was one nation, ruled by one king. It should have meant peace within her borders. But William was dead, and Erzebet floated in the water, dry-eyed and hoarse-voiced, cuddling her little daughter to her. There was a note in her voice that Anne had not heard before. Erzebet had never sounded less than sure. It troubled

Anne for a moment, but Erzebet's hands stroked her hair gently, and in that moment, the joy of her mother's attention was strong enough to make her push doubts out of her mind.

Anne's father had been a vague presence in her life, a figure to whom she had to make obeisance on formal occasions when she was tucked into heavy, jewelled dresses and presented before the court, a fast-swimming figure on trips through the sea; though he was small compared with the sea people, he was so much bigger than Erzebet—than her—that in Anne's mind he was classed more or less as a deepsman. She had paid formal respects to him, anointing his hands with salt water and murmuring the deepsmen's chant of submission before moving on to her grandfather to perform the same task for him, but she could remember few conversations with her father; having confused him so much with the deepsmen, she would have been hard put to describe his face. Erzebet lay on her back, cold waves lapping around them, with Anne's small form curled on her chest, breathing in the fresh, rain-tasting air. Though Anne could hear the strain in her mother's voice, even years later, when she was a woman and old enough to understand, still the strongest memory of her father's death was the peace of the waves kissing her sides, the comfort of her mother's strong arms around her, carrying her face-up under the sky.

So on the day when the marriage was announced between Erzebet, widow of William, heir to Edward's throne, and Philip, the new crown prince, last remaining son of gaunt, shrewd Edward, Anne's feelings were hurt that Erzebet had not taken her for a swim to give her this news. The disappointment was so strong that her eyes stung with tears. A little, cool hand reached out and clasped around hers, and to her surprise, she realised that it was Mary's, her sister reaching teary-eyed and giving her hand a sympathetic squeeze. Erzebet stood, hunched over her canes, facing the court from her dais. There was a stiffness around her eyes and mouth that Anne had never seen before. For a moment, Anne stood before the court, tears in her eyes, perceiving her sister's clasping hand and her mother's set face. Longing gripped her, a deep longing that they could all shed their clothes and jewels and slip into the water together, swim out to sea. She knew it would make her feel better. But whether it would console Mary and Erzebet from their strange, unspoken grief, she was too young to know.

# EIGHT

THE DAY OF the wedding, Anne was packed into the heaviest dress she had ever owned, caked with sharp jewels like a barnacled hull; her hair was arranged in neat locks and trimmed at the ends; new, fine sticks were placed in her hands, and her maid dabbed at her faintly blue cheeks with cosmetics that thickened uncomfortably on her skin and did little to dim the glow. Warnings were given about staying quiet and behaving herself during the ceremony, but these were perfunctory; from those she trusted, Anne received any expression of love with desperate, submissive gratitude, but in the presence of crowds, she seldom spoke at all.

The cathedral was filled with courtiers, hot with the warmth of bodies and candles even though its vaulted ceiling rose high and cool and the doors stood open to let in the light of the sun. Anne sat in her pew, arranged next to her sister, who wore a dress glittering with pearls and gems as stiff and massive as Anne's own. Mary, who was usually decorous in public, slipped a cold, dry hand into Anne's own and held on. Anne did not understand, but the caress was too consoling to puzzle over; she sat quietly like a good girl, letting her hand be held.

Court musicians played a mighty song of celebration as Philip was brought up to the altar. The music was traditional, hautbois and flutes bending themselves to notes sung by deepsmen out at sea—or at least, to the lower-pitched notes of a deepsman's range; the higher tones

were beyond a landsman's ears or a flautist's compass. The accent was
crude, and the notes ornamented almost out of recognition, but Anne
could make the message out clearly enough: it spoke of happiness, of
kingship, of good things, and of marriage. Philip sat in his litter, carried as he was from place to place. Unable to mount a horse, unable to
do more than hoist himself upright with the royal canes, still chair-
bound and stuck, Philip reclined his life away, carried to and fro by
bearers. Attending him at all times were the Lord Privy Sponges, a
post revived in such cases as his, silver buckets of brine over their arms,
moistening Philip's ever-drying skin in a regular, soothing stroke. The
litter lurched forward, the Sponges watching their footing, under the
direction of Robert Claybrook, the Earl of Thames. The man was
Philip's—*adviser,* was the word Anne had been taught to say. Claybrook was a sturdy, alert man of pleasant manners. His friendship was
much sought by those at court. Though his lands were not as extensive
as some, they commanded most of the crucial, capital river, and a man
who owned waterways outranked any landlocked lord in the
country. His friendship was easily given as far as Anne could see.
He even smiled at her and her sister as he guided the litter before the
congregation.

The smile heartened Anne briefly; no one else was smiling. But
when her mother appeared, bent over her polished staffs, making her
slow way unaided up to the altar, Anne's heart clenched. Erzebet was
not a smiling woman, nor a high-coloured one, but Anne was accustomed to an anxious study of her mother's moods and expressions for
any signs of warmth. In Erzebet's pallor and stillness now, Anne read
an unhappiness she had never seen before.

The Archbishop of Stour was at the altar, holding aloft a pearled
chalice. John Summerscales, his name was, a small, white-haired man
with shrunken limbs and bright eyes, quick on his feet for one so
elderly. Anne was used to paying him silent deference, but the man
standing beside him was new to her. Narrow of face, dark-haired and
thin, he was a puzzlement to her, for while he wore the robes of a
bishop, he was a young man for such rank, forty at the oldest and possibly younger. It was hard to tell, for he had the haggard face of an

ascetic. At first Anne supposed he must be one of the severe priests who fasted and did penance with fierce passion for their faith, but then she saw what was strange about him, what had drawn her eye and kept her attention well enough to offer a moment away from worrying about her mother. His left leg dragged behind him, lame and useless, giving him a halting, lopsided gait like no one else at court.

Staffs were forbidden to courtiers, the province of royalty alone. If a man could not stand on his two good feet, he could never stand before the king. Even lame farmers laid down their crutches when the crown paraded by. But this man, staffless and hobbled, walked up to the altar to attend on the Archbishop, his leg scraping the ground behind him, no stick to help him, forcing himself forward on his one sound limb.

The aisle of the Cathedral glistened with water where the Sponges had dripped. As the chant of Mass began, Erzebet stood before the congregation, her face frozen over like a winter lake.

Philip sat staring in his chair, whimpering if the Sponges were slow in their work. As the Archbishop turned to him for a response in the ceremony, he blinked, unresponding.

Claybrook turned and whispered something to him.

Philip blinked, and Claybrook whispered again.

"Yes," Philip said, a deep bass croak. It was not the formal answer required, but it was an answer; the Archbishop evidently decided that it would suffice.

So it was that Anne's mother married her uncle, while Mary and Anne sat hand in hand, Anne trying over and over to catch her mother's unresponding eye. Finally, the Archbishop stood up, straightening his back from bending down to keep a careful ear attuned to Philip's mutterings, and declared to the world that here stood man and wife.

At this, Philip looked up. "Wife?" he said.

Claybrook looked at Erzebet, waiting for her response.

Still-faced, Erzebet tottered over to Philip, her hands white on the heads of her canes. "Yes," she said, Magyar accent thicker than usual, but clear before the court. "I am your wife, my lord."

Philip stared for a moment more. "Wife," he said, then added something in the deepsman language, something Anne recognised from the tune the musicians played, about love.

Erzebet did not move.

Philip reached out a massive hand. His webbed fingers made an awkward grab, catching at the neckline of Erzebet's jewelled gown, then reaching down and digging into the rich silk overlaying her breast. Anne heard her mother's teeth snap shut, and then Claybrook stepped forward, spoke a quick word to the bearers. A shuffle, a grunt of effort, and the litter was hoisted on their shoulders, carried swiftly down the wet aisle, musicians striking up a loud refrain that failed to cover Philip's protests, his voice tolling out, "Wife! Wife! Mine!" as they carried him out of the church.

King Edward rose and stepped before the congregation, raising his hand in a gesture of blessing. At the sight of his gaunt frame, Anne sat straighter than before: Edward had always treated her with an austere kindness, and Philip's grab had frightened her to tears. But Edward looked at no one: not at Anne, not at Mary, not at the Archbishop or the bride or the court. He stared straight ahead of him, at nothing.

The congregation made their way outside, ready to hunt and feast to celebrate the marriage. Anne turned to Mary, still by her side, as small and ignored as she. "Will our mother be all right?" she said.

Mary leaned over and gave Anne a kiss on the cheek, and then a maid came and took her away, and Anne was left alone.

~

No children were to come of the match. Anne never became used to her mother's behaviour after she was married; it was too erratic to understand. The moments when Erzebet would stoop and kiss her, stroking her face and crooning under her breath, rocking her on her jewelled lap, eyes closed, for hours at a time, were spoiled by the knowledge that the next day it was likely Erzebet would stand in court, face forward, looking at no one and with no time or glances to spend on her yearning little daughter. Erzebet was steady and proud as she spoke to ambassadors, greeting them gracefully and holding her ground in disputes, growing stronger and surer under Edward's watchful eye as the months passed, until the king and his daughter-in-law were holding court equally. But in private, Erzebet answered no questions and her kisses came like rainfall, soothing to Anne's parched skin but unpredictable, and as utterly beyond Anne's command as the grey clouds.

It was at the first blessing of the waters after Erzebet married Philip that Anne realised the full import of something about her uncle. It must have been the case even before the wedding, but then Anne was too young to be much interested in him except as a loud-voiced lumbering presence in the background, a figure she was anxious to avoid. Until now, blessing the waters had meant time with her mother and sister in the sea. But this time, as the court gathered itself up and progressed to the creaking of hautbois and the groaning of Philip's litter all the way down to the shore, Anne suddenly saw the inconsistency. Erzebet was of the royal blood, half of the land and half of the sea. So was Mary, so was Anne herself; fin-limbed and supple in the water, quick-tongued enough to speak the language of the sea people. And so was Philip: his clumsy half-tail crippled him on the land, but would have been a mighty rudder out in the bay; his grasp of English was hardly better than a child's, but the simpler rhythms of the deepsmen's language presented no problem to him. Why then, Anne suddenly came to wonder, was he prevented from going into the sea?

It was this question in her mind that made this voyage into the water a serious business. Since that first great voyage out into the bay with Mary, such trips had become a regular feature of their lives together; she had come to think of them as a seasonal treat, like feasting at Christmas and music at Easter. Six times a year, their elders took her and Mary out into the bay to play with these wonderful creatures that spoke their private language, that could dive and wheel in the cold waves faster even than Erzebet, that floated above the dark depths below them like living shadows, fearless as eagles. Anne had loved those trips; stripped naked and free of her tight-bound dresses, the nourishing brine on her skin, strict tutors and staring courtiers left behind, she had been eager to sport with the deepsmen, and had swum to them joyfully, twisting and circling them in races and contests that she never minded losing, so splendid were the feats of agility they performed to outpace her.

Yet that day, when they brought Philip down to the shore with them, Anne realised that while she had delighted in the exchanges between Erzebet and the deepsmen, happy to be surrounded by their native language, she had never thought to wonder why her uncle's voice was absent from the choir.

The litter bearers laid Philip down in the sand. A phalanx stood around him: the Privy Sponges, wetting his grey skin with their endless trails of brine; Anne could see through their shirts the muscles in their arms rise and flex, grown strong with their ceaseless action; soldiers mounting guard; Robert Claybrook, his back to the sea, watching Philip with a careful smile. His son was beside him in recognition of the importance of the day: the whole court always attended the blessing of the waves. Claybrook's son John was a handsome boy a few years older than Anne, with an amiable smile that flashed out every time his father pushed him forward to bow to her and her family; Anne had often wished for him as a playmate, but from the lowliness of her six years, had little hope of attracting the attention of a grown boy of nine. Standing in the shadow of his father, John was keeping one eye on Philip, but his attention kept turning, as Anne's did, to the waves beyond the beach, where the deepsmen were every moment expected.

At the head of the court stood Erzebet. Much of her journey had been made in a litter, as had her daughters'; the walk was a long one for royal legs, and they needed to save their strength for the swim. But as the bearers laid her down, Erzebet gathered her sticks and pushed herself upright without help, the grit of her staffs and the whisper of her feet in the sand a quiet note against the undertone of the hushing sea. Anne, who had been carried in her own little chair, resignedly aware that a place in her mother's was out of the question and finding herself surprisingly lonely that Mary had been placed in another litter as well, recognised the stiffness of her mother's neck and the stillness of her face: Erzebet was not in a talking humour. Anne turned instead to her grandfather, who sat braced on his horse, the stoop of a lifetime on crutches bending his back until it mirrored the curve of his mount's neck. His face was less rigid than Erzebet's, though no happier, but when he caught his granddaughter's eye, it softened just a little.

"Will you swim with us?" Anne mouthed. Her voice was too low for the courtiers to hear, but royal ears could catch a whisper from half a mile away.

"No, Anne," Edward whispered back. "Your mother can go alone, it is time for her to do so."

"Are we not to go?" Alarmed disappointment rose in Anne's throat: was she going to be left behind?

"Yes, you and Mary are to go. I shall stay on the shore." Edward turned his head, casting a bleak look at his son. "Philip and I shall stay behind."

"Why?" Anne wanted to know. Erzebet grew quickly impatient with too many questions, but Edward had never slapped her for importuning him.

Edward did not grow angry, but he shook his head, slowly and carefully. "Pay attention to the ceremony, Anne," he said.

Anne paid attention, but there was little there: the musicians played their usual chant, trills and arpeggios around the central call like lichen around a tree branch: *Come here.*

The music continued, and Erzebet, standing on the shore, raised her face and called. The chant was a grave one, a low, resonating cry that would have been startling from a landswoman, but as Erzebet sang to the depths, Anne relaxed, hearing the familiar sounds that were, to her, part of Erzebet's being, her mother's real language. Mary picked up the chant and Anne followed, their smaller voices straining down to the sound. It was a difficult call for a child to make, but though its equivalents—*help me; mother*—might suit her range better, they were no language for a princess. Anne adapted the call, harmonising, piping her own chant over the deeper one of her mother, trying her best to sing like an adult.

Erzebet's voice blended with the girls' as the waves shimmered sharp-edged on the face of the sea. The sky was white over their heads, and the water reflected back steel-grey, dull and scratched over with turbulence. The call went on and on; no response came, but the women had deepsmen's lungs, able to carry a chant for hours. At the sound, gulls left their perches and circled the court, ready and waiting in case a hunt was to follow, one that might drive up fish within the reach of a sharp-beaked plunge. And against the cries of the white birds, a faint sound emerged, lost on the court amid the squawks and the hautbois and the pulse of the surf, but clear as a footfall to the family's waiting ears. A clatter of water, a sigh and a gasp, then a rush of waves closing over. A deepsman, breaking the surface for air. The first sound was followed by a cascade of others as the troop followed the leader's example, and then Anne's eyes caught them, pale backs turning as the bodies dived again, trails of bubbles cleaving the grey behind them, spray leaping in the air like pebbles flung up by a child's hand. And as the water in the bay streaked white, other voices cut across the family's, stronger, louder, half-buried in the water but, to Anne's ears, slicing through them with the precision of an arrow: *We are here.*

Erzebet lifted her hand, fingers raised in a gesture half of blessing, half of pointing, directing the court's view to those white trails spreading their parallel lines towards the shore. Anne and Mary hushed as Erzebet changed her notes, a tumble of soprano clicks: *We will join you.*

The musicians lowered their instruments: this was between the Princess and the deep. Erzebet's voice was the only human sound from the beach.

There was a pause, pale shapes moving beneath the surface. Then, with a rush of sound and an explosion of droplets, a body burst upwards, rising hip-high in the water. Only for a moment was his face visible before he dropped back beneath, black eyes and white skin, ragged, matted locks and teeth as small and as sharp as a pike's. The answer rose from the waves, from a dozen throats, picking up Erzebet's initial call: *Come here.*

The court stood quietly by, damp sand caking around their costly shoes, as Erzebet began to disrobe at the shore's edge. Her movements were slow and careful, revealing for all who wished to see her fleshly claim to the crown, her supple legs and webbed toes, her rough white skin and hairless sex and long, sturdy waist, marbled here and there with the marks of two pregnancies like the ripples on a wave. It was a sight Anne usually found relaxing, meaning as it did a chance for privacy; the intrusive presence of the court compensated for by the prospect of a real swim, not in a lake but out to sea. But as Anne began unfastening her own dress, she saw the dark patches on her mother's arms and chest, deep purple bruises a hand's width across.

A stir passed among the court, no louder than the fall of a wave. Eyes turned to Philip. Claybrook, standing beside him, looked at his lord for a long, silent second, his normal smile gone. He showed no expression at all; without the smile, he became unfamiliar, almost unrecognisable. His eyes flickered over Philip and Erzebet with a speed that made them seem the only living thing in that still face. Erzebet did not turn her head. She lifted it and froze, a statue standing motionless amid the white foam that frothed and stroked at her feet.

Anne's throat tightened. Under the water, she could go without breath for as long as ten or more minutes, and at the sight of the marks on her mother's pallid limbs, she closed her mouth and let no more air in. She didn't breathe again until she, Mary and Erzebet had waded out past the shallows, and the chilly embrace of the water had taken the weight of her body and floated it out to sea.

~

Under the surface, sounds changed. The rustle of the waves ceased the instant her head dipped below the surface: water stopped her ears, filled them with its ringing silence, a deep solid lull that extended for miles. Sounds were tangible under water, felt against the ears. Against the background of damped quiet, there were endless small ticks and rattles, the clatter of stones rolling over each other in the sea's restless, curving grasp, the clicks of fish signalling to each other in a continual crackling like twigs breaking underfoot: tiny, intimate sounds, small enough to be blown away by the wind on-shore, but here, in the fresh, yielding cold, as vivid as the touch of a finger on skin. Anne listened, coiling her legs to drive herself forward, working her cramped muscles until they stretched out to their full mobility, absorbed as always in the precision and importance of sounds under water, travelling across wide spaces and still as clear and close as if they spoke entirely to her. Distance became palpable, as if her very flesh could reach out and feel the far-off sounds, and she swam faster, water holding her, stroking around her, a present, soothing grasp, carrying everything to her.

Through that dense quiet came the chant of the deepsmen. Just about audible from the beach, under the water it was loud, immediate long before the deepsmen came into view. As she swam further out, the pebbled bottom loomed a greater and greater distance beneath them, the haze of the water blurring it out. Anne, eyes open in the darkening water, felt no fear of the depths, but her chest tingled a little at the sight of it, an excitement and sense of risk she could not explain to herself. Rising to breathe, her lungs more tired than her mother and sister's after holding her breath for so long, she turned like a deepsman, cresting the water in a swift roll, her body turning over and her face breaking into the air long enough for a swift inhalation, then spinning back down without losing speed, bending her back and diving down to her mother. Erzebet, racing ahead graceful as a seal, made no reprimand as she would have on land: here, sound carried far enough that Anne could have swum to the other side of the bay or beyond, and still have been summoned by her mother's voice, even as the fading light hid her in the depths.

In this way, Anne was embraced by the voices long before forms began to appear in the void. As she swam, Anne gathered her wits. Always before now, the joy of speed and the freedom of the water had dominated her thinking, but her mother's bruises, black in the half-light, had made her alert. In this new state of attention, the rattling, atonal harmony called another image to her mind: her father, swimming on ahead, a long dark shape in her memory, in the days before the war took him. The emotion she felt most in those remembered moments was an uneasy bewilderment that this stranger should be present with her mother and sister, a tense doubt as to what he wanted.

But the world was always puzzling then, the appearance of a frog in a stream matter for question, the language and concerns of adults a fathomless mystery, and so the presence of her father had been swallowed up in the general glut of strangeness that beset her infantine world. Now he was gone, and with Philip on the shore and Edward watching from his horse, the swim was like the swims she and Erzebet took in the lakes, a female conclave. Their part in it, anyway. The deepsmen's bass voices echoed around her, but for all their closeness to her ears, the sounds were not oppressive. None of them wanted anything from her.

Swimming through the glittering wall of bubbles Erzebet trailed behind her as she sank from a snatched breath above, Anne discovered that she couldn't remember a word her father had said.

It was on that thought that the first deepsmen came into view. Under the water they were magnified, huge, their pallid skin glowing through the grey, their round black eyes softened in the cloudy brine. Erzebet was there before her daughters, diving deep and swimming back up with one of the men, the two shapes spiralling round and round each other in a column of silver bubbles that rose about them like a fanfare. As the two of them broke the surface, there was a moment of isolation as the mirror-bright ceiling blocked Anne's view of Erzebet, and then the mirror shattered as the two bodies fell back together, the crash of their landing following by a whispered rush as the air frothed back above them. Erzebet descended again, sinking with another man. The words they were saying to each other were simple, *here, with you, me,* but the dance was a twining, supple display almost too fast for the eye to follow. Mary held back, but Anne, determined to understand these new events, braced herself and dived down. No deepsman would follow a little thing like her, but Anne felt stronger, wider awake, resolved to try. Into the dark she swam, the clutch of the water pressing firmer the deeper she descended. Then she turned with a flex of the spine that felt almost forbidden in its ease, and shot upwards, revolving around and around like a spun top, driving her legs hard to launch herself. Closer and closer the surface rushed, and then she broke through, suddenly freezing as the wind blew on her wet skin, an airborne gasp before she was falling with a sharp smack as the water broke, hard and stinging, beneath her.

*Me,* she said.

Erzebet turned and pulled her over. *Mine,* she said to the deepsmen, and again, drawing Mary in, *mine.*

Anne hovered in the brine, waiting to hear what was said.

*Your children,* said the first deepsman Erzebet had danced with, swimming forward. A hard hand reached through the water, felt its sharp-fingered way across Anne's face.

*Mine,* Erzebet repeated. Her pale body, mottled by the shifting light from above, hung opposite his. Her hand on Anne's wrist was tight, and Anne saw that her mother, that sheltering strong-willed body, was, next to the thick-tailed deepsmen, a small figure.

*Man,* said the deepsman. *Your man?*

Erzebet swung her legs to and fro beneath her. Her voice grew louder, making the tips of Anne's fingers buzz. *Man sick,* she said. *No man. Me.*

The white bodies wove to and fro, circling them.

*Me,* said Erzebet. *My children.* Diving again, she coiled her body, swimming in a tight, fluid knot. Before the deepsman could follow her she was up again. Her legs struck out at him. It was a hard blow, shoving through the water around it, but before he could retaliate she was back and clasping him, Erzebet's legs wrapped hard around his single, rough-skinned tail. Then, with a twist and a wriggle, she was away again, dancing and gesturing towards the shore. *Mine,* her voice rang out. *Me. Mine. Treat with me. I am the leader. Treat with me.*

Mary reached out for Anne's hand in the gloom. Anne let it be held for a moment, then she steadied herself. She could see the tension in her mother's stance, the force of will straining her white, marked body. Forward Anne swam, and made for the deepsman her mother confronted. In a few seconds, she was before him, and as Erzebet began her turning dance again, Anne followed, spiralling around him in her mother's wake. Her stroke was weaker than Erzebet's and her speed slower, but she circled him, up and down, calling for her sister.

Mary's name was impossible to say under the water, but she called out, *Take my hand! Take my hand!* And Mary followed.

Up and down the three of them swam, the bare flesh of the deeps-man glinting before their eyes. Then her mother's grip was on their arms again, and Erzebet was waiting before her partner, saying, *Me.* *You,* he said, and the others picked it up. The chant began again, but shifted and changed, becoming sound, a drifting harmony. Anne joined in, piping a sound as close as she could manage to her name. Through the distance, the waves crashed. And in the carrying dark, Anne heard, as if in response, the faint murmur of the Channel, breaking on the shores of France.

In such waters passed Anne's childhood. But when she was thirteen, a bastard was discovered in Cornwall. Though she did not know it at the time, that was the beginning of the end.

# NINE

The story was kept from her and Mary at first, but by then, Anne had been holding her tongue for years. Mary had become a constant presence, and the two girls talked alone, but there were some things Anne could not say to her. Mary had Erzebet's fine brow, her narrow nose; attendant ladies made a point of dressing Mary in clothes to match her mother's. Anne's wardrobe was a more random collection, rich, heavy, valuable dresses, but nothing that emphasised any resemblance she might have borne to her mother. Anne tried not to mind, but she could not explain to Mary how cast out she felt when the three of them appeared together, Erzebet and Mary arrayed as a pair and Anne blue-faced and separate: Erzebet's unpredictable caresses came as often to Anne as to Mary, and so Anne felt little right to complain. Nor could she complain at what was not Mary's fault. Being in Mary's company was a sad comfort. Mary grew taller than her sister and carried herself with a mature grace that eluded Anne. At moments, she almost did look like a mother. But she wasn't, and Mary's fine face was too sharp a reminder of the absent, changed woman. Mary sometimes asked Anne why she would sigh at odd moments, but Anne could not explain it, and after a while, Mary grew impatient and left the subject alone. If it hurt her feelings, she said nothing, and neither did Anne.

Nor could Anne say anything when Philip shouted in public, tugging on her mother's arm. She showed nothing on her face when ambassadors came from abroad, bowing and scraping and negotiating terms that Erzebet struggled to deny. Anne learned quickly that strangers, distracted by the light of her cheeks, could read little in her eyes, and she herself was uncomfortable talking to people whose eyes continually wandered to her cheeks and brow.

Shy, her mother called her, but Anne did not know if that was the right word. The tension in court gripped more every year, thickening the air until the slightest twitch carried through it like sound through water, and Anne, not knowing what to do, did nothing. In consequence, rumours began to build that she was a simpleton. She didn't thrash or yell like Philip, but confronted with diplomats and courtiers who spoke veiled threats and half-promises, she would answer in the deepsmen's tongue as often as English, forbidden by courtesy to ignore them but unable to think of how to answer their half-understood pleasantries. It could have been mere awkwardness on her part, and that was something that most courtiers preferred to believe: one idiot royal was bad enough, but two, one of them a child, leaving only one healthy scion and a daughter at that, was too dire a prospect to contemplate. An awkward-mannered royal was not promising either, but Anne could be disarming. Though her speech was unpredictable, she managed not to give offence. Things at court were frightening; Anne could feel the fear and anger rising like steam from so many men, and the idea of displeasing them intimidated her into silence. Thrashing Philip and frozen Anne. Not, please God, as slow-witted as each other—but still, Anne's off-balance manners gave an impression of simplicity that was hard to avoid, at least in her presence. And before a simple child, people did not always guard their tongues.

So it was that Anne learned the story: a bastard had washed up on the Cornish shores. The case was not as bad as it might be, for no noble names were involved. A fisherman had taken the infant in, a boy child. How he came to be on the beach, none knew, but there was no cause to suspect his arrival was planned: just a sailor's brat, the child of some wretched boatman and a passing deepswoman who had taken a whim to try landsman's flesh. Erzebet did not ask the deepsmen if they had lost a child, did not mention it at all. When she was a grown woman,

Anne planned to ask them the truth of such cases, or at least to consider it, but not this day. Curious though she was, she knew too well the disaster that would follow if the deepsmen had truly lost the child, if they had wished for him back, if it had turned out that they cared, after all, that he was to be burned.

The fisherman who took in the boy claimed to be moved by nothing but pity for his starved condition and a fancy for a child of his own, God not having seen fit to bless him with a family. On the rack he confessed he had planned to sell the child, to rake in gold from some ambitious nobleman, to be the finder of a new, usurping king, but no names could be pulled from him. Anne supposed he hadn't had the boy very long, or he might otherwise have named some courtiers, even chosen some at random, to loosen the interrogator's ropes. His lack of research cost him a dislocated hip; he would be in no better condition to walk to the pyre than his charge.

Anne sometimes sought favour with her mother by passing on the rumours that people whispered before her, and sometimes she succeeded in gaining it. This subject, though, she dared not bring up. Her grandfather and mother went about their duties stiff-faced and drawn, and Anne knew without asking that a sentence would have to be passed. Death was not the question, but mercy: would the traitor and his bastard be permitted strangulation before the flames were lit? To throttle a bastard child would be a lengthy business, straining the executioner's arms for twenty minutes or more before its breath failed. But the issue was not ease. This was to be a clear warning. The word *bastard* was one to make every house in Europe clutch their crowns and reach for their swords. With an army behind him, and Angelica, the first queen who walked out of the water, worked onto his escutcheon, a fresh-blooded half-breed, skilled as a true-born king on the rites and language of the deep and healthier than almost any king in the continent, could take and hold the throne. Once there, courts would have to decide. Treat with him, and they endangered themselves: any sailor's whelp hidden away would take heart from the precedent. But wage war, and they could lose their armies. Soldiers followed men who could rule. And bastards, the perfect balance of humours, had been known to rule well. It was hard to ignore the claims of health and strength.

It took all Anne's will, every minute of the day, to keep from visualising a child on the pyre; her face grew blanker than ever and the impression of idiocy more strong, so completely did the effort dominate her. But the tightness of Erzebet's mouth answered her unspoken question. William was gone, Philip afflicted, Mary a prize for a foreign prince, Anne a quiet uncertainty. England could not afford any mercy to those breeding contenders for the throne.

Nothing was said, no announcement made in Anne's hearing. But through listening to the whispers and keeping her face blank, she learned the date of the execution. Her legs were ill-equipped to carry her from keyhole to keyhole, and her spying was thus confined to fixed places, but her ears were sharp, bred to hear across the echoing fathoms of the deep, and quiet conversations held at fifty yards' distance from her were quite audible. It was easy, with such ears, to find places to eavesdrop; courtiers knew better than to whisper in a prince's presence, but a girl hiding out of sight was another matter. From listening, head still and face slack, she heard the disputes.

The Archbishop of Stour was required to make a pronouncement on the case. Archbishop Summerscales was old and slight of build, but he had not lived so long and risen so high by being foolish, and he was well aware of the cataclysm he would cause by refusing the Church's approval for the execution. It was easy for him to justify it: "God reserves the worst of his fury for traitors" was a phrase Anne heard him use more than once.

The idea that God would approve a burning was one that dismayed Anne almost to heresy. For years, the Church had been a refuge. While Erzebet was observant in her attendance, she spoke little about God outside the cathedrals, but Anne looked forward to the prayers. There the court sat, nothing but the sound of music and voices praising God. The sermons were not what impressed Anne the most. Since she was a little girl, she had loved church for a simpler reason. When the priest called for the prayers, heads were bowed, hands placed together. Voices spoke as one, and there were no conspiracies. People did not watch each other. There was quiet and harmony. It was the only time in her life Anne ever saw Erzebet close her eyes.

Fraught as the world was, Anne listened with hungry ears to tales of the Prince of Peace. She was ready to judge not lest she be judged: every day, it seemed, the world called upon Erzebet to make judgements, and those judgements weighed her down, her back bent further with every month that passed. Anne was not sure if she would ever see a demon, but when she read the phrase "My name is Legion, for we are many," she heard a calling in it. There was no unison among anyone she knew. Men were not a crowd of devils, but she was frightened, and she could feel the fear among them. Fear was possessing the court, and she could think of nothing that would cast it out. Only at prayer did she see the anxious heads bow. Only a true God of Love could so becalm people, even if only for moments.

This was the God Anne prayed to, the God she longed for. The spirit of God that moved upon the face of the waters and said, "Let there be light." She could not believe this God would wish a child slaughtered. But Archbishop Summerscales spoke of God's hatred of traitors. The idea of God hating was unnatural to Anne. If God was in the silences, in the moments of peace, then hatred was a disruption of God, a violation. Anne was thirteen years old and in no position to argue with the Archbishop, but one of them was wrong: either he or she was deeply mistaken about the nature of God. It was for this reason that Anne took to idling in places where she knew the Archbishop might pass close by, hoping for a sign, for some kind of clue that God was not the force of hatred the Archbishop seemed so certain of.

Summerscales endorsed the sentence, and for the most part, he was deferred to. But a quiet conversation Anne overheard one afternoon as she sat studying her Latin in a churchyard walk showed that there was a dissenting voice.

The man who objected was a newcomer to court, the lame bishop Anne had first seen on the day of her mother's marriage. Bishop Westlake, she had learned, was his name. Without having had much conversation with the man, she had still developed a preference for him: his awkward scraping limp was an easy step to identify. A man she could recognise from a distance, and a man scarcely faster on his feet than her, was less intimidating than most people. Westlake had told the Archbishop in a whisper that mercy was the command of God, and the execution of a child was an act the Lord would rue. Anne, hiding behind a church wall, lowered her book into her lap, clasping it so hard that the pages dented under her fingers. These were the words she had needed to hear.

"The child will die, my son," the Archbishop said, his emphasis on the words "my son." "Would you have us rock a broken throne?"

"I would have us do as God bids us," Westlake said. His voice was low, habitually tense, but Anne had never heard him raise it.

"The child is lost," Summerscales insisted. "Shall we set our Church against the majesty of the Crown? Divide ourselves so all Europe can seize the moment for conquest? When the deepsmen abandon a weak prince and the soldiers come from France, where will be your mercy then?"

The phrase "broken throne" stayed with Anne for years afterwards. Later, when she struggled to broaden her forgiveness, she came to think that Summerscales's aims were not as ignoble as they sounded. Perhaps, she told herself until she believed it, his aim had been a Godly one after all: he had aimed to save lives. A schism between the Church and the Crown would have split the country open like a beached seal corpse, a rotted gulf at the centre of a crumbling ruin, ready for the crows to swarm and pick over. She did not believe that a quicker death for the child would necessarily be a disaster if the Church requested it, but it was not in her gift to grant it, and she knew only too well how little ground could be gained by arguing with her mother. Erzebet would have refused mercy. Anne even thought of pleading for the child herself, but to do so would be to admit she knew of the bastard in the first place, and Erzebet was unlikely to forgive such an inconvenient piece of spying, not when she was under this much strain. To beg for a kinder death would elicit a slap and a refusal, and confinement to her room, and a less attentive ear to future requests. Better to save her mercy for times when it would do some good, Anne told herself. That was a sound reason, even if the fact that she didn't want her mother angry with her, that the thought of Erzebet's sharp voice and swift rejections made her limp with misery, was a stronger motivation in her own heart.

Yes, Summerscales might be right that it would do more harm than good for the Church to intercede. There were so many souls in England, so many bodies, and Anne had known for years that war sliced through a nation, gutting it and tearing out its needed men. Perhaps Summerscales had been trying to live in the world while still serving God, to prevent the abomination of a battle. She wished it might be so.

~

Anne was riding the grounds on horseback when she heard Robert Claybrook's voice. As was her habit, she had avoided a noisy gallop, instead sitting quietly on her mount, reins loose in her hands, letting it weave its way through the trees as best it pleased. While she could canter and leap as well as any when she chose, her arms strong as a man's, she preferred sea-racing to land chases, and when left to herself was happier to give the animal its head. She couldn't understand its whinnies, but there was no reason to suppose that they didn't mean something. It was more companionable to let the horse sometimes take its turn at deciding where they should go; she could command it when necessary, but it seemed foolishly tyrannous to order its every step to no purpose.

It was a windy autumn day, and the leaves were dry on the branches, rustling overhead and pooling at the horse's feet. The sound must have covered the light steps of her horse, for Claybrook did not turn as she came within sight of him.

Anne gripped the reins and pulled her mount to a sudden stop.

Robert Claybrook sat on a bay horse in a patch of sunlight, his face dappled with shadows. Facing him on a similar horse was his son John. At sixteen, John was growing tall and stocky, towering over Anne, but his face maintained a cheerfulness that, in this tense court, made him shine out like a misaligned fish glinting within a shoal. Towards Anne and Mary he had shown an agreeable courtesy that Anne, accustomed to curious eyes and awkward addresses, found half-soothing and half-unsettling: it was nice to be spoken to easily, but no one she knew did so, not even her family. Erzebet's occasional passionate attention, Mary's pats and kisses and constrained conversation, Edward's formal kindness: all were easier to cope with than the relaxation that showed in John's face when he bowed before the royal children.

Anne sat still, curious as to how these two spoke when they were alone. In this, however, she was disappointed. John was staring down at his horse's neck, turning his head from side to side as his father said, "You will have to be present," unhappily avoiding Claybrook's eye. Anne recognised the tone, having heard it from Erzebet every time she balked at a formal appearance: Claybrook was scolding his son into performing a duty. Anne knew Claybrook mostly as her uncle's smooth-faced shadow, but from the discomfort in John's posture, and from the tension in his father's, what could the duty be except to attend the burning?

As John looked away from his father's urgings, his gaze lifted and settled on Anne. At once, he straightened and raised his hand to her in salute. "My lady Princess," he called. Claybrook looked around quickly. There was just a moment of hesitation before he echoed his son's hail.

Anne paused. Claybrook was a clever man, she thought; if he considered the subject, he ought to realise that she'd probably already heard the news he'd come so close to letting slip. But maybe he was feeling cautious: a royal daughter repeating unwelcome intelligence could bring a lot of anger down on his head, and though Erzebet was officially supposed to obey Philip, few men would trust Philip's awkward protection over Erzebet's will, even if Philip had been inclined to protect his adviser. Which was by no means certain. Philip tended to obey Claybrook after some persuasion, but showed little interest in his company.

Anne decided to be gracious. Carefully, she blanked her face and gave them a stare of confused simplicity. *I am lost,* she said in the deepsmen's tongue. *I want my mother.*

"My lady Princess, I hope you are well today," John said, kicking his horse and riding around his father in a wide circle, avoiding the man's eye. "Would you like to ride with me back to the palace? I would be honoured." His sentences were simple, as befitted a courtier speaking to a princess of questionable wits, but there was a look of hope on his face. His back was rigidly turned against his father. That anyone should consider time spent with her an actual relief was too flattering to resist; Anne was happy to give him an escape.

"Let us go home," she said. As Claybrook gathered up his reins to follow, she bared her teeth and hissed at him.

Claybrook was a strong man, accustomed to royal whims. For an anxious moment, Anne feared her method would not work. But Claybrook turned his horse with a movement like a shrug, and rode in the opposite direction. Anne supposed that her uncle Philip was enough to make anyone weary of royal company.

Anne turned back to John. Having promised to accompany her, she expected him to look uncomfortable, caught between retracting an offer to a prince and getting stuck escorting a hissing girl. To her surprise, the hiss seemed to have disturbed him not at all. He rode his horse up to stand alongside Anne's, and nodded at her. "Shall we go?" he said, quite as if she had done nothing out of the common.

Having achieved this escape, Anne was overcome with shyness. Her face tingled, a sure sign that the light of her cheeks would be glowing brighter; where Mary blushed a prettier pink, Anne gleamed, and consciousness of this tended to fluster her worse and make her blush more. In darkened rooms, Anne when embarrassed could shine like a floating skull.

Anne could think of nothing to say, but John Claybrook did not seem too troubled by the silence. This in itself was strange: courtiers tended to grow edgy around brooding monarchs. John, though, simply gathered in his horse and rode alongside her, waiting for the blush to fade.

After a while, he spoke. "Do you think there will be a royal hunt soon?" he said.

"I have heard no plans," Anne said. The prospect of a hunt, a proper chase out at sea, with the court in their small boats with harpoons at the ready and her mother and sister beside her driving great shoals to the surface, was a cheering one, but such a hunt had not been seen since her father's death, and with tension so high, it seemed unlikely. Unless the burning of a bastard was cause for celebration. Anne looked at John Claybrook, who was watching his horse with his head angled casually towards her. "I would like one," she confessed.

"I would like to see one," John said. "When I was very young, I saw a porpoise hunt. That was a great sight. My father still has a skull he took."

"I would like that too," Anne said, her spirits rising. Porpoise hunts, like boar hunts on land, were out of bounds for royals too young to risk their half-grown limbs against such a formidable battalion of teeth and muscles. Fish did not fight back, but porpoises were cunning as wolves and stronger than stags: kings of past times had died on such excursions. Erzebet had once told Anne the story of a porpoise hunt where she had fought a great grey beast to exhaustion against the hull of a boat, but with only Anne and Mary to accompany her, she would never make such a trip, not while they were still so little. "It would be exciting."

John grinned. Anne blinked; she had seen people direct such wide smiles to each other in court, but she was unused to receiving them herself. "I would like to see a porpoise in the sea," he said. "They are already beaten by the time we get them on board. They must be a fine foe in the water."

Anne hesitated. Hunting in the water was the province of kings; in so anxious a time, a man could find himself under suspicion for expressing such a wish, even if it was just an idle thought—for no landsman could survive more than a minute under the waves, let alone the long, fierce struggles and dives of a royal hunt. John must have meant no harm, but she didn't know how to warn him off. Better to pretend she hadn't understood, and hope he took the hint. *I swim fast now,* she chattered. *I am more grown-up.*

John opened his mouth to say something, then closed it, turning his face aside for a quick look at the quiet trees and unthreatening sky. "I would like to sail," he said. "At home we live by the river; my father taught me how to row. I would like to go further out to sea."

Anne wanted to keep thinking of hunts, but she didn't want to tempt him into treasonous comments. "Do you catch fish?" she said.

John laughed. "Yes, often," he said. "I like fresh fish. I always eat it at home."

Not understanding the laugh, Anne reached down and patted her horse. "Did you get any porpoise meat after the hunt?"

"Yes, I was blooded," John said, referring to the custom of anointing a child's face with the blood of the vanquished quarry, done once and valid for ever. "My father made me eat a bit of the meat." He grinned again. "It was nasty."

"I thought it would taste like venison," Anne said. John looked at her, and she blushed again, waiting for him to say "Why?" It was a silly thing to suppose.

Instead, he shook his head. "More like rank fish. Venison is sweet with all the grass stags eat, but porpoises are all fish and oil, that is all they eat. Not good to taste at all."

"Maybe that is how you would taste to a porpoise," Anne said. John raised his eyebrows at her, but he didn't show the tense discomfort courtiers usually displayed when she had said something they didn't follow. "You said you ate fish at home."

John laughed aloud, setting a thrush flurrying in haste from its nest overhead. Anne didn't think what she'd said was that funny, but it was a friendly sound, and she relaxed a little. "I hope the porpoises never find out, my lady Princess," he said.

Anne nodded. "Maybe we can have more hunts when Mary and I are older," she said.

It was a hopeful thought, but John's face sobered a little. Anne's fingers tightened on her reins. Mary was fifteen already, a grown girl. If William were alive, if there had been other brothers and sisters, they would have been out hunting well before now. A broken throne. Surely there would be better times at court than this. "Maybe so," John said. "Perhaps, my lady Princess, when you are older you could command a hunt yourself."

"I could ask," Anne said. "I could not command one now."

"Not while you are so young, no," John said. The bluntness of the comment took Anne aback, but he seemed to mean no offence by it.

"I do not think I could command anything now," she said. She hadn't meant to say it, but in her mind was a pyre, bundles of sticks piled high, and a twisting child on the top of it. She lowered her head, stared at the bristling mane of her horse. Skin was flaking from its neck, forming a sticky dust along the parting of its hairs.

Out of the corner of her eye, Anne saw John taking a long look at her. His expression was impossible to read. There was a moment of speechlessness, the silence broken only by the crackle of leaves, red and brown underfoot.

"I shall pray to God to protect you, my lady Princess," said John. "And to guide your hand in wisdom."

It was a courtier's comment, polite and obscure, open to any meaning she chose. She chose to see it as friendship. "Thank you," she said. "We should pray for guidance to do as God bids us." Bishop Westlake's words echoed in her ears.

"Amen."

Anne listened another moment to the leaves breaking under her horse's crushing hooves. "I shall pray for you too, Master Claybrook," she said. "We must all hope to do as God wills. And to know what God wills, not what we will ourselves."

John shook his head, smiled. "We may none of us do what we will, my lady Princess."

⤙

Anne did not attend the burning. John did. A few days before it was due to take place, he was sent away, back to his father's lands, presumably, to go on to the burning from there. She did not get to speak to him afterwards, for he did not return to court straight away, but remained absent for several months.

The day itself, Anne was left with a tutor and set a complicated translation of Magyar into Latin; whenever she glanced at the door, the tutor looked up and slapped her hands, telling her to concentrate. Anne gave the woman her simplest stare, and refrained from asking the question she was so obviously dreading: *where is everybody today?*

A couple of days beforehand, Anne had taken a final decision and, during a quiet class with her mother, asked her out of nowhere, "Should we be merciful to our enemies?"

Erzebet had given her a long, black-eyed stare. Anne's insides had curled up and her fingertips gone cold with fear, but eventually, Erzebet reached out strong arms and pulled the girl, too big to cradle, onto her lap, stroking her hair and saying nothing. Anne dared not speak again, but sat quietly in her mother's arms, head resting against her bejewelled chest and hoping. The next day, Erzebet was gone, and had left Anne's tutor a series of essays and discourses, all arguing the need for strength if a prince is to rule safely. That was her answer, the only answer Anne was ever to have. Anne could not stop wondering what it was that had stopped Erzebet explaining it to her face.

For several days afterwards, Philip thrashed and yelled at the sight of hearth-fires. One of the Privy Sponges suffered a broken wrist when he failed to dodge Philip's flailing arms quickly enough; Robert Claybrook quietly pensioned him and sent him out of court after the doctor was forced to amputate. Even courtiers with candles were subject to shouts of "No! Away! No!" as the mighty body of the king's heir cowered on its throne. Edward ordered fires extinguished; the court retired at sunset, and sat in dim rooms, shivering under their velvet against the chilly autumn damp. After a few days of this, fires were lit again and candles made a welcome return. By this time, Philip had forgotten his fears.

# TEN

I T WAS NOT too long afterwards that more news reached Anne's ears: Bishop Westlake was sick. There was less secrecy about this news; the Archbishop raised censers and prayed for his safe recovery, and the court murmured Aves in the respectful hope that the man would be well again. Anne prayed with them, unhappily aware that there was more duty than good will in many of the prayers: Westlake's lameness had been causing resentment ever since he had arrived. Possibly God would overlook that; her prayers, at least, carried a desperate wish for his recovery.

Edward and Erzebet had treated the man with distant courtesy, but Mary had been cautious of him. "His leg is strange," she told Anne when Anne mentioned that she liked the Bishop.

"He can walk well enough on it," Anne said.

"Slowly." Mary's pretty face was a little wrinkled with distaste: courtiers were sound-limbed, healthy. The expression angered Anne, but she could not express her feelings. Mary had never known how it was to be strange-looking—though it would only sound envious if Anne were to say so. "What does he mean to do in court when he reels like a peasant?"

"Perhaps God called him here," Anne said, feeling an anxious protectiveness towards the one man she had heard express doubts about burning a child.

This was a difficult suggestion to refute if Mary wished to remain pious. "Why did God not make him whole before he called him, then?" she said after a moment's pause, big-sisterly benevolence in her logic. "He looks ill about the court. I wonder what he wants to do here so badly he will hop about to do it."

This was the fundamental question: the Bishop's gait was undignified, and most men would have stayed home with a fine-carved cane to enhance their steps and servants around them who could be relied on to defer to their wishes. Anne did not find the Bishop graceless: his awkward steps were still faster than hers, and his face, which locked into a taut mask every time he was forced to set weight upon his weak leg, had too much gravity to be clownish. Anne did not think it overly suspicious that he should want to be in court enough to walk in on a pained limb: every courtier must have wanted to be here badly enough to leave behind a life tending their grounds and minding their people, giving up the quietness of country living for the uneasy jostlings and uncertain rewards of a life at the centre of the nation. Walking on a bad leg might be no harder than keeping a respectful face as Philip wallowed and babbled. Erzebet didn't trouble to hide her bruises these days, but she presented a pale, stern face to the court every morning.

Anne was too old to shove her sister, but this blithe unconcern made her angry. It wasn't the Bishop's fault he couldn't walk well. He might indeed be fulfilling God's mission in this court; Mary wasn't to know whether he was or not. Since the day she had overheard him talking with the Archbishop, hesitating to give his holy blessing to burning the bastard child, Anne's eyes had followed him about court. He scraped from place to place, always managing not to flinch as his lame leg set down on the ground, but the caution of his movements was familiar to her, reassuring. Every day of her life, Anne retired to bed with weary hands and a sore back, limbs aching from bearing up her weight; sometimes every joint in her legs ached, as if she were some old woman instead of thirteen years old. Meanwhile, nimble courtiers strode from place to place like marching soldiers, towering over her. The Bishop's slow, sore progress was far easier to understand. She had seen, too, his patience as Philip caused endless trouble, the softness of his voice as he spoke to her mother. At Communion, she had knelt before him to receive the Host. Unlike Summerscales, whose hands were doddery and pressed her tongue too firmly in an effort to compensate, Bishop Westlake laid the bread in her mouth with deft, gentle fingers that made her relax, want to lean her head against his hand to receive his blessing. When he made the gesture of benediction over her, it was with a softness that made her feel almost as if he had patted her head instead of simply reciting words over it. And if Mary spoke so coolly about his leg behind his back, what did she say to others about Anne's blue face? Mary didn't know everything, Anne told herself, but the thought that her sister might crinkle up her nose at Anne was more distressing than she wanted to admit to herself.

Now he was sick. A flux, they said, his insides pouring out in a vile, stinking rush that rendered his attempts at dignity useless. That was the thought that hurt Anne the most. His gentle hands and grave voice and brave, schooled face were no guard against the assault of his melting guts. Anne had felt too many curious eyes on her own face not to grieve at the humiliation of her favourite priest. What if he were to die? Anne did not care for the Archbishop, had no desire to confess her sins to that sharp-eyed, wary, rough-fingered old man. Without Westlake, the church was a place of royalty, not a place to pray in peace, a moment of ease and calm out of the shifting, awkward days. Doubtless God had business for Westlake in Heaven, but Anne didn't want him there yet. There were too few gentle people in her life.

Erzebet had insisted that he should be quarantined, but Edward decreed that Francis Shingleton, the court physician, should attend him. Shingleton was a bright-eyed man in his forties whom Anne had spent much of her life avoiding, as his interests were wide and she was aware he had founded a hospital for idiots just outside London. While she herself was protected by her birth from confinement in the dark, silent rooms he recommended to soothe the troubled brain, and Shingleton's cures involved rest and broth more often than anything else (Erzebet having banished his predecessor after a dose of frog's ashes and mercury had carried off one of her equerries), Anne had no desire to have his skilled hands laid upon her, coaxing out of her once and for all the true answer to the question of her wits.

With the Bishop sick, though, Anne's worry overcame her hesitations. There was no need to summon him. Shingleton, she knew, was good friends with Robert Claybrook; all she needed to do was wait. Accordingly, Anne took the opportunity to accost John Claybrook while out riding, some quiet excursions having taught her his preferred routes around the court grounds, on a day when she knew his father and Shingleton were riding in another part of the woods.

John was mounted on his bay mare, his face sober as he traced his way through the trees. Anne trotted her horse up to him with a little more confidence than she felt, hailing him.

John looked up and smiled politely. "My lady Princess," he said.

"I am glad to see you back at court," Anne said. It was a few months since the burning; John had been back several weeks now, but she had had little chance to speak to him alone. It was nice to see a friendly face. She smiled at him, hoping for some pleasant remark, some joke to soothe her anxieties about Westlake's illness, but after a moment disappointment settled in her breast. John's expression was distant almost to wariness.

"I am glad to be back." Although his face was still courteous, there was some tension in his posture.

Anne swallowed, but she was determined to manage this. *I would like to meet him,* she said, resorting to the deepsmen's tongue for safety's sake.

"My lady Princess?" A faint frown of puzzlement creased John's brow.

*The good-to-eat plant man.* Deepsmen had no word for doctor, which strained Anne's invention, but she didn't like to speak nonsense to people any more than she could avoid.

John drew a breath, straightened up and turned his horse around to her. "Would you care to ride with me?" he said.

"I thank you. Do you ride alone today?" Anne got straight to the point. Her heart was beating too fast over her boldness in seeking out the physician for her to withstand much more suspense in putting the question.

"My father is with me in the forest," John said. "He and Master Shingleton ride together."

"Do they look for plants to treat the poor Bishop?" Anne asked.

John shrugged. "I saw them pick nothing."

"I would speak to Master Shingleton," Anne said.

"My lady Princess?" John's face did not change, but his hands lifted off the neck of his mare, as if gathering his reins up out of harm's way.

"I wish to ask after the Bishop, how he fares," Anne said. She kept her face and voice blank, waiting for him to close the distance between them with information. Such a tactic would not work with her mother present—Erzebet permitted no one to be more high-handed than herself—but Anne was learning, since her habit of creeping away alone to listen to people, that a request stated flatly and given no justification was not one that courtiers could easily refuse. It felt strange to assume so adult a posture, uncomfortable, but with the Bishop dying, she was not about to pass up any method that might get her answers.

"May God grant him a safe recovery," John said, his thumbs stroking the worn leather of his reins.

Anne simply kept her eyes on him, not to be diverted. John looked at her for another moment, then, unexpectedly, he almost laughed. The corners of his mouth quirked upwards, and he ducked his head quickly in a half-bow, before sweeping back up again. "As you wish, my lady Princess," he replied. Not waiting for her to answer, he turned his mare around. Anne followed, wondering what she had done that was so funny.

The two older men were riding together. They appeared to be deep in conversation as Anne and John approached at a canter, but she could distinguish little of what was being said over the horses' pounding hooves before John called out a greeting.

The two men turned. Shingleton pulled off his hat immediately, waving it in a neat gesture across his stomach to indicate a bow. Claybrook, who was riding bare-headed, turned his horse and raised his hand. "Good day, my lady Princess," he said. For a moment, his face had been blank, but a smile quickly followed. In repose, his face was not unlike his son's, but though both man and boy were smilers, it somehow lessened the resemblance. John's grin made his face look young, flexible; it was a different countenance from the ageless, agreeable mask his father assumed. "How then, John. I see you have found our princess again."

"I have, Father." Anne looked again at John's face. His expression was puzzling. He was smiling too, but not his usual amused twinkle. Just at that moment, he did look like his father.

"Good day, sirs," Anne said. "I hope I find you well." Observing Edward and Mary, she had learned something useful: the more she referred to herself and the less to her interlocutors, the harder it was for them to disoblige her. Sentences in which "I" and "me" dominated over "you" almost always got a better response.

"Thank you, my lady Princess, we are all well today," Claybrook said.

Anne's eyes were on Shingleton. Fair of skin, short of leg and a little stocky around the waist, he had a look of solidity to him; she could imagine him easily enough ordering soothing compresses and speaking calmly to his imprisoned idiots. His face was quite amiable in its cast; though he wasn't smiling at her, she could see the lines curving upwards around his eyes and mouth that suggest years of sweet-faced friendliness. His look wasn't friendly now, though. His face was pallid, colourless, and there was a tension in his attitude that reminded her of nothing so much as a Privy Sponge forced to keep bathing Philip during a tantrum.

Shingleton was sitting there, saying nothing. Discomfort rose in Anne's chest, making it hard for her to inhale. The three men sat encircling her, each on his horse facing inwards. Little though she knew either Robert Claybrook or Shingleton, Anne could feel something was wrong. She was an intruder here.

"Master Shingleton, I am happy to see you," Anne pressed on. "I was most glad to hear His Majesty my grandfather tell me you were to attend upon the poor Bishop. I hope his case is not too desperate?"

Shingleton's face remained pale, but his eyes studied her, scanning her face with quick movements. "He is most gravely ill, my lady Princess," he said.

Anne waited, but Shingleton did not go on. Was she too young to be told harsh truths? "What ails him, do you think?" she said.

"My lady Princess," Shingleton said, "I could not say."

There was a carefulness in his tone that set Anne's ears tingling. "Are you uncertain of your diagnosis?" she pursued.

Shingleton swallowed. It was only a tiny sound, but she heard the little tick in his throat. "A flux may be caused by many things, my lady Princess," he said. "So many I would not care to guess an answer to the question. My only care is to cure my patient as my lord the King has commanded, and that I strive towards. I have enough on my hands without groping after causes."

Anne did not like to trouble an uncomfortable man, but his caution was frightening. Surely no man who set up model hospitals for treatment of the insane, no man assiduous enough in his study of medicine to rise to the position of Edward's chosen physician, should be incurious about so deadly a disease? "Strange words, Master Shingleton. I understood you were a philosopher?"

There was a silence. Only a few seconds, then Shingleton spoke again. "A philosopher must strive to do good in the world, my lady Princess. It would be an impious man who set aside the good of God's creatures for the good of an experiment. My care at this time is to do his Majesty's bidding."

Anne drew a quiet breath. There it was again: his Majesty's command. Shingleton was not going to tell her anything except that he was answerable to Edward. Did he think she was pushing him to go behind Edward's back? But he had spoken of the care of God's creatures. There had been some warmth in that sentence. Perhaps he minded that the Bishop was sick after all. "Spoken like a good Christian, Master Shingleton. I shall pray for God's blessing on your endeavour."

Shingleton swallowed again, a little louder this time. The movement of his throat under his sandy beard was more free. "You are all goodness, my lady Princess. I hope I will not offend you, but I have been away from my patient for long enough. By your good leave I shall return to him."

"By all means," Anne said. She had wanted to speak to Shingleton so much that it had not occurred to her until this moment that he should have been by the Bishop's side. Why hadn't she simply commanded him back to Westlake's bedside and ridden with him on the way? Out of the side of her eye, she saw Robert Claybrook sitting very still on his horse, and John looking quickly from one man to the other.

Shingleton turned his bay to ride off.

"Master Shingleton!" Anne's call forestalled him: she had just thought of something.

His horse shuddered as Shingleton pulled the reins and turned his head to her. "My lady Princess?"

Anne lowered her voice a little, speaking as gently as she could. "If there is any ingredient or simple you lack, perhaps I could procure it for you," she said. "Is there anything you would wish?"

Shingleton looked at her a moment, then shook his head. "I thank you, my lady Princess, but no," he answered. "I am well provided."

"I thought you spoke of a unicorn's horn." John's voice sounded very loud in the hushed clearing. The two older men turned to him with a start. Their faces were controlled, but Anne could see the furious glares they were trying to suppress. John looked back at them, giving stare for stare.

"Such items are not to be relied upon," Shingleton replied. He opened his mouth to say more, but seemed to run out of words.

"I shall try my best," Anne said. It was there, in the tension of their postures, particularly Claybrook's: they were angry with John.

"Thank you, my lady Princess, but there is no need."

"I would not have your offices hindered by want of ingredients," Anne said.

Shingleton sat quietly, looking at her.

"The king, my grandfather, places faith in your treatment," Anne said. That was the refrain Shingleton had kept returning to; perhaps he would respond if she harped on the same string. "As his Majesty wills, so must we all do. And my heart is saddened by the Bishop's illness. If it would help you, I would be happy to try and procure you such a thing."

There was a pause. "Thank you, my lady Princess," Shingleton finally said. "I can make no promises for the Bishop's health with or without a horn, but I shall try every method. If you may procure one, I shall try my best with it."

"I am sure the princess Anne can be trusted to search for one quietly," John said. There was something in his tone that puzzled Anne, some quality of assertion she could not follow.

"Indeed, my lady Princess," said Shingleton. "It is not good for a patient to have his case discussed all over court. If you were to look for a horn, it must be through your own offices, not spoken of to anyone."

Anne sat on her horse, hands careful on the reins. "I should not break your confidence," she said.

"You are all goodness." Shingleton turned and rode off without another word, leaving Anne sitting watching after him.

Robert Claybrook cleared his throat. "Perhaps you might escort the princess back to the palace, John." There was a tension in his voice, an anger in his glance, that did not bode well for his son.

"So I shall, Father." John gave him a straight look for a moment, then turned around and led the way for Anne.

The two of them rode side by side for a while without speaking.

"I must thank you for your trust," Anne said in the end.

"I am sure you are loyal to his Majesty's wishes," John said.

Anne could make nothing of that, except that Edward presumably wished the Bishop cured if he commanded so good a doctor to attend him. This was treacherous ground, and suddenly she was unhappy discussing it at all.

"I have not spoken to Master Shingleton before," she said, changing the subject. "I was cautious of him. I heard he wished to examine my wits. I do not think he will wish to do so now."

John looked at her and laughed. Anne rode along beside him, listening, the leather of her reins taut in her hands. A unicorn horn might be possible for her to find. She had never heard of a unicorn being seen on land, but such creatures must exist in the sea, for sailors sometimes bought them home. If she went out for a bathe, she might find a deepsman willing to listen to her request. She could find a gift from the land to bring them, perhaps, make a purchase. Though the deepsmen seemed to have few wants.

It was how to get hold of a horn that she was thinking of. That was a problem she could address. Neither she nor John spoke of why such a thing might be wanted.

Perhaps Shingleton wanted the horn as a cure-all: many marvellous properties were attributed to them.

Among those properties was the ability to cure poisoning. But that was not all a horn was good for, and it might not be the reason after all. It might not.

## Eleven

THE TROUBLE WITH Anne's plan was how to get to the deepsmen. The Thames was not too far away, and if she could just make it that far, it would be easier from there: miles out to the sea, but a distance that would take hours to cross on her flimsy, aching feet could be swum in a flash. Even though it wasn't the season for the deepsmen to be in the bay, she could call to them, from the Thames itself if she had to. The sound would travel. It might do little good, but she could ask them to bring a horn next time they came. If the Bishop lived that long. Other, wilder schemes came to mind as she brooded, that she could swim all the way north to the Atlantic waters above Scotland where the sea-unicorns were said to live, find a horn or join the deepsmen in a hunt for one, but by the time John had finished escorting her home and she was being ushered in, ready to dress for another court appearance, she'd accepted that she had to be realistic. If she got to the Thames, it was the best she could do. It was better than nothing.

Accordingly, Anne woke early the next day. Her maid, Alice Grey, usually arrived at her bedside when Anne was still sleeping, sticks in hand and legs bent in a graceful curtsey Anne admired so much that it had been years before she properly grasped that it was a gesture of respect, not a demonstration of Alice's stronger legs. This morning, though, Anne sat up after a restless night and looked around her chamber, facing the first of her problems: the sticks were on the other side of the room, and there was no one to bring them to her.

Swung over the edge of the bed, Anne's legs dangled loosely, grey-skinned and rough in the morning light. While she could coil them like tails, she had never tried walking on them, not without someone by to catch her.

With some trepidation, she set her feet to the cold ground and pushed herself off from the bed. Immediately, she overbalanced, sitting down with a bump. The ground was gritty, harsh; her toes felt long and narrow against it, their bones fragile, their webs easily punctured. As she pressed her weight down on them and levered herself up with her arms, the room rocked around her: it was hard to stand steady. With every joint bowing and bending, Anne wobbled to her feet, clenching small fists and stretching out her arms for balance like a tumbler at a fair. Her progress was no more secure as she attempted to make her way over to her canes; every step, with no staffs to counterbalance her, was a feat, the instability of poising her whole weight over one little point almost impossible to manage. Anne struggled, managed a few paces and then, like a tightrope walker loosing his purchase, fell to the floor with a sharp thump.

The knock was a painful one, and Anne had to remind herself that she was too big to cry. Instead, she gritted her teeth: the Bishop must be feeling worse than she was at this moment. Her staffs were still out of reach, but as she leaned across the ground, reaching out for them, something occurred to her that seemed like a revelation: she could crawl. Her sticks were not yet in her grasp, but what were they, after all, but extensions of her arms? If she could walk four-legged using canes, she could go four-legged when no one was watching.

Anne set her hands and feet to the ground and crawled to get her own staffs, her own dress, her own shoes. Any courtier watching would have been scandalised at the Princess scuffling over the ground like a beast, but Anne was delighted at the discovery.

~

If getting her staffs was the first problem, and dressing herself alone was the second—a humiliating struggle that left Anne dishevelled and exhausted—then getting to the stables was the third. Normally her horse would be waiting for her at the gate, ready for her to mount and set off, crossing the ground at a joyous gallop.

There were hundreds of yards of grass and mud to cross first, though. Anne was inclined to keep crawling, but common sense told her that any groom would be less likely to hand over a bridle to her if she turned up muddy-gowned and prone, royal prerogative or not. Accordingly, Anne braced herself and traversed the distance like a princess, bent over her canes, as upright as she could contrive. The grass was rich with dew, every blade belled with fresh-scented droplets, soaking her skirt as she passed. Looking behind herself, she could see the sweep of darkened green where she'd passed, dragging the dew behind her. It was a shame, spoiling the soft grey haze and the sparkling points of light, but she felt some pride as she saw how far she'd made it on her own.

The stables appeared out of the mist, fine wooden buildings with dozens of mounts. Anne wondered for a moment how she would manage to saddle her horse if no stable hands were up yet—without her canes propping her up, she would fall, but with them she'd be unable to lift the heavy leather saddle—but to her relief, a groom appeared in the doorway. His name, she knew, was Maydestone, a pleasant-faced man of around thirty with wiry arms that could hold the tossing heads of even the shyest horses. Anne had always liked him: like all royals, she found mounting a horse difficult without a block to clamber from—she could have pulled herself up by her arms, but that was indecorous in public—and Maydestone's love of horses was such that he tended to concentrate on stroking and placating the fidgeting animal rather than wondering where to look as the princess made her ungainly ascent. However, he might present an obstacle this morning if she couldn't explain herself convincingly.

"Good morrow, Maydestone," she said. If she could take the initiative, it might make it harder for him to wonder why she was out unchaperoned.

"Your Majesty." Maydestone gave a deep bow, and Anne sighed internally at the sight of his straight back and strong legs. With such a body, she could run all the way to the river. He wore a respectful smile, but she noticed that it was a little softer than when he spoke to Erzebet or Edward. It was the same when he spoke to Mary, she remembered. Though Anne did not feel young, she recognised the face of a man who liked youngsters when she saw one.

"I would like my horse brought," she said. In the rain-softened earth, her sticks were sinking, leaving sharp little burrows and smearing their sides with mud. It was an effort to maintain her balance.

"All alone this morning, my lady Princess?" The question set Anne's heart thumping in her throat, and she felt her face tingle. She drew a breath and told herself that his tone had been friendly, trying not to blush; her face shining in the misty air would look outright macabre.

"I am. I mean to go riding," Anne said.

Maydestone clearly weighed the situation for a moment. "Where do you mean to go, my lady Princess?" he asked.

"Down to the riverbank," Anne said, too anxious to lie completely. She opened her mouth to ask that he bring her horse before her legs tired any further, but stopped herself: there was no need to remind him how odd it was that she'd be out by herself.

Maydestone looked at her for just a moment. Though his hesitation made Anne's face prickle with nerves, her opinion of him improved: evidently he was caught between thwarting a royal here and now and referring the matter back to Erzebet, and on the whole, he was managing the situation tactfully. "I shall be back before I am required at court," Anne said, letting tension sharpen her voice. There was a dry note of irony in her voice, she noticed; it was a tone Edward often used to reinforce his commands. "Bring me my horse, please, Master Maydestone."

Maydestone bowed again. He had a look of cautious kindness in his face that Anne found a little puzzling. Erzebet granted her requests or didn't grant them, but always with the same stern mien. People giving her things just to please her wasn't common.

Maydestone, however, turned on his heel and returned with her horse a few minutes later, saddled and bridled and ready for riding. Kicking the block that stood by the stable door forward for her, he turned to the horse's head, stroking its nose and whispering to it as she wrestled her way onto the block, strapping her canes to the saddle in their usual place and taking a firm grip. Maydestone's attention, as usual, was away from this undignified scramble; he carried on speaking in a low tone to the horse, telling it about its beauty. The softness of his voice gave Anne a momentary pang; whether it was possessiveness of her horse or some other envy, she couldn't have said, but there was a sting of jealousy that distracted her for a moment before she remembered she was on a crusade. With a bounce from her wobbling legs and a good pull from her steady arms, she was up and ready to depart.

"I thank you," she said, interrupting his murmurings with the horse. Maydestone looked up, as if disturbed from a private conversation, then blinked and bowed to her. Anne gathered her reins and dug her heels into the horse's side, turning away at a swift trot before he could say anything else, out alone into the green and grey morning.

The Thames was perhaps an hour's ride away, Anne reckoned as she hastened along. From here, it would only be a narrow riverbank, but it should be enough. The further she rode, though, the more her spirits sank. Deepsmen sometimes offered to share fish, it was true, but she had never seen her mother bargain with them for goods like a merchant. And how long would it take them to hunt down a sea-unicorn and bring its horn to her? Days, weeks? The Bishop could not survive poison that long; he would live or die by Shingleton's skill and God's will, and those things would be decided in the next few days. It was nice to be out, to see the glittering grass slip swiftly away under her horse's cantering feet, to canter at a good speed without a court to keep stately pace with, but the smell of wet earth and the cool mist on her face were lonely comforts. The further she rode, the more Anne felt the pressure of her isolation. Always a tutor with her, a riding master, a room full of people, talking obscurely and whispering one to another; she had found their presence oppressive, but being out so early, with the mists obscuring everything, was a new sensation. Even in the bay, she could follow her mother's calls in the dark. The castle was already invisible in the mist; she could see hazy shadows of trees here and there in the white, but colours looked cold in this early morning light, and there were no signs of human life in any direction. Though she was determined to be brave, Anne gripped her horse's mane, her hands tiny against its broad neck. Her heart had not slowed since she had left Maydestone behind. She tried not to think it, but it was frightening to be all by herself. Without her mother's voice in the void, she was lost.

The river was impossible to see in the mist, but she could hear it, a cool rush of sound carrying easily through the wet air. This was an underwater morning, visibility clouded by the damp, sound her guide: the sensation was familiar from trips into the sea, but the luminescence of the mist around her, the bright white and the solid clump of her horse's hooves below, were disturbing and strange. Anne thought again of the Bishop, but it was hard to visualise his face: no church bells had sounded, and the bubble of the distant Thames and the creak and sway of trees far off were the only signs of movement in the world. The further Anne rode, the harder it was to believe that time existed outside this moment, that anyone but her was real at all.

~

The river, when it appeared, was something of a surprise: a dark split in the earth, cutting a dingy stripe through the white air as she rode into view. Anne was almost bewildered as she faced it: after all her bold plans, there it was, nothing but a little runnel of muddy water, slippery-sided and striped with long, trailing weeds, their tendrils flowing in smooth straight lines down the path of the current like catkins hanging from a bough. She had followed the sound of it, but she realised now she should have followed the court paths, the landmarks she couldn't see in the mist, should have gone miles downstream, because here, the river was shallower than she had expected. Disastrously shallow: if she lay face down and called, perhaps the sound might carry, but there were weed-choked beds for the sound to travel past, rocks and dips and cross-currents cutting off the echoes, and the chances of a deepsman hearing her from this vantage point were shockingly, heartbreakingly bad. Anne sat facing the river, the inadequate stream of her hopes clotted with reeds and mud, and tears started in her eyes. Her night of planning and morning of sneaking had come to this: a weedy stream, too empty to carry even a forlorn question out to sea.

Anne sniffled, and dropped her horse's reins. She had come all this way. Even if she did no good here, she should try. Leaning over its neck, she realised something else: there was no groom to catch her as she dismounted, no block to aid her descent: there was nothing to do but fall off onto the wet ground if she wished to get down.

Things couldn't get worse. Anne screwed her eyes shut and leaned sideways, letting herself fall. The knock as she hit the ground winded her, and she struggled to catch her breath: she could hold a lungful of air for fifteen minutes or more, and often did when situations around her got so tense that she wished to disappear; to be deprived of her cache of oxygen was terrifying. Her back hurt as she tried to straighten it, and her cramped lungs couldn't open out; air groaned and scraped in her stricken throat, and Anne dug her fingers hard into the grass, trying not to panic. Closing her eyes, she pulled and pulled, fighting against her closed lungs until a mouthful of air dragged its way down and opened them out, flooding her chest with cool, soft mist. The relief was so great that she sat for long minutes, breathing and breathing, faster and deeper than she had ever done before, gorging herself on air.

Bruised and muddy, spendthrift in her breaths, Anne decided she would complete her quest. Her clothes were heavy, but she could unbutton and untie them herself, and once she'd wriggled out of them, she could crawl again, dirty knees and palms far less of a concern than spoiled fabric. The reeds around it were stiff and sharp-tipped, but she pushed them aside, reckless in the ridiculousness of her mission. The water was cold on her face as Anne dipped her head below the surface, the fresh taste of earth in her mouth, and called.

*Bring us a horn,* she cried. *Bring us a horn. Bring us a horn.* She repeated the chant, waiting for it to carry, waiting for the sound to carry forward. Anne lay face down in the water for a long time, sending her voice to carry on the current.

There was no answering call.

Anne sat up in the river, hip-deep and filthy. Splashing herself with the cleaner surface water, making deep cups with her webbed hands, she managed to get herself almost presentable, if dripping wet. To her dismay, she realised that there was no way to slip into the palace without explanation now. Erzebet would know she had been out alone. She would be angry. Maydestone would be punished for giving her the horse to ride. What was she to do?

Faced with the ruin of her clothing and the clammy cold of her hair, Anne's fear returned. She wanted her mother, unreasoningly, even though her mother would be angrier at her than anyone else for this morning's work. She wanted Edward, even Mary, anyone to take her home. But the Bishop was dying and Anne was trapped in this plant-thick, unswimmable river, and there would be trouble before anyone could make things right, and maybe nobody could.

The exhilaration of breathing again had passed. Anne had to bite her lips to stop herself from whimpering. The water around her legs was comforting, but even getting back onto her horse was going to be difficult without a block, even if it would stay still for her clamberings. Crawling out to the bank, Anne lay down and curled up, confused and wretched.

It was some time before she heard the sound of hooves. So startling was the noise that Anne sat up in panic, grabbing her clothing and dressing as fast as she could. The effect was untidy, but it was the best she could do. A moment's anxious debate with herself, and she called out: "Who is there?"

There was the sound of a horse being reined in. "Your Majesty?" It was Maydestone's voice.

Anne swallowed. "Come to me, please."

"Can you ride to me, your Majesty?" Maydestone's voice sounded out of the mist.

Anne shook her head, as if he could see her. "I cannot get on my horse."

There was a pause, then the sound of hooves again. "Can you call to me, your Majesty?"

Anne was swallowed again by fear. Why had Maydestone followed her? How was she to explain herself? Idiocy seemed the only possible excuse. Anne composed her face in its stupidest lines and called again: *I'm lost. Bad place. I'm lost.*

Maydestone rode out of the mist, mounted on a slightly shabby black horse, less elegant in its lines and paces than her own. "Are you hurt, my lady Princess?" he said.

*Let's go back,* Anne said.

Maydestone dismounted, crossing to her and taking her by the arms to examine her. "Are you hurt?" His voice was slow and clear, and persistent: he did not sound like a man who would be put off by answers in the wrong language.

"I am not hurt," Anne said. "But I cannot get back on my horse. You must help me."

She was trying for imperious, but Maydestone persisted, even as he gathered her up and set her on the saddle of her waiting horse. "Why are you wet, my lady Princess? Were you in the river?"

"Were you sent to look for me?" Anne's nerves overcame her desire to be opaque. If Maydestone had been sent, it would be a measure of the trouble she was in.

Maydestone tugged her skirt straight with the same brisk gesture he'd have used to adjust a bridle. "No, my lady Princess. But no one followed you for half an hour, and I grew concerned. I beg your pardon, but it is a misty morning." His voice was not quite conspiratorial, but it had a businesslike air of acceptance as he spoke of her misbehaviour.

"I should not have ridden off," Anne said. Back on her horse, mounted like a princess, her muddy, wrecked skirt was becoming shaming. She hung her head, uncertain what to say.

Maydestone held her horse steady. "Why did you do so, my lady Princess?"

Anne considered for a moment speaking like a princess, commanding her privacy, but her state was too foolish. "I thought I could call into the river to ask the deepsmen for something," she said.

Maydestone frowned. "I do not understand, my lady Princess."

Anne gave an unhappy sigh. "I thought I could ask them to bring a unicorn's horn next time they come," she said. "I hear the—" Caution suddenly made her swallow. She had no reason to tell this man all she had heard. "I heard the Bishop—Bishop Westlake is sick. I read that such horns were good in cases of flux, but the doctor had none in his store." She screwed her eyes shut, too embarrassed to say more. It had been such a far-fetched plan.

"Why, my lady Princess," Maydestone's voice said in the darkness behind her eyes, "why did you not ask an apothecary for one?"

Anne opened her eyes. "An apothecary?"

"A man who sells simples and medicines," Maydestone said patiently. "There are apothecaries in every town."

"I—do not know any," Anne faltered.

Maydestone pulled on his beard for a moment. "I could go for you if you wish, my lady Princess," he said.

Anne looked up in sudden hope.

"My lady Princess," Maydestone said. "Did his Majesty ask for a horn?"

"No," Anne confessed. "It was my own idea." She cast around. The dress she wore was less jewelled than one for state occasions, but it was still ornate, with a few pearls sewn around the neck. And it was already in a bad state. A lost pearl could pass for truly "lost"; she need not account for its disappearance. Reaching up, she took one of them between her nails and gave a sharp tug. "Buy it with this," she said. "If that will suffice. Please go to the town and fetch one. You need tell no one. And say nothing to the apothecary except that you want one, nothing at all; ask him nothing, tell him nothing. But please fetch one. Will you need another pearl?"

"No, my lady Princess," Maydestone said, catching her hand as it reached up to pluck another one from her neck. "That will be ample, I think. More than ample."

"Then keep the surplus," Anne said. "Only be quick, please. The Bishop is sick."

Maydestone bowed. He didn't smile, just bowed obediently, then turned his attention back to her horse, but Anne had already learned something: some people could be trusted to oblige her if she asked. Whether Maydestone saw profit in the opportunity or was simply trying to save himself trouble when he realised she was out without permission, she couldn't say, but she had come through the morning's work, and heard about apothecaries. She was better off than she had expected. And she had learned something else, too: difficulties and all, it was possible to manage alone.

Erzebet was furious about her disappearance, and the state of her clothing on her return. Punishments followed, but Anne minded less than usual. Maydestone returned the next day and brought a piece of horn with him, enough, the apothecary had said, to treat three men. Anne, after some strategic planning of her usual ride, managed to slip it to John Claybrook, with instructions to pass it on to Shingleton.

Whether it was the horn that saved him or not, a few days later, it was announced that Bishop Westlake was out of danger. Edward ordered prayers of thanksgiving from the whole court. Mary bowed her head dutifully; Erzebet put her palms together with a fierce glare towards the floor. Neither of them looked at Anne, but then, neither of them knew she had got the medicine. Why she didn't tell them, she couldn't quite have said, but her instincts pressed her to secrecy. She bowed her head and gave thanks, pride and pleasure making her face glow with eerie light.

# TWELVE

ON THE DAY the end began, Anne suspected nothing.

Her lessons began as usual: she was closeted with her tutor, Lady Margaret Motesfont, a thin-faced woman with narrow brown teeth, whose satisfaction in following the progress of a fine piece of rhetoric was seldom matched by satisfaction in her pupil's work. But Erzebet was due to make an inspection later that morning, so Anne applied herself, one ear cocked for the church bells as they tolled the passing hours, and one eye on the vellum, her pen scratching, struggling to trace answers to Lady Margaret's difficult questions. The subject that day was an argument from Louis, King of France, a piece weighing the merit of the landsmen's souls against the deepsmen's, the question of what form of man most represented God's image corporeally and spiritually. It was as well-argued as most such tracts, which was to say, its arguments were familiar, though Anne found it a little flat in expression and lacking in passion for the goodness of God; though she did not say so, she suspected that it might receive a little less attention were it not by a royal author. Then again, the language of the deep, Louis's mother tongue, was hardly fit for poetic flourishes. The Bible spoke of the God that divided the waters and placed the fir-mament between them, but it was impossible to express the word "fir-mament" in the deepsmen's language: it stopped at *surface,* the place where the water met the air, and anything beyond that could only be conveyed by the word *up.* As Anne persisted with Louis's arguments, laid out in his stark French, tracing the inevitable conclusion that the person of the king mingled elements in the most perfect combination under Heaven—a conclusion she had little personal reason to quarrel with, but seldom applied to herself, being more interested in the notion of God as light than God as king—at the back of her mind was Erzebet, her forceful, blunt sentences in the deepsmen's tongue and her sharp, laconic, careful English. The argument itself was not one that Erzebet had ever much bothered with; she merely sat on her throne while rhetoricians repeated it, still as a stone-faced Virgin.

Eleven o'clock tolled, and Anne looked up in hope. Erzebet was a punctual woman, and finally she was due.

The door remained closed, and Lady Margaret tapped the table, summoning Anne's attention. "Continue, if you please."

"My royal mother will be here shortly," Anne said. "We should stay for her."

"We will continue with the lesson, my lady Princess." Margaret's face was stern, and Anne felt herself disliked. The pedantry of her tutor, Margaret's love for books of argument and impatience with Anne's adolescent understanding, made Anne the more eager for her mother's appearance. Conscious, though, that Erzebet had little sympathy with Anne on days when she had scanted her education, Anne bent her head again to her book, feeling an antipathy to King Louis that had nothing to do with the fact that he was French, and a rival king at that.

Quarter past eleven rang from the steeple.

"My royal mother is late," Anne said. "The clock has struck the quarter hour."

"I heard nothing," Lady Margaret replied.

"Perhaps not, it is far away," Anne explained, trying to excuse Margaret's landsman ears. "But it has sounded."

"We will continue, my lady Princess." Again, the tone was firm, but there was a little rattle in Margaret's throat, a trace of hoarseness, that made Anne look up sharply.

"Do you not wonder where my royal mother is?" she said. At the back of her neck, a tendril of anxiety began to coil.

"My lady Princess, please continue with your reading." Anne's eyes were focused on Lady Margaret's mouth as she spoke, the sight of it filling her vision as Anne's hands grew cold and unsteady. Somehow it was hard to look away from it, ivory-dark teeth, straight on the top row but crooked on the bottom as if badly shuffled; a flake of loose skin peeling from lips suddenly gone white.

"Where is my mother?" Anne's voice came out in a gasp. She inhaled and inhaled, her ribs swelling and clamping inside her dress, but there wasn't enough air in the room.

The sound of Lady Margaret's swallow was loud as the click of a gate-latch. "My lady Princess, we must stay until we are sent for."

"I want to see my mother." All Anne could think of was the bruises she had seen, indigo clouds stamped on white skin, Erzebet's stillness, her rigid refusal to flinch as Philip shook thick fists before his courtiers.

"We must stay until we are sent for." Margaret's voice was pinched, but her eyes were black and her skin clean of colour. The folds of her skirt did not hide the hands that she gripped together in her lap.

"Has my lord my uncle—where is my uncle Philip?" Anne said. The need for an answer was so intense that her teeth chattered as she spoke.

Lady Margaret shook her head, taking a grasp on the fine leather binding of the book she had held all morning. "His Majesty has kept to his chamber all morning, my lady Princess."

Anne shook her head, terrified. Always, she had avoided Philip for his clumsy gestures and loud cries. She would have owned to being frightened of him, somewhat, but not until this morning, with fear pounding suddenly in her chest, did she understand how frightened she must always have been. Philip never kept to his chamber. He was carried from place to place without consultation of his wishes, and while he might be taken for an airing when there was an ambassador in court he might offend, he was never shut up. What had he done to her mother?

"Take me to her."

Lady Margaret shook her head, fast as a shivering dog. "We must stay till—"

*I want my mother.* Anne blasted out the sentence in the deepsmen's tongue at the top of her voice, a voice made to carry across the Atlantic tides. Her own ears buzzed, and Lady Margaret flinched, gathering the book to her chest like a blanket.

*I want my mother. I want my mother. I want my mother.*

Lady Margaret turned her head aside, but Anne's lungs were royal, and could carry on a chant for hours.

"My lady Princess . . ." Margaret shouted over the din.

"I want to see my mother." Anne switched to English, repeating the phrase in an endless stream. Her voice rose and rose. Fear was surging through her, a riptide in her chest, and the angry satisfaction of seeing her tutor grow exhausted under the barrage of sound was a salve, a shallow hope that she might, for a moment, mistake her terror for fury.

When Lady Margaret burst into tears, Anne's voice faltered for a moment. Margaret was a strict woman, dry, fonder of the treatises she taught than of the act of teaching them, and Anne had thought her capable of no emotion beyond scholarly appreciation and impatience with fuzzy thinking. To see her weep was to see the world upended.

Anne swallowed, too frightened by Margaret's display to feel pity. "I want to see my mother," she said. "Take me to my mother."

At Anne's drop in volume, Lady Margaret looked up. "I shall say I acted on your orders," she said, as if to herself, still crying quietly, her hands forming fists over the leather bound volume cradled in her lap. "I shall return to the country. You wish to see your mother, my lady Princess? Come with me."

Both girl and woman were gasping with tears as Margaret seized Anne by the arm and dragged her from the room. Anne made a grab for her sticks, but Margaret was walking at full pace, speeding up to a run as if pursued, and Anne's legs slipped and scurried as she tried to follow, kept upright only by the clutch on her arm. As the girl stumbled, Lady Margaret did not slow her pace, but instead took hold of her with both hands, gripping Anne with a painful force, like a woman clutching at bedclothes in a nightmare. Anne, dazed with fear, gripped back.

Margaret raced and Anne staggered across the palace until they reached a hall where soldiers stood guard. Standing amongst them was Robert Claybrook, delaying an anxious-looking Francis Shingleton, who was attempting to hurry in through a doorway. Behind the open door, Anne heard the sound that had been building in her ears since she and Margaret had begun their frantic journey. Someone was screaming.

Claybrook looked up as they skidded to a halt. "Lady Margaret, what do you mean by this? You cannot bring her here."

"My lord, she commanded me to bring her, she was not to be dissuaded." Lady Margaret, tall as she towered over Anne, looked thin and small against Claybrook's soldierly height; the hand on Anne's arm gripped tighter.

"This is no sight for her." Claybrook took hold of Margaret's shoulder, pushing her backwards. "Take her away at once. This is no place for the princess to be."

The motion of Claybrook's arm loosened Margaret's grip for just a second, and Anne made a desperate lunge and broke free. Her legs scrabbled on the floor, and, reeling, she fell to her knees, scrambled forward and collapsed inside the room.

Someone lay on the bed. Dark wings rose around her, bedsheets soaking in blood. The woman thrashed and shrieked, raking the air. The room was full of people, Shingleton hovering anxiously, but none dared go near the flailing claws, the curses that tore out of a throat half-clotted with gore. With every jerk and turn of her body, the woman scraped off more skin, rags of flesh sticking to the blankets in clumps. What lay on the bed was a wet, red-yellow hulk, no face remaining, no features but a screaming voice. The smell of her wounds was like nothing Anne had ever encountered, like nothing on earth. In a corner, a priest was swinging a censer; outside, a bonfire had been lit; herbs were strewn in bundles on the floor, but the smell of scored flesh choked everything. The room was veined with drifts of smoke, and Erzebet ripped at the stained sheets, entangled in a web of blood and skin before Anne's stinging eyes, as if Hell had reached up and grasped her mother in a wet, enclosing hand.

## Thirteen

Erzebet lingered for hours before she died. Once Anne's ears had tuned themselves to the screaming, she couldn't stop hearing it, not when Robert Claybrook lifted her up and carried her out of the room, not when Lady Margaret took her from him, a shaking, mute, wide-eyed bundle, and bore her away. Anne clutched at Margaret as if terrified of being dropped, her legs wrapping round the woman's waist with a wrestler's grip until Margaret tried to pull her loose, pushing against the clinging girl and gasping for breath. Anne hung on, staring at Margaret's white, familiar face, hysterically waiting for her to say something that would make it all right. Lady Margaret carried Anne to the other side of the palace, back to Anne's chamber, where she tried again to unlock the girl's legs from their suffocating grip. Anne was not to be loosened. Lady Margaret paced the chamber like a woman soothing a baby on her hip, staggering under Anne's weight, until attendants came and pried Anne loose, unwrapping her limb by limb. They put her on a chair and covered her with a blanket, poured wine into her mouth, but Anne could not swallow. The wine ran over her chin, her lips too loose to fasten on the goblet, and Anne made no attempt to clean herself. She sat smothered in her blanket, legs lolling from the chair, red wine smearing her white and blue face. People fussed around her, spoke to her, but the screaming, distant and muffled through rooms and rooms of closed doors, drowned everything out.

It was hours before Erzebet's voice gave out, and hours more before she finally died. Anne did not move in all that time. Lady Margaret lifted her from her chair and laid her on the bed, but though the girl lay still on her pillow, she gave no sign of sleeping. Her eyes stayed wide open as the dusk set in, staring into the dark.

The funeral was planned for London. Anne sat in a rattling carriage for hours of the journey, saying nothing, looking at no one. Custom laid down the rules for what was to follow: Erzebet was to be buried at sea. The mass of courtiers would accompany the funeral ship to the water's edge, the more powerful men would join them on board as they sailed out to the bay, and Erzebet's body would be cast into the deep. There would not be a grave to visit. Erzebet would go back to the sea, where she had taken Anne so many times to dive and spiral under the rocking waves.

A new dress was given to Anne the morning of the funeral. Her maid Alice tried to interest her in it as she pushed Anne's unresisting hands through one sleeve then the other, telling her that it was the gift of my lord Thames, a fine gift, my lady Princess, but Anne made no response. The weight of the dress, unusually heavy even for a formal gown, bowed her legs and tethered her arms, and Anne was more aware of the drag of her skirt than the words of her maid. She stooped over her sticks without being asked, obediently following the procession.

Mary sat beside Anne in the church as Archbishop Summerscales, who had married her mother to Philip years before, recited the funeral rites, with Bishop Westlake in attendance. He had recovered from his illness, looked as well as he ever did, but the thought was little comfort now. Anne wondered if he knew she had found the unicorn horn for him. If it had made any difference. Her faith in its power, anything's power, to counteract poison, was broken.

Mary cried throughout the ceremony, and reached for Anne's hand, but Anne merely lifted it in her own, and with her other hand, dug sharp fingernails into Mary's pink skin. Mary snatched it back, crying harder under her breath, and shuffled away from her sister on the pew, fidgeting to and fro till Anne reached out again and placed her nails against Mary's wrist, not digging in but holding them there, poised to scratch. Mary, who had been taken riding the day of Erzebet's death and had spoken to Anne of the "fever" of which she had been told their mother died, drew in a deep breath and held it, staying still and silent until Anne withdrew her claws and laid them back in her lap. Mary's eyes were accusing, bewildered, but Anne kept her gaze straight ahead on the gold censer that an altar boy swung, releasing choking clouds of incense into the air. She couldn't look at her sister's face and see Erzebet's brow and cheeks, reproduced in miniature, see them smeared with the tears of the girl who hadn't heard their mother scream.

The procession to the burial ship was a long one, and the voyage down the Thames out to sea the work of hours. Philip's sedan creaked on board, Privy Sponges following in attendance, and Edward limped on after him. Anne had seen little of her grandfather since her mother's death, but the sight of him loosened something in her, just a little. Stumbling on her heavy dress, she edged up to him, putting both canes in one hand and reaching to touch him on the arm. Edward, who had always answered her questions with patience, turned to look at her for a brief moment, and then there was a yell from Philip and he turned aside, gesturing for guards to attend him.

Philip, disturbed by the rocking of the boat, was pointing into the Thames. His voice blared out in the cold morning: "Want! *Want!*"

Anne froze on her canes, the carved ebony handles cutting into her palms, pressing patterns through the webs between her fingers. They were new, elaborately carved with waves, skulls, symbols of mourning. Like the new dress, they were impractical, too ornate to rest weight on comfortably, and Anne's hands were already stamped with their carvings, but she had not thought to ask for replacements. It seemed inevitable that the world was heavier now, sharper-edged.

Philip was thrashing, pointing overboard. *Swim,* he yelled in the deepsman's tongue. *Want to swim.*

Robert Claybrook hurried to attend on Philip, a sober, pallid John at his heels. John turned and gave Anne an uncomfortable glance as her uncle tried to grab Claybrook's arm, but Anne was too heartsick to wave at him.

Mary hastened to Anne's side, the scratches of the church apparently forgotten in the tension of a threatened royal tantrum. Anne didn't turn, but she didn't move away.

"A-are you well, sister?" Mary, red-eyed, was quieter than her usual self. Any hopes of a kiss or pat, those little reassurances that had sometimes come from her big sister, seemed remote. Mary was just a girl, two years older than herself and under the impression that their mother had died of natural causes.

Anne didn't look at Mary. Instead, she swallowed, and spoke her first sentence since Erzebet's death. "Why do they not let him in the water?" she said.

Mary bowed her head; her canes clicked heads as her hands drew together over her body. "They say he could make love with a deepswoman," she said. "As he could not with a queen. Then the next prince of England could never leave the sea."

Anne had seen Philip bathed naked once or twice, before her father's death, before his marriage to her mother. His flat-fronted abdomen, bereft of any genital protrusion, had meant little to her at the time: she had only been young, and the deepsmen were similarly streamlined, any manhood concealed behind a neat slit level with their hips. She had not thought of it since. The bruises on her mother's arms took on a new and sickening significance. Erzebet and William had had the genitals of landsmen, as Anne herself had. Philip had roared with lust and grabbed at her mother, but built as he was, as Erzebet was, how could there be any way of satisfying it? The sight of Philip, wallowing and bucking in his sedan, was suddenly too repulsive to watch, and she closed her eyes, turning her head aside. Philip always lashed out when he was frustrated. Tears were gathering in her throat, closing it tighter and tighter until it hurt to swallow.

"He will be king, will he not?" she said, opening her eyes to look at Mary.

Mary took a hoarse breath. "Grandfather may live a long time yet," she said.

"God willing." Anne crossed herself, a moment of genuine prayer. Erzebet could have held the throne. But she and Mary were young, unmarried. If Edward were to die, Philip would be all that was left.

Edward stood, watching his son. His lined, sunken face bore no particular expression, but the wrinkles around his eyes, the creased forehead and the downward strokes of the mouth, all gave him a cast of misery. His crown was on his head, a bright silver circlet polished for the occasion, but age was shrinking his flesh and the band was loose, sitting a little crooked, a little too low over his face, pushing the flesh into bunches below. Though Edward had always been grave and calm, in the cocked slant of his crown there was a cold breath of the ridiculous—like a boy wearing his father's hat—that made Anne shiver under her gown.

Philip was still thrashing in his chair, shouting. As the Privy Sponges attended him, wary of his flying fists, Robert Claybrook darted forwards and held up his hand, gesturing for them to wait.

Edward stood, bowed over his canes. The two men regarded each other, and Edward said nothing.

"Water," Philip said, pointing at the bowls of brine the Privy Sponges carried to wet his skin.

Claybrook didn't turn towards Philip. Instead, he motioned to the two Privy Sponges and they laid their bowls and sponges down on the deck.

"Water," Philip said.

Edward stood and watched. Philip demanded a while longer, then stopped, patting at his face. The rasp of skin against drying skin was quiet against the lap of the Thames on the boat's side. *"Water,"* Philip insisted.

Crystals of salt were drying on his face, the skin rough and brittle beneath. Anne stood silent, her heart beginning to pound in her ears.

Philip stared at Claybrook, who stood with his back firmly turned; at Edward, withered hands clasped over his sticks as his son gradually dried out. The wind blew cold across the Thames, and Philip began to whimper. His big webbed fingers patted again at his cheeks, his neck, their grey pallor growing starker and starker as the dry air rushed over them.

It was a full two minutes before Claybrook turned and gestured to the Sponges, who began their work again. Philip whimpered louder as the brine first touched his face, but Claybrook made another gesture and the Sponges paused in their work.

Philip fell silent. He said nothing more as the rest of the party boarded, and the ship cast off to make its way down the Thames and out to sea.

Erzebet's body lay wrapped in its winding sheet, ready for burial. Nothing was visible but a thick white bundle, unstained cloth, layer upon layer, swaddled like a baby. Anne stared at it, thinking of Erzebet's fierce voice, her strong hands, her black eyes. The need to rip open the sheet was so strong that Anne gripped her sharp-carved canes harder than ever, fighting the sense that if she could just let Erzebet out of the cloth, if she could help her escape it, then she'd come out as stern as ever, quite all right.

Court musicians began the burial song; from below, the drummers beat against the hull, sending the echoes through the water to call the deepsmen. The music on deck would be all but inaudible to them until they reached the ship and surfaced, but Edward lifted his voice in harmony with it, singing out for the court to hear, a tribute to Erzebet. There was nothing else they could do for her now. Mary followed, and after a moment, so did Anne, singing away the hours as they floated downriver: *We are coming. Dead body. We are coming. Dead body.* The sound of the drums thrummed through Anne's chest.

It was only when they finally made it out of the estuary, the grey waves opening in an endless vista before them, that the thought of the deepsmen came clearly into Anne's mind. She had never swum with them when a body was buried at sea, but she had seen her father's burial. At the time, the reigning emotion had been confusion, an uncertainty as to how she was supposed to mourn for this man she had seen so little of, but she remembered now the speed with which the deepsmen surfaced, the rapacity of their hands grabbing his body to take it down. They did not move like pallbearers. She had seen them grab like that before, but only in one set of circumstances: when snatching a fish out of the water to eat. The way they had grabbed her father's body looked nothing like mourning. It looked like hunger.

And what of her mother's flesh, melted and soaked with poison? Would it be torn apart by the deepsmen's sharp teeth, swallowed down their cold throats to kill them? If England were to poison its deepsmen allies, what then for its fleet? Would there be no deepsmen to see them safe across the Channel, or worse, mortally offended survivors ready to smash their hulls if they tried to leave port? The boat was preparing to drop her mother's corrupt flesh into the arms of the deep, and maybe it would bring death with it.

Anne drew breath and changed her chant. *Not safe. Don't eat. Not safe. Don't eat.* Mary gave her a wet-eyed glare, a look of furious, unforgiving grief, but Edward merely gazed at her for a moment, then lowered his head in a slow, resigned nod. The lines on his forehead pressed close together as the crown tilted down his brow.

The deepsmen were waiting for them, a boiling mass of bodies, lithe and dark in the water. Arms and legs flashed above the surface, but they moved so fast around the hull that they could have been fish, porpoise, anything. There were no faces to be seen from this high up.

*Not safe,* Anne cried across the waters.

The white package was carried across the deck. The Archbishop hastened forward to bless its final descent, and Westlake halted after him, lame leg dragging. He came to rest by Anne, who stood clutching the rail. The carvings on her sticks were too painful to hold, and she had dropped them, clutching the smooth wood as her mother's body was lifted over it, throat sealed with tears, legs and back aching, ready to collapse.

As the body was released, falling in a white flash to the waves below, there was a crash of water and spray shot upwards, splattering on the deck. Summerscales and the bearers flinched back as if the droplets themselves were poison. Anne stayed where she was, the few fragments of seawater clinging to her cheeks and lips all that was left of her mother.

The deepsmen gathered around the body, circling it, patting it with uncertain hands. Murmurs of *not safe* rose from below. As the water soaked through the white shroud, weighing it down to sink into the dark, the Bishop looked at Anne, his hair blowing untidily around his sad face.

For just a moment, he rested his hand on her shoulder.

And that one moment went straight to Anne's crushed heart, sank in so deep she thought she might never recover.

# FOURTEEN

THE DAY AFTER the funeral, Anne went to the Bishop.

She had said almost nothing to anyone, only chanted the burial rites then fallen silent as the body went under. She returned to the palace, letting herself be ushered from place to place. She was unresisting, but she wouldn't touch her food.

All night, she lay huddled under her blankets. Every rush of wind outside her window, every creak of wood outside her door, made her eyes fly open, staring into the dark. Clasped in her hand was a crucifix Erzebet had given her the previous New Year, a silver-and-pearl cross that felt smoother in her hand than the sharp-edged diamonds and sapphires she was often expected to wear, given by courtiers with some idea of complementing her blue face. It seemed to Anne that it was for the sake of the crucifix that she was staying awake: if she were to fall asleep, it might slip from her hand into the bedclothes, be bent by a careless roll, lose a pearl among the linen, even slip out of sight, not to be found. The thought of anything happening to it was so horrifying that the little cross felt charged with danger, but she couldn't bear to put it aside. She lay awake, whispering soundlessly into the creaking, rustling quiet: *Mother of God, protect me. Holy Queen, help me. Stella Maris, save me.*

In the morning, she rose hot-eyed and tousled, and addressed Alice: "I wish to pray with Bishop Westlake."

It would have been easier if Westlake had come to her, but Anne wanted to go and see him. She refused offers of bearers, help with her canes. She laid aside her carved mourning canes for the ones she usually used, smooth oak. Her maid Alice protested a little at the impropriety, but Anne didn't answer except to say, "And I want another mourning dress. This one is too heavy. See to it." Erzebet had had no patience with impractical things.

Anne walked by herself to meet Westlake in the chapel. The going was difficult, but her walk this way was about the same distance as his. If he could limp halfway, so could she. When she got there, he was already waiting. His face was grave; though lines scored his mouth and brow, he did not have the crumpled appearance Edward had. Rather, the wrinkles seemed like scars, cuts of expression made in younger skin, a frown of thought on his brow and the remnants of smiles around his mouth—along with deeper twists made from an expression she had often seen, the stern pinching-in of his mouth as he rested his weight for step after brief step on his damaged leg.

Anne hesitated before him, gripping the familiar wood of her canes for comfort. Her heart was pounding in her throat. Over her black dress, the pearl crucifix had been a reassuring adornment, but now it felt light, as if it were about to float away.

Westlake got to his feet and motioned her into a chair, saying only, "My lady Princess." Anne struggled as usual to sit without toppling, a complex balancing act that required keeping her canes in hand at all times if she wished to retain any dignity, but Westlake did not offer to help her, merely seating himself, slowly, one hand gripping hard on the back of his chair as he extended his left leg with steady, careful grace. Except for his hand on her shoulder, no one had touched Anne for days but Claybrook and Lady Margaret when they had carried her away from Erzebet; Westlake's failure to fuss awkwardly around her chair as most courtiers did, uncertain how to help and too dutiful to touch the princess uninvited, was soothing, but it did not make it any easier to talk to him.

"How are you this morning, my lady Anne?" Westlake said. He spoke quietly, as if he actually wanted to know. Her name came easily off his tongue. It should have sounded wrong, was probably a mistake: "my lady Anne" was the address for a noblewoman, not a princess. But at the sound of it, something tugged inside her. So very few people called her by name.

Anne looked at her hands for a moment. "Why did you come to court, my lord Bishop?" she asked.

"My lady Princess?" Westlake looked at her curiously, apparently unoffended.

"Your leg must trouble you," Anne said. "If you stayed at home, you could have a staff to help you walk. But you come to court."

Westlake did not look uncomfortable at the question. "I wished to serve God, my lady Princess."

"Could you not serve him at home?"

The Bishop did not answer for a moment. His eyes rested on her, dark blue-grey like a faded garment. "Do you wish to talk about your mother?" he said.

The question was a shock, too overwhelming to answer. "What happened to your leg, my lord Bishop?" Anne said in an unsteady voice.

Westlake smiled. It was a small smile, his mouth stretching only slightly outwards, but it softened his face a great deal. "I fell from a horse when I was about your age, my lady Princess, and broke it. It had to be set."

"Did it hurt?"

"I was fortunate not to die of the injury, my lady Princess. And more fortunate that the surgeon did not need to remove it. I can only thank God for his favour."

"But you were unlucky to fall," Anne said, anxiously aware that this was questioning God in His own house but too miserable to abandon the conversation.

Westlake smiled again. "That was my bad riding, my lady Princess. I am lucky God smiles even on such poor horsemen as myself."

For just a moment, a smile warmed itself at the corners of Anne's mouth. The movement was her undoing: the moment she felt it, her face remembered how to feel, and then she was crying, her eyes clenched shut, her mouth beyond her control, everything in her slipped loose from its moorings.

Westlake reached out and took hold of her hand, clasping it between both of his. He was not a warm-blooded man, and his touch was cooler than most courtiers', but the pressure of his palm either side of her chilled fingers, like blankets and mattress cradling a sleeper, was the only comfort in a swaying world. Anne cried and cried, gripping her small, webbed fingers around Westlake's hand, until she lost track of time altogether and there was only the sound of her sobbing voice.

It was a good while before she managed to draw breath and swallow, trying to rein herself in. Westlake removed his hand long enough to draw a handkerchief from his sleeve, and, tilting her chin up, wiped her eyes. Anne swallowed again, blinked, struggled for a voice to speak with.

"I—I do wish to speak about my mother," she said. The word *mother* was somehow no harder to say than any other word.

"Is it true you were present at her death?" the Bishop asked.

Anne nodded. "What is your Christian name, my lord Bishop?" The question was an intimate one, but it was too disorienting to know the man's surname alone, so Anne decided to exercise her royal prerogative.

"Samuel, my lady Anne." He said her name kindly, showing no resentment.

"My lord Samuel. I do not wish, I, I do not wish to speak of it."

Samuel Westlake did not push the question, merely sat and waited for her to speak again.

"Is your health recovered, Samuel?" The name was reassuring, and Anne said it again.

"I am very well, I thank you," Westlake said. "I heard that in your kindness you sent me medicine in my illness." His eyes were on her again, and despite their dark colour, there was a brightness to them that made Anne uncertain how to look back at him. "I am most grateful, my lady Princess. I have prayed many times that God would smile upon you for your charity."

Anne blushed, placed an anxious hand up as her cheeks glowed their embarrassing blue. "I did not know if you had been told," she said. "I did not tell the doctor to tell you it was me."

"No, my lady Princess, but Master Shingleton mentioned your kindness when I was recovering," Westlake said. "I must thank you again for your goodness. It was a most Christian act."

"Did Master Shingleton use the horn?" Anne said.

"I believe he did," Westlake nodded. "Though I was too ill to ask what was in his medicines at the time of taking them."

Anne was fingering her pearl cross, thinking of the pearl she had given to purchase the horn. Erzebet had been angry with her for spoiling her dress, but Anne could not regret it. The dress had not been Erzebet's gift. "I am glad you are well, my lord Samuel," she said. "I do not wish to see—suffering is a curse difficult to bear."

"We must look to our Saviour, my lady Princess," Westlake said. He patted her hand again as he said it, and Anne thought of Christ upon the cross. Just at the moment, thoughts of the Five Wounds, the scourging and the crown of thorns and the nails, were too painful to consider.

"I have prayed to the Virgin," Anne said. "But I do not know what to do."

Westlake picked up her hand. "You have been kind and charitable to me, my lady Princess," he said. "If I may counsel or comfort you in any way, I am your man."

Anne looked at him, towering over her in his chair. "I thank you," she said. "I do need your help."

"Name your wish, my lady Princess."

Anne hesitated. "I—have heard of your charity, your mercy," she said. The burned bastard was in her mind, the slaughtered child Westlake had wished to spare. Erzebet had held her when she asked for mercy. Erzebet had also ordered the child burned alive. Her mother was dead, and Anne was lost in an incomprehensible wilderness.

"Name your wish, Princess Anne," Westlake said. "I say again, if I may help you, I am your man."

"Samuel . . ." Anne said. "My mother died of poison. Someone put poison in her bathwater."

Westlake crossed himself, not taking his eyes off Anne. "May God receive her Majesty's soul."

"Someone killed my mother," Anne said. "I need you to help me find out who."

# BOOK THREE

# DURANCE

## FIFTEEN

Henry could hardly believe the stories John told him.
John said that the king was an old man, weak and fragile in body, but that nobody ever challenged him. John said the king had had two sons, but one of them had lately gone to war in Scotland and been killed, and the other one was stupid and couldn't walk. John said it was only women and an old man on the throne now: Princess Erzebet, who came from a long way away, and two little girls, younger than themselves. And, John said, the king was still on his throne.

Henry was eight when he first met John. This boy was like nobody he had ever encountered, in the sea or out of it: quick with a smile, easy to laugh, fast and energetic on his feet. To begin with, John laughed a lot at Henry, whenever Henry fumbled words or said something strange. Henry, who hated to be laughed at, began by hitting John in angry retaliation. The blows, even from a boy as small as Henry, were heavy ones, usually knocking John off his feet. Allard had never learned how to discipline Henry, too aware that any reach for a cane would likely land him flat on his back with his protégé throttling him, and attempted to deal with such outbursts by a firm "No, Henry." Henry was, at first, too angry at being mocked to listen.

Soon enough, though, he stopped hitting John. John never retaliated; instead, he simply got to his feet and faced the other way, turning aside if Henry, slow on his bent legs, tried to get round to face him. This cold-shouldering made Henry far more nervous than he was prepared to admit: if he couldn't see John's expression, there was no knowing what he might be planning, and in addition, John was his friend, a bright spot in a world of didactic adults, the first time in his life that Henry, accustomed to the flickering round of fear and safety, flight and hunting, had ever been entertained. John was funny; sometimes even Henry, fierce-faced and inexpressive, couldn't help but smile when John laughed. Amusement was such a new sensation, bringing with it a lightening of his tense muscles, a brief surcease from thinking ahead and watching all sides and waiting to see whether what happened next would be safe, that he was in no way prepared to give it up. It was easier, after a while, to keep his fists to himself. John might ride away for the day after a quarrel, but he would be back the next, cheerful and lively as before, apparently with no sense of grudge.

While Henry couldn't quite admire the recklessness of forgetting injuries so easily, trusting again so soon—John had the memory of a mackerel when it came to past arguments, or so it would appear from his behaviour—he also was willing to trust John. John did not push books or weapons into his hands, or force clothes on his limbs, or drop food he hated on his plate. John, in fact, never made him do anything. He was willing to do what Henry said, and to do it happily, with no stern gaze or note-taking or whispered asides. John did not seem to want anything from him. Therefore, Henry considered what John said to be more believable than anything Allard told him.

"If the king is old and he has no good sons left, why can we not go and take the throne now?" Henry asked.

Allard's answer would have been long and involved history, but John was straightforward. "Because you are too young. You need to lead an army into battle against the king's forces, and you need to be grown up to do that."

"Could I not start?"

"My father knows a lot of men who can raise armies," John said. "He is waiting to see who will join him. The king fares ill enough now, but he will get worse as he gets older. And when he is older, you will be bigger."

"But I have to hide now," Henry said. "I have had enough of it."

"You would feel worse if they catch you before you have an army at your back, deepsman," John said amiably.

This was true in theory, Henry knew. Allard had told him that the king would kill him if he was caught, though he had not gone into details. "I can fight a grown man now," he said. "Landsmen are weak."

"You could not fight an army, and that is what they would send. And it would be all of us in trouble, not just you." John, unoffended at the slur on his kind, did not look too frightened. It was puzzling, because the thought of an army, thundering down on him with hundreds of black-hooved horses, sharp swords out and ready to swing fast through the air, was definitely frightening. But John had never seen a battle in the short years of life he had lived, and perhaps did not realise what it would be to be in one.

"I could be the king's son," Henry said. "I could marry his daughter." The deepsmen sometimes formed pairs, and it seemed like something he could do. Landsmen seemed to take such bonds more seriously—as far as he could understand from Allard's explanations, marriages were supposed to last for ever, even if the couple grew tired of each other or a better offer came along—but he was unlikely to do better than a king's daughter anyway. It didn't sound like a bad idea.

John laughed. "You mean Erzebet? His daughter-in-law? She is married to Philip, much good that will do her. You do not want her, Henry, trust me. You would be happier married to a shark."

"Nobody would marry a shark," Henry said. In his mind, Erzebet stood before the throne, a rock in her raised hand. She could go, when he took down the king.

"Another shark?" John grinned at him.

"Sharks do not marry, they just fuck," Henry said.

"Do not say that in front of my father," John told him. "He will only hit me for teaching you bad language."

John taught Henry a lot, but Henry was teaching John too. To begin with, John had had a patient air when he explained things, as if talking to someone stupid. Henry, who had no patience at all with stupid people and saw no reason why anyone else should, determinedly argued and questioned and tested John's logic until he succeeded in driving home the point that he wasn't stupid, just foreign. John's swordsmanship improved rapidly with hasty, strong-armed Henry as his sparring partner. The two of them rode together on Allard's grounds, John explaining the names of animals, Henry pointing them out, quicker-eared when they rustled in the bushes, able after a few days' study to predict the directions they would dart, the paths they would take, the best direction to throw a stone in order to bring one down.

Language was a question of its own. Little though he was interested in Latin, Henry picked up English as quickly as he could, realising that a spoken refusal would get him out of unwelcome tasks more effectively than feigned incomprehension, that a spoken demand was easier to grant than vague pointing, and that it was harder for people to discuss him when he was there listening to what they said. He did not care to be discussed. But when it came to understanding things, John's mind was set in a different pattern from his, and it could be difficult to make things clear to both of them.

John, for example, explained to Henry that Allard's grounds were near the coast. "Coast" was a difficult idea. "Where the land meets the sea," was how John put it, explaining that England was part of an island, but Henry, accustomed to flying through the water, could not think of land and sea meeting. Land carried on under the sea, down along the sea bed. Land was simply where the water ran out and there was nothing left to hold you up. John often came with fish for Henry to eat, telling him how he had gone out on a small fishing boat, but however John explained the mechanism of nets, Henry found them difficult to picture, struggling to understand that his image of John plunging his hands into the water to catch fish for him was in some way inaccurate. The day John brought a net to show him was worse: Henry's hands, flexed together between the digits with webbing, could find no purchase on the interlocking strings, and the thing slipped out of his grip, a frustrating tangle of lines and angles he instinctively found ugly.

It was Henry's language, though, that gave him an advantage.

One day as they rode together and a brown creature swooped over-head, Henry gestured upwards, saying, "What is that?"

John squinted upwards. "A bird."

Henry shook his head. "The thing you showed me yesterday was a bird. This one is brown." Colour was a new concept in itself, to have words for the shades of things, all the panoply of tones that the landsmen's sun revealed away from the grey seas. Henry had lost most of his fear of red things, but the complexities of colour were still of interest to him, and he wasn't prepared to ignore them when John seemed to be making a mistake. "And it has a different shape."

"Oh." John waved a hand. "That was a crow yesterday. This is a swallow."

"What is a bird, then?"

John shrugged. "Something that flies. Like a crow or a swallow. Both are birds."

Henry considered. The creatures he had seen sometimes flying past his chamber window came to mind, the ones he had seen dive into the sea. He had refused to discuss them with Allard, but he wanted to know about them nonetheless. "There are birds that fly past my room" he said. "They are white, with grey backs." Colour was such a useful abstraction, once you understood how to talk about it. You could describe things that weren't there.

"What kind of bird?" John said.

Henry shrugged in puzzlement. "I do not know. Allard called it a bird. You know . . ." He gestured in frustration. "One of those white birds that can swim."

"*Swim?*"

"Yes, a bird that can swim. A—" Henry gave up, naming it in the deepsmen's language. There was a word for it there.

"What's that?" John perked up, a mixture of amusement and interest on his face.

*Gull,* Henry chirruped. "That is what they are called."

"You have a name for birds in the sea?"

"Yes, these ones can swim." Henry was growing impatient. "They sit on the sea and then swim into it to catch fish."

"Oh, *gulls*," John said, catching on. "Gulls dive under the sea sometimes. Grey backs, white breasts . . . I see. How deep can they swim?"

"About from here to here," Henry said, indicating roughly fifteen yards.

"Truly?"

"Yes, they swim with their wings," Henry said. "Gull," he added to himself. It was a convenient word to say, short and contained within the mouth.

"What was that word again?"

*Gull,* Henry said, using the deepsman's expression.

John imitated the word. The sound was ridiculous, and Henry laughed out loud.

"Hm." John tried again.

"You say it very ill," Henry said happily.

"Can you understand when I say it?"

Henry shook his head. "I know you are trying to. But if you said it to a deepsman, he would swim away."

John made a few more attempts, but his voice, unbroken though it was, lacked the range to deliver the high word at a steady enough pitch.

"You are just squeaking like a bird," Henry said.

"Perhaps a gull would understand me," John said, grinning and blushing slightly.

"Gulls are stupid," Henry said, mostly for the fun of saying the word "gull" again.

"Then they might understand me," John said. "If I sound stupid enough."

Henry shook his head again, enjoying the foolery of the idea. "There are many kinds of stupid. You are only one of them, John."

"The best kind," John said. "Say your word for gull again."

*Gull,* Henry said. The word had never been difficult to say, had only been part of his everyday language. But faced with John's inability to say it, the landsman's slowness of his tongue and narrow scale of notes his voice could produce, Henry sat comfortably on his horse, enjoying the feeling of being clever, able to make sounds impossible for a landsman. He knew that when John was gone he would have to be careful and studious again, guarding his words against the adults who pestered him, but he felt, for the first time, that he could afford a moment of hubris, just as a game.

John never mastered the pronunciation of the deepsmen's words. His ear wasn't fine enough to pick out the words a court hautbois imitated when playing an attempt at a deepsmen's language—something Henry realised he himself could probably do the day John brought one along and played it, much better than Allard played the flute—and likewise John never managed to make a sound clear enough that any deepsman, even Henry, could have deciphered without knowing already what he was trying to say. The language depended too heavily on sustained sounds, on variations of pitch that were beyond John's hearing in many cases and beyond his tongue in all of them. Some words remained inaudible to him, even if Henry tried to transpose them down into sounds that would have baffled a deepsman; other distinctions, simplify them as Henry might, eluded him. For the most part, what John could hear, a deepsman almost certainly would not understand; certainly no deepsman would have understood anything John tried to say. But with Henry as his teacher, he added words to his understanding if not to his speech, until Henry could make at least a few remarks in his mother tongue and have John understand him.

Movement had always been confined to Allard's lands, but when John's father came into his life, the rules tightened around Henry, becoming ever more frustrating. Hearing John speak of going hunting on his father's grounds, Henry wanted to go with him. Horse-riding, once mastered, was a tremendous advantage, letting him travel as fast as he wished without recourse to his weak legs, and outside Henry rode everywhere. The upshot of this was that he tended to spend most of every day outside, however much John shivered in the snow or sat resignedly under a tree dripping rainwater down from its leaves. Allard's land had little hunting on it. The boys chased rabbits through the fields, Henry swinging a spear with steady accuracy to pierce and scoop up the shrilling, thrashing little bundles of fur—which he gave to John, having no taste for red meat himself—but John spoke of deer, creatures almost as big as his horse and fast on their feet as they flitted through the forests. Though Henry had learned hunting in the sea and was used to prey only big enough to give a handful of meat, he remembered the dolphins, the dominance fights, the clash and swirl of opponent against large opponent. These fights were the province of adults. Henry needed to measure himself against such creatures, to test himself. The idea of deer wandering the green fields, out of his reach and blithely unconcerned about him, offended him. He could not quite overcome his dislike of land animals; even horses, useful though they were, were jolting and wayward in movement, overheated in smell. Henry was a steady rider, harsh to any mount that refused his commands, but he knew better than to hurt a horse too badly. That would end their usefulness. A creature similar to them but huntable, happily wandering free while he had to stay within a few square miles, was maddening.

Demands to visit the Claybrooks' land met with no success, though. "The time is not right, my lord," was all that Robert Claybrook would say on the subject.

"Why not?" Henry was not to be put off. "John can take me."

Claybrook gave a stern look to his son. John shifted a little on his seat, looking uncomfortable, and gave a surreptitious shrug, which Henry noticed.

"Do not blame John," he said. "This is my idea. I wish to see deer. There is nothing to hunt here but rabbits."

"My lord, the journey cannot be risked." Claybrook smiled patiently as he said this, but Henry did not trust his smiles. They came too steadily onto his face, not flashing out in quick response to a joke as John's did. Claybrook could be relied upon to smile before he spoke, and Henry disliked smiles that came with such politic predictability.

"Why do you call me 'my lord'?" Henry asked. "That is not my name."

"Your title, my lord Henry."

"Of what am I lord?"

"You are royal by your birth, my lord Henry," Claybrook said, gesturing as if to bow.

"Not when the king is so far from me," Henry said. "I have more to do before I can be royal."

"As you say, my lord."

"Do not call me that when you refuse to do as I say," Henry said. "If you will not let me on your land, I am not your lord."

John laughed, and Henry relaxed a little, turning to him. "What does the king do when men disobey him?"

John opened his mouth to answer, but his father interrupted. "We cannot risk you being seen," he said. "There is too much danger to all of us."

"Have you not found an army yet?"

Allard stepped in. "Henry, you must listen to Lord Claybrook." His hands, narrow-fingered with knotted knuckles, were gripped together. "If you were seen, you would be taken."

"By who?" Henry, on the whole, preferred Allard to Claybrook these days. Though his preoccupation with books and insistence on learning tiresome facts never waned, Henry was at least accustomed to him. Allard provided food, tried to find fabrics that Henry hated less than others, made sure his horse was well shod and stabled. His anxiety around Claybrook was irritating, but in necessities he could be relied on. Nevertheless, it was hard to respect a man so twitchy in movements, always scratching with his pen or fidgeting with his fingers, who deferred so clearly to Claybrook's regular smiles and neutral phrases. Half out of childhood habit, Henry bared his teeth a little at Allard as he spoke.

"You must stop asking!" Allard's anxious frustration was preferable to Claybrook's patient courtesy; at least it was clear what he was feeling.

"It angers you that I keep asking," Henry said. "But you do not answer me when I ask why the risk is so great. Why are you so certain I would be taken? Are there soldiers surrounding the land?"

"No. The risk is not worthwhile," Allard said, with a nervous glance at Claybrook.

"Is it so great?"

"No, but the price is," Allard said. He turned on his heel, looking angry, and picked up a book, opening it before Henry. "This is the price. For all of us. Do you wish this to happen?"

Henry studied the lines on the page. Reading had never interested him enough to motivate study, especially as Allard was always there to read things for him, and pictures, flat scribbles on a flat page, were difficult for his eye to take in. A little figure stood atop a triangle, swirls going up around him. "What is this for?" he said.

"It is a burning, Henry." Allard sounded angrier still, whether at Henry's incomprehension of the image or at the image itself Henry couldn't tell. "That is a stake, and those are flames. Princes do not care for bastards ready to threaten them. If they find you, they will burn us all."

Henry swallowed, keeping his face blank. The fire was lit in the hearth, its flames crackling over the flaking logs, sending out a heat that tingled uncomfortably on his skin even from yards away. Tiny motes of ash swam up the chimney, lifting up from the cracking logs beneath.

Henry raised his head and stared straight at Claybrook, refusing to show fear. "That will not happen to me," he said.

Nevertheless, he dropped the subject of visiting Claybrook's grounds.

It was a few weeks later that John rode in on his own, a jerking sack tethered to his saddle. Henry, who had been riding Allard's fields throwing spears at points on the ground, looked up in interest. "What have you there?" he said.

John grinned, a little breathless. "My father thinks I am practising riding on his land," he said. "I crept away. Look what I have." He untied the sack and it fell to the earth with a flurry, something inside it struggling.

"What is it?"

"A fox. I found a burrow and set a snare for it. This will be better to hunt than rabbits."

The sack convulsed on itself, and a narrow face emerged, a tawny orange shade that Henry didn't care for at all. The next moment dark, slender limbs followed, the creature thrashing its way out of the sack.

"Let me have one of your spears," John said, looking excited. Henry tossed him one without looking, eyes still on the bag. "We should have dogs, really, but it will run when it gets out."

The sack tumbled over, and then the fox was running, dragging coarse threads behind it, shaking its limbs free as it dashed across the green field. John shouted "Come on!" but Henry, accustomed to grabbing at prey the moment an opportunity arose, had already started his horse forward, spear in hand, following the bounding creature as it leaped from tussock to tussock, its feet barely brushing the ground. To Henry's eyes, the fox was flying, not the unpredictable lollops of a hopping rabbit but smooth, fast, fast as a dolphin through the air, and he grasped his spear, nothing in his mind but excitement and a predatory fervour. Everything about the fox—its size, its speed, its unforgivable colour—concentrated itself to a fine point, a red scrap of life racing across the green, ready for his spear. Behind him he could hear John yelling, John whose horse was finer than his but less obedient, and he called back, "Go ahead! That way!" For there were trees ahead, and if the fox got in between them, it could sleek in and out away from them while their horses stalled and swerved. John veered his horse around and the fox darted away, staying out on the open field.

This was different, Henry realised, this was new. This wasn't the dive and strike through the sturdy currents of the sea: this was rough ground and varying terrain, places to negotiate and footing to watch and his friend behind him to direct as they ran their quarry down. Light-footed rabbits left few tracks in the grass, but the fox trailed ravelling threads of sack, and flower heads swung as it streaked over them: Henry's horse and the fox were both fighting the ground for footing, an interplay between the land and the prey, Henry and the prey, everything swinging in and out of balance as the seconds flashed by.

The fox was fast, and the boys chased it over the field, John laughing and Henry silent except for shouted commands. John's riding wasn't quick enough, and before Henry could warn him, the fox wheeled round and dashed for the trees again. It was only a small copse, Henry knew, having explored it over and over on days when John was away and there was nothing to do but ride and practise, but a fox could slip through it any one of a dozen ways. Henry slowed his horse a little and gestured to John.

"Go around that way," he said, pointing to where the trees were thickest.

"Where are you going?" John asked, breathless.

"Go!" Henry said, not waiting; this was no time for discussion. John peeled off, making for the section that Henry had indicated.

Henry slowed his horse, picking his way into the copse. Light shone through the trees, vivid green overhead, and Henry closed his eyes; the earth beneath him was too dark and overgrown, he'd never find the fox if he let every movement distract him.

A mild breeze rustled the leaves overhead, but it was quiet among the trees. Henry sat still. Over the breathing of his horse, he could hear the clopping of John's, twigs snapping under its hooves—and . . .

There. "Go left," Henry said to John. "Go left and shout."

"What?" John's voice was muffled. "Can you see me?"

"No, I can hear you," Henry said. "Do what I say."

Henry heard the rustle of clothing that suggested John was shrugging, and then his horse pounded forward, John's voice yelling: "Angelica! Angelica!"

There was a scrabble, a clatter of leaves, and the fox dashed out of the undergrowth. Henry leaned forward, thrust his arm down, his spear slitting flesh and piercing down to bone with a sharp, delicious crunch. The fox shrieked, and Henry shoved his spear forward, spitting it to the ground, sliding off his horse as John came out of the trees, grabbing warm, dirty fur and digging his claws into the fox's neck.

Hot blood clogged the webs of his fingers, and then John was on the fox as well, clubbing its head with the butt of his spear, three sharp blows that Henry felt through his blood-stuck hands, and with each blow the fox diminished, grew slower, until, with the last blow, it was still.

Henry wasn't out of breath, but the triumph was choking. He had killed a land creature, got his own hands on it; the staked rabbits were small prizes to this. The strangeness of a hot-blooded victim, to a boy used to hunting chilled silver fish, was too bewildering to think of, so instead he smiled at John, baring his sharp teeth in a joyous grin, holding up handfuls of the fox's flesh.

"Better than rabbits?" John said, wrinkling his nose at the smell.

Henry leaned down, taking the fox's sharp-toothed, wet jaw in his hand. Careful of his webs, he placed his palm against it and gave a hard shove down. Bone split apart, and then the jaw was dislocated, held on only with a strip of bloody-backed fur that Henry severed with a nail. There it was in his hand, the trophy, familiar from the battles with dolphins: the jaw and tongue, a pink scrap amid black gums and white teeth, nestled in his palm.

"Do you want some?" Henry said, offering it to John.

John looked a little distasteful. "Can I take the tail?"

"If you wish it." Henry smiled at him as John happily took out a knife and started sawing at the body. "Why were you shouting 'Angelica'?"

He shrugged. "That will be your battle cry when we go to war," he said. "Angelica came out of the sea like you. That is what bastards say when they take thrones." John spoke distractedly.

"Bastards?"

"Like you. Deepsmen on land who are not kin to the king." John spoke distractedly, being more interested in the fluffy, white-tipped brush he had secured, busily cleaning it and stroking the fur.

Henry was still too delighted with his kill to be much involved in the explanation. *We win,* he said in his mother language, and raised the fox's jaw to his mouth. The tongue was red-tasting, meaty and less to his liking than fish, but this was his victory, his trophy to take, and this was how kills were celebrated in battles back in the sea.

He sank in his teeth and jerked his head back, capturing the tongue in his mouth, a narrow scrap of well-won meat. Blood wet his lips, the taste of gain, and he lifted his face to the treetops, swallowing his prize whole.

## Sixteen

ALLARD'S WIFE, MARGARET, was a woman Henry seldom saw. He had little desire for her company: even from a distance, she did not look reliable. In his presence, she displayed an attitude similar to that he'd seen her show around the estate's guard dog. That barking, grim-jawed beast had frightened Henry when he was little, and he supposed that was what lay behind her behaviour, but he had mastered his fear of the animal, riding to its kennel one day when he was unobserved, dragging it out by the chain when it barked at him and laying about it with a stick. The dog was almost as big as he was, but he was able to lift it one-handed, and the animal went from snarling fury to cowed whimpering by the time Henry was done with it. Afterwards, he left it a piece of fish he had kept from his dinner, and it gave him no more trouble.

While he had no desire for Margaret Allard to attack him, even if the idea had not been ridiculous—her husband had been no match for him at seven years old, and Margaret was far smaller—he could not respect her timidity. What he mostly felt was a sense of unease: a woman so constantly frightened was like a fish that might dart in different directions. Henry had never consciously tried to scare her, and her tense-handed wide-eyed fear in his presence deepened his mistrust of her. Her high voice and swaying movements were interesting, different, and he would have liked to get closer to her, test the heft of her body and the texture of her flesh, but, unwilling though he was to confess it, she made him uncomfortable.

As a result, when she fell from her horse and broke her leg one day in Henry's eleventh year, he was not overly concerned. She meant something to Allard, who went around stiff-faced and wet-eyed, but her injury had little effect on Henry's own life.

Her fate, though, hung in the balance, and Henry discovered he was supposed to care about this. John came around looking grave and said earnestly, "I am sorry about your mother."

The phrase alarmed Henry for a moment, and he gave an angry scowl. "What do you mean?"

"Her accident," John said, puzzled. "How is her leg?"

Understanding dawned: John was talking about Margaret Allard. "Mortified, I think," he said. "Why do you call her my mother?"

John was not often short of words, but this question seemed to quiet him. "Will she die, do you think?" he asked after a moment.

"Perhaps," Henry said. She wouldn't starve with people to feed her, leg or not, but wounds festered on land.

"Has she seen a surgeon?" John seemed concerned about the woman. This was amiable of him, as Henry didn't think he knew her very well.

Henry shook his head. "I have seen no one come," he said.

"Why not?" John looked frustrated.

Henry shrugged, a gesture he had learned from his friend. "Maybe Allard thinks a physician would see me and tell the king."

"My father will find one," John said firmly. "We shall need a physician when we have an army, we could begin now."

"If you wish," Henry said. A physician might be useful, and Margaret might as well be treated as not. "But why do you call her my mother?"

John looked at him a moment more, then sighed. "Because you live with her, and she and her husband care for you, or have their servants attend you, and they try to advance you. That is usually what a father and mother do. By adoption, that is what I thought they were to you."

"You look like your father," Henry said. "I do not look like Allard. I only live with him." A thought struck him. "You have your father's name. Does this mean people think I am called Henry Allard?" The idea of people going around behind his back, applying names to him without his knowledge, was a disagreeable one.

"Perhaps," John said. "Not a name you should keep when you are king, though. The Allard family is a small one, not powerful or rich. It is not a strong name—that is, a name that will make you sound strong." Years of experience had taught John to speak to Henry as literally as possible.

Henry wasn't surprised. "Do you call me Henry Allard?" He didn't want his friend misnaming him in secret.

John shook his head. "Just Henry." He reflected for a moment. "Did you have another name, before?"

Henry froze. He did not like to talk about his time in the sea, even with John. "Yes," he said. "But you could not pronounce it."

"What was it?"

"It means nothing," Henry said. "Could you find a physician for Margaret? I would like to meet one."

John sighed. "I will ask my father."

John must have asked to some effect, as two days later a physician arrived. The days had passed unhappily in the house: Margaret lay behind a closed door, but Henry had occasionally caught the sound of her, harsh, guttural moans he had not known a landsman could produce. The moaning voice troubled him. He did not especially like Margaret, but she lived in his house, and it nagged at him to hear her hover between life and death with no decisive action taken either way. Allard, he felt, should be doing something for her. His reluctant concern did not mean he liked Margaret any better—if anything, he felt some resentment of her for driving him to worry—but still, he was troubled by a sense of responsibility.

So, when Henry was ushered to his room by Allard because the physician was due, Henry objected less than he otherwise might to the idea of confinement. Allard was white, his hands shaking, as he herded Henry upstairs. Henry, who disliked the crutches he was supposed to walk on, climbed the stairs on all fours by way of asserting himself, but then went quietly to his chamber and stayed by the door, listening for what would happen.

It was some time before Henry could hear anything more than murmurs, strain his sharp ears though he might. There was a pause, whispers, the sound of instruments.

After a while, there was screaming. Henry had never heard such sounds before, not from any man or woman. Margaret was shrieking like a spitted rabbit, high, harsh screams mingled with human sobs, and the noise of it froze Henry in fascination for a moment, listening with intent ears to this new, strange sound. Then he decided that this would not do, that the surgeon must be making matters worse, possibly even taking advantage of Margaret's weakness to do something to her. He might attack or injure her or take her flesh for food, and no stranger was to do that to someone in his household, however tiresome they might be.

Ignoring his sticks, he crossed the floor on all fours and reached for the door, only to find it locked.

Furious, Henry considered breaking it down, or at least trying to. Soberer thoughts prevailed: it would take a while, and by the time he had succeeded, Margaret would probably be dead. Instead, he called out: "Allard! Allard!" Allard was worried about people seeing him, and frightened of Henry making a noise when strangers were in the house. If he couldn't protect his wife, maybe the fear of discovery might stir him to action.

There was a sound of running footsteps, and Allard appeared in the door, pale as a deepsman. He looked at his charge, but seemed to find no words.

"You should stop the surgeon, he is hurting your wife," Henry told him.

Allard stared for another moment.

"Can you not hear her? You should do something."

Allard came into the room and sat down on the floor beside Henry, careless of his neat clothes.

"You should stop the surgeon," Henry said again, louder, as Allard seemed in some kind of stupor.

Allard looked at him, then, to Henry's discomfiture, reached out and stroked the boy's shaggy head. "Her leg has mortified," he said in a hoarse voice. "The surgeon has to amputate it to save her from dying."

"Amputate?" The word was unfamiliar.

"Cut it off." Allard wiped his mouth with the back of his hand.

"But then she will be no use," Henry said. Having said it he realised that she would still be faster than he was, given a crutch, but Allard withdrew the stroking hand. The woman had never been much use, for all Henry had seen, but Allard seemed distressed at her pain nonetheless, and though he thought Allard's attitude towards her unreasonable, Henry sensed a need to rephrase. "Will this not make her worse?" he asked. Cuts let in diseases in this dry, contaminated world, and to create a gaping gash where there had once been a limb sounded like madness to him.

"It may save her," Allard said. His voice was barely a whisper. "And she will die if he does not do it." The screams had stopped, leaving a grim silence behind.

Henry thought of the cleaning fish in the ocean, little pecking silverlings that nibbled parasites off his flanks. That was as far as medicine had advanced among the deepsmen. If you were injured in the sea, you recovered or you died with no one mauling you in the meantime. "Is the surgeon wise?" he asked.

Allard drew a breath, grasping his hands together. "He is the King's surgeon, Henry. If he is not, there is no one better."

"Then he must do what he can," Henry said. The damage was done now; they might as well make the best of it.

Allard reached out and patted him again. Henry did not much care for the caress; his head was vulnerable and best left alone, in his view. However, Allard tended to pat him when he was pleased. There was an advantage here worth pressing.

"Will I meet the surgeon?" Henry asked. "You said he worked for the King."

"Why do you say that, Henry?" Allard's hands were shaking in his lap, his eyes on the door.

"He could bring me to the King, or kill the King for us. He can use a knife," Henry said. Personally he preferred a direct route in conflicts, but if no one was going to let him meet the King for years, perhaps this surgeon might be a useful short cut.

Allard closed his eyes for a moment, then got up and headed for the door. "I must go to see my wife," he said, and closed it behind him. Henry heard the lock click shut.

It was more than an hour later that it opened again, and a stranger was ushered in, Allard hovering tensely behind him.

Henry looked up from the floor, where, frustrated at the enforced idleness, he had been whittling away at one of the canes he was supposed to use for walking with a dagger he was supposed to use for fencing practice. The man standing in the doorway was sturdy, well-fed looking without being flabby: rosy-faced and sandy-bearded, almost fox-haired in colouring. Henry refused to show it, but his heart was beating faster and he held his breath; he was actually a little reassured by Allard's presence. It was years since he had met a stranger.

The man crouched down, bringing himself as low as Henry. People seldom did that in his experience, and Henry sat still, waiting to see what else the man would do.

"Good day, Henry," the man said. His voice was cautious but gentle, as if speaking to a small child. "My name is Francis Shingleton."

Henry stared.

"Would you like to speak to me?" the man persisted.

"Why would I like to speak to you?" Henry demanded. "Why do you ask? Do you mean to offer me something?" His tone was harsh, but in fact the man did not seem that bad. He was clearly wary, which was only sensible of him, but he didn't have the fixed smile Claybrook did. Possibly he was all right; it would be interesting to see how he reacted to being challenged, anyway.

"Your father said you wanted to meet me," Francis Shingleton said; his tone was matter-of-fact.

"Allard is not my father," Henry said, with a little less aggression. The man had a point: he had said he would like to meet a surgeon.

"But you wanted to meet me?"

Henry was not about to concede it. "What were you doing to his wife? Will she live?"

"I hope so." The reply sounded honest. "It is in the hands of God now. These cases are always difficult."

God was a phrase associated with the nasty cross of straight-edged wood; Henry associated remarks about this distant being with a refusal to take responsibility. "You mean you do not know," he said.

"That is right. I do not know."

Henry nodded. The man gained some credit in his eyes for admitting his ignorance. "Sit down, Shingleton," he said. "You will be uncomfortable like that."

Shingleton rose to his feet and found himself a chair. "I cannot say for sure whether Mistress Allard will live," he said. "But she is more likely to live now than before the surgery. Her broken leg would have killed her, left untreated." Henry scrutinised the man's hands. There was only a tiny trace of blood, just inside the rim of the thumb-nail.

"How much can you do if someone is sick?" Henry said.

"Not enough." Shingleton's eyes were on him, looking at his hands, his limbs, his face. The gaze was direct, but Henry didn't feel intruded upon: he was just as curious to see a surgeon. "But we must do what we can."

"Who is 'we'?" Henry didn't like this referring to persons absent. "Do you not mean *you* must?"

"I must, yes." Shingleton nodded. "But others like me as well, my lord Henry. People should do as well as they can with the knowledge they can master."

"When did I become your lord?" Henry said. "You called me Henry when you came in."

"Did I?" Shingleton frowned, rubbing the backs of his hands together.

Henry sat up. His legs were folded under him and he couldn't get up from the floor without help; seated on his chair, Shingleton towered above him. As there was no way around this, Henry braced himself more solidly, staring straight into Shingleton's clean face. "Allard says that you are the King's surgeon. The King would burn you if you did not tell him I was here. And he will burn me if you do. What are you going to do?"

"Henry." Allard started forward a little, hands gripped together.

Henry turned to look at him, but said nothing: he saw no need to defend a fair question.

Shingleton looked into his lap for a moment and sighed. "I would not send anyone to the stake," he said. "I do not care for burnings."

"Would you not wish to save yourself?" Henry said. Risking burning for your own ends was one thing, but risking it to save an eleven-year-old half-blood you had never met before today was too unlikely to gamble on.

"I am sworn to heal the sick," Shingleton said. Under Henry's black stare, he was starting to look a little sweaty. "That is my calling."

"You do not want to get into battles," Henry said.

Shingleton shook his head. "No, my lord."

"But you are the King's surgeon. The King must always risk battles."

Shingleton looked back at him. "I never travelled with an army."

"Do you treat children?"

Shingleton looked startled at the change of tack. "My lord?"

"You speak to me as if I were a child."

"Excuse me, my lord."

"I am not condemning you, I wish to know. Do you treat many children? What do you do when you do not wait on the King?"

Shingleton swallowed; the sound was loud in the closed room. "I have a hospital for idiots, my lord. But I do not think you are one."

Henry let the man sweat another moment before giving him a smile. "No. I am not. But I hear the King's son is. My friend John says so. Is he right?"

Shingleton drew a breath.

"Shingleton, you can say so in this room," Henry said impatiently. "The King will not hear you."

"Yes," Shingleton said. "He is an idiot. Her Majesty Erzebet is not, but she will not bear him children. Her two daughters are young. I do not wish to see blood, and I fear for the throne. That is the truth, my lord Henry."

This was good news to hear from an outsider, a man unprompted by Allard or Claybrook. Henry nodded. "So you will not tell the King of me?"

Shingleton shook his head. "It will come to a contest for the throne. Now, or later. I thought before today the threat would come from Spain, or from France. Not from our own shores."

"I am not a threat to anyone but the King," Henry said. "And he is old, and his son is an idiot. If you will be good to me now I will be good to you later."

Shingleton nodded. "Can I ask a favour, my lord?" he said.

"Yes." Henry did not wish to be friends with this man, but he had decided to think well of him. He was not a soldier, but would be of use if he wasn't pushed.

"May I examine you?"

"I am not sick," Henry said. "I am never sick."

Shingleton looked almost hopeful. "That is good news indeed, my lord. But I would like to learn. The house of Delamere—cousins have married cousins for generations." Delamere was the King's family name, Henry remembered. Maybe he could take it for himself later; it was better than Allard. "You are newly out of the sea, my lord, you are healthy. I would like to learn what a healthy King should be, in body." His eyes were bright.

"If you like," Henry said. "But do not touch me. I do not like to be touched."

～

Shingleton examined Henry, studied him with care and interest. By the time he was finished, the child-idiot tone was gone from his voice. He spoke to Henry the way Allard spoke to Claybrook: with deference.

The following week, Shingleton visited again to check on Margaret

Allard, who was beginning to recover. He also came to see Henry. When he appeared before Henry, he did something no one had done before: hingeing his straight landsman's back and legs, he lowered his head and bowed. The sweep of it brought his head almost level with Henry's.

## Seventeen

W HILE HE KNEW that they would need soldiers, for a time Henry was happy playing with John. As they grew older, though, his friend was called away to court more often. These absences, which could last months, left Henry bored and angry, difficult to please and, in the privacy of his own mind, sad. There were too many adults towering over him, and all of them put demands on him. No one was any fun.

Thomas Markeley, his old arms instructor, took John's place as a sparring partner during the lonely weeks when John was away. Henry liked Markeley well enough: a man of few words who tended to handle Henry much as he handled a horse, with brief instructions, pointing him in the right direction and giving him the occasional pat. Markeley was easy to understand. He had also been a soldier, and Henry studied him, trying to learn what he needed to know about such creatures.

John said that most people—"the people" was the phrase he used, an awkward concept to understand, as unlike the concept of a tribe, "the people" did not seem to include all the people in England—were more like Markeley than like anyone else Henry knew, but that most were not soldiers. They grew things, dug the earth and planted seeds (John having planted some in a patch of earth to prove to Henry that this was how plants came about, a little patch of greenery Henry sometimes visited when there was no one to play with). They kept animals captive and slaughtered them when it was time to eat. They made things. From this, Henry had formed an impression of the people of England as hungry and frightened. They kept their prey close to them where it couldn't escape, but if the prey took sick and died, they couldn't swim across the miles to find more. They stayed on little patches of ground, facing starvation if the ground didn't yield food. They were forbidden to gather what they needed: it was called stealing and ended with a rope choking the life out of them. The king led them and told them what to do, but they couldn't see or hear him. He was out of their reach, experienced only by report—but they must all know that he was old, that he had no good sons. Somehow he managed to keep away kings from other tribes, but Henry was certain of something, even though Markeley always changed the subject back to weapons when asked directly: the people needed their king to be strong, and he wasn't. They would be frightened of other kings, and, more importantly, they would be ashamed.

This could be used to his advantage, Henry thought. People would want a strong king. If he managed it properly, offered them what they lacked, they ought to be pleased about it.

He would have liked to share the thought with John, but John was away.

~

Boredom was not something Henry had ever had to deal with in the sea. Every moment was a hunt, shoals of silver food bristling before him, dolphins crackling their threats across the leagues of water, avoiding the pinching fingers of the other children, questing across blue, empty deserts to find the currents that would take the tribe to its next destination. He had been active, frightened, alert, every waking moment. Taken into Allard's house, he had remained frightened. But the years had passed and no one threatened him; the soldiers he heard so much about remained distant, unseen. He had learned, studied—at least with weapons—because he hadn't known any other kind of life. John had introduced him to the idea of company. Left alone, he found the practice a little wearisome. He persevered, hefting his axe day after day, because there was nothing else to do. Sometimes, when the weather was too hot, he kept to his room, staring out of the window, one hand idly turning the crown Allard had given him when he was small.

The occasions John returned, Henry was too happy to see him to complain about his absence. He knew that John had to go to the court to learn about it. When he was sixteen, though, and beginning to chafe at this round of coming and going, training and promises with no sign of progress, another absence was called for, one that was neither welcome nor expected.

"John should go," was the first Henry heard about it. Claybrook was already discussing the topic with Allard and John when Henry, who had heard rapid hoofbeats from across the estate and ridden back from his explorations to meet them, made an awkward entrance into the room.

Allard looked even more nervous than usual; Henry could hear his breath scraping in his throat. "Will you not go too?" he said.

"Yes, I must." Claybrook gave an impatient wave. "But separately. I will have to join his Majesty's party. And I will have to return to court afterwards. Philip takes more and more care, and her Majesty is less and less willing to help. I could not ride back to tell you about it. John will be free to return. He can go on his own: he would be in the way if I was caring for Philip. It would be natural enough to send him home after such a sight anyway."

"What is to happen?" Henry broke in. John was sitting in a corner, looking smaller than usual. The sight made Henry angry and anxious.

"Henry." Allard turned to him, reached out a hand and then thought better of it. "There is news from court. There may be no need for us to be alarmed, but it is most serious."

"What?" Henry didn't want preamble; in the time it took Allard to talk about the news, he could simply have said it and spared Henry some frightened seconds.

"It may not be—"

"John, what has happened?" Henry gave up on Allard, who after eleven years still would not learn that he should give straight answers.

John shrugged unhappily. "They say someone has found a bastard, and they are going to burn him." Henry froze. "Not you, we think. In Cornwall, far south of here. They say he is young, only four years old or so. And they have caught him. But it will stir the country up. People are talking about whether they will really burn the child or kill him first, give him an easier death. But we do not think they will. Princess Erzebet is looking very fierce about it."

Henry shook his head, urgency swamping him. "Do we have soldiers now? We could stop them, could we not?"

"Henry, we cannot." Allard sounded almost as unhappy as John.

Henry turned on Claybrook. "You talk of soldiers. Why have I seen none? We could go to Cornwall and stop them doing this."

Claybrook gave a polite smile. In this conversation, it looked utterly wrong, and Henry glowered. "We are not yet ready, my lord."

"He may be right, sir," John said to his father. "I do not think the people will wish to see a child burn. Henry and I are well grown now. Maybe this would be a good moment to strike."

"Not unless we wish to put this child on the throne," Claybrook said, a sharp edge in his voice. "And it is Henry we wish to crown, not this Cornwall infant."

"He could be my son," Henry said. "You say that the King is weak because he has not enough sons. This boy could be mine."

"You are too young to be his father, my lord," Claybrook said, as if correcting a mistake.

"I am not a fool, I know this," Henry snapped. "But if we could take the throne, then I could say he was my son and that would make him so. You say England needs deepsmen boys. There would be two of us." In fact, Henry had ill memories of deepsmen boys, but this child was smaller than him, weaker, and could not hurt him. With Henry's dominance assured, the infant might be useful. And whether or not he would like the child, Henry could not stand the thought of a burning. If England could burn one bastard, it could burn another, and the child's death would bring him a long step closer to the scorching pyre.

"This boy would be a threat to you, my lord." Henry noticed with anger that Claybrook's voice, so biting when speaking to his son, had turned back to courtesy and calm when addressing Henry.

"I could settle such a threat if it happened," Henry said. "But it is not coming from him now."

"This is useless talk, my lord," Claybrook said. "It cannot be done."

"Why do you not want to save the child?" Henry demanded.

Claybrook gave him a politic smile. "England would accept one bastard on the throne, my lord. England would become used to him in time, if he could hold it. But England would never accept two bastards at once. One bastard would become a king, if he were strong enough. But the king is king by birth. Two bastards together would destroy the very notion of kingship."

"England would accept a king that ruled," Henry said, his voice unfamiliarly choked as fury made it harder to speak. "You are—are talking songs. These are thoughts, not real things." His vocabulary was beginning to desert him in the cold haze of his anger.

"My lord," Claybrook said firmly, "we have not the soldiers."

"Then *what have you been doing for eight years?*" Henry looked over and saw John sitting silent in his chair, gnawing his knuckles as Henry shouted at his father. Henry drew a breath, held it, held it, let the seconds stretch as his lungs settled around their hoard of air.

A silence hung in the room.

Henry let the breath out of his lungs, drew another. "John, could we raise soldiers?" he said.

John swallowed, avoiding his father's eyes. "Probably not fast enough," he said. "And possibly not many enough. The burning will happen soon. It takes many days to bring an army together. Weeks, usually."

"Could it be done?"

"Possibly." John looked at Henry, his shoulders hunched as if to hide him from the adults staring at him. "But probably it would fail. And then we would go on the pyre together."

Henry looked at John for a moment, refusing to drop his gaze.

The air in the room was too thick, too windless for comfort. He lowered his voice, sitting down on the floor. "Can you go to this burning?"

"My lord . . ." Claybrook began.

*"I do not speak to you."* Henry did not shout, but his words rang around the room, resonant as a cry in the sea, and everyone flinched at the sound.

John shrugged. "If I must. You will wish for news straight away, yes?"

"Will you stay awhile after you come back?"

John nodded. "Yes, I can do that."

"Then you should go. Go alone. Do not bring a servant, no one who will make a noise or want to talk to you while you are there. Listen to what the people say, and tell me about it."

"I will do that." John's face, normally pink of cheek and bright of eye, was dull in the half-lit room.

"You do not look well," Henry said. "Will it make you ill to see it?"

John straightened up, shook his head rapidly, his curls flying about his face. "It will not kill me," he said. There was a moment when his face struggled for composure, but then his old grin was back, almost as wide as before. "I shall be as brave as a soldier about it, Henry. It may do me good to see what we face, make me cautious."

"If you cannot watch it, you should tell me so," Henry said.

John shook his head again. "No," he said. "We will see more deaths than this before we get to the throne." He smiled again. Henry could see that the smile was forced, but he was not going to hurt his friend's pride by pointing it out. "After all, it will not be you on the pyre."

John rode away that night. Henry had insisted on accompanying him to the edge of the estate, and with Claybrook already gone to catch the royal party, Allard made no objection; his face was sad and frightened, but he knew better than to quarrel with Henry in his current mood. Henry and John rode quietly together, no sound but the hooves of their horses drumming against the damp earth. The air was cool on

Henry's skin, damp and pleasant, and the moon cut a sharp slice of light in the black sky above. It was a bright night, easily bright enough to ride by.

At the edge of the grounds, Henry patted the neck of John's horse and said, "I will see you soon." John looked at him and nodded, his mouth pinched shut, his face grey in the moonlight. He turned his face without speaking and, after a moment, kicked his horse to a trot and set off.

Henry sat by himself, listening to the sound of the hooves as it faded in the distance. In the still, moist air, sound carried far, and he could hear great distances: owls hooting from miles away, the rush of a river, the scuttle of mice in the underbrush. In that great quiet, John's horse was the loudest thing for miles.

After a few minutes, when he was sure that he was out of John's earshot, he followed.

~

John was easy to track. His horse pattered along, a steady, sustainable pace: John had never liked to press his animals too hard. Neither did he like to be alone; Henry could hear him whispering under his breath: "Good beast. On we go . . ." He sang songs to keep himself company, talked to his horse, clattered his teeth together to make noise to go along with him. The sound of his loneliness made Henry sorry that he was trailing so far behind, but irritated him a little as well. Henry knew about hunting at night. If this were in the sea, with all the noise John was making, a shark would have taken him in the first ten minutes.

Hour after hour they kept on. He did not know where the burning was to be held, but the distances were still greater than Henry, used to cantering in circles within a few miles of land, had ever ridden in his life. The trees did not change, the earth smelled fresh and black and the wind parted before him as it always did, but despite the danger of the journey, the openness, the wild risk of discovery, something in Henry relaxed. After years imprisoned, he was travelling the miles again.

The thought of the bastard had driven him almost mad when he had first resolved to follow John. Henry was too old to think he could somehow rescue the poor landed brat, but he had to go anyway. They were going to burn him. Were it not for Allard—it was a thought that had never spurred him to gratitude before, but he felt a surprising stirring of it now—that would have been him. This child, his kinsman, was headed for the pyre, and Henry had to see it. Even if the boy didn't know he was there, Henry had to be near him. Whether he was destined for the throne or the fire, Henry didn't know, but the flames were something he needed to see. The thought of them made his heart pound so loud in his chest he could hear it over the noise of John's horse, and that made him angry. He was going to face the flames, match his courage against them and stare them down.

～

It was early the next morning, grey dawn seeping through the sky, that Henry finally decided he had hidden long enough. John's horse stopped pacing in the distance and Henry heard a slithering dismount, the familiar voice saying, "Good girl. Just a little rest and we will go on . . ." It was time to make his approach. As the sky whitened, Henry could feel his chest constrict; a dark sky was like a dark sea overhead, soft and expansive, deep enough to hide in, but with light capping the day he was beginning to feel exposed. They were on a dirt road, tufts of long grass straggling at the sides and brambles leaning toothed, drunken legs this way and that, and Henry didn't like it. He'd never seen this place before.

John sat shut-eyed on the ground, his horse cropping the grass beside him. He didn't see Henry coming. A small flare of frustration briefly warmed the chill in Henry's bones: John shouldn't be so easy to track. It was careless. How would he survive if they were ever hunted?

"You should not close your eyes on a strange road," he said, riding forward, and John's eyes flew open. He stared at Henry, his mouth hanging open and his face pale.

"Good morrow," Henry continued, seeing that John wasn't going to say anything. The sight of his friend speechless made him uncomfortable, and there was nothing to do but carry on and wait for John's spirits to catch up. He hoped it would be soon; Henry was not good at being the cheerful one. "I am coming with you."

John looked frantically back and forth, up and down the road. There was no one in sight; brown puddles shivered in the wind and the grass bobbed beside them, but the road was clear. "Get back into the woods!" John leaped to his feet, making a grab for Henry's bridle. Henry's horse turned its head and Henry grabbed at the reins, steadying it. "Henry, hide yourself! Get into the woods! What do you do here?"

"I am coming to the burning," Henry said. "Leave my horse be, you will frighten him."

"To Hell with your horse, Henry. Do you mean to have us killed? How did you follow me?"

Henry shrugged. "I could hear you from a mile away. I wish to come to—"

"Henry, you can't! Go back, please. You will be killed. We will both be killed if you are seen, and if you are not seen my father will kill me when we get home anyway. Henry, please go back." John's face was drained of colour, his eyes wide. His hand, reached out for the bridle, was frozen in mid-air, and Henry could see it shake.

"I will not give you up if anyone sees me," Henry said. "But I shall come to the burning."

"No you will not. Not with me." From the ground, John was far taller than Henry, but secure in his saddle, Henry could see the top of John's head, an unaccustomed sight. "Henry, I cannot take you with me. You must go home."

Henry leaned down and patted John on the shoulder. John flinched like a nervous animal, but Henry felt no aggression, just a sense of friendship. He wasn't going to get John hurt. "I do not know the way," he said. "I only followed the sound of your hooves. I will get lost."

"Then I will take you."

Henry shook his head. "I will not let you. You cannot fight me, John. Either we go to the burning together, or I go on alone and try to find it by myself. You can sit in the mud beside this road and wonder where I am."

John swallowed, looking at Henry's sharp, small teeth and narrow nose, his black eyes and white skin. "Your face will reveal you, Henry. You would be taken the moment you saw another person. You cannot go into a crowd."

Henry gave him an innocent stare. "Then you must protect me, John. You are my friend. Protect me from my folly."

John looked for a moment, then shook his head. It was a gesture Henry had often seen before, when an argument had broken down with John laughing and giving way. He wasn't laughing now, though. He drew a deep breath, and shook his head again. When he looked back, his face was set more in its own lines—though still pale as bread. "Is that your only cloak?" he asked.

Henry nodded. It was thin wool, grey and warm-smelling, and kept out the cold but little; he had never much cared for warm clothes.

"We must change, then," John said. "Mine has a hood. Here, take it." Henry shrugged off his own cloak and reached down for John's, a dark grey affair of heavier fabric. "Put it on and pull it over your face. I swear, Henry, if this does not work then we must go home."

Henry settled the cloak around his shoulders and pulled up the hood. It weighed down on him, thick and oppressive, blunting the bite of the morning air, smothering him from the world. John pulled Henry's thinner mantle around his own frame, shivering. "You landsmen are always cold," Henry said. "My cloak is too small for you. Look, it barely reaches your knees."

"I am a good friend to wear it," John said, clapping his arms around himself. "Raise your hood."

Henry pulled the hood up around his face. The fabric, warm from its former wearer, covered his ears, shuttered his vision, enshrouding his head in dullness. To be so screened from his surroundings made Henry more nervous than before, and his hand twitched, wanting to pull it off.

"Further forward," John said. His teeth were chattering. "How far forward can it go?"

Henry reluctantly covered his face. The cloth hung down on his forehead, like a ceiling blocking out the sky. The further forward the hood, the more vulnerable he felt, but John seemed to relax. "Well," he said, "that is not perfect, but if you keep your head lowered, it will do well enough. Pull it down. Keep it over the tops of your boots, so nobody can see your legs."

The folds of the cloak were difficult to arrange, but Henry twined his legs back, tucking the cloth over them. "Good enough?"

John shook his head. "We are lucky I am taller than you. That cloak is barely big enough as it is." He pressed his hands against his forehead, fingers splaying over the white skin. "I do not like this, Henry."

Henry bared his teeth from the depths of the hood. "I do not like this hood, but I wear it to please you."

"Why must you see this burning?" John lowered his hands, looking up at his friend.

Henry did not know how to answer. He shook his head. "I wish to know what is happening," he said in the end. "And I wish to know the worst that can happen to me."

"If you wish to know that, let us go home now and I will set fire to a cat for you," John said.

Henry shook his head again. "I wish to know what I am fighting against."

❧

John said little on the rest of the journey, and Henry said nothing either. The two of them plodded side by side, down the road. The first time someone passed them Henry's hands tightened on his reins so fast that the horse shied, but the traveller only raised his hand and nodded, saying, "Good morrow." John hailed him in return, and they passed on. The stranger was a man dressed much like Allard, with yellow hair and a pink face, startling in his unfamiliarity, but gone down the road, no threat, no danger. Henry resisted the urge to turn and stare after him. *If all goes well,* he told himself, *I shall rule that man one day. I will not have to hide from him. I will show him my face, and he will bow.*

As the numbers of people increased, though, Henry grew uncomfortable. John was right, many of them wore cloaks, and as they thickened on the road, becoming a crowd, a shoal of cumbersome horses and riders, more and more of them pulled hoods up covering the bewildering variety of faces, as if to shield them. There was nothing in any of their features that needed hiding. They just drew up their hoods, covering their heads from what surrounded them.

The pyre had loomed immense in Henry's mind, casting a black, flickering shadow over his spirit, but the sight of it was so mundane that for a moment he couldn't believe this was what they had come so far to see. A tall stake of wood, roughly hewn and set in the ground, surrounded by bundles of fuel, a simple cone heaped around a stick, like a pile of snow with a spade stuck in it. It was not tall like a tree or black like ink. Just a fireplace heaped up in an open field.

"Henry." John's voice was low, too low for anyone but him to hear. "We should stay at the back of the crowd. If we are too close to the front, we will have to dismount, and then you will have to walk."

And then people would see his legs. Then he might as well climb up on the pyre and lie down to sleep out the last few minutes of his life. Henry said nothing, but pulled hard on his horse's reins and dug in his heels, forcing the animal to back up.

Having followed John all night, ridden so far and tired his horse to get here, Henry expected the burning to begin at once, but it was hours of waiting before anything happened. People arrived, people upon people. Henry was no judge of clothes, but they had more the look of Claybrook than of Allard or the servants; tall people, people on fine horses with servants attending them. More and more. Henry hung at the outskirts of the crowd and backed up his horse more with each arrival, and they kept on coming. The sight was overwhelming. In all his life, he had known fewer than a dozen people. Now there were scores of them, thronging together, a great gathering, all strangers, numerous, various, terrifying.

It was some time, too long, before an unfamiliar sound came to Henry's ears, piercing and sharp. He looked up, reached to tug on John's arm.

"Your hand," John hissed, pushing him away.

Henry hid his webs back in his fists, folding his fingers around the reins. "What is that?" he whispered.

"The fanfare. The King is coming. Can you not understand it? It is meant to be the deepsmen's language."

Henry listened, frowning with angry concentration. There was something of the creak and drone of his mother tongue there, and he knew court musicians were supposed to imitate the deepsmen's language with their instruments. Probably there was something to hear in that displeasing mix of sounds, but he wasn't about to converse with it. He shook his head. "It means nothing," he said.

There was a rustle, the snort of horses and the sound of voices whispering, and the crowd pushed back. Henry found his legs being jostled by other men; to his alarm, he could feel knees, calves, the clear shape of others being pressed into his skin. If he could feel them, they could feel him. "Back up, back up," he hissed to John, yanking hard at his horse's mouth. The animal, over-driven and exhausted, jumped under his pulling, and Henry loosened the reins in panic: if the creature reared now, it would tumble him onto the ground, legs strewn out for the world to see. Heart thrashing against his ribs, he took a gentler grip and pulled back, trying to see John around the suffocating hood.

Preoccupied with his battle to get out of the crush, Henry missed the royal litters' arrival. When he looked up, there was an array of people, a man, a woman, both crowned and stiff-backed, and something else, a fat shape slumped beside the woman—but they did not have their faces to him, and he couldn't see. His hands convulsed in frustration; if he had his axe, he could ride up to them now, three hard swings and this whole parade would be over with. If it weren't for the crowd. They were too far away from him, and he couldn't see their faces. They could be landsmen, could be deepsmen, could be anything.

There were no speeches. The crowned woman raised her hand, and brought it down again. There was a murmur, and then men were coming forward, dragging behind them a shuffling, lurching figure, whose weeping rang in Henry's ears, got inside them like an itch, a burr he couldn't dig out. He looked at John, desperate and bewildered. "That is not a bastard," he said.

John shook his head, raised a hand to shush him. "That is the man who found him," he said. He opened his mouth to say more, then stopped, shook his head again and laughed. It was not a happy sound.

The man wept, and when his leg touched the ground, he groaned.

Guards climbed up the pyre, dragging the man after them. Yanked his hands above his head, tied them with rope, left him hanging there, lopsided, his face contorted, his body flopping with sobs, helpless as a dying cod. His voice, coming out in broken lumps, was the only sound in the field.

Other men followed. In their arms they carried someone, a shape Henry recognised instantly. Two tails, pallid skin, a thick sturdy waist and a fan of webs between its fingers. A child. His child, his brother. It struck Henry, as the child was tied up back-to-back with its finder, that the boy might actually be his brother. His mother had found a landsman to her taste once before. The thought gave him a passing moment of hostility towards the little shape on the pyre.

Then two men stepped forward with lit torches.

Flame caught quickly on to fuel, lapping round it like a climbing vine, ragged edges roaring in the wind. The man's sobs rose quickly to screams, but it was the child's voice that Henry heard: the shrilling cry of an animal, the shriek in the language he had not heard for many years from any throat but his own: *Help me! Help me!*

A man in robes was standing grim-faced before the pyre, making square gestures and muttering something in what Henry supposed was Latin. One of his legs was faulty and he stood at an angle. As the heat washed over him, stinging his skin, it seemed to Henry as if the whole of creation was lurching, sick and crooked in this dry, hard world where no water cushioned you, where you landed as you fell with nothing to break the blow.

The child screamed for his mother. *No help to you now,* Henry thought, ash in his throat. *She pushed you out here to meet this.*

There was a racket coming from the royal gathering, the lumpen shape of the man beside the queen rocking and yelling in his chair. People were standing beside him, squeezing water over his skin, and the sight made Henry so sick with anger that his stomach heaved. With another twist in his heart, Henry recognised a man standing beside them, directing their motions. It was Robert Claybrook.

The flames were rising and the screams were fading. Henry caught a glimpse of bubbling skin as they finally tore their way upwards to close over the child's head. On the firewood below, something frothed and hissed: fat melting off as the meat cooked. The smell was no worse than any other roasted joint, any other hearth fire Henry had ever encountered. Now it seemed he had always been right in his hatred of both.

The fire roared for a long time and no one spoke. With the sight of the child gone, Henry had no more reason to stay. They were at the back; they could set out and go. As Henry turned to tell John to come with him, he looked down, and horror broke through his body in a wave of cold that blotted out the heat of the fire.

His leg was uncovered. Something, some movement, had pushed the cloak back, and there it lay, a limp snake down the side of his horse, accusing him.

Henry covered it with a frantic tug, and looked around him. All eyes were still on the pyre. No one was looking at him. He was safe, surely he was safe; if anyone had spotted him, he'd be burning right now, thrown in with the others; why waste wood when there was a fire already lit? A laugh coiled in his throat; he was getting light-headed and stupid. Time to go.

Henry backed his horse out of the crowd, slowly and carefully. The movement was enough to get John's attention, and the two of them set out together.

A little way down the road, they heard a voice hailing them: "John? John!" Recognising Robert Claybrook, the boys stopped their horses.

"Dismount," Claybrook said. The fire had flushed his face, making it scarlet, and his voice was hard. Henry slithered down after John; the horse would need rest soon anyway, or it would collapse.

"John." Claybrook's voice was clipped. "Who is that with you?"

"Henry, sir." John spoke to the ground, barely above a whisper. The sound of it hurt Henry's ears.

"The fault is mine," Henry said quickly. "I followed him all the way and would not go home; he stayed with me to make sure I concealed myself well."

Claybrook gave Henry a brief look. His eyes glittered as he turned back to his son. "You brought him here," he said.

John did not look up.

"Answer me."

John lifted his head a little; his face was haggard. Henry could see his legs were shaking. Claybrook stood over his son, and raised a hand.

Henry stepped between them and raised his arm, poised to strike a backhanded blow.

Claybrook fell back. He took another quick look at John, then at Henry standing with his hand still raised.

Henry stood braced. "If you punish him for this I shall know it," he said. "It was my doing. Punish me, if you can. But I will know it if you touch John."

Claybrook stood frozen before him for a moment. Then he turned, walked back to his horse and gathered his reins in his hand. Henry could hear his ragged breathing as he went. "I must return to his Majesty," he said.

Henry stood, beginning to stagger, watching him ride off, but John pulled on his sleeve. "We must go now, stay ahead of the crowds," he said. Henry nodded, and the two of them clambered back into their saddles.

They went down the road in silence.

"Let us go through the woods," Henry said after a while. John turned his mare without saying anything, and the shade of the trees covered them both.

"We can rest when we get to Allard's land," Henry said. "Sleep in the woods for a few hours." The idea of it, earth against his back and the clean smell of leaves, birds chattering in the trees and the grass sighing and bending under the wind, and dark, oblivious sleep, filled him with yearning.

"He will be worried about you," John said. His voice was very small.

"Yes," Henry said. "I suppose I must say I am sorry."

## EIGHTEEN

THE OLDER ANNE grew, the more she played stupid in public. She went to Mass daily, prayed for protection, for guidance, for something to get her through the day. Before the court, she kept her face blank, retreating again to the church as soon as the formalities were over. A girl whose salt-limed brain was too withered to hold more than one idea at a time, and that idea being harmless love of God—such a girl was safe. Such a girl might never find herself thrashing on a bed of blood, screaming her life out after a bath of poison. Or as safe from such a fate as was possible for a girl who was third in line to the crown.

Anne spent her days with Bishop Westlake as much as she could. Since her tutor, Lady Margaret, had dragged her to Erzebet's deathbed, she had spoken not another word to the woman, but had gone to Westlake for any further education. She should not have been able to arrange such matters for herself, but Erzebet was not there to organise them for her.

They prayed together, and studied, and spoke. They spoke of Erzebet's death, her murder.

Anne cried at night, and slept with a chair wedged under her door, and every morning when she woke up, her body was chilled with fear. The love of God held her in the day; there were glimpses of the Holy Spirit, when she longed for it enough. But grief was an icy chill that crowded other thoughts out of her mind. She would see her mother in Heaven; this she believed. But she wanted her mother back now, and that, God could not provide.

An icon of the Virgin stood in her chamber and watched over her as she slept, but its blank, landsman's face was so strange to her that she had to close her eyes before praying to it, whispering words of entreaty in the cold dark behind her eyelids.

～

Samuel Westlake was not a man to discuss what he had heard in confession, even with his adopted princess, but other information was at Anne's disposal. What he could tell her, though, was painfully little.

Erzebet had died scorched to the flesh with poison. That poison had come to her through her bathwater. Though she did not share her husband's fragile skin, Erzebet, like most monarchs, enjoyed bathing; she would become curt and irritable if unable to wash herself at least every other day. Anne knew this; usually she herself bathed attended by maids, but there were some memories, from early in her life, in which Erzebet had sat in a tub while waiting women poured in brine from wooden buckets, dancing baby Anne in the water and trickling cool droplets over their bare skin. There had been a day, weeks before she died, when Anne had been bathing as usual and Erzebet had come in. The maids had set their buckets down to curtsey deeply, and Erzebet looked around in impatience, waving her hand and saying, "Carry on. No need to stop."

Anne had smiled up, droplets trickling down her face and pattering in the water around her. "Good morrow, my mother."

"Anne. Are you well?" Erzebet halted over to her on her canes. "Bring me a chair, Jane," she said, turning to one of the maids, and Jane hastened to seat her mistress beside the tub.

"I am, thank you." Nakedness didn't trouble Anne, being accustomed to swimming bare-skinned out to sea with her mother, but still, she was uncomfortably shy. When they swam, activity bound them together: there was a task, motion, purpose. To sit trapped in a wooden bath while her mother sat beside her was unfamiliar, and the thought of saying something foolish made Anne's cheeks tingle.

Erzebet reached out, tucked a lock of Anne's hair behind her ear. "Good girl."

Anne bit her lip, too pleased to dare answer.

Erzebet sat quietly. There seemed to be nothing to say.

"A-are you well?" Anne managed.

Erzebet looked at her daughter. There was a pause before she answered, just a few moments, as she exhaled. In a lesser woman, the sound would have been a sigh. "I am well in body, Anne. The state is never quite well."

"Are you tired?" Erzebet looked worn. There was a bruise on her collarbone that the rich dress did not quite hide, and her face was pallid, her eyes dark-rimmed. Though Anne's heart beat hard at asking the question, she needed to know.

Erzebet rarely smiled; her sharp teeth stayed sheathed, and her face was grave in cast. But there was a little softening of her lips as she said, "Somewhat. But we must always work, Anne." Her hand trailed down into the bathwater, little drops from the sides of the tub marring her fine-worked sleeve. The gesture was a weary one, absent-minded, as if Erzebet hadn't noticed she was dabbling her fingers in the soothing brine. Anne wished desperately to reach out and take her mother's hand. She almost did, but she had not quite the courage. She sat and gazed at her mother's face, soaking up her presence, knowing that very soon, she would go away again.

Erzebet hadn't been concerned about bathwater. She had swirled her hand in it idly. Food, she was careful of, and wine: tasters stood attendance, and whenever possible she would insist on fish carted from the sea in buckets, brought to her table knocking their tails against a trencher and killed safely before her eyes. But a bath had been a haven, a resting place. She had no fear of water.

Brine. That was what she had loved. Landsmen might bathe in river water or well water, but for Erzebet, for Philip, for Anne, the water was saline, rich and strong. But Erzebet had not died on the coast, spent much of the year away from it. Seawater wasn't easy to come by. Instead, attendants poured ladlefuls of salt into their buckets, stirred them with long sticks, making up the best palliative they could.

Those bowls of salt sat open in the bath chambers. It would be easy to add something to them. And once it was added, Erzebet was condemned, death flowing in a white, whispering stream to dissolve in the bucket of water, ready to eat its way into her flesh.

~

Philip asked frequently what had happened to Erzebet. That, at least, was probably what he meant when he tugged on Robert Claybrook's arm, saying, "Wife? Wife?" The tugging was forceful: Anne could see Claybrook's tall body jerked to and fro by the force of Philip's importuning.

The court met infrequently these days. Edward had been handing over power to Erzebet for years, but with Erzebet gone, disputes were beginning to be settled in private. Robert Claybrook and a neighbouring noble, John Forder, had a disagreement about some waterway rights; rather than bring it out in public, Edward spoke to the two men apart. It was Samuel Westlake who passed the news on to Anne: Edward had allocated the rights to Claybrook in very little time. The man who had charge of Philip could not easily be gainsaid.

What Edward was doing was sending out ambassadors. Frequently when Anne saw her grandfather these days, he had a portrait in his hands. It was at a private audience that Anne learned the reason.

Edward had gathered the remnants of his family together: Philip, Mary and Anne. There were a number of miniatures spread out on a table beside him. Anne, sitting quietly on a chair near her uncle, kept her hands folded in her lap, hoping that if she stayed still, Philip would not notice her: his sudden shouts were hard on her bruised nerves. Her uncle sat, unattended by the Privy Sponges for once, swathed in wet clothing. A white cloth wrapped around his head gave him the air of a corpse laid out for burial, and Anne shuddered. His great blank face staring out of that dank mass of fabric looked barely conscious.

Edward made no preamble. "I shall announce this to the court in due course," he said. "But you should know, Mary, Anne, that I have sent ambassadors to the courts of Spain, France, Venice and Flanders, asking whether their sons are interested in an alliance."

"An alliance?" Mary's pink cheeks were paler these days. Though still short in stature as a princess always would be, she was growing, rising above Anne, the beginnings of a swell at her chest. Since Anne had started going to Westlake for her education, the two girls had spent less time together. Though Anne could not forgive Mary her innocence of the true cause of Erzebet's death, she had been surprised at how pleased she felt at seeing her sister. Mary looked taller, but not happier. The gap in their ages seemed smaller now than it once had, and Anne could see that her sister was looking young and lost.

Edward's face was grave. "You are young to be married, my dear, but not too young. We must look to the throne."

Mary said nothing for a moment. Then she swallowed, and gave her grandfather a brave smile. "As Your Majesty says." Her face was wan.

Anne spoke up uninvited. "This is good news for you, Mary. You shall be Queen. You will have a fine husband." Anne, simpleton of the court, fully expected Mary to be the great prize in marriage. Beautiful Mary, heir presumptive, next in line after Philip. The throne of England stood ready for the man who married her. Mary could command her own price.

"I shall see to it," Edward said. "I have had limners working to take portraits of the princes of Europe." His tone was reassuring, though the words were formal. Anne considered for a moment. Portraits were by their nature flattering; she had seen enough rosy-cheeked, delicate-featured paintings of herself to have realistic expectations about how accurate they were. But the issue was a crucial one. Idiocy was in the family, the tree was tangled root and branch, cousins marrying cousins until catastrophes like Philip came forth, thick-tailed and staring. Most of the courts of Europe were peopled by close relations. Angelica's line had branched, but it had interbred, tangling in on itself. The choice was not an easy one. Their father could be free of his choice, more or less, because he was finding a wife, but a husband, a King, was a political choice as much as a fleshly one. To bring a wife to court, to integrate her and subordinate her nationality to his, was one thing. But to bring in a husband, a man who would hold the throne himself? A man who could father healthy children and also be accepted as a King of England? At that moment, Anne could think of no one.

She looked at her sister. Mary sat, head lowered, hands still in her lap, her eyes fixedly down. The idea of children being born by that small body was a frightening one. Anne resolved to pray harder, maybe take the veil, take herself out of the succession altogether rather than lower her body into such turbulent waters. But who would care for Mary if she were gone?

"There is also the question of your husband, Anne." Edward's voice cut across Anne's anxieties; he spoke gently, but she started nonetheless.

"Me?" She couldn't think of anything to say. Mary was the older one, the prettier, the pink-faced beauty of the family. Mary would have a husband. But her, Anne? Her blue face and meagre body traded out to some foreign man?

"We face a problem, Anne," Edward said. "We need sons for the throne. You know that. We will find a husband for Mary, he can rule with her, and if they have sons, all will be well. But we have to be sure. If, God forbid, ill health should befall your sister, we could not afford you to be out of the country."

Mary looked at Edward, then at Anne, her face pale. Edward put it carefully, but there was no doubt what he meant. Not every woman was able to bear children. Not every woman survived childbirth. If Mary's body wasn't strong enough for the task, Anne would be needed. England might be pinning its hopes on Mary's pretty face, but it could not afford to go without a spare.

Mary lowered her eyes, her mouth closed. It was a good effort, but Anne had felt eyes on her faulty face too often not to know humiliation when she saw it. She leaned towards Mary, reaching out her hand; things were changing too fast, but she could not see her sister's face shutter like that without reaching out to her. Mary did not clasp the fingers Anne extended, but she didn't pull away either. She sat still, her countenance controlled, as Anne squeezed her dainty, fragile hand.

"But this presents us with a difficulty," Edward was saying. "If you were to marry into a foreign court, your choices would be greater. But to find a prince willing to leave his own court and live in England with little promise of the throne—that will be difficult. If we wish to find a good husband for you. And we do, Anne. I have sent ambassadors. But you must understand why you may have to be patient."

As Edward explained, Mary's fingers curled around Anne's, and Anne felt humiliation burn cold in her own cheeks. More than humiliation: horror. She had not thought of it before, had not considered herself married; it had been her mother's attention she wanted all her life, not a husband's. But Edward was right. For any prince to come to England and live all his life as the husband of a spare: that was a poor marriage to offer any man. The kings of Europe had sons enough, but what father would throw away a precious son on such a bargain? Edward did not say it, but she knew what he meant. For any prince to be willing to come and strike such a bargain, there would have to be something wrong with him.

"We shall find you a good husband." Edward's tone was earnest; his head was bent from decades of hunching over staffs, but he leaned forward a little. His manner had always been too formal to reach out to them; he had never embraced and kissed like Erzebet, never clasped hands like Anne and Mary, but there was concern in his face. Anne gripped Mary's fingers tighter, newly grateful. Since Erzebet had died, there had been few caresses.

"I understand your Majesty," she said, her voice not quite steady. There was nothing to do but be brave. Would Edward marry her to a diseased prince? The idea was inconceivable, he was her grandfather and he was leaning forward as if he loved her—but he had married Erzebet to Philip. Philip's idiocy was legendary throughout Europe, but he was not the only monster to come out of the house of Delamere. There was more than one king with a son he would be pleased to see carefully disposed of, married to a reasonably healthy girl, out of sight, ready to beget sons that might survive the inbreeding better than their father had. Philip could beget no one, but there were others who could. Anne struggled desperately to believe that her grandfather would not sell her to such a man.

"You must find Anne a good husband." Mary's voice was sharper than usual. She sounded peremptory, royal, but under the abruptness was a note of hysteria.

"Our ambassadors will see to it," Edward said. "We do not take this lightly."

"I will—" Mary stopped. For a wild moment, Anne wondered if she had been going to say that she would not marry well unless Anne did. That would have been reckless, throwing the nation into hazard, hundreds of thousands of souls, to speak up for her sister; it would have been sinful. If that had been her thought, she would have had reason to bite it back. But Anne knew, even in that moment, that she would never ask Mary what she had been going to say, for fear of hearing that it might be something else.

There was nothing to be said. Time with her family was a rare thing, but Anne needed to be alone. If she could get into church and pray, if she could reach out to God, perhaps there would be some comfort. She had to get out of that room and pray, before she lost her courage.

"You shall be a happy wife, Mary," Anne said. "I shall pray for us both." With an effort, she levered herself out of her chair. Her intention was to go closer to Mary and give her a kiss, but as she spoke, Philip roused himself from his stupor.

"Wife?" he said. His voice echoed around the room; Philip could never moderate his volume, and it rang off the stone walls loud enough to make Anne's ears buzz.

"Philip," Edward said. The word was clipped, but Philip seemed not to notice.

"Your wife is in Heaven, my uncle," Anne said, making her way for Mary and using a phrase she had heard Claybrook say to Philip many a time. The words were spoken numbly: it was hard to imagine Erzebet in a state of bliss. Since her bloody death, Anne had tried hard, but however many times she tried, she couldn't remember seeing Erzebet smile.

"Wife," Philip said. His great hand reached out and caught Anne as she reached past him, locking around her wrist and pulling her to him. His fingers, dank and sticky, fastened themselves around her ankle, reaching under her heavy skirt to grab it.

"Wife," he said.

Anne gasped, struggling like a hooked fish, trying to get away, but Philip was impossibly strong. She could hear her grandfather making sharp commands, but Philip wasn't listening. His grip was hard enough to bruise, and he was pulling her to and fro on his lap, rubbing her body against his; she could feel the tension as he dragged her back and forth, yanking her arms like a child shaking a frustrating toy.

Anne turned her head and bit, sinking her teeth into Philip's hand. There was a roar of pain that sang in her ears, and he shoved her. Anne hit the floor so fast that she rolled over like a dropped bundle, skirt tangled around her legs and her side smarting from the crash against the stone flags. She looked up dizzily, tears closing her throat, unable to speak.

"Philip, you must not seize people like that," Edward said. His voice was trying to sound sharp, but there was a quaver in it, an old man's shudder. The skin on his face was fragile, like cobwebs that might tear at a touch. It suddenly struck Anne that her grandfather was dying.

## Nineteen

Anne did not know how she lived through the time that followed. Day followed day with nothing but a crushing sense of anticipation, a dread of something unknown. Every morning she woke tight-chested and breathless, the air of her room pressing down on her as if she had dived fathoms too deep. Day after day she presented a limpid face to the court and hid whenever she could, riding her horse by the river and staring into its brown depths, wishing to dive in, shake off her heavy gown and swim away into the sea where no one could find her. But the sea was no refuge. Edward could not accompany Anne and Mary; no deepsmen would follow a king so old and frail. Anne dreamed of joining the deepsmen, of growing long and muscular like them, strong enough to fight for herself, but her small body was no defence against anyone. The next blessing of the waters, Mary and Anne set off together into the deeps while a reduced court sat on the shores, none of the usual retinue but only Edward, Robert Claybrook, Archbishop Summerscales and a few other great men, watching silently as the girls stripped and submerged themselves in the grey surf, ready to swim out. Edward had spoken to them quietly on the way, advised them on how to speak—childish words asking for friendship, for care—and Mary was prepared to begin such a chant, but at the thought, Anne's heart sank. The deepsmen would not long protect a country with only children at its helm. It was strength they respected, not appeals to their better nature. Anne pinched her mouth tight and gripped Mary's wrist as they set out, telling her quietly in the underwater language: *Be careful. Stay silent.* And Mary only nodded, twisting her wrist out of Anne's grip and reaching to take her hand. To stay in sight of one another was in no way necessary, but Anne held her sister's hand, grateful for the momentary comfort.

Out in the bay, the deepsmen seemed vast, long-bodied like horses and great-armed like blacksmiths. Mary began by chanting a greeting, but the voices boomed around them: *Are you alone?* Had they no support, or was it down to them, two young girls in the sea?

Mary's hand tightened on Anne's, and Anne steadied herself in the water. There was nothing for it but a bold face.

*Click,* she said, naming the strongest of the deepsmen. It was guesswork, memory, terrible risk, but if she didn't dare it now, they were lost. *Rattle.* The names were untranslatable, but she remembered them from happier times, like the names in a favourite story from childhood. Anne held herself up in the water and named each of them, identifying them. She named each of them in turn, then put on her boldest face. *My sister,* she said. *Me.*

There was a moment's pause and then Click reached for her, a strong arm darting out to grasp her shoulder. Anne dived, swimming down, remembering the motions Erzebet had swum through, wrapping her legs around his waist then swimming away, brushing her body against his, a dance to and fro, offering and retreat. His skin was rough and cold in the water, but as she swam in and darted back, his grip did not connect with her, his crushing hands and black claws stayed out of her flesh.

Mary floated in the water wordless, watching as Anne swam in and out. *I am a princess,* Anne told herself in the solitude of her own mind, as she forced herself to continue, stroking his skin with placating hands. *They are not of my kind. This is nothing. I groom an animal for my country.* It was not impossible if she kept her teeth set and concentrated on the cold of the water against her skin, ignored what her hands were doing. It was not difficult. Compared with the grabbing hands and baffled lust of her uncle, it was not difficult. Anne swam and caressed, offering all she could in the name of England, striving to keep the deepsmen content with the only thing she could give.

~

Edward did not ask on the shore how she had kept the deepsmen loyal, and Mary did not speak of it to her. The girls sat in their coach on the way home, dripping wet, one on each side. Anne saw tears in Mary's eyes, but Mary cried too easily these days. The weight still sat on Anne's chest, the dread of something terrible happening. The moments with the deepsmen in the sea had not lifted its pressure. Therefore, what had happened could not be terrible. Anne sat alone, salt water running down her cold skin, and lifted her head. She had to carry on living.

~

She did not speak of what happened in the sea when she made her next confession. It could not be a sin to keep England safe. She was not certain, but could not ask Samuel. She could not speak of it.

If she was wrong, if she had sinned, then she was committing a mortal sin by making an incomplete confession, by taking Communion when she was not in a state of grace. If she was wrong, then every breath she drew, she drew in sinfulness. But there was no other means she could think of to keep the deepsmen placated, which meant she would have to do it again next blessing of the waters, and the blessing after that, and the blessing after that, until she was old enough to fight. She could not afford to hear anyone tell her that she shouldn't do it.

More and more, Anne prayed for solitude. She did not want to be lonely, but it was hard to think of an alternative.

# TWENTY

ANNE AVOIDED PHILIP whenever she could, but there was no help for it: he seemed to like her. Pink Mary with her landsman's prettiness was of little interest to him, but Anne realised, as the pressure built every day, that she had caught his eye. The blue of her face that sent most people's eyes out of focus as they addressed her appealed to him like a shining toy. Anne could not don a veil, not as a princess of the court, but she could not keep the colour from her cheeks either. Whenever Philip was nearby, her heart began to race, her grip to weaken, and the phosphorescence lit up her face in a blazing, frightened blush that brought Philip leaning his massive trunk towards her, reaching out to pat her skin with sharp-nailed paws.

Anne stopped appearing in court whenever she could. She spent her time with Samuel Westlake, who, though he could not but notice how his charge had grown anxious and subdued, only grew kinder and calmer when he spoke to her, forcing no confidences. Anne was not comforted by this: the fears weighing her down were so great that she longed to unburden herself, but she could not. They were matters of state; her responsibility. She could not share them without betraying herself as a princess never should. Erzebet had not confided, and her daughter would not either. It was too difficult to talk about. She would have liked to tell Samuel something, if only that she was oppressed by fear, that her body was losing the memory of ease, that she could not sleep and when she dozed she had nightmares and the days were all too long. But Samuel was too tactful to ask. Anne would have liked him to insist, to force her somehow to speak, but since he did not, she couldn't tell him.

The day that Edward announced Mary's betrothal, though, she could not avoid the court.

Anne found little she wanted to see these days, but she could not help but look about her. The court had thinned of late. Edward had spies, she knew, and it could only be expected that with the throne so weak, there would be plotting. But there had been no scandals. A few great names had been quietly sent back to their estates with soldiers to guard them; many more middle-ranking nobles had followed their example and gone home. Possibly they were tending their lands; possibly they were raising armies—though with no alternative to set on the throne, there would be little point in a rebellion. Possibly some of them had simply sickened of the sight: frail Edward, lumpen Philip, two small, frightened girls, all that was left of the Crown of England. Anne would have wished it so, but she was too sad to believe it. It took a strong stomach to be a courtier.

There were musicians still in attendance, and they played the fanfare for good news. Anne had heard such fanfares since she was a baby, and had never much questioned them, but, alert and anxious, she could hear in their strains the original deepsmen's phrase they were supposed to represent. It wasn't about good news. It meant *good hunting; good prey.*

Edward had always stood on his feet, even though his gnarled hands trembled on his canes, but today his legs had failed him. He sat on his throne, its silver chasing rising above his shrunken body, like a child on a grand carved chair, and announced the good news: negotiations would soon be concluded for a marriage between Mary, nearly fifteen and the heir to the throne of England, and Louis-Philippe, second son of King Louis of France.

The court huzzaed dutifully, but Anne could see the glances. Louis-Philippe was not the Dauphin; that would have meant Mary leaving for France, a foreign princess in a foreign court, as Erzebet had been. The choice of Louis-Philippe could mean only one thing. The throne of England was to go to a Frenchman.

Anne's throat clenched. She remembered the arguments she had read on the day of Erzebet's death, King Louis's discourse on the souls of the deepsmen and the landsmen, the divine blood of kingship. The words had sunk so deep into her memory that she could no longer judge them as arguments, hearing them only as the music that played in the background of a great disaster. But they had been coherent. Louis was no Philip, no idiot: Louis could hold a throne.

Louis would have his son on the throne of England. England was going to be swallowed up by France.

Mary raised herself to her feet to do obeisance to her grandfather. Her legs were even less steady than usual as she rose, though, and Anne could see, with a flutter of panic, that there were tears in Mary's eyes. Anger momentarily writhed in her chest: it could have been worse. Mary would have a husband who was probably not an idiot, who would not maul her with thick, clawed hands, who could carry a sentence to its conclusion and protect her, if he chose. It was terrible, but it was no less terrible than any other alternative Anne could think of. Stern-faced, stoical Erzebet glimmered in Anne's mind. Erzebet would not have wept.

Anne pulled herself to her feet, tottered over to her sister and embraced her. From the outside, it might look touching, the congratulations of a simple-minded princess. But as she locked her arms around Mary's neck, Anne hissed in her ear: "Control yourself. We are before the court. Do not let them see you like this." Mary's breath was hot on her ear, and Anne felt a salty tear press against her own cheek, briny and soothing. She tightened her grip and whispered, "Show them a still face. Be silent."

Mary's arms came around her, and her sister held her hard for a moment. Anne shut her eyes. Even with everything going, the embrace was a second's worth of comfort, and comfort had to be taken where it could. Mary clung around Anne's neck like a child, and Anne shivered. Since Philip, since Erzebet, Mary had seemed somehow younger than her. Anne wanted to pity her sister, wanted to feel charity, but if she pitied Mary, betrothed to an acceptable man, what would that let her feel about her own life? She gripped Mary close, trying to hold something together.

Philip had sat dully in his place, and Anne kept her face carefully averted from him. Beside him, as always, stood Robert Claybrook. Claybrook was leaning over him, whispering in Philip's ear, and Philip was shaking his head slowly, a look of unwillingness on his face. As Anne watched him out of the corner of a carefully downcast eye, Philip leaned forward. It was a meaningless movement, nothing more than a gesture of impatience with his counsellor's advice, but the suddenness of it made Anne jump, her canes unsteady and her legs weak. The moment of clumsiness was enough to unbalance her, and, canes skidding and legs crumpling, Anne landed in a heap on the floor.

Anne swallowed. Collapsed before the court; so much for princely dignity. In another moment, she would be crying like Mary.

She heard the scrape of Samuel Westlake's awkward gait before she saw him, heard it at once; he must have started forward without pausing to think. The thought of that warmed Anne just a little, and so she sat still, waiting for him to reach her side and help her up. His progress was slow, his lame leg dragging behind him, but his hands were firm as he pulled her to her feet. Anne swallowed again, and forced her voice to be steady. "I thank you, my lord Bishop."

Westlake bowed and turned to resume his place. To do so, he had to cross the dais, and at the sight of his halting limp, Philip looked up, curiosity in his face.

"Stop," he said.

Westlake turned. His haggard face seldom showed emotion, but Anne could see he was frozen before his prince.

Philip shook off Claybrook, who had laid a cautious hand on Philip's massive shoulder, and picked up one of his canes. Leaning forward, thick flesh bunching at his waist, he proffered it to the Bishop. Take," he said. Take."

Anne glanced at Mary, hoping she was using the distraction to gather herself; in fact, Mary was just as distracted as everyone else.

Staffs were the right of princes, no one else. But the rights of princes were subject to exceptions, if a prince so chose.

Westlake stood with hands carefully tucked by his sides, and looked at Edward. The King's face, withered and tired, turned from the court to his son and back again. There was a few seconds' pause before he raised his hand, gesturing for Westlake to take the staff, a gesture less of bounty than of resignation.

Westlake reached out and took it, shifting his weight onto it with just a tiny, barely audible sigh. The fine wood clicked against the stone floor all the way back to his place in the crowd.

Philip watched him go, chuckling a little to himself and batting his great palms against his lap. Edward watched him for a few seconds, then turned back to the court. "Letters have been sent," he began, "issuing an invitation—"

"Marry?" Philip said, his bellows voice blasting over his father's frail one.

Robert Claybrook leaned down, whispering in Philip's ear.

"Marry!" Philip said, his tone rising. He had caught the word "marriage" from Edward's announcement, Anne realised with her heart beating in her chest, and now he was getting interested. "Wife!" Philip said.

Anne's face blazed. She put her hands to her cheeks, ducking her head and spreading the webs of her fingers over the treacherous light, but she couldn't turn away, not with all eyes upon her. *Do not let him look at me,* she prayed in desperate silence, *Mother of God do not let him look at me, Mother of God do not let him see me . . .*

"Wife!" Philip said, leaning off his throne and reaching towards her. "Here! Here!" His great arms were grappling the air. Philip could not stand alone, but he was leaning forward, his demands ringing around the room: he was calling for Anne to be brought to him. Every drop of Anne's blood screamed for her to run, to grab her canes and stagger a ridiculous broken flight from the room, but she couldn't do it; idiot or not, a princess could not run. Erzebet had stood bruised and stern before the world, Erzebet had—*oh God I want my mother*—

There was a thud and a clatter, and a muffled snarl of pain. Robert

Claybrook had been leaning over Philip again, trying to hold his arm back, gesturing to the Privy Sponges to stand back and withhold their brine. A single swipe of Philip's arm had brought him down. Anne gripped her canes desperately; Philip had knocked down the greatest landowner left at court. This wasn't knocking down some servant; he had toppled his minder. Everything was falling apart.

The click and scrape of Westlake's gait was an undertow to the tumult in Anne's ears, barely noticed, but when she looked up, there was Samuel, whispering to Edward, who was gesturing with a taught, shrunken hand. And Samuel was making a careful progress over to Philip.

He spoke quietly to one of the Privy Sponges, who handed him his bowl. Westlake's voice sounded softly under Philip's yells, and he stood, calm as a tree, before the thrashing prince, dipping his sponge and reaching out with a careful hand to moisten Philip's brow.

The distraction slowed Philip down. He turned his head and blinked at Samuel, water dripping down either side of his face.

"That is good, my Prince." Samuel spoke quietly, so quietly that Anne doubted any ears but a deepsman's could have picked him up. "That is good, Philip. Be calm. All is well. All is well . . ."

The words subsided into a croon, and Samuel stroked the sponge over Philip's face, his arms, caressing him as a nursemaid might bathe a baby. His voice was a quiet sing-song, and Philip leaned back, closing his eyes.

Samuel's glance flicked over to Anne for just a second before returning to Philip, but by that time, the blaze of her cheeks was starting to diminish. She stood, silent and still, and as the sponge ran over Philip's forehead, his face creased. He was smiling.

# Twenty-One

Henry had always dreamed of water, of grey dark seas and vibrant depths, the glitter of salt in shafts of sunlight and the flick of fish through the moving currents. After the burning, though, he dreamed of fire.

Months passed. Henry trained with his weapons out of doors, worked his horse, waited. John came sometimes, but Claybrook was nowhere to be seen.

Robert Claybrook talked of the arts of war, but he brought no soldiers with him. He smiled and traded words and told Henry, *No, no, no,* all his life, *Wait, not yet, no.* Robert Claybrook had stood by the pyre as the child burned, and under his command had daubed the idiot prince so that the heat of the blaze did not distress the royal skin.

For eight years, he had waited for the favour of this man. He had waited on land that he could have ridden over any time he chose. It had not even been difficult to slip off Allard's grounds; he just had to climb on his horse and point its head forwards. There were woods beyond, and roads, and mud, and it was not different from the mud and trees of home. There were people in their hundreds and thousands, and he could not fight them all, not without help, and Claybrook stood among them as the hot, rippling air spilled from the pyre.

And the princes, the princes had come to the burning as well. Henry brought his axe to his chamber and slept with it beside his bed, waking up suddenly with the flutter of fire in his ears and grabbing its handle, gripping the solid wood in his hands. It was never hot in his room; the cold air of night always came as a shock when he jerked awake. But the question that came to him in the night was a simpler one than any other he had thought to ask before.

You could not ride a horse for ever. An all-night plod had been enough to exhaust his own; it stood panting in the stables and shivered under its blanket, and Allard had pleaded with him to leave it alone for a few days' rest. Henry had obliged; the pleasure he felt at seeing Allard again had surprised him and he was in no mood to hurt the man. But the burning had taken place only a night's ride away from Allard's land. And the princes had been there.

The next time John came riding in to visit, Henry charged him. John had come in waving and hailing, with a sack on the back of his saddle that must have been a fox. The sight of it pained Henry; it would have been good to chase the animal, ride it down, pin it with a spear and rip his frustrations out of its wet, twitching flesh, but afterwards they would simply celebrate their victory and Henry would feel he had accomplished something, and then they would be friends and he couldn't ask John for the truth. John had been subdued since the burning, his smiles forced, his easy gestures constrained, and Henry had been too pained by the sight to make John unhappier. If he was going to ask, he had to ask now.

Henry turned his horse's head and made straight for John, turning the butt of his axe outwards. The haft caught John squarely in the chest and he tumbled, landing so hard that he rolled for five feet before coming to a stop, doubled over, clutching at his ribs, breath rasping in his throat like a creaking door.

Sliding off his horse, Henry landed beside him, pushing John back and sitting on his chest, webbed hands braced against pale throat. John had grown tall, looming more than a head above his friend, but there was no match in strength between them; Henry could wrestle John down with one arm. John's eyes were wide, but he made no effort to struggle, lying flat on the ground and fighting to get his breath back.

Henry waited.

John managed enough breath to say, "What in God's name are you doing?"

"Where are we?" Henry said.

"What?" John's face was flushed now he'd recovered the use of his lungs, and twisted in pain as Henry leaned on his bruised ribs.

"Where are we?"

"Henry, get off me, what ails you?"

"Where—" Frustration was choking Henry, and he had to struggle not to shake John like a fox. The sight of John's suffering hurt his heart and he didn't want to continue, but he had to have answers; John's failure to provide them made him angrier. Why was John making him do this?

"What do you mean 'Where are we?' " John gasped, slapping the ground with one frantic hand. It was a wrestler's gesture, a token of submission he had taught Henry years ago, though Henry did not always acknowledge it at the best of times. "What are you trying to ask me? I do not know what you are asking me, Henry, and if you would get off my chest I would try to answer."

The sound of anger in John's voice made Henry tighten his grip, fearful that John would get up and leave. "How far are we from the court? We did not have to ride far to the burning." The word *burning* was dry in his throat like a cough. "And neither did the court. Where are we? I want to know, John."

John's voice was stifled under Henry's grip. "Twenty miles from London. The court is there now."

Twenty miles. Henry's hands loosened, and he sat back. Twenty miles. All his life, "the court" had been a mythical place, far beyond reach, a season's journey away. And all the time it had been less than a day's travel. "Why did you never tell me this?" he said. The pain of the discovery was sharp like betrayal. It had been so close.

"I thought you knew—" John's voice stopped abruptly as Henry's hands closed on his throat. John's eyes screwed shut, and he slapped harder at the ground.

Henry loosened his grip.

"My father—thought you would ride off if you knew," John said, gasping. "I did not wish to lie to you, but you did not ask."

Henry swallowed. John's ribs were an uncomfortable seat, but he did not move. "Does your father intend to make me king at all?" he said.

John put a hand up to guard his throat, struggling to push it between his vulnerable neck and Henry's clutch. "I do not wish to talk to you unless you promise to stop choking me," he said.

The defiance made Henry angry enough to start choking John again. John had known this all along, and had said nothing, and now he was demanding terms. But Henry caught himself, just. He did not want to hurt his only friend, and what else was he to do? "If I get off you, will you tell me the truth?" he said.

John nodded, his eyes warily on Henry's gripping arms.

Henry withdrew his hands and slid off onto the grass. The two of them sat hunched side by side, staring at the ground between them.

John drew a breath. "My father means to set you on the throne, perhaps," he said. "But he is not sure. Things are happening at court, and he does not yet know which way the wind blows. William, the Prince, was killed a little before your father told mine about you. He thought England would fall faster. But Erzebet married Philip, and she was strong while she was alive, and my father was adviser to the prince, and hoped he might have influence that way. But Philip is an idiot, and hard to steer. And of late, Philip has taken a liking to another man, a priest called Samuel Westlake. He does not wish to end on the pyre, my father, and he has never thought the time was right."

Perhaps. That was the word Henry heard. All these years of training, of promising, of waiting. His whole life, built on the word "perhaps." He turned aside, too chilled to speak.

"I think you should move against the King," John said. "Edward is old and sick now, and Philip—my father thinks that he can steer the country if Philip is on the throne, but Philip cannot go in the sea. There are only the princesses, and they may take husbands, I have heard a rumour that the King is searching. I think you should move soon. But my father still hopes for Philip. He—is not sure he can trust you."

Henry sat silent. His thoughts clamoured so loud that he could not speak. He had not been in the sea for eleven years. But bastards were burned. The only safe place for him was on the throne.

≈

Later that day, Henry approached Allard and asked for a map. Allard was so pleased to show it to him that Henry felt a little guilty, but he bent his head over the page and studied the shapes. His reading was still poor and he had to ask Allard to spell out the words, but when he closed his eyes, he could feel the lie of the land, the direction in which to travel. He couldn't call and hear his voice echo off rocks miles away, or be guided by the crash of waves in a far-off bay; the air on land was too thin to carry sounds. But if he thought about the sun, rising east and sinking west, and distances to cover and the shape of the land he would have to travel through, he could make it. It was not impossible.

≈

Henry said nothing of his plan to anyone, not even John. It was lonely, like being a child again. Henry did not like to dwell on that time, but the shadow of those days and weeks and months in a single straight-walled room, his first months on land, pressed down on him now. It had been cold and frightening in the sea, and dry and frightening on land, and few people had ever pleased him. He remembered, with a force that almost weakened him, how he had longed for home in those days, how the sickening angles and implacable peculiarities of the landsmen had horrified him, and how hard it had been to wrench his mind into new currents of understanding. He had not wanted to understand. Before he could speak he was free of their plots and demands, or at least free from the obligation to listen to them. But he had learned speech and could not go back, and the time in that room was something he did not intend to return to.

Only one thing stood out from the memory of those days. Allard had spoken to him of Angelica, the miraculous woman who walked out of the sea, ready to bring the Venetians freedom. A fine story. The strange thing was that Allard seemed to believe it. John too, even Claybrook; they accepted the story without question, without thinking about it. That was a reason to hope.

Henry had never believed in fairy stories, but he was too old not to understand the concept of planning. Angelica wasn't a miracle, that was obvious. What she was, what Angelica, Mother-Queen of Europe, Star of the Sea, had been, was clever.

Henry had lived in a locked room for months before he uttered a word of English. He had never heard a word of it spoken in the sea. Or Italian, or Latin, or any other landsman's tongue. Angelica walked naked out of the sea, a gift of the ocean speaking perfect Italian. And if you believed that, you must be a fool.

Angelica wasn't a miracle. She was somebody's bastard. Somebody like him, a sailor's brat, as likely as not pushed out of the sea when she got too big to drag in her mother's wake. Henry had refused to waste emotion wondering who his natural father was—unanswerable questions were a stone around your neck—but he remembered the boats, and the spawning of the deepsmen, the spinning dance as partners swam round each other, the woman's hands descending and rubbing at the man until a slit opened, a narrow tube wormed out to infiltrate a corresponding slit that opened in her abdomen. He had always been aware of his own different construction, aware that landsmen were made like him, and, remembering the clever hands of the sea women, could picture how his mother must have pleasured his father in the water. His mother was not exceptional in beauty, even among her own tribe, and could have had little more than a passing interest in the man. His father had been stupid, madly, profoundly stupid to risk his life for a swim with her; the penalties for sailors who consorted with the sea women were horrific. Perhaps he had even died for it, before Henry was born, if his captain had caught him at it. If the ship had been willing to stop long enough to pick him up at all; he might even have drowned, abandoned to the waves rather than brought home for execution. Whether the captain had punished Henry's father on ship, or had overlooked it, it was a crazy thing to do. Stories about romance could not account for it. The explanation that seemed more convincing to his mind was less sentimental: after enough months at sea, some men would fuck anything. That was all he cared to know about his father.

But if it happened now, it could have happened then. Hundreds of years ago, some Venetian salt-fisherman had gone for a swim, or a boatman had leaned over the side and saw a face in the depths; some deepswoman had taken an interest in a curious new body. And Angelica had been born, and kept with her mother until she became too much of a burden. Perhaps.

But thinking about Angelica's story Henry realised something else. John had brought him fish when they were children, had caught them in a net. At the time, he had not connected the ideas, but he had hated the sight of that ugly mesh, so easy to tangle up in, so hard to pull out of. John had gone out in a boat, and he'd dropped a net to catch fish.

Suddenly a memory came to him: the tribe swimming up to the dark-hulled ships, chanting as loud as they could: *Don't drop, don't drop*—something. Why had they wanted anything to do with the ships in the first place? The ships dropped fish for them, but they could catch fish for themselves. Full bellies every few weeks hardly seemed worth centuries of fealty to these land-bound creatures.

But he remembered something else, too. The dolphins, and the deepsmen, who hunted each other for sport. The red fox he and John had chased through Allard's grounds. It was the way of the living to hunt, and to care little for the death of foreign creatures. Even the landsmen, John said, hunted porpoises. If there had been no Angelica, what would have stopped them from hunting deepsmen?

No one had explained this to him in the sea. He had been too young, had taken the custom for granted. But he thought he understood, now, what the word had meant. *Don't drop nets.* Because if a sailor would risk burning to fuck a deepswoman, why wouldn't he drop a net to drag one out of the water, all those miles away from land

and whores and women of his own kind? If a landsman would hunt a porpoise or a deer to entertain himself, why not a deepsman?

You could stay down in the water for a long time. You could avoid the boats, if you did not swim in waters they crossed. But his tribe had swum the same route, each of the five years he had lived in the sea. You needed the current. There were only so many areas where there was enough to eat; you could not wander the vast tracts of empty water, starving; you could not, if you lacked the strength and numbers, move into new waters, not unless you could beat out the tribe already using it. Deepsmen did not measure their territory on maps, but they had to follow the fish. If your route met the route of the ships—or worse, if you depended on a coastline—you could not avoid them for ever. Now he remembered meeting other tribes, the tension, the shouts of challenge, he remembered with new understanding one of those insults: *ship-followers.* Tribes that had other routes, perhaps, could afford to ignore the sailors, could afford to despise the tribes that had made peace with them.

Allard had said that the deepsmen attacked Venice, invaded it for no reason at all. But Allard knew nothing of the sea. Angelica had. There were shallow waters around Venice, and people in boats. A bad territory for a tribe to hold. Perhaps Angelica's father had been a salt-farmer out for a swim. Or perhaps he'd been a sailor who caught a deepswoman, fucked her, and threw her back like an unwanted fish. But the landsmen loved to have enemies. That, Henry had known all his life. They drew pictures of the world and divided it up with lines, into England, Scotland, France, they fought years of wars among themselves. There was nothing in the world that would have made them scruple to fish and fuck the deepsmen.

Angelica, perhaps, had been pushed out of the water when she'd grown big enough to be a nuisance. But she'd remembered enough of her old ways. Perhaps she'd grown up being owned by somebody clever, too; someone ready to make his move when the time was right.

The deepsmen hadn't invaded Venice for sport, or to save it from the French. There had been a war before ever the landsmen knew they were waging it. The deepsmen could have been driven off, perhaps would have been, if there had been no go-between—but this time, there was. Angelica had been clever, and had taken the battle onto their ground. And once she was there, she had held it. What had Allard said? The Venetians didn't want her children and grand-children to rule in other countries, they wanted Venice to keep its advantage, to hold its empire. Of course they did. But Angelica had made it happen. Henry could picture her face now, not the flat-painted icon Allard had shown him, but a face like his own, fierce, grim, steady-eyed. Angelica hadn't cared about Venice. She had cared about her own people. Her own coastal tribe, who had lived at risk too long in the shallow waters around Venice. Tribes in the water were wary of each other at the best of times; an empire of deepsmen, an alliance between the tribes, was inconceivable. This was no story of some invis-ible God sending aid to the landsmen. This was a woman whose ambi-tion had refused to be chased back, who would not flee when she could fight. Angelica had brought the battle to the landsmen, and had tri-umphed so thoroughly that they never knew what they had lost, any more than her own people truly understood what they had won. She'd fought for her own kin, had fought so hard she had overturned the world.

You couldn't avoid these landsmen, not once they knew you were there. Henry knew, deep down in his gut, that the landsmen were a threat to his people. Even back in the sea, where life was hard and clear, the landsmen's boats had been a mystery, a cause of silences and withheld explanations and rough arms holding him down. The lands-men brought madness in their wake, and once they'd seen you, they wouldn't let you go. If you let them have control of you, you were lost; only if you had the upper hand were you safe. And you couldn't ignore them. Angelica hadn't. You waited till they were weak, you found a place to attack, then you drove in and made them need you, until they quailed to hurt you for fear of hurting themselves.

And England was weak now.

A washed-up bastard squeaking on the shores of Cornwall to face the raised fist of a tyrant queen was one thing. A grown bastard speaking

English, washed up on the shores of a dying king and idiot heir, might be quite another. Claybrook was a bad man, and had no plans to bring soldiers to Henry's aid; he would stand for ever while the fire burned, hair blowing in the scorching wind, and Henry wanted none of him. Claybrook would wait, and wait, and Henry would grow old and die on a few square miles of countryside, always waiting for the blow to fall. Let the court become uncertain enough, let Claybrook decide he needed an advantage, and what was to stop Claybrook selling Henry to the court, finding a bastard and burning him to prove his loyalty?

You did not find safety by staying still, hoping the current would carry it to you. You went out and you hunted it down.

So it was that one day Henry, maps memorised and his horse saddled and fed, rode to the edge of the land on which he had been imprisoned for thirteen years, drew a breath long enough to carry him over the edge, and set out for the sea.

The journey was not going to be a difficult one. He had only to travel south. Henry's sense of direction was good, and he had composed a basic navigation chant as he studied the route, sung it to himself in the privacy of his bedroom often enough to fix the details in his mind. There was a river in London, a great river that led past the royal palace, and a great deal of it ran through Claybrook's land; that, Allard had once explained, was why Claybrook was such a powerful man at court. If Henry could reach it, he could swim his way along. He could hide on the banks, watch, wait for a time when people were gathered, pick the moment to emerge.

The road as he travelled it was a familiar one. He had not much considered it before he set off, London occupying his mind, but it clenched around him now. To go south, he had to pass along the same route he had taken before. It made sense, of course: the princes were in London, and would have wanted an easy journey—but this route he had to follow was through the lands on which the little boy had burned.

What was the boy's name, Henry wondered as his horse tramped through the woods. The navigation chant was running through his thoughts; it was, he realised, the first time in a while he'd been thinking in his mother tongue. His cloak—John's cloak, which he hadn't given back—was up around his face. The smell of smoke, meaty and oppressive, had got into the fabric, and filled his nose even as the cloth covered his ears. But this was caution. He was on some other man's land; from a distance, he was best off looking like an anonymous shape.

What was the boy's name? He must have had one. Henry had had a name in the sea. Whistle, that was it. It was so many years since he had heard it. Once it had been part of him. All he owned; you didn't carry possessions in the sea, didn't take anything with you that would slow you down. No crowns or thrones, no rich garments or disguises. You slipped into the translucent depths, and the water would hide you. He had been hungry and frightened and no one had much liked him, but life had been simple. You didn't wait. You fought for what you wanted, and if you didn't get it, you starved. If someone called him Whistle now, would he answer?

There were no rites for the dead in the sea. Corpses sank, and fish ate them. But he would have liked to have known the boy's name. It had been years since he'd heard a deepsman's name, even his own. No one on land could pronounce it.

The earth made little noise under the hooves of his horse. The beast's breath huffed, the saddle creaked. He could hear these sounds through the thick wool of John's cloak. But he couldn't see out of the corners of his eyes. His mind was preoccupied, dwelling on the lost names of the sea.

When he first heard the sound of cantering horses, he turned his head, but fabric blocked his view. Henry kicked his horse and started hurrying on himself, just in case. It wasn't till he had ridden several hundred yards that he realised the horses were following him.

There were hoofbeats, several animals, and they were gaining on him. Henry leaned down to his horse's neck, kicked its sides, pushing it to go faster. It sped up, but there were trees in the way, fallen branches to leap over, it was a woodland path and he didn't know it well. In the end there was nothing to do but reach forward and kick, trusting the beast to avoid the trees, to keep its footing.

The jingle of metal and the pounding of hooves came at him from the side, and then there was a man in view, shouting, "Stop! You there, stop!" Henry turned his head, kicked, kicked, but the man was dashing towards him, leaning down, and the next thing he knew there was a hand grabbing at his bridle.

Henry's horse, overtaxed and frantic, shied back, rising on its hind legs with a sudden jolt that shook Henry in the saddle. As the man made another grab for its reins it reared again, and Henry was falling, the ground slamming into him, leaf litter and earth and horse's legs all around him.

As the man who had been reaching for his horse dismounted, Henry was filled with a wild disbelief. This couldn't be. An hour ago, he had been safe, this had not been happening, and if he had ridden in another direction he would be alone now, alone and secure. He could reach back in his mind, touch that time, it was so close. It seemed impossible that he could not undo the terrible mistake that had led him to these people.

A hand was gripping him. Henry kept his head down, desperately hiding in his hood, but then a hand reached forward and yanked it from his face. There was a cry of, "There!" and Henry saw, in the red faces of the four men surrounding him, the scarlet skin and fair hair and blue eyes that were so alien beside his own features. He was exposed, white-skinned and black-eyed and sharp-toothed, his face naked before strangers.

He could fight these men. Landsmen were weak. All of them had swords hanging from their belts, and Henry reared up and made a grab for the nearest. His hand closed around its hilt, but the owner's arm chopped down on his, forearm on bony forearm, and Henry lost his balance, his weak legs toppling him back on the ground. If he had his axe, if he had something to lean on—

Something looped around him, pinning his arms to his sides. A rope. A man was crouching at his side, a dagger in his hand, pointing it at Henry's throat. "Be still, bastard," he said. "Do not stir." Skilled hands were tying Henry's wrists behind his back, rope cutting into his skin.

There was something in the way these landsmen moved. They each acted separately, yes, but together they were more than him. One standing over him, one looking to their horses, keeping look-out, one at his back tying his hands, one at his throat with a blade. There was a kind of synchrony to their movements that he remembered from his days in the sea, so many years ago now, when the tribe had closed in on its prey.

They had hunted him in a pack. They were armed, they acted together, and together they had run him down. Henry had wanted the sight all his life, and now, for the first time, he was seeing soldiers.

## Twenty-Two

PHILIP HAD NEVER much cared for Mass, and today was no different; as Archbishop Summerscales stood at the altar, intoning the liturgy, he lolled in his pew, banging his hands against the wood of his seat to entertain himself with the noise, occasionally saying something in the deepsmen's language—*move on; hungry.* The deepsmen didn't have a word for "bored," though clearly that was his problem. Robert Claybrook rose from his seat to try and calm Philip down. He leaned over his prince, spoke quietly into his ear.

"No," said Philip, giving him a push. It wasn't aggressive, just the light shove of a child uninterested in a toy being offered him—but Philip was strong, and Claybrook took a hard step back to maintain his balance.

Summerscales raised his voice a little, but he was an old man, no match for Philip's bellow.

"Mary?" Philip said. He seldom bothered with names when people were actually around him, but since Mary had been sent to France—an insult to the Crown of England, that she had to cross the seas to meet her consort when it was her country that would be ruled, but one that Edward, coughing now and growing more fragile by the day, was in no condition to dispute—he had remembered her name well enough to ask about her. He didn't seem to miss her, but the explanation (Princess Mary has gone to visit a friend, she will be home soon and happy to see us) seemed to please him, and he enjoyed hearing it repeated.

Anne sat alone in her pew, hands pressed together. Mary had given her a gift before she left, a silver and gold crucifix. It hung on the wall of Anne's chamber. The pearl cross that Erzebet had given her Anne wore daily, she would not part with it; Mary must have realised Anne would not want a pendant, must have put some consideration into the gift. Anne had not thought to give Mary anything. She had been carried in a separate litter down to the docks as the court went to see Mary off; they had embraced briefly, too briefly for conversation: everyone's eyes were on them, and Edward had been coughing, Philip complaining, the captain of the ship—a man of consequence, brother to the Baron of Tyne—standing on the gangplank, ready to carry Mary up himself. He wasn't quite managing to keep from turning his eye to the flapping sails, haste to get underway in every line of his body. Mary had whispered, "Pray for me," and Anne had kissed her cheek, anxious at Mary's departure. That Mary had asked for her prayers tugged at her: Mary knew how much time she spent in prayer, knew it was the right thing to ask. And then the captain had come forward, lifted Mary up, and Mary's weak legs dangled awkwardly as she was carried on board before Anne could think of an equally suitable farewell. Anne raised her hand, but Mary was slung in his arms like a parcel, her head concealed behind his shoulder, and Anne did not think that Mary saw her wave goodbye.

Philip pushed at Claybrook again as Claybrook attempted to explain it. He turned his head, saying again, "Mary!" He spoke pointedly to Westlake.

Westlake quietly left the altar where he had been standing in attendance. The click and scrape of his cane on the stone floor caused most people in the chapel to turn their heads aside, reluctant to witness his offensive ownership of a royal object. Reaching Philip, he sat down beside him. Anne could see in the stoop of his legs that it was easier for him to sit than it had been before Philip had given him a staff.

"Princess Mary has gone to visit a friend . . ." Westlake said, his voice cheerful and calm. The explanation was, in fact, of Westlake's devising. Mention of sailing the sea, ships and marriage were all subjects that agitated Philip and led to demands, frustration, raucous clamouring for things he couldn't have. Claybrook had attempted to reason with Philip, but he had had to accept the formula Westlake improvised one day when Philip had pulled him over to question him: it was incomplete, but it worked. Philip never tired of it.

Samuel's leg was easier, but there was something in the stillness of his hands that made Anne anxious. Philip was on the pew opposite hers, she was out of his reach, and Samuel was good at calming him down before the word "wife" occurred to him. The dread that he would grab at her did not retreat, but it calmed, just a little, when Samuel stood between them. Samuel's face was impassive as ever, but Anne could still feel it. He was tense about something.

Robert Claybrook bowed, backed away to his own seat. His face was as stiff as an icon.

As Philip subsided, Westlake rose again, ready to resume his place. He walked past Anne, a little slower than usual; slower than she knew he was capable of. As he passed her, he did not turn his head, but he spoke in a whisper that only her ears could ever have caught.

"My lady Princess, I must speak with you alone."

Anne lingered after the service was over, hands blamelessly folded and eyes closed, trailing a rosary over her fingers. No one would disturb the Princess at prayer. The congregation filed out, and Anne waited, whispering under her breath. "Holy Mary, Mother of God, pray for us sinners, now and at the hour of our death . . ."

It was some time before she heard Westlake's approach. She finished her decade and laid down her beads. "What is it, Samuel?" she said. "Have you any news of my mother?"

"News of my mother" was how she referred to Erzebet's death and the questions it had created; it was the only way she could describe it. There had been too little news. Samuel had sent men to make discreet enquiries of apothecaries, but no poison had been found capable of creating such devastation, no one remembered selling any. He had sent spies and asked questions, to no avail. The thought of an answer made Anne's hands tremble a little, and she folded them carefully in her lap.

Westlake shook his head. "No, my lady Princess. It is another matter."

He stopped, and Anne looked at him in bewilderment. Self-contained Samuel, her grave confessor, was shaking.

"What is it, Samuel?" she repeated. "If something troubles you, be assured of my aid."

Samuel swallowed. "My lady Princess," he said. "I have news that I must trust to someone. I do not know what to do. Can I trust your silence?"

"Of course." Anne reached out and put an anxious hand on his arm. "What is it?"

Samuel cleared his throat. "I must explain something to you, my lady Princess. You know—you do know, I am certain, that a bastard was executed this year."

Anne nodded. Erzebet's static face and oblique lectures on the need for a prince to be strong. That empty day when everyone was gone and no one would tell her where.

"There were rumours, my lady Princess . . . No one likes a burning." Westlake rubbed his face. It was a strange gesture for him, freer than usual. Anne had never seen him sit so loosely, as if he were not observed, as if he were alone. "It was a hard business, the burning of a child. And there were rumours afterwards."

"Rumours?"

Samuel nodded. "The burning took place on Robert Claybrook's land, not far from here. His priest is a man from the North, John Bridgeman, a good man—a cousin of mine, my lady Princess. We went into the Church together, though he never rose so high as to come to court. But the people of his parish, they were afraid. They swore they had seen a ghost there."

"A ghost?" Anne shook her head in nervous bewilderment. Bad omens meant disaster for England, the wrath of God, even. God wanted his people to be merciful. Samuel had been right all along, and

Erzebet—Erzebet had been wrong. They should not have burned a child.

"The child's soul, they said, seated on horseback, the child grown into a man. I did not—well, vengeance is the Lord's, and he judges as he chooses. His ways are not known to us. But the rumour troubled me, my lady Princess. So I asked my cousin to spare me a favour. Some of his parishioners are soldiers, good men, trustworthy. They had not liked the burning either." Samuel rubbed his face again, raising a little colour in the cheeks. "I asked my cousin, and he asked them. They kept a watch on my lord Claybrook's land. They did not tell their master they did so."

Anne blinked. This was a great betrayal of their lord, even if a bishop had asked it. They must have hated the burning. It must have been terrible indeed.

"My lady Princess, I thought it might be a ghost. But I thought it might be a man of flesh, also. I—I do not care for burnings. My lady Princess, I was there, blessing the flames, praying for those people's souls. I hope I shall live and die an Englishman and loyal to your Majesties, but I wish never again to see such a sight." The colour stayed in his cheeks, and his voice rose. Anne swallowed. The sight of Samuel angry was so strange, so unfamiliar, that she drew back a little, frightened. "But I could not stand by if there was another bastard in the land."

Distracted as Anne was, the word took a moment to filter through. "A—another bastard? Do you think it could be?"

Samuel turned to her. She could see his pupils, wide and black, filling his eyes. "My life is in your hands, my lady Princess," he said. "The soldiers found him. I have him locked in my house."

BOOK FOUR

DISCOVERY

## Twenty-Three

Henry could remember the first time he saw a building, a great towering rock of straight-sided stones, Allard's arms wrapped around him and the jolting steps leading to a square, oppressive room, bound hands and rank food and nothing to do but bite his sticks and worry at the walls. The sensation of ropes around his wrists filled him with a childish terror, a panic so stark that as the soldiers tied him to his saddle, the trees of the forest stiffened around him, forming bars, an enclosing canopy of leaves trapping him, and he leaned up on his saddle as if to swim up through them, break the green surface and draw breath in the white, clear air above. But as he yearned upwards towards the green, a man came and placed a sack over his head, and Henry heard the coarse-woven hemp rustle in his ears with the sound of a crackling fire.

❧

It was a long ride, a harsh one. At nightfall the soldiers stopped to rest their horses and built a fire to warm themselves; one of them pulled up Henry's hood and offered him some meat. Henry saw the man's face, blue eyes and sallow skin, but gave no answer, instead baring his teeth and snapping at him. The soldier dropped the hood with a jump and left him sitting there, saying only, "We had better tie his legs." So Henry slept bound hand and foot, the open air parting around him, sounds on all sides of rustling leaves and shrilling birds and the scampering of small-footed mice, all within his hearing and out of his reach and no help to him now.

~

Blindfolded, he was brought to a house and bundled inside. Henry fought the arms carrying him and, outnumbered as he was, gained nothing for his struggles but a sudden drop to the floor, cracking his head, followed by a swift recapture and a march up some narrow stairs, his body swinging in a helpless pendulum between his stretched arms and legs.

A door creaked, they entered a room, and the soldiers dropped him and left him. Henry scrambled up immediately, pressed his bound hands against his covered face to bring the sackcloth to his sharp teeth and began chewing. His mouth filled with grit and threads, but he persisted, teeth and jaws aching with haste, until he had a hole in the sack wide enough to let the ropes through, biting until they too parted, leaving him free to untangle his head and unbind his feet, ready to fight.

But as the hours went by, he found that his speed had been wasted. He sat in an oak-floored room, whitewashed walls and beams overhead and nothing to see through the narrow window but a green lawn, and nobody in sight. It was a full day before anyone came to the door.

~

The creak of the hinges flooded Henry with terror; his mind flashed full of soldiers, strong numerous men ready to drag him to the stake. Mixed with the fear was a desperate anger, fury at the *waste* of it, all those years preparing himself, learning how to use weapons, bracing himself for a conflict that would never come. Sixteen years, sea and land. Even in the ocean, he could have lived another decade before some predator took him, maybe two or even three, a lowering mouth and sharp teeth and a swift severing of his life. Not this. Not blazing red flames and hundreds of strangers crowding round while he screamed his life out on the pyre.

The door opened, and no soldiers came through it; only a man with a pale face and lame leg, leaning his weight on a stick, a stool under his arm. There was a moment of hope at the sight, that perhaps this man might be something like him if he had to walk on a cane, that he might help Henry rather than burn him—but then the anger settled back, gripping his muscles tight against the bones. Henry recognised his face. This was the man who had stood before the bonfire, had stood in the shuddering heat and muttered Latin while the little boy burned. The man was here for his life.

Henry retreated, bared his teeth. If he only had his axe, he could deal with this man.

The man stood over him, tilted his head for a second. "Do you have a name?" he said.

Henry clamped his mouth. He was not going to plead.

The man settled himself on the stool. *"Losquerisne Latine?"* he said. Henry swallowed. Latin, the bane of his childhood, the language this man had chanted at the fire. He did not speak it, would not, was furiously glad he had never learned.

*"Français? Italiano? Deutsch?"* The man paused, then shook his head. "You would hardly have swum here from Italy, would you? Come now, my boy, answer me. I know you understand me."

Henry fought the impulse to shake his head. He was not going to give this man the satisfaction.

"Perhaps—look at me," the man said. Holding his fingers together, he sketched a gesture in the air, a wide-armed wave that ended palm-to-chest. It was a motion Henry had seen before, not a deepsman-to-deepsman pose—no landsman could reproduce those out of the water, and probably not that easily in it either—but he had seen adults of the tribe showing it to children as they swam up to greet the ships. No one had explained what it meant, though. Henry kept his face blank, said nothing.

His questioner sighed. "My name is Samuel Westlake," he said. "I would like to know yours. Will you favour me?" The question was met with silence, but, to Henry's discomfort, it did not seem to bother the man. No smiles like Claybrook, no anxious scribbling like Allard;

he simply sat there, let the silence hang. Henry felt in that moment a longing for Allard, his anxious courtesy and his long explanations, that was stronger than anything he had ever felt in Allard's presence. Allard had been right. He should have stayed home.

Westlake nodded. "You have lasted a long time," he said. "Whoever took you in should be congratulated. What did they call you? Richard? William? Philip? Henry? Edward?"

Henry could not quite suppress a flinch at the sound of his own name, but he caught himself quickly, hoping the man had not noticed. The word *Henry* had leaped out of the litany like a slap, leaving him shaking. How was this murderer able to grab so quickly at his name?

Westlake caught the flinch, and shook his head. "My dear son, there is no mystery. No one would have taken you in who did not have thoughts of the throne. If they wished you to wear a king's crown, you needed a king's name. There are only so many names to choose from."

So that was all the thought Allard had put into his name. The homesick nostalgia that had gripped him a moment ago was replaced by a heartsick fury. The name had come to him when he was still unable to speak, when English was a foreign tongue and the words meant nothing. It had been bestowed without explanation, like a law of nature. But there was no art to it, nothing profound. Just a choice off a list. The country had a Philip alive, and an Edward, a William recently dead. Allard had preferred Henry to Richard, and that was all. Even his name was not his own.

"I can hardly keep guessing," Westlake said. "And in your position, I would not care to hear myself constantly miscalled. I can call you Richard and Henry and William in turn, if you wish, or you can tell me which is the right name. It is your choice, my son."

Henry shook his head. Was he even Henry any more? He could just as easily be Richard, be William. Be *Whistle*. Nothing had been true.

It was a second before he realised his mistake. He had made a landsman's gesture, an Englishman's gesture. No one shook their heads in the sea. He had shaken his head like a landsman, and Westlake had seen him do it. Had seen he understood English, just as clearly as if he had opened his mouth and spoken his useless, phantom name.

Desperate, he lunged off the floor, striking out a sharp-nailed hand against this probing man who had come to destroy him. Henry swung hard and Westlake was knocked from his stool, but the next moment Westlake had swung his cane around, a swift swipe to protect himself. The blow was not well-aimed, but it struck Henry's forearm with a crack, wood on bone, and Henry drew his arm back before he could help himself. In that time, Westlake had struggled to his feet, ungainly but fast, and was standing over him at the door, out of reach and far enough away that Henry would have to crawl to reach him. His stick was held firm in his hand; the gesture was not exactly a threat, but Henry knew the value of a weapon. He had choked Allard to stop Allard beating him, but this man was out of reach. And Allard had wanted him alive.

"There is no call for that, my son," Westlake said. "I am not here to hurt you."

Henry stared at him, but he did not believe him.

"I had heard rumours," Westlake said, leaning on his cane. Taking the man's weight, it became a prop again, not a weapon. "I sent men to find you. You are lucky, Edward—is it Edward, You are lucky I found you before anybody else did. I might be able to keep you alive. But you will have to trust me. If you will not speak to me, I will not know how to help you."

The tone was not unkind; the words were not a threat. But Henry had spent a lifetime locked in narrow rooms with men towering over him, promising him safety if he stayed obedient within his prison. He blinked up at Westlake for a moment. Then, mouth sealed, throat closed, a pocketful of air held guarded within his chest, he turned his back.

## Twenty-Four

"THE BOY WILL not speak to me, my lady Princess," Westlake told Anne.

Anne sat unmoving. The shock was too great for words or gestures; deepsman's call or English, she could express nothing. There was a little heat in her hands, a small point gathered at each wrist. Her face did not glow at all.

"My lady Princess, I must know," Westlake said. His face had come unloosed; normally stiff with resolve, with the endless strain of bearing up his dignity while his leg dragged pain behind him, now it was moving, eyes blinking, mouth open, blood in the sallow cheeks. The openness of it was almost embarrassing. Anne had confided her secrets to his gravity, cried before his reserve, leaned herself on his steady, contained patience. Now it seemed she had exposed herself to a man of flesh and blood like any other.

But Samuel had been kind to her, and he was asking her for help. Just at that moment, nothing else seemed important.

Anne reached out and took his hand, clasped it. Anything to soothe the fright in his face. "I am not angry with you, Samuel," she said. "I shall protect you." That was the image before her eyes: Samuel marched between soldiers, a heaped bonfire before him. The boy conjured up no image in her mind; Anne knew little of boys.

There were a few seconds when she heard Samuel breathing, his rapid gasps slowing as if by will. "I am most grateful, my lady Princess," he said in the end. The words did not seem to satisfy him. "I am your man."

"You are my friend, Samuel," Anne said. She wanted to keep talking about their friendship, to stay in this little bubble of kindness. If they moved out of it, they would be back into the current and the hard, dangerous fact that was starting to make itself felt: that Samuel had committed treason, had hidden from the Crown a criminal usurper who had been planning to kill them all.

"We must plan, my lady Princess," Samuel said, and the bubble flew upwards as bubbles must, disintegrating around them. "We shall not be discovered by the men I sent after him; they are not talkers. But I found him because of rumours. If one man can hear a rumour, any man can hear it. I may not be the only man looking for this boy."

"You are the only man who found him," Anne said. Erzebet would have had a plan by now, she thought. But then Erzebet would have been angry. Erzebet would have raised her hand and sent Samuel to the stake without a word. The uncomfortable thought possessed Anne that it was her mother's absence that freed her to treat Samuel's news with mercy. Erzebet would have thought that mercy a mistake.

Anne shook her head. It was a mistake God would forgive. She did not want another silent day while the world went to watch a burning child.

"I do not wish the boy to suffer," Samuel was saying. "But I cannot hide him for ever. I thought of smuggling him out of the country, but that would do him little good. He would face the same dangers on any other shore."

"He might pose greater dangers to us," Anne said. Erzebet had taught her to use her head. She had to think. "How many countries would turn down the chance to march upon England with an English-born king to place on our throne? He could strike an alliance at any court in Europe."

Westlake nodded, rubbed his face. "You are right, my lady Princess. But he cannot live here. I had wondered—do you think he might be better taking shelter in the sea?"

There was a look of hope on his face, and Anne shook her head again, frustrated at the gulf in his understanding. This man was her friend. He did not know that what he suggested was impossible. "The deepsmen would not take him," she said. "Not for ever. To them we are visitors, not kinsmen. I—if he were to stay . . ." It was not a comfortable thought. Anne had no illusions left about the deepsmen, the wonderful diving angels of her childhood, the relentless creatures she must appease over and over, but it was not easy to say such things out loud. "I do not think they would accept his presence in the sea," she said quietly. "And they have no charity at all for those they do not accept."

Her face had begun to tingle at the thoughts, but Westlake was too preoccupied with the problem to notice. It was urgent, desperately urgent; she could see it in the tension of his arms. For all they knew, there were already soldiers knocking on his door.

"Besides," he said, answering her without a pause, "we could hardly ask the boy to stay in the sea for ever. He could walk back up the beach whenever he wished. No, whatever we do for him we must do in England. You are right, my lady Princess."

Anne wondered if Westlake had thought of giving the boy a knife and letting him choose a quicker, kinder death than the flames. But if Samuel wasn't going to suggest it, she wasn't either.

"Has he a plan?" she said. The words "the boy" told her nothing; perhaps if he was clever he might have a solution worked out already.

Westlake shook his head. "He says nothing, my lady Princess. He has not spoken a word since my men first laid hands on him."

Anne looked up, startled. "Then are you even sure he is English? Or that he has his wits?" The thought of Philip loomed in her imagination: huge-bulked, brass-lunged, thick-handed. If the boy was another such idiot, another rapacious block . . . if the boy was such a being, then she was not sure she wanted to help him.

Westlake cleared his throat. "He seems to understand me," he said. "I do not know, not absolutely. But he does not seem stupid. He listens. He just does not reply."

Anne felt a sudden, unexpected sense of kinship with the captive boy. She had faced too many situations, surrounded by demands, questions, threats, where she had no way out. She could not hide herself among the crowd, could not claim ignorance, irresponsibility. Her face and form spoke loud, a clanging bell proclaiming to everyone who saw, here was a royal body, a body politic, a body expected to have answers. What other refuge was left except silence?

"Does he answer you in the deepsmen's language?" she said.

Westlake bent a swift, interested look at her. Her secret was out, it seemed: asking such a question was admitting that she hid behind idiocy, behind her mother tongue, when she did not feel like speaking. Even if it was only Samuel who knew, Anne felt a shiver of vulnerability at being so exposed, but she shook it off. There wasn't time to repine.

"No, my lady Princess. I tried him with sailor's signs too, but he did not respond even to those." Samuel made a brief gesture of demonstration, signing the word "friendship" in the sailor's pidgin that was sometimes used between traders out where the princes could not reach. The language was a crude one even compared with the deepsmen's limited vocabulary: sailors and swimmers seemed to find little beyond brief offers or requests for assistance that they could companionably discuss. It was not a form of speech that could be trusted for more important issues, questions of power and planning: the demands of a second language quickly exhausted the deepsmen's understanding, and the effort to convey the complexities of royal affairs in it was not one they were eager to make. Princes, speaking their tongue and visiting them regularly, were worth forging a bond with, but sailors were alien to their eyes, travelled along routes they could not follow for ever, and presented a different set of men in every ship. Such men were offered passing courtesies rather than serious discourse, and the pidgin was accordingly limited. It was a practical language, not a political one, and common to sea and land people both; it would hardly incriminate the boy if he displayed an understanding of the signs. Samuel was right: this was refusal to speak, not failure to understand. "He says nothing at all, gives nothing away."

"He cannot stay so for ever." Anne said it without thinking, because it was the truth, the absolute truth of her life. However cornered you were, eventually you had to find an answer, even an inadequate one, even a foolish one. You were never left alone for good.

Samuel said nothing, rubbed his face again. She could hear the joints of his ankle click as he shifted in his seat.

"Do you wish me to meet with him?" Anne said.

Samuel looked up at her, as if startled.

"Come now," Anne said. "You cannot have failed to think such a thought."

Samuel almost smiled. "No, my lady Princess, I have thought it. But I did not expect you to suggest it."

"We must decide at once," Anne said. "We have no time for this." This was a moment in time, suspended as in water, with dark, violent shapes swimming fast into view. If you could not hide, you had to act, or you would be dragged under.

"The boy is violent," Samuel said. "He made for me. I could not see you injured."

"I am stronger than a landsman," Anne said. She did not wish to allude to Samuel's bent leg, the crooked list of weakness that a predator would spot in an instant, but she would if she had to.

"I—" Samuel bent his head, rubbed it in thought. "If he were to injure you, there would be no saving any of us, my lady Princess. How could you account for such an injury?"

Anne remembered a misty morning, a failed quest that saved Samuel's life none the less. "There is a man in the stables. Robin Maydestone. He has been kind to me. If I command him to say I fell from my horse, I think he will say so."

Samuel was looking at her, his eyebrows rising further up his face the faster her answers came. "He is still far bigger than you, my lady Princess. It is rash to risk your life."

"My life is at risk by this boy's birth!" Anne snapped, hearing Erzebet's bite in her tone. "He aims at my throne, my country; do you think he will leave my head on its shoulders if I do not find some means to stay him? Do you think my grandfather will be pleased with me if he knows I have talked to you thus? This is not a moment to pause in the tide, Samuel; if we stay, we shall drown."

Samuel's hand had wandered to his staff, closed his fingers around it, as if unaware of its own movement. "I think we might try another attempt first, my lady Princess," he said, cradling the wood. "If you were to see him, you must have an able-bodied man with you. I cannot protect you well enough."

In all the time she had known him, Anne had never heard Samuel allude to his leg. He had answered few questions about it once, and never mentioned it again; he had never spoken of himself as weak. The jolt it gave her was enough to make her pause and listen for a moment.

"Who have you in mind?" she said.

"I do not know for certain," Samuel said. "But the surgeon, Francis Shingleton, can be trusted, I think. We spoke of many things when I was sick. He does not like burnings either, my lady Princess."

"And he has a hospital for idiots," Anne said, filling in the pause. "If the boy is simple-minded, then perhaps he may know him to be so."

"That was my thought, my lady Princess," Samuel said.

"Can he be trusted to keep silent, do you think?" Anne said.

"I hope so," Samuel said. His voice was quiet.

"Well." Anne spoke into the hush. "If he cannot, then I suppose we will know of it by and by."

## Twenty-Five

W HEN THE DOOR opened again to admit Shingleton and the girl, Henry was so startled that he did not know which of them was more alarming.

Shingleton: the man who had examined him, the man he had conversed with. No fighter, but not untrustworthy; that was what Henry had thought. It angered Henry, but the fact was that new faces frightened him; he had lived five years with a small tribe and eleven years captive with a handful of familiars, and unfamiliar faces were cataclysmic. To see Shingleton here was no guarantee of safety, he knew if he reasoned about it, but still the fact was that his face was known to Henry and he couldn't help relaxing a little at the sight of it. This was wrong, his reason told him. He should not be pleased to see this man in this place. The lame man who had captured him was no part of Claybrook's plan, or he would have said so. This was some new circumstance, with flames flickering around its edges. He must not let himself be stupidly calmed by the sight of a known face. He might still talk himself onto the pyre.

But it was the sight of the girl that drove everything else out of his mind. She entered tottering on two sticks, white-faced and webhanded, and she was a princess.

She was tiny. The princes had occupied Henry's mind so long that even though he had caught only a distant glance of them, they were huge in his mind, long-bodied deepsmen with great limbs and weaponed hands. This girl had pallid skin with a faint blue sheen like you saw on fish deep, deep in the black, and on tribesmen from those darker waters. Her hair was an array of matted locks like a deepsman's, but arranged into neat rolls that swung too long around her face; a huge jellyfish dress concealed her legs—but she was no landswoman. Under the skirt, she was low-slung, her legs bent under their own weight, so her body sat near the floor as if she was crouching. Her back was bent, hunched over like a cripple's. She shuffled on her sticks, and stared at him, black eyes in a white face, thin lips pinched together—but under those lips, the teeth would be sharp. Her hand could grip a rock, he was sure of it. This was what kept him hidden, trapped in a stupid house with people who lied to him. This withered girl.

She stared at him. She was in that moment so profoundly ugly that he wished for a spear.

~

Anne could not show anything, not before Shingleton. But this boy was extraordinary. He crouched on the floor, face closed and hostile, still as a rock in the current. His back was straight. The elderly curve of a prince's spine, the aching hunch garnered from years of leaning on canes, was absent. This boy was straight-spined like a commoner, like a soldier. His supple legs splayed over the floor, his webbed hands and white face and dark eyes were all princely, but he was sound, strong, unbroken.

Anne had seen her grandfather, withered and ageing; she had seen her uncle, flesh-slabbed and rolling. She had few memories of her father. Looking at this strange boy, she wondered for a long moment if he had looked like this.

~

The lame man came in and closed the door behind him. "Francis Shingleton," he said indicating the surgeon. "This man will not hurt you, but he wishes to speak with you. This is the boy, Shingleton. I think his name is Henry or Edward, or Philip or John or one such name, but he will not tell me which."

Shingleton had not told the lame man—Westlake, that was it—had not said that he knew Henry. Shingleton was keeping quiet.

"How do you do?" Shingleton said, and Henry said nothing.

"And this—" Westlake seemed to pause, then cleared his throat and said, "This is her Majesty Princess Anne, the second granddaughter of King Edward."

The girl stood quite still. He looked at her and she looked at him.

*Who are you?* she said in the deepsman's language. Her accent was a little foreign, not that of his own kin, but he understood it. The language he had gone without for so long, had heard only in his own throat and, once, from a distance, in the screams of a dying child. She had been part of that: for her to speak this private language was an outrage that made him grip his hands on the floor.

"I am Anne Delamere," she said. "I have no other name. *Who are you?*"

There was no answer to give in the deepsmen's language but *Whistle,* his old name, his old self. But Whistle had been pushed up on a beach eleven years before and left to die. It was a long time since he had heard his native language spoken in a woman's voice.

"Can you speak to him, Shingleton?" said Westlake. "Is he simple? You act simple, my son, but I do not think you can be."

*I know you know what I say,* the girl said. Henry could not stop seeing how tiny she was, frail as a dead leaf. She was right; even if he was just out of the sea, he would understand the language she was using now. But she did not say it to the men, she said it to him.

Henry remembered with a sudden force the day Allard had placed a crown on his head. It had horrified him, but it had become his toy, his one cheerful thing. Most likely he would never see that toy again. But crowns were made of silver, he knew now, and the one Allard offered him could not have been. He had never thought to ask. It was probably only a bauble of tin.

*I am here,* said the girl, *I hear you. Who are you?*

It struck Henry hard that if he were in their position, he would give up soon and try beating the prisoner for information.

Anne's hands were shaking. "Excuse me," she said to the boy, and turned aside. It was foolish to want to be polite to him, but she was too afraid to be otherwise. Tears stung in her throat, and she wasn't sure why. "I do not think it polite to talk over any man's head, but perhaps our guest will forgive me. I believe I might speak to him more freely alone."

"That cannot be, my lady Princess," said Westlake. Out of the corner of her eye, she saw the boy twitch. She turned back.

"We have much to discuss," she said. "If you will not speak English to us, perhaps you might speak our mother tongue to me."

The boy's face stiffened further, and he closed his arms around his body.

"If we are to save you, we must speak with you to make a plan," Anne persisted. "Please, sir. I know you understand me."

Henry swallowed, and raised his head. There was nothing for it but speech. "I understand you," he said. "I do not trust your salvation."

Everyone stiffened. The sight of them tensing made Henry tense in turn; were they poised to spring? Both men opened their mouths to speak, but the girl raised a hand and they stopped.

"There were rumours of your presence," she said. "You would have been caught soon. We do not wish to see you burned, and we found you first. You should trust us, or we cannot help you." She gave him a bleak, black-eyed stare. "You have little choice."

How did she get grown men to be silent with a flick of her hand? Henry had wished all his life for such an impact on people, but he had had to shout and tussle for purchase. He shook his head. "I do not believe you."

"My lady Princess." That was Shingleton's voice. Henry was so afraid of betraying their acquaintance that he hardly dared look at him. Measured against the girl's impassivity, his own face was treacherous, an unschooled horse that shied when it should be still. "I would like to speak to the boy alone, with your Majesty's permission."

The girl gave him a sharp look. "Why?"

Shingleton glanced at him. "My lady Princess, we do not know the state of this boy's mind."

"He is no simpleton," the girl said. Her arms were crooked in front of her body; it was a frightened pose. But still, there was a clip to her voice, an assurance. She did not speak fast or loud: she spoke without clearing her throat or looking around her, as if she knew without reflection that people would fall silent when she spoke. "It is easy to pretend to be a natural, Master Shingleton, and he is not one."

Shingleton shook his head. His hands were folded very carefully before him. "Not a simpleton, perhaps, my lady Princess, but other things affect the wits. And, my lady Princess, perhaps it would be wise to ascertain his wits before we let him speak too long with you."

"I give nothing away," she said.

"How do you endure them calling you 'my lady Princess' every time they speak?" Henry heard his own voice cutting into the conversation. If Shingleton had his way, the girl would go out of the room. He needed to speak to Shingleton alone, but perhaps he would never see her again, and the question had surfaced, suddenly and unbearably. "They would serve you better if they called you nothing."

"How do you mean?" said the girl. "Master Deepsman?"

There was something in the way she added the last words that reminded him of John, but there was no humour in her face. "They call you their lady Princess when they want you to follow their wishes instead of your own," Henry said. "If what they have to say would please you, they would have no need to princess it."

The girl looked at him, her ugly face glowing in the shadowed room. "How long have you been longing to be called a king?"

There was a silence. It was not practical to hit the girl with two men standing by. Henry turned his face to the wall and withdrew into speechlessness. It made it easier for Shingleton to ask for time alone with him.

Anne retreated to the next room, with Westlake halting after her. A wish possessed her that she had not seen this boy. She could not blame him for his silence, his mistrust; she had hidden too many years behind a dull face not to recognise the freezing of an animal when predators are gathered all around. But if Shingleton could not talk him around, if Samuel could not, then he would not help himself. And if he would not, then he would have to go.

It would be easier to endure the death of someone she had not met.

"Perhaps Shingleton can prevail upon him, my lady Princess," Westlake started to say.

Anne cut him off. "Let us say a decade," she said, taking out her rosary. Better to hear the whisper of prayer than the crackle of flames.

It occurred to her as they started on the Hail Mary that she did not know the name of the boy she was praying over.

~

Shingleton closed the door, checked the lock, craned his neck at the crack.

"Whisper," Henry said in irritation. "I can hear you."

Shingleton edged closer to him. "The princess Anne has ears as sharp as yours, I would warrant." There was barely any sound: Henry had to lean close, training his short-sighted eyes on the movement of the man's lips. "Are you hurt, Henry?"

Henry shook his head. "Can you get word to John Claybrook?" he said. A longing for John's face, his laughter, was tugging inside him, but he felt some despair as well. Robert Claybrook had lied to him. It was John he trusted—but John was dependent on his father, and John had not an army at his command. All his life, Henry had loved John as a follower, but a follower was little help to him now.

Shingleton nodded. "I will ride to the Claybrooks straightway. Westlake will not follow me, he has not the men to guard you and go after me as well. Henry, how did you come to this?"

"Not 'my lord Henry' now?" To hear his name repeated so baldly cast Henry back into childhood, stiff-sided rooms and his hands bound and sickening food in exchange for speech. Where was there escape from captivity?

Shingleton didn't answer. "When Bishop Westlake told me he had a deepsman boy in his charge, I almost fell down on the spot. I had no idea if it was you. I thought he might have told me so that I could have notice to fly."

"Would that be like him?" You needed to know the habits of your captors. Henry had lived all his life on that rule.

Shingleton nodded. "He is a man of God." Henry shook his head; God had never meant much to him. "He has little taste for killing."

"How far can I trust him?" Henry asked. The quietness of the conversation did not bother him, but Shingleton's strained face as he struggled to make out what Henry said was frustrating.

"He will not betray you if he can help it," Shingleton said. "But last time there was a bastard found, he could not."

Henry saw Westlake again in his mind, standing before the blackening bodies.

## Twenty-Six

ANNE DID NOT tell her grandfather. She went to greet the court as usual, and showed nothing on her face as she scanned the rows of faces. Earls and Dukes, great counties and rivers in their rule, men who could raise armies, men who could hide a bastard and make for the throne.

Behind one of those faces was the knowledge of the hidden boy, but she could not see which one. Any more than they would see behind her set face the knowledge of where their lost usurper was now.

❧

Henry was with Westlake when he heard the sound of hooves outside. The sound was terrifying: hoofbeats meant soldiers now, people coming out of the shadows to find him. Westlake was still speaking to him, trying to explain once again why Henry should trust his captors; his landsman's ears were too dull to hear the sound from far-off.

Henry turned his back and huddled his arms around himself. It was no good to trust anyone.

Then he heard a sound over the hoofbeats, faint and distant, muffled by the air—but he could hear it. If he lowered his head and blocked out Westlake's words, he could hear it.

"Henry? Can you hear me? It is John. Shingleton came. I am coming to visit the Bishop."

Henry closed his eyes, shielded his face in his arms so Westlake couldn't see the desperate hope. The voice was getting closer, surfacing, bringing him nearer and nearer to breathing clean air.

"Henry, when I come in the house, make a lot of noise, and I can insist upon finding you. Do you hear me?"

"Are you unwell, my son?" Westlake said, seeing Henry drop his head and shield it.

Henry said nothing. He would be making enough noise by and by.

～

Anne sat before the court. All of a sudden she wondered whether the same man who had hidden the boy had killed her mother.

～

"My lord Bishop, I have a spiritual matter I wished to discuss with you," Henry heard John's voice saying below. The sound of it was so familiar that Henry almost paused, rocking a little with relief. It would almost be funny to hear what story John could make up as an excuse for visiting. But there was no time to hug pleasures to himself, and he wanted to see his friend.

He clenched his fist and banged on the door, raising his voice in a brazen deepsman's call; yelled at the top of his voice, yelled for eleven years behind walls. "Let me out! Let me out! *Let me out!*"

～

Anne sat and shook. She should have asked herself this question before, but the sight of the boy had driven other thoughts from her mind. She had been thinking of pyres, executions, Erzebet's stiff face as she ordered death for other people. Not her own end, not her wet red face as death came for her.

It could not have been this boy. To poison Erzebet's bathwater would have taken speed and stealth, the ability to pass from room to room unobserved. But had he known of it? Had he been consulted? Had he ordered it, even?

Anne gripped one hand over another, and debated in cold terror whether or not to open her mouth and tell her grandfather the truth.

~

There were voices downstairs, a clatter of feet. There was the sound of a scuffle.

Henry thought of John, riding his horse fast, running on long limbs. He thought of the lame, gaunt man who had locked the door upon him.

He was not afraid as he heard the struggle. John would win, and then he would come up the stairs and find him.

~

Who could have put the poison in the water? How could it have been accomplished?

By anyone, that was the terrible thing. The salt was not guarded, and Erzebet had not been in that room since the day before. Anyone, anyone with sturdy limbs and a straight back who could run colt-footed from place to place instead of dragging like a split-limbed snail could have slipped into the room, shaken a packet over the salt and slipped out again. It could have been anyone.

And Samuel—Samuel had been poisoned. Or made ill enough to need a unicorn's horn to cure him at least. And Shingleton had been reluctant to say whether that was poisoning or not. Why would he be so reluctant?

Only if he didn't want to cross a powerful lord. Because he did not know who to accuse and feared the consequences of a mistake? Or because he knew who was responsible and dared not take a stand?

Only her weak legs kept Anne in her chair, kept her from leaping to her feet and running to find her horse and ride over to Samuel, crying out: *We cannot trust Shingleton! We have made a mistake!*

Shingleton had been at her mother's bedside. And if the king's surgeon had been in the room to examine the salts, he could have told any story he wished if discovered.

Anne's mind raced on ahead of her, over the green to Samuel's wooden door, but her legs stayed slumped in her chair, loose as wet cloth.

As John rattled at the catch, Henry heard the sound of Westlake's dragging steps following him up. So John had not hurt the man. That was weak of him if they were going to make an escape, but then the door pulled open and Henry was so glad to see his friend that he forgave him his hesitation in battle.

Henry reached out a hand, his face opening into the first smile he had felt in days, but John stepped back, casting a quick glance over his shoulder. "You do not know me," he hissed. Then he raised his voice. "Bishop, what is this?" he said.

Held down by the weight of her body, Anne drew a deep breath and bethought herself. Why would Shingleton make an assay at Samuel?

If she kept her thoughts light and careful, handled them only between her fingertips, she could understand why someone would kill her mother. If they had a bastard, a man to take the throne and beget sons, the country would probably welcome him. If he was strong enough. And this boy was strong-limbed, and strong-willed, too: he had not begged for mercy. Her grandfather was dying. Her uncle was simple. Her sister and she were young girls, a prize for anyone looking to marry onto the throne . . . but neither girl had ever given any sign that she could hold the rudder of power out of the grasp of a foreign husband.

It had been a mistake, all those years, to hide her wits behind a staring face. She had traded privacy for safety, kept her thoughts secret and left her throne unguarded.

She had wasted her care in the wrong places. She had made a lifelong mistake.

Anne thought these thoughts with cool fastidiousness, as if judging someone else. She held them at a distance, examining them like soiled rags, and decided that they were correct. She had played the fool, and lived a fool, and she had been wrong.

So yes, there were reasons to remove Erzebet. As Edward ailed, there was no other prince strong enough to stand against a bastard reaching for the throne. But Samuel? Samuel had never hurt anyone.

Samuel . . . Anne lowered her eyes. For a moment her face tried to settle itself in dull lines, laying over a mask of stupidity to give herself privacy to think. But she was done with that. She had trained her face to look stupid, and now it did. It would be a disadvantage.

She would have to work on that. Meantime, she looked at her folded hands, trying to look demure instead of stupid, and thought about Samuel, letting his face rest in her mind.

Samuel was favoured by Philip now, it seemed. He could soothe Philip, calm him down, control him as no other courtier had ever managed. But Samuel had been sick before that had happened. All he had ever done that she knew of, the only thing he had ever done to mark him as different, was to walk into court on a lame leg and speak privately to the Archbishop about the doubtful wisdom of burning a bastard.

But not this bastard. Someone else's, a child no lord had had time to invest in. It made no sense.

Anne was done with guarded foolishness and hoping for answers. It was time to try her wits against the world. Erzebet, she told herself, looking at her sharp-clawed, well-tended fingers, Erzebet would be proud of her.

~

Westlake appeared behind John on the stairs. His clothing was untidy, he lurched on his lame leg, but his face showed little pain. Only, it was a little greyer than before.

"What is this, Bishop?" John repeated. His voice was conveying a good impression of shock, disapproval, disbelief.

Westlake shook his head. "I fear you are undone, my son," he said to Henry. "Forgive me."

John turned around to face Westlake. "Have you been hiding this—this bastard?"

Westlake looked at the floor. "Only a few days, I swear it. I have planned no treason. I found the boy and hoped to save him from execution. That is all." Around his neck there hung a cross, a sharp-cut pendant that Henry felt an instinctive dislike of every time he looked at it. But now the man's hand was clutching it as if it were a spar.

John stared at him a moment. Then he reached out and closed his hand over Westlake's, pinning the cross between his fingers. "Swear," he said. "Swear before Christ."

Westlake's face showed no colour, only stillness. He looked at John with dead, hopeless eyes, and raised the cross. "I swear before Christ," he said. "I wished only to save him from the pyre. I do not think it pleases God when we burn his children."

Henry looked at John's face. From here, he could hear his friend's breathing, a cautious, shivering set of breaths like an unstable staircase. Henry remembered the day they had ridden out to the burning, how sick John had looked at the sight. "You were present at the last one," John said. "You blessed the flames."

Westlake dropped his head, his fingers still around the cross. "I prayed for the child's soul," he said. "I could not save his body."

"And is it the body or the soul of this man you wish to save?" John said. His eyes were bright and blue, staring hard at Westlake's pallor.

"You may leave my soul alone," Henry said. "You will be with us, or you will not leave this house." It was what he would have said to a stranger, so he said it to John. It troubled him a little, though. He did not think he was good at lying, and he was so tired of being lonely. He wanted this conversation done with.

"There is no call to threaten," John said. "If you do not threaten the throne, I will not threaten you."

"We do not," Westlake said, so quickly that he was speaking before John finished. "I swear before Christ, we only mean to save this man's life. It is a hard fate, caught between the land and the sea, and I do not wish to see anyone punished for it. Do not betray us, and I will pray for you every day of my life."

John sighed, ruffled his hair. Henry sat back on the floor, wondering how long he would have to act before he could plausibly give in.

A few hours later, as Anne was riding over to Westlake's house, John Claybrook accosted her.

Anne had set out as quickly and discreetly as she could. Since the day he found her a unicorn horn, Robin Maydestone at the stables seemed to have taken a fancy to her, and indulged her requests for horses at odd hours with an affectionate grin under his bowing. Anne had assumed that this might be because he had a daughter of his own, or perhaps because he didn't. She should have asked; playing stupid had left her ignorant. In any event, it was proving useful when she needed to slip away. It was a cool day, the ground soft under her horse's hooves and taking sharp impressions with each step, and Anne let the damp air drift over her skin while her mind raced. She needed to know what this boy, this man knew. Never mind what Samuel said, to *Hell* with what Samuel said if he stood in her way. This bastard had been raised by somebody, and that somebody was somebody she needed to know about. Erzebet's scorched face jostled at the back of her mind, and she kept her mouth closed to keep in the sickness.

When John Claybrook rode up behind her, calling "My lady Princess!" Anne jumped so suddenly that her horse shied under her, jerking its head against the tug she had given its reins.

John cantered up and caught at its bridle. Anne grabbed for the reins, trying to back away: some courtier following her, however pleasant his manners, would be a disaster just now.

"My lady Princess, I come from the Bishop," John said quietly.

"I am going there." Anne turned her head aside. She was not going to discuss this.

"My lady Princess, I found the man he was hiding."

Anne dropped the reins. Her horse stood, stamping a protesting foot, as John held on to its bridle. "What man?" she said.

"My lady Princess, I know you know." John had always been friendly to her from the height of his superior years, but Anne did not feel herself a child any more, and she was not going to be addressed as such by any nobleman's son.

"You speak out of turn, sir," she said. "Tell me your business or leave me."

John looked at her, his normally cheerful face anxious. "My lady Princess, forgive me. But I . . . there is no cause for alarm. I am your man."

"Explain yourself," Anne snapped, her heart pounding. "I am out of patience."

"My lady Princess, I—I went to speak with the Bishop, to speak with him on a spiritual matter. But there was a noise from upstairs, and I went to see what it was. I found he was hiding the bastard in his house."

Anne frowned to stop her usual look of frightened idiocy coming back. "What story do you tell me, sir? You accuse a man of God."

John shook his head, persisted. "It was not the Bishop who told me you knew of this, my lady Princess. It was Henry. He mentioned a young deepswoman. It could only have been you."

"Henry?" So that was the name, Henry. A cautious choice; there had not been a Henry in the family for several generations. So Samuel had persuaded his name out of him in the end. It cost Anne a pang of unreasonable disappointment that she had not been there to hear the boy confess it himself before she steadied herself.

John blinked, shook his head nervously. "That was his name, he told me. He said he had spoken with you and you had been kind to him."

"He was wrong," Anne said. Her voice was clipped. That did not sound like the sullen, cautious boy she had seen. Surely her careful courtesy could not have made such an impression on him: she had not been kind, merely wary. Diplomatic of the boy to say so, perhaps. You would think a lord would raise a bastard for diplomacy, if nothing else.

"My lady Princess, I can help you. My father can help you. We none of us want to see another burning."

"Do you question the Crown?" Anne's voice rose. It was one thing for Samuel to tell her, secretly and in a quiet place, that he did not care for fires. It was one thing for her to question, in her heart of hearts, if

she could have watched such a sight. For a passing courtier to make
such judgements on her mother's decision, that hard-won decision
that had frozen Erzebet's face and brought a single embrace when
Anne questioned it sideways, was another thing entirely.

"My lady Princess." John held on to her bridle. "I can help you.
Let me help you."

Anne gathered herself, invoked her mother's cold face. "Will you
tell your father of this?" Because Robert Claybrook could raise an
army, march on the capital with a bastard at his side. But he had power
as Philip's keeper, would have more when Edward died; he could be
powerful without risking himself in battle. It might be very advanta-
geous for him to hand Henry over. Or to claim him for a cause.

John could ride straight home and tell his father, and then the
secret would be out, the property of great men. Could she stop him?
She could not stop his tongue, unless she had him placed where no one
could hear him. It would be easy enough to do. A story of an assault, an
attempted treason; she could lay any word against him. But he would
talk, even if she had a headsman silence him, he could talk before the
axe fell. Certainly he could talk to his father.

"I believe he can help, my lady Princess."

Anne shook her head. She would believe a great many things, but
not that a man like Claybrook would be motivated by Christian charity to a foundling bastard. A man of the Church, a man of medicine,
men with only their own faith to recommend them, might be moved
by such abstract concerns, but Claybrook had land, waterways,
wealth. He had too much to lose. "Be silent with him," she said. "Say
nothing until I tell you otherwise."

John hesitated. "He will know if I am absent, my lady Princess. I
must say something. And we cannot keep it from him for long. This
must be known, sooner or later, whatever is done."

"Tell him you visit a sick friend," Anne snapped. "Do not tell me
you are unable to lie, Master Courtier."

A shadow of his old grin passed over John's face, then he was serious again. "As you command. But as your courtier I know it my duty
to advise you, and I advise you to let me tell my father. He can help us."

"A sick friend," Anne said. "Or a fever of piety. Or you will find that I can speak too, and my words will be such that you may die of them."

Henry waited as the night fell. Claybrook knew he was here. He could talk, now, could accuse Claybrook and go with him hand-in-hand to the stake. Not Allard. Allard had been good to him, Henry saw it now. He had tied him up in a locked room and forced questions upon him, but now it had happened again; it could only be that this was how landsmen were. As a landsman, Allard had done his best. He had not made false promises like Claybrook.

But Claybrook was ready to threaten. There would be no choice for him now. Claybrook would have to rally his soldiers at last. There was no safety except on the throne, and no safety for Claybrook unless he could put Henry upon it. He had not planned it so, but now he could force Claybrook's hand. When John came tomorrow, he would send a message. They marched on the capital, or Henry named his keeper.

## Twenty-Seven

THERE WERE QUESTIONS to be asked, answers Anne needed. And the boy was in her grasp. All she had to do was ride back to her grandfather, say a few words. "Bishop Westlake has most vigilantly set spies upon our enemies, and has captured a traitor." Credit to Samuel, credit to her, and the bastard curtained in flames, swallowed up in heat. It was a fine threat. With such a threat in her hands, Anne could force the name of her mother's murderer out of him.

John Claybrook was downstairs when she arrived at Samuel's house. "My lady Princess," he said, standing up, "my lord the Bishop will not let me see the bastard."

"No need to rise, Samuel, thank you," said Anne, as Westlake prepared to pull himself to his feet. "You did well. You are not to see him unless I say so, my lord John."

John flushed, closed his hand and opened it as he bowed.

"Have you told your father?"

"My lady Princess?"

"Yesterday I told you not to tell your father," Anne said. "Have you obeyed me?"

The flush deepened. "Yes, my lady Princess. I did as you bid me and told him I had to visit a sick friend." John shrugged. "He was most Christian about it. He gave me some wine to take him."

"Most Christian," Anne said without warmth. "Where is it?"

"The Bishop brought it upstairs for Henry."

"I am surprised," said Anne. "Deepsmen do not like wine."

"He—is no deepsman, my lady Princess . . ." John's face was confused.

"No," Anne said. "But he is no king either."

～

Samuel was waiting for her, but she brushed him aside. "I will speak with him alone today." Anne headed for the stairs, Samuel limping anxious attendance.

"My lady—"

"I can call you if there is trouble," Anne said with some bitterness. "That door does not keep in noise very well."

Samuel bowed. "Your forgiveness, my lady Princess. I am sorry."

"It cannot be helped," Anne said. "Did he thank you for the wine?"

"No, my lady Princess," Samuel sighed. "He barely speaks to me at all."

"I will have him speak to me," Anne said, and went up the stairs.

～

The bottle of wine was resting between Henry's hands as Anne came in. They had tied one of his legs to a bolt in the wall, and one of his wrists was shackled to it; he could sit up, but not reach the door. The bottle clinked against the fetters as he weighed it. It was a gift from Claybrook, it had to be: John had no cellar of his own. The thought of such a cheap peace-offering made Henry want to smash it, but he restrained himself. Perhaps he would drink it first. Claybrook could give him more later, and he would. Henry would see to that.

The girl stood in the doorway. Henry could still not get over the femaleness of her; land women had been a rare enough sight in his own life, but they had been tall creatures, entirely foreign. This girl, down on his own height, smaller even, with her webbed hands and bent legs, was an aberration. Though he had never seen that blueness

of skin on members of his own tribe, he had seen it on others occasionally: tribesmen from colder waters, further to the north where the
waters were dark in winter even during the day, tribesmen with strong
arms and great lungs, who could dive deep. Meetings with them had
been fraught at best: he remembered the displays, brandishing of rocks
and shows of strength, the men of each tribe breaking for the surface
and leaping high in the air, higher than their competitors; cries to carry
across the fathoms: *I am strong. Do not trifle with me.* Deepsmen did not
draw imaginary lines to separate themselves; they judged on territory
and kin, and unfamiliar faces were occasions for challenge. He
remembered, distantly, the insults and shrieks when unfamiliar tribes
came within earshot of each other: *Weakling. Ship-follower. Stranger.*
Not "my son," not the lame man's weird courtesies. You did not pretend, in the sea, to be kin when you weren't, and this girl was no kin to
him. Even her dialect, when she spoke their shared language, was not
the one he had grown up with; he understood it, but the groan and
shrill of her voice fell in alien patterns on his ears. She was a foreigner,
this girl. So many years had he spent looking at landsmen that her
face, featured like a deepsman's with her small sharp teeth and black-
set eyes, seemed grotesquely alien. He would have liked to defeat her,
somehow, beat her down in a fight or make her obey him, to stop her
face from troubling him any further. He wanted to eat her tongue.

She came in, hunch-backed and grim, and stood before him. Out
of the sleeve of her dress, she drew a knife.

"I wish to know," she said, "what you know of the death of
Princess Erzebet."

Henry stared up at her, saying nothing.

The girl twitched her knife before him. "You are to answer me,"
she said, and there was a fierceness in her voice that made Henry see
bared teeth, sharp claws, the sea breaking its currents around her feet.
"Tell me what you know, or I shall send you to the pyre today. And I
will hurt you before I send you." She opened her mouth as if to say
more, then closed it again. Henry gripped the fetters. If she had said
more, he might have thought she was bluffing, working herself up,
but she said only what she meant. She meant what she said.

"If you come near me I will fight you," Henry said. He was not going to show fear to this woman, not for anything. "And I am stronger, and if I hurt you before you hurt me you will suffer."

She looked at him for a moment, then opened her palm, dropped the knife. It quivered in the floorboards, point piercing the wood. "I can throw," she said. "Can you catch?"

Henry reached forward in a lunge, the fetters yanking against him as he made for her.

"That was a noise the men will have heard," the girl said. "I can have them shackle your other arm. I have only to give the word."

She could, and he would be bound and helpless with her knife before him. Henry wrenched his chains again, sick and unsurprised. He would have begun the threats sooner if he were in her position.

"I have—handled deepsmen." The girl's voice was low in her throat, a hoarse throb that cut the air. "And I can manage you, Master Deepsman. You are in my land, and it is me you must answer to." She reached down and plucked the knife from the floor, wobbling on her staff but steady-eyed. He could see the tension in her fingers.

"I answer to no one," Henry said. If she came close enough, it would come to bloodlust between them. He could fight. And it would be good to grapple her, force her down and tear the certainty out of her; that measured voice could scream for mercy, he was sure of it, and those pale little arms would feel good gripped in his fists. Wasn't this what it all came down to, a cry of claim against claim? *Mine,* her hand was saying. Why else would she so clearly be gasping to plunge in the knife?

"Answer me about the death of Erzebet, or I shall begin by unmanning you." Her lips dragged over the last words, as if she was unused to saying them, but Henry saw the angle of the blade.

Henry was back where he was born, chest convulsed with dread, and only fury to keep it at bay. So he concentrated on her stupidity until its magnitude made him want to slap her; she was not even asking the right questions. "I know nothing about the death of your Erzebet," he said.

"Answer me," she said. Her hand lowered the knife a little, as if testing its edge against the air.

"What do you want of me? She died of a fever. I did not give it to her." John had told him this, he remembered; he had thought it good news, one less obstacle to the throne. Fevers meant burning skin, hot and painful; it had given him a moment of angry gladness. That moment seemed a long time ago now. Henry clenched his teeth together, to keep from blurting out the insults that crowded inside him. If he berated her for asking the wrong questions, he might point her to the right ones.

*Did you kill her?* The question came in his mother tongue, and it shook Henry badly. The urge possessed him to grab her face, press his hand hard over that neat little mouth and silence this sea-water call, but he could not reach her.

Henry inhaled, finding himself oddly breathless. He could carry air in his lungs for a quarter hour, but this girl, this fragile ugly girl, was making him gasp as if he had been fighting. She would answer for it later, he told himself; it was a reassuring thought.

*I did not,* he said. *She is a stranger.* You could lie in the deepsman's language, but it was difficult to equivocate with so simple a vocabulary. In the sea you needed only statements and challenges: *The prey is there. Do not trifle with me. I want that.*

The girl turned the knife in her fingers. "Tell me what you know of her," she said.

Henry shook his head. "You are foolish, Princess, and you ask me things I cannot answer. I know nothing of this Erzebet of yours. I heard she died of a fever, and I was happy to hear it because it meant one less prince between me and my goal. Do you think I should weep for her?"

"Do not lie to me." The girl's voice was quiet, but as she stared at him, she bared her teeth suddenly and the knife went back in her grip. "Do not lie to me, *do not lie to me!*"

Henry felt an angry pulse of pleasure at the distress in her voice. "A fever took the tyrant bitch before she could burn me," he said. "I saw what she did to my brother and I know what she would have made of me."

The girl was blinking now, her voice a hiss. "Do not tell me he was your brother," she said. "I have been in the sea, and I do not believe you."

So she was not sentimental. Good. "He might have been," Henry said, telling the truth. It was an idea he had not told to John, even; he could not tell his laughing friend so weak-minded a thought. "My mother must have liked to fuck landsmen, after all, just like yours. I saw him burn."

The girl stopped for a moment, stood over him. "My mother did not fuck landsmen," she said. Her voice caught over the word, as if she were unused to coarse language, and Henry gritted his teeth in satisfaction. "My mother was a prince, not an animal. My mother married an imbecile who cannot go into the water in case he fucks a deepswoman. Do not talk to me of fucking or I will tell you what imbeciles do."

"I thought you meant to begin by unmanning me," Henry said. "If you wish to begin by talking to me, that is a lesser threat." He had not really meant that Erzebet fucked landsmen; if he thought about it, this girl must have been the child of a half-caste, her parents the children of half-castes, back and back, generations of hobbling spiders like her. She had understood what he meant, which was odd in itself; John or Allard would have frowned, made him explain. But the word *animal* was a strange one on his ears, one he had never thought of. Animals were creatures you hunted, spitted on spears or choked with your bare hands. They were prey. Out of the water, he knew no animals that could threaten him like the creatures of the water: no sharks, no porpoises, no poison fish. Only landsmen, with their swords and their numbers and their incomprehensible rules. He had two languages, and now he was trapped, he was, for the first time in his life, speaking to a person who understood both of them.

There was silence as the girl stared at him. Then, knife still in hand, she dropped to the floor, letting go of her crutch and collapsing into a sitting posture with a suddenness that must have been painful. He saw her face flinch for just a second, but she was still out of his reach and he couldn't get to her. She sat opposite him, a wasteland of skirts all around her, and fingered the blade.

"What would you do," she said, "if I gave you this knife and told you to take your choice between self-murder and the pyre?"

Henry looked back at her. "I would take it and wait until someone came close enough to fight," he said.

Her voice was almost interested. "Do you really think there can be an escape for you?"

"I shall not give up my will."

She nodded, more to herself than to him. "A king does not speak so bluntly, Master Deepsman."

Henry shrugged. "If I gained the throne, I would have diplomats to speak for me."

"Is your name truly Henry?"

He hesitated. John must have made a mistake, let it slip, as he had told it to no one. John needed a sharp warning when he next appeared. But it could betray nothing, and it was strange, somehow compelling, to hear this girl speak his name. "In their language," he said. "Back in the sea, it was something else."

"What was it?" Her black eyes looked up at him, attentive.

*Whistle,* he said. It was like speaking a dream, some lost childhood memory that had sunk and resurfaced, changed with the salt water. "But it has been a long time since anyone has called me that."

*Whistle,* the girl said. She sighed. "We have only one name, here on the land. But the deepsmen have names, out in the bay. You cannot explain them to a landsman."

Henry shook his head. "We are not alike, you and I."

"No indeed." Her eyes were on him still. "You have seen the depths. The great waters out beyond the bay."

He shook his head again. "You do not track them by sight. Everything is blue."

"That I could have known," she said. "I do know that."

Henry braced himself. "Why are you talking to me? Where are your threats? You have asked me only one question, and that one was useless."

She shrugged. "I am poor in kinsmen, Master Deepsman. *Whistle.* Do you truly know nothing of Erzebet?"

*I don't know,* Henry said. "I only heard she died of a fever."

The girl curled her legs under herself. Her face was glowing in the indoor shade now, a bright, cold blue. It was a sight he had not seen for so long, a colour of home. On that enemy girl, still, there was something beautiful about it. "She was poisoned," she said. "Someone put poison in her bath and it stripped the skin from her." He could hear her take a breath, another one, panting like a landsman.

Henry frowned. Had Claybrook not known of this? He had told Henry she died of a fever, and Henry had believed him. Or had he known, what then? Would Claybrook have knocked out the tyrant that stood between him and victory? If he had done so, why hadn't he raised an army as soon as she was dead? It was a sudden gulf of ignorance, and at its appearance, he felt the fear coming back. He was lost in weeds, sounds bouncing back and no clear echo to guide him.

He raised the bottle, turned it over in his hands. Perhaps some wine would be good for him.

"I saw my mother die," the girl said, and Henry realised that it was her own mother she was talking about when she spoke of Erzebet. He had known it, he could have told it, but the word *mother* meant little to him. Erzebet was a tyrant, a bare-toothed killer of his kind, and this girl was something else. The fact that she would be upset at the loss of Erzebet was not something he had considered. It wasn't the words she used so much as the fact that she said them at all. She did not seem talkative. Erzebet's death must have meant something to her, for her to speak of it for no purpose, only to hear herself say the words.

"If you call her a tyrant bitch again," Anne said, "I will cut you."

"People die," Henry said. He had seen plenty of people die in the sea. It had not made them his friends. But the girl had a knife, and he did not say that.

~

The boy was an animal, Anne told herself. No, he was not an animal. He called her mother a tyrant bitch, he spoke of fucking as if it mattered not at all, as if nothing, none of the things that clasped and crushed her, could touch him at all. He was appalling, but he talked to her, he had seen the sea, he was probably telling the truth when he said he had no hand in Erzebet's death. He just didn't care about it all.

What would it be like, to be so unburdened? He had no courts to please, no country to care for, no deepsmen to manage with nothing but quick hands and shut eyes. Men did not bear down on his body; he kept his own space, pretended nothing, no concern he did not feel, no loyalties he did not owe. Even with a gyve on his wrist, he spoke his mind.

She had wanted to cut him, for being so unconcerned with all that mattered to her, for being so distant, so far from home, so isolated. But he was not Philip, she told herself, he was not a deepsman from the bay.

"Do you mean to tell me who hid you all these years?" she asked him. Somebody must have. He cared nothing for her family, but he must have one of his own.

Henry looked at her. "Do you wish the truth?"

"I do."

He cocked his head. "My—father will notice I am gone, and he will seek for me. If he cannot save me, I may name him to save myself. But I will wait until you push me to that point."

Anne swallowed. She had tried, she had tried hard to be good all those years. This casual casting-off of his family should have been horrifying. But at the same time, some part of her ran out to meet it, like a figure glimpsed in the distance. The freedom of disloyalty, the safety of solitude. When duties penned you in on all sides, ingratitude could save your life.

"Do you think you could withstand it if I had you put to the question?" she said. If he could think only of himself, so could she. If he was free to owe nothing to anyone, it freed her to owe nothing to him. He did not ask to be a stone around her neck. Something was running through her at the boy's self-centredness, something she did not expect: an answering pulse of relief.

Henry seemed to consider the question seriously. "I think so," he said. "Could you withstand it?"

Anne shivered against her will. "If it were easy to withstand, it would not be useful," she said. "But it would not be me suffering, it would be you."

"True." Henry did not smile, did not make it a joke. He simply conceded the point.

"If your father saves you, it will be the worse for me," Anne said. "Is he your real father?"

"I doubt it," Henry said. "And perhaps it would be the worse. But if you mean to kill me now, you will have to come close to me to do it. And if you meant to burn me, I believe you would not have hesitated. It is not a thing one can do if one wavers."

"If one does it with one's own hands," Anne said slowly. "But to give an order and have you burned where I cannot see you would not be so difficult."

He seemed to have no answer to that. Instead he grimaced, and pulled the top off his bottle of wine. It sat in his hand, dark and clean.

"Do you mean to drink that?" Anne asked suddenly.

Henry frowned at her. "Why not? It can hardly matter if I am drunk here."

People drank wine without checking it all the time, of course. Most people did not have to fear poison. "Do you know who brought it to you?"

Henry shrugged. "The man called John. He said it was a gift."

Anne nodded. "From his father. Most Christian of him." The scent of alcohol rose from the bottle, heavy and choking.

A Christian gesture. But Claybrook was not a Christian man.

An English bastard, full-grown, was a serious threat to the throne. People might accept a princess's marriage to a foreign prince, but an English, clean-blooded, rational bastard to set on the throne—if he could hold it for a few years, he could hold it for ever. Every royal house in Europe would be courting his alliance. And bastard though he was, he was English. Many people would rather have a new English master than an old French one.

Perhaps Claybrook was being wise, playing both ends of the game. Waiting. Making no move on the outcome, sitting on the edge of a battlefield until he saw which side was carrying the day. A gift of wine, a simple enough gesture. And yet . . .

His son John had come round to talk to Samuel. John had never shown an interest in Samuel in his life.

They were a present family, the Claybrooks.

The memory of him came to her, hard and cold, of Claybrook standing before the door of her mother's room. Erzebet's screams had blinded her, blotted out all other impressions. Her ears had always been sharper than her eyes. But Claybrook had been there. Claybrook, who might have been anywhere else in the country, was on hand that day.

Claybrook could have wandered into Erzebet's bath chamber if he wished, added something to the salt. But Anne thought of the pyre. The heat, the ultimate, fatal threat. Samuel had found no poisons that answered the case. What else could have scorched Erzebet's skin? Anne had dismissed the idea of boiling water, for who could have wrestled her strong mother into a steaming bath? No one, no landsman, if Erzebet had her wits about her.

But Erzebet sleepy, Erzebet drugged from a harmless cup of wine sent to her through some uninformed servant . . .

Claybrook was a tall man, long of arm. He could easily have lifted her mother. If there had been something in her wine.

"Do not drink this," Anne said, clutching the wine away from Whistle. It was a danger to her, to lean in and out, but she was fast and he was not expecting it, and the bottle was in her hand and out of his reach again before he could stop her. "Do not."

"Why *not*?" His voice rose, close to a shout; Anne could hear the hoarseness, the strain, under the threat.

"I do not . . ." Anne turned, struggled for balance. "I wish to test something."

She went to the door, called for Samuel.

"Tell no one of this," she said as he came up the stairs, one step at a time. "Do not tell John Claybrook. I wish to send a message to Robin Maydestone at the stables. Tell him I wish for a dog to be sent. He will have dogs, yes? An old dog, one that is sick or turned savage, one that he does not care for." She thought of Maydestone's gentle hands on the horses' flanks, the way he crooned to them. "Not one he loves," she added. "Warn him he will not see it again."

"Yes, my lady Princess." Samuel's face was bewildered, and he hesitated for an explanation.

"Go swiftly," Anne snapped. "Take it from him, bring it at once."

The door closed behind her, and Anne sat down again, leaning against it, careless of her rich skirt crumpling on the floor. Henry sat across from her, his eyes never leaving her face.

"What do you want with a dog?" he said.

"I want to test the wine," Anne replied. The situation chilled her to the bone, but she almost laughed. "I can tell you are a prince by hope, not by connection," she said. "If you have never had a wine taster."

"Do not laugh at me."

Anne laughed again, her eyes stinging. "I do not trust my lord Claybrook's wine."

"Are you going to cry?" Henry said. He sounded less alarmed than interested.

Anne swallowed, shook her head.

Henry said nothing, and neither did she. They waited together for the dog to be brought.

~

It was a long wait before Samuel returned. "He is downstairs," he said quietly. "He wished to bring it himself, and I could not dissuade him."

Anne gave Samuel a sharp frown. "That was ill done, Samuel. I would have thought you could have found something to say that would make him stay."

Westlake shook his head. "The man is not a fool, my lady Princess. He is fond of you and wished to see you. He would quickly grow suspicious if I argued."

Anne shook her head. "I must go downstairs," she said to Whistle. "Do I need to threaten you to make you stay silent?"

Henry looked at her, ignoring Samuel. "You have already done so," he said. "I wish to see what you mean with this dog."

Anne and Samuel struggled down the stairs together, to meet with Maydestone, who stood in the door. Under his arm was a hound, scraggly-limbed and sticky-eyed, white hairs clustering on its muzzle like the greying of an old man. He bowed, and the dog whimpered as he shifted his grip. "My lady Princess, the dog you commanded," he said. Anne remembered the day by the river, the day Maydestone had helped her back onto her horse, and the memory of kindness was so strong that she almost reached her arms up to him, to be carried away, taken to her chamber and tucked in somewhere safe. She pulled herself up.

"I thank you, Master Maydestone," she said. He bowed again. His eyes flicked behind her, to the room, innocuous enough in appearance. Not plotting, not scheming, but curiosity, no doubt. That was to be expected.

"Master Maydestone, you have done me good service, as ever," Anne said, getting in the way of his vision. "I shall remember this." There was a silver bracelet encircling her wrist, and she slipped it off, weighing it in her hand a moment before passing it to him.

"My lady . . ." Maydestone's hand dropped a little, as if the bracelet was heavier than it should be. Surprise stretched over his face, almost dismay at the size of the gift.

"Say nothing of this to anyone," Anne said firmly. Maydestone's expression relaxed. A bracelet was no price for a used-up old dog, still whining and pawing its feet against the air, tucked under Maydestone's arm—but for a dog and for silence, that was a different matter. That was understandable.

"As you command, my lady Princess," he said, bowing again. He set the dog down. For just a moment, he tousled its ears; then he straightened up and shooed it into the room. It walked a few steps, unhurried, then lay down, splaying out emaciated legs behind it.

"I thank you," Anne said, and closed the door.

Henry heard the voices downstairs. The girl would return. She had threatened him, she had warned him. He no longer knew what to feel about her, except a desire to keep talking. If they kept talking, perhaps he might know what he felt.

She came in awkwardly, carrying a wretched-looking dog. He made no move to grab her as she shuffled over the floor, within his reach.

"Help me feed the dog this wine," she said. "I cannot do it alone."

The dog whimpered, scratching a little at the floor, and suddenly Henry's heart quickened. This was a fox to catch, a creature to hunt. He leaned forward, rolling onto his hands and knees, and crept across the floor, silent as a bird, drawing nearer and nearer. The dog laid its head down between its paws, rheumy eyes closing, huffing a little sigh—and then Henry was on it, wrenching it up off the ground.

Anne was beside him quickly, the wine in her hand. "Pull its head back," she said, "and open its mouth."

Henry grabbed the dog's jaws, forced them open. There in its mouth was the tongue, grey-pink and ready for his grasp—but this was not a killing hunt, he must leave it alone. Already the girl was pouring wine down the dog's throat. The beast coughed and struggled, its throat convulsing against Henry's wrist, and Henry gripped harder. The wine trickled down, an unsteady stream, splashing and thinning, foaming pink as it mingled with the dog's spit.

Anne set the goblet down. "Very well," she said. "Now we wait."

It was not a long wait. To Anne, it was no surprise, not really, as the dog thrashed and twitched, paddling at its belly with its hind paws, whimpering out its life on the cold stone floor. Henry sat frozen.

Anne swallowed. "We may not have much time," she said. "But I would have you tell me what you know of Robert Claybrook."

Henry looked at her, this girl who poisoned a dog with the wine meant for him. Anger choked him until he could wish for nothing more than a rock to smash her skull. This girl, this black-eyed, blue-faced freak of a girl who had saved him and killed the dog, with wine from the man for whose favour he had waited all his life.

He almost reached to slap her away. It was the sight of water gathering in her eyes that stopped him. What was he to do with a creature so incomprehensible?

"I think you should tell me," Anne said. "I think—I believe we may have an enemy in common."

# Book Five

# CONQUEST

## Twenty-Eight

King Edward's health failed with a suddenness that surprised even the most ambitious of courtiers. Princess Mary was still in France, her courtship with Louis-Philippe mired in treaties and diplomacy. Prince Philip was in his chamber, attended as always by Privy Sponges, staring into space and saying little. Princess Anne had been missing all day, and nobody knew where she was. By the time she returned to the palace, unblushing and oddly silent, Edward was already lying in his bed, speech struck away from him.

As Anne sat by his bedside, ambassadors were already being assembled to make the journey across the Channel. Mary would have to come home with a husband. Philip could sit on the throne, make a suffering king, but it would not hold. Mary must come home bringing the new heir to the throne, the French king of England. Otherwise England would flounder and sink. Philip was a broken rudder, and the country needed more.

Air dragged in and out of Edward's thin body, a long pause between each breath. His arms tried to lift up, point and give directions, even though his shaking hand could not have held a pen and his dry eyes creased in puzzlement as he tried to make out the words people said to him. He was going back to the sea, back to his deepsman's blood, English a complexity beyond him, every breath a quest, a fragile body clinging to life moment to moment. He was so weak,

Anne thought, watching his thin arms fall back onto the covers. In the sea, he would have drowned.

A few weeks and Mary would bring a husband home. She was perhaps in his company right now, a stranger unable to console her. Anne found herself longing for her sister. Though matters had been tense between them, Mary had been present at every grief of Anne's life, at William's death, Erzebet's marriage, Erzebet's end. She had been older than Anne and far above her, or she had been ignorant of the truth and frustrating, but she had been there. Now she was away, and Anne felt a sense of dislocation. Without Mary there, the grief had an air of unreality, a nightmarish absence she could not quite manage.

But soon Mary would be back. And Edward would be gone, his body falling to the deepsmen below, ready for their hunger. And after them, little scraps falling to the fish below his bones floating down to the eels and scavengers of the depths. Anne saw her grandfather's hand rest brittle on the bed, the bones rising through the skin as if in anticipation of their imminent fate, and his dark-blooded veins, thick and round as worms, lay over them.

Anne could have wept for her grandfather. But she could not let him see her tears, could not let herself see them. That way lay fragility, brittle bones under parched skin, a laying down of life and waiting on a bed for the end.

This was the conversation she replayed in her mind to keep herself from crying as her kind, frail grandfather lay breathing his last:

"I think we must help one another," she had said to Henry. She had heard of a life lived on an estate, of Claybrook's patience, of a courtier who had smiled and bowed and tended to her idiot uncle, playing for control of his wayward prince, and all the while raising a bastard hidden carefully away, in case an opportunity arose to use him.

And Henry had said, in the same tone he had told her he answered to no one: "Then you must marry me."

~

Erzebet had married a creature. Anne, who had seen the bruises and the set face and the merciless commands, knew such things could be borne. And before that, Erzebet had married a man, Anne's father, a man Anne had never known. Anne sat, feeling her heavy dress press on the edges of her skin, her small body. She was not beautiful like Mary, she had little to trade in her own self, but her flesh was royal, saline and scarce, and every pound of it would be valued for the power it could bring.

When Erzebet was a child, Anne had heard, a great-uncle had been found guilty of conspiring against the Magyar throne. His brother, the king, had not been forgiving, and the prince had been executed with a hot iron crown. They said he screamed to God and his skull cracked like ice lifted in warm hands. But Mary could not do that to her if she secured herself quickly.

Anne had asked Erzebet about the story once. Her mother had given her a straight, searching look, her face showing more desire to understand Anne than willingness to let Anne understand her. And she had nodded. "He died like a coward," Erzebet said. It was a double disgrace on our name, to be a traitor and to be a coward."

Could any man bear a burning crown without screaming? Anne had wanted to ask, but she could not put such a question to her mother's implacable face. Erzebet bore a silver crown and the husband it brought with it, and she never flinched. Erzebet screamed herself to death after burning in water.

Anne wanted to know more about her mother, wanted to find letters or history, something that would tell her how it was done, to marry a frightening stranger and be a queen. But she could do it. Erzebet had done it, and so could Anne.

Anne thought of Venice, weakened from an empire to a city under the weight of its loyalty. After Angelica's time, after her children were old, the Venetians had refused all bastard alliances for centuries in aristocratic fealty to their Angelican bloodline—they had married only royals, true descendants of the Dogaressa. Cousins married cousins until the line gave way, producing such horrors that finally they had been forced to abandon their pride. The daughter of Jean le Bâtard had married a Doge a century ago, and since then, the Venetian princes had produced fewer monsters. But their empire was gone, could not be retrieved. It would be whispered abroad, she was sure, that England was going the way of Venice. Conflict with France had kept Jean's bloodline out of the English courts in the century since his usurpation. William had travelled far to find Erzebet—and if Anne and Mary had been saved from Philip's taint, it could only be because, four generations back, one of Jean's brood had married into the Magyar line. This, Anne had not been taught in her lessons, but she knew it, deep in her blood.

She could marry Henry. It would save men from the flames. It would quicken the royal line. She would not think about Mary.

≁

Anne summoned to her Thomas Wade, the master of ceremonies for visits to the sea, and told him she wished to call upon the deepsmen.

He bowed deeply, but she could see the doubt upon his face. One by one the English Delameres had been falling, first William, then Erzebet. Mary was away, and now Edward. And Philip had been struck down at birth, had cankered in the muddied waters of his mother's womb. Until Mary brought Louis-Philippe, there was no one left but little Anne. The deepsmen might desert so weak a nation.

"It shall be done," Anne said. "Let it be known." And with Edward dying, each breath weaker, there was no one to countermand the order.

Anne assembled at the shore the greatest names of the court. Thomas Wade, the master of ceremonies, a man who had presided over every shore she had visited since she was a little girl. George Narbridge, Earl of Tamar, lord of Cornwall and the white shores of the south. John Forder, the Earl of Ouse, who held most of the eastern coast, lord of East Anglia and the Wash, where the great river that gave him his title opened out into the sea, a man with too many armies at his beck. John Greenway, Earl of Severn, guardian of the west coasts, Wales and all its peninsulas and bays, and the River Wye besides; his younger brother Robert, Lord Mersey, whose lands stretched up to Lancashire. Their father had held those shores and rivers alone, inheriting domains from his wife's family as well as his own, but sickness had carried him off and the brothers had divided their land. Erzebet hadn't liked it, hadn't trusted the chances that their heirs would manage as peacefully together as they did, but she had been unable to break their father's bequest; she had revived the Earldom of Mersey for Robert by way of a boon, and had been watching for suitable wives for both their sons, some means to tie the broken coast back together. And Thomas Hakebourne, Earl of Tay, ruler of the cold shores of the North, the Humber Estuary, the Spey and the Clyde and the Tweed, a man Erzebet had called loyal unto death. Hakebourne had gone up to Scotland with Anne's father, fought armies to a standstill, thrown his life at the battlefield and emerged with Erzebet's favour. Erzebet had not quite this spelled out, but Anne was aware that Hakebourne was a third son. Erzebet's choice was a sharp one. With no estates of his own to inherit, Erzebet's favour was the only thing that stood between him and a life as a lieutenant or a monk. It had been the kind of loyalty Erzebet liked, the loyalty of gratitude. The loyalty of a man who knew how poor his other choices were. Hakebourne stood beside the water, bull-shouldered and stern-faced. Anne had heard his name in court far more than she had seen his face; mostly he had remained in Scotland, ruling with a steady, relentless hand. But he had heard her summons and he had come at once. He had bowed before her. He stood, among the other men, ready to watch Anne walk alone into the water.

And Claybrook, too, the murderer; Claybrook, Lord Thames, was there. The great house of Claybrook. He was of her court, and he would bend to her rule. Anne dismounted from her horse and made her own way to the shore, disrobing without aid, stripping off garment after rigid garment until her skin, her fragile, royal flesh, was clothed in nothing but air, cold wind wrapping round her and icy water tingling beneath her feet.

"Our great house has suffered," she said, raising her voice. "God has seen fit to test our nation with misfortunes. And we have not broken beneath their weight. We shall endure. I stand before you and speak with my grandfather's voice; I go forth into the sea bearing his blood in my veins, and that blood is the blood of England, and shall never be washed away."

"Amen," came a voice. It was Hakebourne's, and after a moment, the other men followed him. They stood, crossing themselves, and watched her stand, their prayers ready to carry her out on the tide.

Anne turned on her shaky legs, sank into the cold rocking waves, and swam out to the bay, where the deepsmen waited, where Henry waited to join her.

## Twenty-Nine

"How do you keep them with you?" Henry had wanted to know. Because Henry had lived in the deeps, had swum with the tribe until it cast him out. It wasn't his strangeness, he understood now, that had driven his mother to carry him through the waves and shove him up on a beach to die. It had been his weakness. He wasn't as fast as a deepsman child, he was small, cloven, narrow-lunged, a weight that was slowing her down. And with a sea full of sharks, of dolphins, of whales and currents and easy chances to die, who would keep a burden with them? Who wanted someone you had to save, over and over again?

He had never been allowed to see the ships, had never been taken to meet the kings. But he knew that this weak girl would have no way to impress the deepsmen, no strength to show. All she had was a need to be saved. So: "How do you keep them with you?"

Anne made a gesture. Henry had never known a girl, had lived a lifetime of lonely flesh, but he understood it. John had said there were landsmen women who traded their bodies for money, and though money was something Henry had never handled, he recognised the concept. Even in the sea, a woman struggling to keep up, a woman unable to fight the other women, might dance her way through the water to a stronger man, trade quick hands for a strong arm to defend her. Once or twice, when he was a baby, he had seen his mother do the same thing for men who threatened him. She had protected him, until she tired of it. When John had told him landswomen did likewise, his main emotion had been frustration that John couldn't bring him one, but smuggling foxes was one thing, smuggling women who could tell others what they had seen was another, and you couldn't hunt a woman from horseback. Secrecy meant celibacy, little though he might like it. He hadn't thought of his mother, back then.

Her face was impassive, and Henry studied it. This was the condition of a weakling, a ragged loser struggling for scraps. He would have thought, given that she was reduced so far, she might be less haughty in her demeanour. But something inside him twitched as she moved her hands.

"Would you do the same for me?" he said. The girl was ugly, he thought, but the question was there before he considered it. Whether it was a request, a question, even a political question—she was bartering her alliance, after all—he didn't think. He asked, and having asked, found he truly wanted to know her answer.

The girl stiffened, her body growing still within her clothes. It was a second before she spoke. "Go out to the bay with me, bring the deepsmen around, come back to land with the deepsmen behind you, and marry me to secure our claim," she said. Her voice was low, but she spoke steadily. "When you have done that, I will do anything you wish."

Henry thought of the throne, safety, the girl's hands. She was a quarry, a prize. For that, he would go in the sea again.

Henry knew he would have to stake his claim to the throne out in the bay. He did not say to Anne that he had not seen a deepsman, had not spoken to one, had not been in the water since he was five years old.

≺

Anne went down to the sea escorted by nobles. Henry went to the sea alone, hours in advance of her, slipping through the field with his face covered. Westlake knew of it, but neither of them, not even Henry, told John.

"What did you mean to do, riding around alone?" Anne asked Henry. "Did you think you would come and kill us all by yourself?"

"No." Henry heard no anger in her voice as she asked the question. "I only meant to come out of the sea, make myself known. It worked for Angelica, and you cannot tell me she was born speaking Italian. She must have hidden somewhere until she knew the time was right." He thought of that picture, the flat image of a graceful woman that had hung over him in childhood. "I thought it might be my time."

When Anne thought of Angelica, she could only see Erzebet, but she was learning to respect strategy. "You know," she said, "that was not a bad idea."

Henry slid easily off his horse as he reached the beach. The journey over the sands was not difficult: a simple crawl on all fours, nobody watching, a slow but secure progress across the cold grit and strewn pebbles. It was only when he reached the water that he stopped.

For eleven years, Henry had seen the water in his dreams, remembered it, thought of it, judged the world by its standards. But he had never in his life entered the sea. He had been born into its pushing waters, had swum through it, a grey expanse where light carried only a few feet but sound carried hundreds of miles, a place with forests and mountains you could fly over, a weightless infinity where every direction was possible and freedom to move never came up against a solid surface. He hadn't known there was another kind of world. Now he was returning to it, entering it like a landsman, ready to take off his shoes and wade in, upright, walking on his legs.

Henry was frightened of the deepsmen. He saw that now, clear and stark, sitting on the damp sand with the waves hissing at him a few feet away. He always had been. His mother had been the solid thing in a fluid world, had dragged him by his hair out of the path of many dangers, and he had been frightened of her. Five years following a woman, struggling in her wake, bleating to keep up. He was weak, had always been weak. He could wrestle a landsman down, but landsmen had kept him prisoner nonetheless, had locked him up and trapped him like a fox the moment he tried to ride out for himself.

A tide of panic overwhelmed him. What was he doing? Taking

the word of some girl that he could follow in her wake? Sacrificing himself like a soldier for a princeling whose mother would have burned him alive? John wasn't here to make him laugh, there were no studious men to take notes or make explanations, there were no women here, proffering comforts they would never provide. He was alone. He recognised the feeling, understood it. It was honest, clean, real. No more lies: he was by the sea, and he was frightened.

Henry reached out a tentative hand to touch the water. The wet sand bucked and glistened as he pressed down upon it, bouncing back into shape as he removed his palm. Then a fizzing spray of water rushed towards him, slapping against his outstretched feet. Had the sea always been this rough? He had known it was, had told himself often enough, but his body had forgotten.

Behind him lay the land, armies and stakes and executioners. Before him the sea, with its harsh giants and tearing teeth. Henry gave a quiet, bitter laugh; caught between fire and water, that was him. It was a division he'd heard landsmen make, fire and water, but it had never made sense to him—nothing could live in fire—until now.

Given the choice, it had to be water. But he was not going to crawl in like some landsman.

His clothes had been a nuisance to him all his life, and Henry peeled them off without regret. There was a line of rocks around the edge of the bay, and above them, a cliff. It was a difficult climb, but once he'd started, he found he could keep going. Clambering had always been easier than walking. Even as the rocks pressed into his legs and hands, Henry felt his spirits lift. He could see a long way from up here. He'd never seen the sea from above. From below, its gleaming ragged roof was a bright, permeable heaven, but from this height, the waves looked solid, iron-dark and heaving with dense, sharp-tipped waves. From above, you'd think a diver would shatter on its surface.

Henry turned on the cliff and braced himself. He was going to fly down like a gull. There was going to be a moment, an instant in his life where he forsook the ground and swam through the air.

He let go of his perch and dived. There was a wild, flashing moment of absolute freedom, and then the water crashed around him.

Cold. Pressure. The light over his head. Henry looked around him disorientated. He had struggled for years to learn how to use his eyes: now, faced with the thick, translucent darkness, light melting into obscurity almost within the reach of his hands, his first instinct was to swim back to the surface and look around. Accustomed to breathing in and out, constantly squandering air like a landsman, Henry found his chest clamping, flexing inwards as he forced himself to keep his throat closed. And the *weight* of it: wherever he moved his limbs, water smothered round, pushing against him, blocking his path. He had thought he could float, chase along easily, but he was swimming against a path that resisted his every movement. This was *exhausting*.

Henry closed his eyes and went limp, letting himself tumble through the restless water. This was the dreamland of his childhood, the unthinking dive and sway and bitter-salt purposefulness of a deepsman's life. He had remembered it for so long; he couldn't now, all of a sudden, be afraid of the dark in the place he had always thought of as home.

As the cold clasped his skin, Henry thought about opening his mouth and inhaling. Forget about the girl on land with her wild promises and alien loyalties, forget about taking the throne to lord it over a people he'd never met and never cared for, forget it all. It would come to death in the end, one way or another, a fire or a sword or a shark's maw. Why not get it over with? At least if he was dead, he could stop fearing the end.

It was fear that kept his mouth closed. Henry rolled over in the water, and as he drifted, he could feel his muscles locking down, knotting themselves around his ribs. It was familiar. That was how it had felt in the sea. A tense chest and guarded heart and fear wrapping round you like an octopus, warning you, guiding you, saying to you every moment: *Take care, watch out. This will not last, but just at this moment, as long as you can keep it, you are alive.*

Henry smiled. He didn't have a place, but this, this was him. This was what he remembered, land or sea: the instant-to-instant watch and weigh of a cautious animal, hazarding and husbanding and spending its life as wisely as it could, balancing itself over the precipice and managing, instant to instant, not to fall.

He could do this. He could remember this. The deepsmen would be coming; Anne was going to call them. They would be big, and they would be aggressive: it would be difficult. But nothing was easy. And after all, Henry thought, after all these years, it would be satisfying to have something to fight.

# Thirty

Henry did not hear the deepsmen as they approached, nor the sound of Anne as she entered the water. The waves clattered over his head, and he floated in silence, listening. But he heard the sounds from the beach, the weird, creaking music the landsmen were playing to summon them. He lay, drifting on the waves, and waited.

~

Anne swam out to sea, the current brushing over her like a caress. The peace of solitude was such a relief that for a few minutes, she simply swam, slow and steady, rolling over to feel the water stroking her skin. The deepsmen were starting to call for her, but she held off answering. It was time to call Henry. Anne gathered herself, slipped up to the surface for a breath, and called. She did not answer the deepsmen's signals: *We are here, where are you?* She gazed into the blackening gleam, and called, clear and steady: *Whistle. Come here. Whistle.*

She knew the currents in this bay, and she was accustomed to swimming. Following the deepsmen's voices, she reached them before him.

Out of the haze they loomed, long-bodied and great-armed, suddenly more alarming than she'd expected. Erzebet's iron will had kept her strong, and she'd bartered all she had to keep them friendly, but here, confronted with their massive bodies, Anne realised something, grasped it with her eyes and body instead of just her understanding:

these deepsmen were huge. Henry was small. She'd only seen him crouched down, chained and hunched, but she had weighed him up. Everything looked larger under water; Anne had assumed that in the sea, Henry would be magnified to a deepsman's bulk. Now she saw her mistake. He was bigger than her, but that was no great boast: everyone was bigger than her. She'd been weighing him up against Samuel, against John Claybrook. Henry would be more than a match for them; shorter, yes, because of how his legs bent under him, but he had a deepsman's great chest and arms, thick with muscle and heavyset. He could have grappled any landsman in an instant. But he couldn't grapple these men. Henry might be sturdy against courtiers, but he carried a landsman's blood in him too, and no landsman was as brawny as these people of the ocean. Against these deepsmen, he was a mouse confronting rats, a cat against dogs. He was outmatched.

Anne curled in the water, twisting and coiling to keep their attention on her. She couldn't say it now, not while the deepsmen were before her, but she called in her mind: *Whistle, come here. Prove me wrong. Help me.*

No one had seen him enter the water, she thought. If he lost, no one would come to help him. Erzebet wouldn't have laughed, wouldn't have found it funny—but she would have realised in advance what struck Anne now: at least it would solve the problem of what to do about him. She could placate them again, let whoever fought him claim her as a winner's prize. Her throat burned with bile at the thought, and she swallowed, taking a sip of sharp brine to calm herself. She would live. She would survive. But if Henry failed now, he would die in the water, and she couldn't help him. Louis-Philippe would take the throne with Mary, and Henry's body would wash away. No one would ever know he had lived.

~

Anne's voice had echoed across the water, calling: *Whistle.* Henry did not take the time to be surprised at the long-lost name. He was home; he was ready. There were voices mingling with hers, and all of them were different. After the unfamiliarity of the water, he understood them, the pitch and timbre, all different, all speaking together. He did not recognise any of them; their dialect was unfamiliar. He did not know this tribe.

It didn't matter. He was going to make it his own.

~

Anne danced, and waited. Hands were reaching towards her, ghostly pale in the darkness. As she slipped out of their reach, a cloud passed away from the sun, and a streak of light struck down through the water, silver pale, salt glittering in its beam. It was beautiful. The brightness of it struck her hard: this glinting moment, ready to pass, easy to snatch away. She was alive.

Hands reached out again, a large palm folding around her narrow wrist. A peremptory rattle of sounds: *Come on.* This was the deepsman she had humoured before. Her fingertips tingled as his hand squeezed around her forearm, a memory of rough, slick flesh. Anne tugged back, but there was no way out of his grasp. She had to do something, now, at once. He could drag her down. His lungs were massive, his body immense, and there was no way she could outlast him. She needed air, needed to move before she drowned.

*Whistle,* she cried again. She was not drowning, she wasn't: she had air enough. She was just breathless at the sudden grab. She could last. *Whistle, hurry.* Where was he? Silence yawned around her, stretching in every direction, and for a long, choking moment, there was only an arm pulling her forward and the rustle of the sea.

Then a voice out of the void: *I am coming. This is mine. I am coming.*

And Anne kicked back, striking out with her sharp-clawed feet, and fought her way free. It wasn't much of a blow, not by the standards of the deep, but it was fast and sudden and she gouged her nails against the coarse skin of her captor, her suitor, her subject—she ground in her nails and the man holding her arm let her go.

And the voice sounded again: *I am here. This is mine. Do not trifle with me.*

It was coming from the other direction, Anne realised. Instinctively she turned her head, but the deepsmen, used to the blindness of the water, made no such movement. Instead they gathered together, swimming back to back in a coiling spiral, a great long column that sank a whirling shaft into the depths like the pillar of a cathedral, a sleek, turning regiment of bodies shining white against the black in a single ray of light. It was a fighting stance, one that she recognised with a foolish stab of loneliness: backs to each other, united in trust, in motion and watching for whatever threat might come, ready to face it together. Her bastard was coming, and they had banded. She was making them unite. This was how much she needed this.

The sound continued, around and around. He was doing something Anne had never seen: circling, out of sight, calling as he swam. It couldn't possibly work as a flanking movement, not when they outnumbered him: all they had to do was split up and follow the sound, and they could lay hands on him easily. But his voice echoed out of obscurity, and the deepsmen gathered together, waiting.

Henry swam in a spiral, yelling out his claim. This was a hunt, a chase. He had seen his family do it a hundred times: surround the fish, circle them, drive them into a ball. When the threat could be coming from any direction, you massed ranks and kept on the move and hoped for the best. The deepsmen did it to fish, but they did not do it to each other. That was why it was the right thing to do now. The deepsmen were a frightened people. If something was new, they would not take the risk of attack. Hide and circle, watch and wait: he knew how to do this. Now it was time to come out of the dark.

Anne swam backwards, keeping in sight of the deepsmen. *Whistle,* she called.

A voice answered her: *I am here.* And a body swam out of the depths.

It was Henry, Whistle, gleaming in the grey light. Anne had seen women naked, deepsmen, but the sight of him darting past her unclothed gave her a moment of alarm before she pulled herself together. He was circling, following the path of the waiting deepsmen, and he called to her: *Which? Who is in charge?*

Anne pointed her arm and bounced her voice forward, driving the sound towards the great-armed titan who had grasped her wrist. *That one,* she said. *I do not want him.* Her arm tingled in the cold, and she cried out again, loud enough to echo off the shore: *I do not want him!*

The deepsman changed his path, rising up the centre of the spiral like the eye of a whirlpool, his tribe swimming round him. *Who are you?* he said. *Do not trifle with me.*

Henry swam out beside Anne, pausing in the water. He hung very still, and his arm came around her. Rough skin brushed her waist as he pushed her behind him. *Mine,* he said, taking up as bold a pose as he could strike. *I will fight you for her.*

The deepsman raised his arms, thrashed his great tail. The force of it swept a current forward that rocked Anne where she floated, and she thrust her arms out, paddling frantically to stay upright. *Do not trifle with me,* the great voice groaned out. *I am strong.*

Henry did not look away. *Challenge,* he called back. *I will fight you for her. Mine.*

~

The man was immense, Henry saw, half as long again as him. This was something he would never survive, not if it came to a clash of tails, the wave-shattering smack of bone against bone. He couldn't kill him. If he was going to bid for the throne, he had to subdue this tribe, not destroy it. The deepsman towered before Henry, and fury twisted in Henry's throat: he was a stranger, small, fighting alone. He tasted crab meat in his mouth. *Just let this girl look away,* he said in his mind, *and I will eat your tongue.*

He couldn't outswim this tribesman. If he had stayed in the sea, he would have been his subject, always, inescapably, until he died. But he was not going to be the subject of any man, ever again.

He dived down, and the great arms reached to grab him.

❧

Anne's throat closed as she saw Henry swim forwards. The deepsman reached out and took hold of him, and the water heaved around them as the great tail swept out again. Whistle was small against him, a boy against a man, but the tail did not connect: Henry had parted his legs, let the wave sweep between them. He did not call, did not look. He lunged back, and the arms gripping his shoulders pulled at him.

The cold of the water bit into her skin, and Anne watched, her heart pounding in her throat. Henry could not get himself out of the deepsman's grip. The tail struck out, and the water rocked; Anne tumbled over, somersaulting to steady herself. Everything around them was tossed as if by a storm, and Henry was struggling, pulling himself back, the massive hands digging into his shoulders. His legs were snaking to and fro, twisting like banners in a high wind, but he couldn't avoid it for ever: the deepsman had him, and he was going to break his legs.

Teeth shut, Anne looked, and in the gloom, saw something she hadn't seen before, so fast had Henry flown by. There was a dark band around his waist.

He hadn't told her about it, hadn't warned her. He didn't trust her. But he had thought ahead, and he was hers, and she was going to help him.

Anne drove herself straight up, broke the surface and snatched a mouthful of air. For a brief second, the thin sounds of the land cut through the air, and then she was underwater again, swimming down to join the fight.

❧

As the girl flickered at the corner of his vision, Henry's first thought was, *No, stay out.* Deepsmen had little time for chivalry, but a dominance match was a one-on-one issue; if she joined in, then the tribe would too, and they would both die. The two of them couldn't fight them all.

But then he felt hands tugging at his waist, unknotting, and his rope, the rope he had carried with him across the bay, was being looped, ready for him to use.

Henry sprang back again, reached out and grabbed, and the rope was in his hands. The deepsman kept hold of his shoulders, and Henry braced himself, feet against the deepsman's chest. That was all he needed, a little purchase.

And, with his arms outstretched before him, the deepsman's wrists were level. Henry reached out, and wound the cords, and pulled them fast. *There,* he thought as he tugged on the knot. *See how you like that.*

The deepsman let go, suddenly grappling with himself. Henry floated above him for a moment. The sea was movement, endless and unconstrained, and if you couldn't swim, you drowned. Rope could be gnawed through eventually, Henry had learned in those first painful months as a captive in Allard's hideaway—but the sickening dismay of constriction, the panic and horror it induced, was something he had never forgotten. Even with a lungful of air, this tribesman could not think.

He was confined. He had lost.

Henry flicked himself downwards and grabbed the tribesman's legs, pulling him down into the dark. *Mine,* he said. *Yield. Yield to me. Yield.*

And, kicking and thrashing in the blue abyss, he heard the reply: *I yield.*

*The tribe,* Henry said. *Everyone yield.*

The beaten deepsman's voice carried upwards, and he heard it, crackling all around him: voices, each of them blending to the same final, blazing, longed-for, hard-won answer. *We yield. You are the king. We yield.*

The girl's voice echoed from above him, a shriek of triumph: *Us! Us! Ours!*

Henry bent his head to gnaw the deepsman free. The taste of salt filled his mouth.

~

So it was that Anne, Princess of England, walked naked out of the sea, and beside her walked a young man no one had ever seen before, a straight-spined young man balancing on his curved legs. He stood with his back steady, unbowed by a prince's hunch, but his eyes were black to the edges and his teeth were sharp, his hands webbed across, and in his hand he held a lock of hair, pulled from the skull of a deepsman out in the bay.

Henry looked across a beachful of people, ornately dressed old men, long-legged young ones, a profusion of horses stamping at his presence. He had not seen so many landsmen at once since he had watched his brother burn. A spasm of shyness gripped his throat, and for a moment he could not speak. Then his fingers tightened on the lock he had torn from his beaten adversary, and he raised it aloft.

"I have heard how your country fares ill against the French," he said. Anne had told him to mention France, to say nothing of himself. "They will not come to you now. I have taken this from the king of the deepsmen as token of his fealty, and I come now for yours." They were courtier words, liar's words; Anne had made him memorise them. She thought a speech was in order.

A man stepped forward, a man with a grey face and white hair. "Who do you come from?" he said. "Whose bastard are you?"

"Lord Wade, please." Anne's voice wasn't conciliatory; it was sharp.

There had been more to the speech, but Henry decided against it. He looked the man in the eyes. "Do you want a French king?" he said. "I have come from the sea, and I have beaten the deepsmen. They will do what I say. So will you. Give me a horse: my legs are tired from standing."

It was a long moment that passed, and then a man came forward. Samuel Westlake, Henry saw. He leaned his weight against the horse as he approached, and then handed the reins over. Henry took them, and mounted up.

# Book Six

# TROTH

## THIRTY-ONE

ANNE SAT ALONE in the chapel, her hands clasped. She couldn't kneel, but she was praying. Samuel had explained to her that it wasn't royal privilege not to kneel before God, but a consideration for a prince's weak legs; that no prince should ever consider himself too high to kneel, in spirit, before the Creator.

Anne hadn't argued with him, but it hadn't seemed relevant to her. Samuel was interested in theology. God, to Anne, was both infinite and simple: to pray was to be cradled in light. She reached out within herself now, tried to relax, open her soul, feel the blessings of God around her. When she prayed best, she could vibrate with the sacred, feel the atmosphere coil and hum with blessings, Holy Presence in every drop of air, every fibre of herself, her own body and the bench under her and the stone beneath her feet ringing with divinely omnipresent as salt in the sea. Christ had said to man, *You are the salt of the earth,* and Anne had listened. When she prayed, she could taste it: God, the flavour of every thread and scrap of the world.

What she prayed for was blessings upon her marriage. That had been quickly arranged; Henry could be crowned as her husband, she had declared herself intent, and who was to stop it? There had been some talk of getting Philip's consent, some notional royal blessing, but Henry had stopped that: when one man wanted a woman in the sea, he said, and another man tried to stop him, they fought for her. Did Philip wish to fight? He said it dryly, and several people laughed, as if he was making a joke. It could have been a joke, a reference to Philip's infirmity, his unfitness to fight being his unfitness to rule. They thought it meant a resolute and witty king. In that moment Anne understood just how much everyone disliked her uncle.

Anne didn't think it was a joke, though. She was not sure if she should be afraid of Henry.

But marrying him was the only option, and it might be a good one. She could have sons, lots of sons, a shoal of them to lead out to the delights of water, to help her guard the shores. The idea of childbirth seemed inconceivable in this moment, procreation unreal, but she reached out to God, asking for strength. In this moment, she was safe in the arms of the Lord; what would follow, would follow. And whatever became of her, it could not be a worse death than shrieking in bloody sheets, skin boiled from her body. She would marry Henry, and God would support her.

Anne sat in the chapel and prayed. She could find no form of words appropriate to the situation, but God would forgive her for that. God forgave. There was infinite mercy in Heaven; this she believed. There had to be, when there was so little mercy on earth.

Anne opened herself to God, and felt God around her. The living heart of the world beat within her chest.

～

Henry was surrounded by men he didn't know. They had escorted him to a palace, a stone building broader and higher than any he'd ever seen before, with buildings and buildings around it. This was London: no estate, but a reef of landsmen, wood and stone, thickets of people and dwellings. The city made him nervous; there were too many obstacles, blind spots on every side. There was no way to know what would approach.

Seated at a table, uncomfortably swathed in rich clothing too narrow around his chest that some servant had brought from a royal wardrobe—Robert Stone, he had asked the man's name, told him the clothes were too tight, made him promise to find or make new ones, noted his name and the speed with which the man bowed and retreated—Henry was talking to too many people. The men from the beach. Anne had said they were important men, they controlled the land on the coasts, and the rivers. Claybrook was among them; Henry could barely look at him, so choked with anger did he feel. But Claybrook's land included most of the Thames, Anne said. The great river that led out to the east sea. Ridiculously, she even addressed him as "Lord Thames." Until they could bring him down, he was a man of consequence.

He looked around the table, trying to weigh these men up. Lord Wade, the man who had spoken to him on the beach, he had decided against; the man was sharp, but not sharp enough. He had the wit to know he must be a bastard, but not the wit to hold his tongue until he knew what to make of Henry. The man had spoken to him, demanded to know whose bastard he was, as if he was somebody's horse. Henry intended to be king, and was quite prepared to fight for it. He had seen deepsmen in the sea circle each other and pose, striking the water to show their strength. But only a stupid man would posture at an opponent he couldn't beat.

The others? He weighed up their stances, trying to get a sense of them. Samuel Westlake sat silent at the end, his eyes flitting around the group. They all seemed to have multiple names, a quirk Henry felt he could soon tire of. He had accepted as a child that landsmen tended to have two names, one for themselves and one for their family. It made a certain amount of sense; deepsmen didn't have family names, but you could refer to other tribes by naming their usual haunts. Landsmen's names were more random, but he'd grown used to it. Now, it seemed, landsmen *did* sometimes name themselves for their territory—but, insanely, only one man per territory got to do so. There were even two brothers in the room—Greenway, Anne had said— who he was expected to address by different names. Henry was entirely unwilling: the custom was stupid, and more than that, offended him. Why should he address one Greenway man as Severn and the other as Mersey, but none of their families, none of the people who lived by Severn or Mersey waters? No man was a river, or owned a river: land and water were where you lived, not what you were, and it was arrogant to claim a whole rushing body of water for your own. Henry had every intention of ruling England, but that did not make him England, and if he wasn't doing it, he didn't see why his subjects should. He was not about to give Robert Claybrook any more titles, that was for sure. It struck Henry, thinking about it, that Allard had never called Claybrook "Lord Thames," or not in his hearing. But everyone else did, to Claybrook's face. Claybrook must have been very determined to keep him ignorant of his location.

The whole business was angering, and Henry had stuck to addressing the men by their actual names. He could see it causing a flicker of insult every time he did it, but they could just put up with it. If they didn't like it but did not protest, it was a secure sign of his dominance.

There was a man from the west, of Wales, called Forder, a man seeming too large in his clothes, restless and watchful, as if ready to charge at any moment. The Greenway brothers disturbed him a little: they looked to each other more than to anyone else. For a moment, Henry's heart twitched; then he gathered himself. If they could be loyal to each other, they could be loyal to him, if he could persuade them. Do well by each, and the other would follow. Anne had said their best chance was the largest man, a man called Hakebourne. Henry studied him: big, still, watchful. Not making a judgement, holding his nerve. He could use such a man.

There was another man at the table. Narbridge. Lord of Cornwall. It had been in Cornwall his brother was found. This was the man, this tall, loose-limbed man in fine garments, who had handed his brother over to the queen. The man was bright-eyed and alert, paying attention to all in the room, but Henry was having none of him. Anne said he was loyal, but Henry did not wish to know. The man was a burner of bastards, and soon, when he had the crown on his head, Henry and he were going to have a reckoning.

"What is your position on France, my lord?" the man called Forder was saying. He was leaning forward, his shoulders taking up too much room, blocking the other men's lines of sight. His restlessness was rattling Henry; restless men were either skittish and untrustworthy or aware of some danger coming in, and either way Henry didn't like it.

"What is France's position on us?" Henry said. The question had been toned like a trap, as if Forder knew the answer and was waiting to see if Henry got it right.

"Well, my lord, Prince Louis-Philippe has been expecting to take the throne as consort to Princess Mary," Forder said. He had an air of impatience, and Henry cut him off.

"This I know," he said. "If France will keep to their shores, we will have peace with them. It is their choice. Louis-Philippe will not be king. It is for them to decide if they wish to fight it out. That is what I mean. Is there more to your question, Forder?"

The man bristled at the sound of his name, but Henry was not going to concede.

"Will you send ambassadors?" Forder persevered, his tone becoming dryer.

*Ambassadors* was a word Henry had heard, but he had never seen one. You sent men to speak for you. When they were out of your sight, when you couldn't correct them, could you trust them to say what you would say? Henry had never seen a landsman speak with the bluntness he required. He could send a letter, perhaps, except he couldn't write.

The new clothes gripped Henry's chest. He was too hot. "That will be to discuss with the queen my wife," he said. He didn't like this juggling. Maybe Anne would understand it.

"My lord Prince," said another voice. Hakebourne, the man Anne said she liked. "It is for us to support our God-sent king. We have been granted an Englishman to rule us, and we shall defend God's gift."

There were some nods from around the table—the brothers, the two men whose faces were alike, even more so than most landsmen's.

"God-sent?" Henry said. Nobody had sent him, nobody but Anne. The word *God* was two crossed sticks, the strange object that Allard had brandished at him, a nasty piece of wood that Allard seemed unaccountably fond of. There were too many unfamiliar things in this conversation already: France, marriage, God. He almost said, *I came myself, not because I was sent. I came on my own, and it was hard work to come.* He stopped himself. The man's words were strange, but he seemed to be offering support. "Your loyalty is noticed," Henry said. "That is good."

Claybrook sat and watched, and said nothing.

"How soon do you wish the marriage, my lord Prince?" Hakebourne said.

"Soon," Henry replied. "We must move quickly, yes?" The idea of marriage itself was still a curious one. Anne had fought beside him: she had said she would do anything he wished. They had taken the same side, made a side between the two of them. Exactly what some word, some dance that involved walking into a stone building and answering questions put by some person who had to obey them anyway would do to make that alliance any faster was beyond him. It was an inconvenience. He had always known landsmen had a passion for objects. Now it seemed they had a passion for forms of words as well, things of language as well as things of wood and metal.

It was tiresome and confusing. But they wouldn't let him be alone with Anne. He had seen her white flesh gleam through the blue water, had seen every inch of her shimmer in the waving light, had seen the drops of brine run from the tips of her hair down her body as they walked on shore, globes of water hanging from the lobes of her ears, glistening in collar-bone, gilding her breasts. Though he had not, since childhood, had his hands on a woman, he wanted his hands on Anne. The girl had agreed to him, chosen him; she was his, and the landsmen were keeping her away for reasons that made no sense. If it were one man, he could have fought him; he had fought a deepsman for her already, and could fight again. But against this barrier of words, this landsman idea that they all seemed to hold, there was nothing he could do except go through the form. It would work, but he didn't like having to do it.

*When I am king, we shall speak plain,* Henry said to himself. *And there shall be no more tangles of words.*

≈

Anne had wanted to tell her grandfather she was getting married. Edward lay clinging to life like a filament of seaweed wearing away, waving in the water, down to its last thread. He could no longer move his arms, but he could still whisper. Anne wanted to ask his blessing, to speak to him at least; this last link to her family's past.

Nobody else thought it was a good idea. Henry had shrugged, saying she could if she wished but it made little difference to him. Anne had found herself facing a roomful of courtiers all trying their best to dispute her out of it. Their reasons had been various, mostly to do with troubling a dying old man.

Less than a week ago, they would have hung over his bed, ready to pump answers from his wheezing lungs. But that was before Henry had arrived.

Anne looked at Hakebourne, who had said nothing. "What say you, my lord Tay?"

Hakebourne weighed the moment for a second before answering. "We follow you, your Majesty," he said. It was a careful answer, succinct, blandly loyal. There was just the slightest emphasis on the *you*.

Anne understood again the desperation that had been driving everyone she knew. If Edward were to refuse his consent, that would leave no king but Philip. Anne had been afraid of Philip, his hard-nailed fingers and clutching paws, his booming voice and lashing arms, but the speed with which he had been sidelined unsettled her.

There was Mary, of course, and her husband. England might have accepted a Frenchman on the throne when there was no alternative, but now it would fight. Anne was trying not to think of Mary, not to imagine her sister's face. But as the men around the room turned to her and spoke of following her, as if Mary had never existed, she was starting to wonder what she had done.

"Your Majesty," Samuel said. Even as she thought of her family, Anne noticed the change of address. "His Majesty's thoughts should be on Heaven now. If you were to pray with him, you would do him better service."

Anne's eyes stung. They were talking in public, but it was not like

Samuel to so mince his words. Even Samuel thought that the chance of Edward's refusal, the chance that he might cling, in the end, to his own son rather than to some strange boy come out of the sea to depose him, was not worth the risk.

Even if he did refuse his consent, Anne thought, nobody would listen. It would sigh out in a whisper, and every man in the room would suddenly find his ears had dulled. Could anybody make out what his Majesty had just said? They would fear not; alas, it was impossible to discern.

Henry had walked out of the sea, and England had slipped from her grandfather's weakened fingers. A bastard who should, by law, have burned—and now a week later, everyone in the world would side with him against their king. That was how fast the world could change.

"I shall pray with him," Anne said, her voice shaking. "I am sure he will take our prayers to Heaven with him."

She did not tell Edward she was getting married. She sat on his bed and held his hand, whispering prayers to the Virgin. His fingers were so frail, the webs between them so dry, that she half expected them to crumble in her grip. She sat with him and prayed, offering him nothing but her company. Anne did not want his last moment on earth to be the sight of his loyal subjects turning away from him, deafening their ears to his speech.

～

After that, it was only a few short days before Henry and Anne found themselves preparing to go into the cathedral and swear marriage.

Anne was attended by maids, trussed into a jewelled dress. Not since her mother's wedding had she had such finery plated over her skin, and the thought made her heart shiver. Philip, grabbing at her mother's body, yelling over the music, *Mine! Mine!*

Philip was not to be at the wedding. She had thought he would, had assumed Samuel would be at his side, calming him, trying to keep him from shouting about wives and clutching at the nearest woman, but Henry had refused. "If the man will make trouble, leave him else-where," he said. "He will not be king; who will object?"

And Henry was right. Edward had nothing to say about the mar-riage, because nothing had been said to him. Philip could barely speak. Mary was overseas, not to be informed until the marriage had taken place. Anne had a foolish wish to write to her, to tell her the news, to have Mary be part of this great change as she had been part of so many others, but she pressed it back. She had taken the decision when she chose to save Henry. There was no way back, she could only go for-ward, and it would destroy her to repine. Was it wrong to marry without her family, to cut at a stroke every last tie she had? She could think of no other alternative; the country seemed to wish it. After the first moment of shock when she walked onto the beach with Henry, it was alarming how quickly everyone had taken to the idea of their new king. Anne was there to tether him to England, she thought, this flot-sam washed up on their shore. Moor him to the dock before the chance was swept away. But what seemed to be sweeping away instead was the Delameres, carried away on the current, sinking out of sight. She was the last of her kind. If she had not been there to legitimise Henry's claim to the throne, or if she had not been willing, would she be here now, caked in pearls? Or would she too be drifting out to sea, cut loose from her country?

Erzebet would have blessed the marriage, Anne thought. She would have let Heaven take care of Heaven, and turned her will back to England. Anne had prayed to the Virgin, thought of her mother. But somehow it was hard to pray and think of Erzebet at the same time. That still, grim, fierce-eyed face was a shadow in the glow. It was easy to say decades for Erzebet's soul, but that resolution, that wolfish, headlong passion to live, that tension and courage and stiff-backed self-sacrifice that Erzebet had shown in every memory of Anne's life . . . Perhaps Jesus had looked so on the cross, Anne thought. But then again, perhaps not. Jesus would not have looked so angry. And the mother of God had never worn so hard a glare in any icon Anne had ever seen. Erzebet would not have wept at the foot of the cross. She would not have let her children be sacrificed.

Her mother wanted her to live, Anne reminded herself. God would take her; God took souls up to Heaven. And Erzebet had understood, as nobody else had, the vital importance, in a prince, of practicality. Her mother's spectral blessing was all she could take down the aisle. As she climbed into her litter to be carried up to the altar, Anne gazed ahead, her face still, grasping after God in her heart. That heart was beating in fear and doubt, but God would protect her. Erzebet would have done it. Anne was going to marry Henry and secure the crown of England, and there was an end on it.

～

Henry sat before the altar, waiting for Anne to be carried up to him. This church was a building he had little liking for. The ceiling was curved, columns rising on all sides; larger than the rooms of his childhood, it was at least spacious. But the windows were coloured glass, blue and green, impossible to see through. It was a cave, this room, a cave with a concealed entrance; though he was too old for such delusions, he still found himself short of breath, as if frightened he would run out of air because he couldn't see the sky. Rows of landsmen stared at him; making him uncomfortable. The urge to tell them all to do something was strong; if he could command them, then their stares would be fair enough, but he was expected to stay quiet in this stupid place because of this stupid ceremony. This, Henry decided, was the last time he would go through such a ritual.

The cross on the wall was getting on his nerves. A great looming anchor of a thing, its rigid angles casting a shadow behind it, with a grotesque corpse-statue pinned to it; Henry was uncomfortable being too near it. The corpse was only painted wood, but it still seemed corrupting to him, unclean. Here on the land, meat rotted quickly and lay where you left it. It was dirty to leave bodies lying around.

Musicians were playing all around him. He remembered such sounds from the day of the burning. If he strained to hear, he could pick out some vague echoes, like a voice speaking through cloth, but the words were nonsense. John had said, so long ago, that the music was supposed to speak of good news, of love, of majesty. All he could pick up were random phrases: *There's good eating here; Do you want to fuck?; Do what I say.* If you talked to the landsmen face to face they seemed capable of reason, but put them in charge of things, of objects and language and sounds and they became idiots.

He wished he could talk to John.

~

Anne settled at the altar, prepared herself for the ceremony. She wished that Samuel could have conducted it, but the Archbishop of Stour, Summerscales, held precedence. *When I am Queen,* Anne thought, *I will see to it that Samuel is the next Archbishop.*

Music played around them, speaking of love and good fortune. Though she had little faith left in the musicians, knew by now how difficult it was to bend the deepsmen's language to court formalities, she still wondered whether she was right to hope. Perhaps life would go forward from here. With sons, England would no longer be gasping air in a sealed cave. Perhaps Henry would love her.

What she felt for Henry, she did not ask herself. He was a chance, a knife to slice through a tangle of weeds. Anne lowered her head in prayer, reached out for the love of God, asked him to sustain her. She could do this.

~

The girl beside him was spattered with jewels, so many it looked as if she'd rolled in them. Her body was invisible in the garments, her bowed legs encased in an ornate skirt, her arms crusted in silver thread, her chest plated in fabric; even her hair was bridled and haltered in jewels. It struck Henry that after today, he could take her off into a room alone and pull the clothes away.

Everything about Anne suddenly seemed overwhelmingly female: the high pitch of her voice, the littleness of her hands, the small body and soft face and strange, plaintive expressions. What was he supposed to do with a woman? When he had first seen a landswoman, Allard's wife, he could think of nothing to do but scratch her face. She hadn't liked it, but he'd had no other ideas. Now, when he had an idea, what to do with this girl? The tears that had so intrigued him with Mistress Allard now felt like a threat, a demand for something he couldn't supply. Even armoured as she was, the girl seemed maddeningly, gallingly desirable—but that face of hers showed no expression, she kept closing her eyes and moving her lips for no reason he could make out, and, torn between watching the lips move and fretting at the pointlessness of someone speaking to themselves, he found himself growing angry with her. What was she thinking? He didn't know what he wanted from her, and she wasn't telling him. In that moment, he wasn't sure if he wanted to caress her body, or grab it and shake some answers out of it. He could not be the subject of some fragile girl's whims.

＞

As the vows were read out, Anne followed, trying to mean them, reaching out for faith. *I did not need to do any of this,* she thought as she swore to God that this man beside her would be her husband. *I could have spent my days in prayer. I could have joined a convent, dropped out of the succession, let Mary take the throne with her French husband.*

*I could walk out of this cathedral right now. I could take my sticks and leave. Something else would happen. England would happen without me.*

Anne crossed herself and swore her life to her king and country in the living presence of God.

＞

Later that night, stripped by her maids and wrapped in linen, she found herself confronting the living presence of her husband, which was another thing altogether.

Ushered in by attendants, Henry had barely spoken to her since the ceremony. The two of them had been carried side by side to the celebrations, had sat and dined. She could feel the tension of his body a foot away. Anne picked at her food, smiled and made pleasant answers; Henry, she saw, tasted very little. "Have you no appetite, my lord?" Anne said, trying to start a conversation. And Henry simply looked at her with his black eyes, and said curtly, "I do not care for meat."

Now she was alone with him, and he was staring at her, perched on the foot of the bed and sitting quite still. Helplessness overwhelmed Anne; she could still herself and live through anything if she had to, but her husband was just looking at her and making no move. Anne closed her eyes for a moment, prayed for strength. It seemed something was expected of her.

When she opened her eyes, she thought, for a moment, that she saw it, the light of God. But it was just her own blue face, blushing in the darkness.

Henry was staring at her in frustration. What were women supposed to do? If this were the sea, he could have swum around her, waiting to see if she would dive and flirt, offering a coiled body for his enjoyment. But she was just standing there, doing nothing. A landswoman's body was not the same as a deepswoman's; there were cloven legs, a crevice between, something darker and stranger than a deepswoman's swift-stroking hands and flat-fronted slit. Henry had seen people couple in the sea, had seen landsmen couple from a distance, but, it was occurring to him with frustrating force now, he had not seen what he needed to know. Though John had explained happily enough how such things were done—years ago, fewer years ago than it seemed, when nothing more complicated than boredom and confinement and the dread of something unknown were troubling him— there was nobody to explain to him now. He had seen her naked in the sea, as she had seen him, but she swam with her legs together and had given him no clues. She had him at a disadvantage.

Again, the urge to shake her overwhelmed him, to try his sharp nails on her white-grained skin. They were supposed to be friends, he and she. Why was she not making things easier?

Anne swallowed, seeing Henry's hands twitch. Memories rose in her mind. Philip's hands, savaging under her skirts. The bodies of the deepsmen, her mind a long way from her loyal fingers. Offerings, prizes, tokens of exchange. The skin on a man's body that she had never touched in safety.

She could live through it. She could pledge her life away. There would be Heaven some day, and her soul could hide within her body till then. But in the meantime, her soul could curl up small, and her body could do what needed to be done. At least on her wedding night, perhaps, there would be no bruises in the morning.

Anne, hanging on to one of the bedposts for support, slipped out of her linen robe and dropped it on the floor. Her face tingled as she reached into her mind for a phrase she had heard in the sea. No one had translated it for her, but she knew well enough what it meant. She had heard the deepsmen call it to Erzebet, had heard Philip cry it when he wasn't crying *Wife,* had heard the strains of music that claimed to speak of love. This was her mother's language, a secret language that no one on land understood, no one she didn't trust. God could hear her heart, but no one listening would make anything else of this shrill little bird-cry, no one but Henry, who needed to hear it.

*Do you want to fuck me?*

The girl's skin gleamed grey and lilac in the glow of her face, and as Henry heard her speak, something in him gave way a little. At last, she was talking like a person.

*Yes,* he said. *Come here.*

Allard had told him not to use coarse language in front of ladies, but what did men keep ladies with them for? The girl wasn't dancing, wasn't posing, but if she could be direct, she was human after all.

Anne hauled her weak legs onto the bed and moved towards her husband. She wanted to say something else, but she couldn't think what.

Her skin under his hands was dry and cool, and smelled faintly of home. No one had taught him how to kiss, nor what to say. Henry was not gentle, but the girl in his arms made no attempt to resist as he bent her this way and that, learning with his hands the secret of royal flesh.

BOOK SEVEN

APOSTASY

## THIRTY-TWO

"A FTER THE CORONATION we shall send word to your sister," Henry told Anne. "Not before."

"As you say." It took her a long time to bring that answer forth. Henry was right. If they paused now, if they did not take the throne, there would be deaths. Henry would go on the pyre, and so, perhaps, would she. So would Samuel, and Hakebourne, and the men who had supported them: the great families were all throwing their weight behind this new leader, and they would not give him up on Mary's say-so. Not on the command of an English girl who was sent abroad to become French. They had to hold the throne, and if Mary objected, they would be stronger if they were already crowned. Anne wondered whether Mary's marriage had taken place yet, whether even now an ambassador was coming with a proclamation. The man would be surprised when he reached England. Had she beaten her sister into the marriage-bed? How would Mary be changed when they next met? She bowed her head, trying not to worry about whether her sister was all right. It had to be this way. If they secured themselves fast, there would be no need for a conflict.

"What else?" The two of them were riding together, a trip around the park. There were too many people for privacy in the palace, too many people on the streets; Henry had ordered a space cleared and they had retreated there to discuss things. Anne was already learning that Henry was best appealed to straight; court formalities exasperated him.

"My uncle." Even as Anne spoke, she was not sure what her wish would be.

Henry shrugged. "He is in the way, and nobody likes him. But if you do not want him harmed, that is all right. He is no threat. We could send him somewhere where he will trouble no one."

Philip could be sent away. She would be away from his wandering hands. Anne inhaled a breath of clear air. "Someone could look after him. Nobody too ambitious, though."

"We could put him somewhere with water," Henry said. "The man would do better there anyway."

Anne twined a finger in her horse's mane. "He has always been forbidden to go into the sea."

"Why? He does no good on land." There was a certain sadness in Henry's voice that unsettled Anne. Though he had shown little feeling for Philip beyond a matter-of-fact contempt, the idea of him trapped on land seemed to trouble Henry nonetheless. He had already proposed that the two of them visit the Thames together, go and swim alone, proposed it more than once. There never seemed to be time, and Henry grew more morose with each delay.

It irritated her husband when she didn't look at him as she spoke, so Anne made herself meet his eyes. "They say he could—fuck a deepswoman. Breed an heir that would challenge the throne." *I do not curse,* Anne thought. *I speak to my husband in his own language.* Henry had an inability to see obscenity that was, after the first trying night, not without compensations. Anne's body still felt liminal, uncertain as to its own privacy, uncertain as to how much right she had to claim her flesh as her own. But whatever her anxieties, it was at least difficult to be embarrassed in the presence of someone as physical as Henry. Even in his sleep he said nothing in English, just the quiet chirrups of a deepsman: *We must move on soon. Let's drift. I don't need to surface yet.*

"Him?" Henry shook his head, almost grinning. "Your landsmen have been worrying about that all these years?"

"Well, yes." Anne looked down at her hands, looked up again. "Is that funny?"

"No deepswoman would want him," Henry said.

It was a thought that had never occurred to Anne. She did not want to be near Philip, but with royal seed such a thinned commodity, she had always thought that just her own feelings. "They must want landsmen sometimes," Anne said, gesturing towards Henry's own half-caste body.

Henry shrugged again. "Healthy landsmen, yes. They get curious, I think. But a sick fish like your uncle? That man is no father for anybody's child. Your people fear too many of the wrong things."

Anne thought to ask Henry what he feared, but she didn't want to know. It was too refreshing to be around someone who did not seem afraid. "So we could send him away, to someone who would care for him. I must think of someone."

Henry brightened up, an idea striking him. "I can think of a man," he said.

Anne blinked. "Do you know anyone?"

Henry thought for a moment. "We will have to arrange it. I do not want the man hurt. But we could send him to my father."

The suggestion startled Anne so much that a rein fell from her hand and her horse tossed its head. Henry leaned down and passed it to her. "Your father? You know your father?"

"Not my real father," Henry said "The man who took me in. He is a—scholar, I think you would say. He always wrote about me when I was little. He would be interested in your uncle."

Anne looked at Henry in open curiosity. "I do not remember my father well," she said. "Was he good to you?"

Henry thought about it. A crowd of images: bound hands, stone walls, the stick he had choked Allard for wielding on him. Salt in a bowl, a pen forever scratching. Raw fish. Lessons. Angelica. A painting on his wall, a story, a life on limited grounds. How far had he come from that frantic little fish, pissing himself on the way up a staircase, frightened of corners and blind to speech? It was a question, but he had no answer. Henry had lived on land most of his life, but he still did not know how much he liked the landsmen.

"He was not a bad man," he said in the end. He thought some more. "I think he liked me," he added. All the times Allard had warned him to stay on bounds, had spoken of pyres, had checked him from running away seemed different in retrospect. Claybrook had played him like a tool he could abandon, but Allard, he thought, had honestly not wanted him hurt.

Such a man as Henry's father should technically be burned as a traitor. For a moment Anne panicked: how were they to save him? How could they explain it? Then she shook her head. In a few days' time she would be queen. If she didn't want a man burned, she could order him spared, and that would be that. It was hard to take in.

Both of them were silent for a moment. Then Henry's face darkened.

"Claybrook," he said.

Anne drew breath. "Claybrook."

Each waited for the other to speak.

"John is my brother," Henry said in the end. "I want him spared."

"Did he know of the death of my mother?" Anne's voice was stiff. She had faced Henry with a knife in her fist, but she was married to him now. It was more difficult to know how to argue with him having pledged him her hand.

Henry shook his head. "No."

"Are you sure?"

"Yes." He had said no; why was she pressing it? John hadn't known. "He told me a great deal about court," he said shortly. "He did not expect any of it to be repeated to you. He told me your mother died of a fever." John hadn't told him how near London they were, but that was a lie of omission. It wasn't the same thing. People either lied or they didn't, but John had known Henry was frustrated about his surroundings, and could have lied to him about where they were to keep him quiet. Instead, he kept quiet himself. He could have lied, and he hadn't. If John said it was a fever, he thought it was a fever.

Anne sighed. She wasn't so sure. But John had been pleasant to her over the years. She was not eager to see him dead. And if his father were dealt with quietly, John would inherit the Thames, would be a powerful man with a king who considered him a brother. It would not be in his interests to betray them.

Perhaps they could poison Claybrook, she thought. God would not want it, but it would solve a lot of problems. "John will be against us if we kill his father openly," Anne said.

Henry shook his head. Personally he wished to take an axe and deal with Claybrook simply, but John was likely to be unhappy about it. His wife was right: this was a difficult thing to solve.

"If we claimed it was he who found you and raised you, perhaps we could execute him for it instead of your father," Anne said. "That would at least be done in the light. It would look ungrateful, but we could try to pass it off as justice. A king so just he punishes even criminals who help him."

Henry stared at her, dismayed, and angry that it sounded feasible. "That is a crooked plan," he said. "You would lie to many people."

Anne looked up at the clouds, stretched back in her saddle. The action bared her throat to the sky, and Henry struggled not to be distracted. "Yes," she said. "It would be better if we could think of a straight one. But I cannot, can you?"

She didn't say it as a challenge, only a question. Henry didn't answer.

"We cannot move till after the coronation, in any case," Anne said. "We can strike harder with our backs braced against the throne. Has Samuel talked to you about the ceremony yet?"

"Not yet." That was another dull conversation Henry did not wish to go through. Only days after the wedding, and again he was expected to totter into some great cavernous room and talk nonsense at an old man's prompting. Once he had the crown on his head so no language-tangled landsman could argue about it, he was going to see to it that less of his time was wasted that way.

"Oh, and after Archbishop Summerscales dies," said Anne, "I wish Samuel Westlake to succeed him. You would be happy with that?"

Henry wasn't sure what an Archbishop did, but Westlake was a sharp man, who hadn't mistreated him when he had the opportunity, and Henry felt he owed him a favour. "As you please," he said.

～

Much to Henry's disgust, Westlake chose to discuss the coronation with him in the same cathedral he had been married in. Henry would have preferred outside, anywhere outside, but the day was a rainy one, and while that would not have troubled Henry landsmen seemed to be fussy about their clothing and hair; it was difficult to make them concentrate when the weather was against them. So, back in the dislikeable chamber they went. Empty but for the two of them, it seemed bigger, but the obscuring windows were still a nuisance. There were faces and hands sketched in among the colours, but they were nothing like real faces. Just crude images, as much like a real face as a court tune was like a real word. Court landsmen seemed to have a compulsion to mimic real things, and to do it badly. There was something uncomfortable about being surrounded by these glass corpses. Being penned in on all sides by something so useless was like being smothered in cloth, rolled up and bound in landsmen's muddle-headed thinking.

"That is the Annunciation," Westlake said, seeing him staring at one of the windows. Henry had been trying to see through the glass; there were more white patches than usual in amongst the blue and red, and he was hoping he might get more of a view.

"The what?" Henry's first impulse was to assume that "annunciation" was the name of that particular window, or perhaps the usual name for a window that faced south, but it was easy to be misled when landsmen took to naming imitations of things.

"The Annunciation. The Annunciation of the Angel Gabriel to the Virgin Mary that she was to be the mother of God."

That helped not at all. *God* and *Virgin Mary* were words his wife was fond of muttering to herself, and while she was welcome to play with such words if it pleased her, Henry was becoming tired of hearing them from other people. They were recurring with greater and greater frequency; landsmen could not seem to stop mentioning them. He had the sense that they were word-objects landsmen toyed with when nervous, the way a man riding might fiddle with a rein. Allard had tried to explain something of their significance when he was very little, but Henry had classed it as Latin, something pointlessly abstruse that he didn't want to learn. If he tried biting Westlake now to make him stop talking nonsense, Westlake could hardly tie his hands as Allard had, but it seemed that such behaviour wasn't acceptable among landsmen.

Best to ignore it, perhaps, and ask his wife about it later. "What do I need to know about this coronation?" Henry said.

"There are some speeches you should memorise," Westlake said. Henry noted that there was no "your Majesty" or "my lord" in his speech. He spoke plainly, an older man to a younger. Henry wasn't sure if he liked this or not.

"Speeches? What do I have to say?"

"The usual oaths of kingship," Westlake said. His tone was neutral, polite. "To uphold the law and the Church, to protect your people."

"The church?" Henry said. Protecting his people sounded fine, but churches were buildings, and there was more than one of them. "Why do I have to uphold a church?"

"*The* Church," Westlake said. "To keep the laws of God, and to help your people do the same."

He would rather have asked his wife, but Henry decided that this conversation could not go further without clarification. "You keep talking about God," he said. "Explain this to me."

The man's face did not change very much. Eyes flicked to Henry's face, lines around Westlake's mouth slackened a little. He stared at Henry, not moving forwards or backwards. "Has no one spoken to you of God, my son?"

"My son, is it now?" Henry said, annoyed that a straight question was being met with such a frozen reaction. "If I ask to know something, it is because I do not know it already. If you will not tell me, I will have to ask someone else."

"My lord, were you ever baptised?" Westlake said. He seemed to be gathering himself for something.

"What is baptised?"

Westlake paused for a moment, cast his eyes up in thought, then turned back to Henry. "Did someone pour water over your head and put salt on your mouth while saying a form of words, perhaps when you were a child?"

"I ate salt for myself," Henry said. "Do you mean being bathed?"

Westlake shook his head. "You have had no religious education, my son," he said. His tone was not harsh, but his eyes were dark, the pupils in them wide. Though he wasn't fidgeting, the man had an air of unease. "May I ask you a question?"

"Ask," Henry said. He saw no point in asking permission to ask something else; by the time permission had been asked, they could already have got to the question.

"In the sea," Westlake said, "do the deepsmen ever speak of God? A creator? A saviour?"

Henry thought of the sea, the endless motion, the hunger and search for food, the ears attuned for predators, the changing light and crackling, clicking sounds of fish. He wished he was there now, instead of in this tiresome conversation. "Deepsmen do not chatter like landsmen do," he said. "They speak to the point."

Westlake looked down at his hands, clasped over the head of his cane. After a moment, he drew a breath. "It is given to us to convert the heathen," he said. "My son, I must take up your day and ask you to listen to me. I have much to explain to you."

Henry did not understand the word "heathen," but he was not pleased at the thought of sitting all day in this building listening to Westlake lecture him. With all his soul, he wished he could get off his bench, crawl out into the rain, be outside with the wet air pattering against his skin. The memory of the fight returned to him, that desperate, direct clash of arm against arm. It was dangerous, but it was clear, and it made no demands on him beyond his own survival. But the landsmen referred to this subject so often, it was becoming uncomfortably clear that he had better find out what they were talking about.

"Go on," he said. The rain sighed outside the windows, and Henry sat back, bracing himself for a frustrating day.

～

An hour later, Henry was horrified.

He wanted to talk to Anne about it, but he felt too much concern to begin: these landsmen words his wife was always muttering turned out, on explanation, to be worse than "marriage," worse than "coronation," worse than all the ceremonies and formalities and bundled-up words the landsmen spent their lives pondering. The landsmen weren't just strange. They were stupid, bone-deep stupid. They were mad.

Allard had explained to Henry, or tried to, some story about how a landsman named Jesus had died because of bad things he had done. That was as far as Henry had understood. Now it seemed that this dead landsman, who had planned his life so ill he had ended up nailed to a stake instead of burned at one, was speaking for someone else, this God that everyone kept talking about. That this Jesus had risen from the dead a few days later, Henry believed no more than he believed that Angelica had naturally walked out of the canals speaking perfect Italian after a lifetime in the sea, no more than he believed that he himself had been sent by some invisible creature after a lifetime in the waves worrying about the England he'd never seen. He had emerged telling the landsmen that story, and even they must know it wasn't true, not if they thought about it. But they didn't seem to want to. They kept referring it back to God. Landsmen believed stories, most particularly stories that suggested that someone who appeared at the right time was sent by some thing, some thought-thing or word-thing that they'd never met, instead of just being a clever person who had thought about how to make a memorable entrance.

A man might come back after three days' hiding; it was not impossible. But the landsmen seemed to think he'd come back again, some day when the world ended—a thought that, in itself, was inconceivable. Creatures died; the world was what creatures died in. A broken back or a gouged throat created not a shiver of notice in the world, in anything except the dying creature. The world was what happened before you were born and kept happening after you died; there was no need for some dead landsman to come back and have everyone living die at the same time and tear up the world while he was at it. Everyone would die anyway if they waited. It seemed to Henry that the landsmen were confused, that they hadn't seen enough dead things to know how easily the water kept flowing after a death, that however much you dreaded the end nothing stopped the tides. And no landsman could destroy the world anyway, however clever he was at dodging in and out of seeming dead. The world was too big, and landsmen too little. And if anything were to have an effect on the world, it would not be a landsman. There were too many other kinds of creatures in the world, speaking ones and mute ones, clever and stupid. The landsmen did not have the final say over existence.

But it seemed, listening to Westlake speak, that they thought they did. The world, the hard dazzle of sound and sensation, colour and motion that had overwhelmed Henry since the moment he entered it, was not real to them. They thought it was something else, just a picture, an angelica created by some other mind they couldn't see or touch. They were all ideas without sense.

It struck Henry, listening to Westlake tell his stories, that the nastiness of the landsmen's possessions, the straight lines and enclosing roofs and binding clothing, could be explained by this. They didn't notice them. They looked at clothes and thought of ceremonies; they looked at buildings and thought of their owners. Always the ideas, and never the things themselves. They couldn't feel what was up against their skin: the world, thriving and struggling and vitally, irrefutably real.

The thought made him forgive Allard for a lot, unexpectedly; for the tiresome Latin and scratching pen, the horrible clothes he'd forced on Henry's limbs and the words he'd forced into his mind. He had thought he was doing Henry a favour; he'd had no idea how false his gifts really were.

But this did not mean Henry was going to swear to uphold this landsmen's God. Bad people lied, and he was not going to be one of them. He had learned English and how to dress himself, had learned to hold a conversation and not let the vividness of the world distract him. But life was notice, attention, the real world and the living body moving through it. This Henry knew, with every fibre of his self, and he was not about to forswear it.

# Thirty-Three

"Your Majesty," Samuel said to Anne, "we face a problem."

Anne put down the manuscript she was reading. The room she was using had been a place Erzebet was fond of, a library room with illuminated volumes and bundles of letters kept tied together. Anne had taken to going there when she wished for privacy. Her hope, which she did not confide, was that she might find some letters her mother had written, something to tie her to a past, some word of advice. So far, she had found a great deal of theology, some letters to Scotland her mother had written before the war overcame them, and little else. Erzebet's handwriting, fair for a prince and as legible as a pen directed by webbed fingers was ever likely to be, was sharply familiar to her, and the words stood out. *There should be no discord between princes.* The royal house was one blood, one kind, Erzebet had said, and there should be union between them. It was commonly said in border disputes. Maybe Erzebet had even believed it at the time. Erzebet had seen her husband lost in the maelstrom of Scotland. Without deepsmen to guard their borders, what could princes be but a pack of dogs snapping and snarling over scraps? Strange to think that the deepsmen, so warlike in themselves, could be the keepers of peace. Nothing united a pack of dogs so fast as the distant wolf's howl.

*Between princes,* Erzebet had said. The king of Scotland, King John, had been a cousin of her husband's. *No discord between princes.* Not, *There should be no discord between family.* Once the borders were passed, a cousin became a prince, and a prince was his country. A prince was where he was now, not where he had come from. It endangered a nation's people to think otherwise.

"Has my lord a dislike of the ceremony?" Anne said, stretching out her hands as best she could. Henry had a limited tolerance for boredom; it was going to take a lifetime of diplomacy to smooth the tension between his finite patience and the time-crusted formalities of court life. "Perhaps we might shorten it. There seems to be a fashion for haste these days."

Samuel was leaning forward on his cane, both hands gripped over it.

This was so unlike his usual stance that Anne felt a prickle of worry. Usually Samuel stood straight as a guardsman, his stick a careful prop to keep him from listing—but today he hunched forward, as if to keep from falling headlong. The stoop of his back was almost royal.

"Your Majesty." Samuel hesitated, then swallowed. "He will not swear to uphold the Church."

Anne frowned. "He will not take the vow?"

Westlake had always looked her in the eye. Used to bowing and scraping, or to tall courtiers staring over her head, it had been one of the things Anne loved him for. Now he was looking at his hands. His knuckles were white over the head of the cane. "He declares he does not know God, nor does he wish to. Your Majesty, the boy is— unregenerate. He will not govern a Christian people, not as a Christian king. He swears he will not hear the word of God."

As Samuel had begun to speak, Anne had felt a shiver. Thoughts flickered through her mind: her husband turned his back on God, would drag her to Hell. Hell, the separation from God—and Henry embraced it, avowed it. By his own choice, he was carrying Hell around with him. How could he bear his life?

Oddly, it was the word *unregenerate* that soothed her. She thought of the deepsmen, white ghost-bodies massive in the hazy sea. They did not speak of God. They had no self-consciousness. She thought about Henry, saying the word *fuck* without a blink, of herself, a stricken scrap of flesh in a crushing gown, calling over the waters of her mother's funeral: *Not safe, don't eat.* Henry had lived among the deepsmen. No one had spoken to him of God.

Anne opened her mouth to ask whether Samuel had spoken to him of the love of God, had tried to open his soul to the bliss of the Holy Spirit. Then she stopped. Of course Samuel had. No righteous priest would act otherwise, faced with such a heathen. But Henry was not much of a listener. Not to things he didn't understand.

"Does he oppose the Church?" Anne said quietly.

Samuel looked up. His face, weathered and wan, looked at her with a young man's bright eyes. There was tension there, the hardness of conviction. "No, your Majesty," he said. "But he says he will have none of it himself. He says . . ." Samuel stopped for a moment, then took a breath. His shoulders hunched a little further, as if anticipating a blow from above. "He says that if landsmen wish to be fools and fear dead men, that is their concern. But he will none of it himself."

Anne swallowed. Would God punish her for her husband's blasphemy? Would he punish her husband? She looked at her hands. Samuel was calling her "your Majesty." She was a vow away from the throne. Never in her life had she been stronger. She lowered her voice, gently. "God forbade Eve to eat the Apple of Knowledge," she said. "That is how sin came into the world." She drew a breath. "Apples do not grow in the sea."

Samuel looked at her again, a rapid glare that came up quick as a wince. "Your Majesty, you cannot be joking."

"I do not joke," Anne said. "I will swear to uphold the Church. Samuel, you have been my spiritual father; you know how I love God. We will have a Christian England. But for all the theologians' talk of the image of God, the perfect body of the king and the Star of the Sea, our lord Jesus Christ came to us as a landsman. When God sent a Flood to cleanse the world of sin, it cannot have been anything but a festival for the deepsmen. If He had wanted to purge sinners in the sea as well as on land, He would have sent a fire, or turned the waters to blood. It has been the landsmen who have felt His scourge when they strayed. Perhaps the deepsmen are unfallen. And my husband is so very like a deepsman in his spirit."

Samuel took a step towards her. She had never heard him raise his voice, but there was an edge of distress in it now. If he had not always been gentle to her, she would have thought him angry. "You cannot break the covenant between the king and God, your Majesty. Nor change the duty of a king to his people. We cannot be a Christian people with a heathen king. It is blasphemy. We cannot have a heresiarch prince."

"Henry is no heretic," Anne said, trying to be calm. "He had no faith to betray. We will be a Christian people: *I* will protect the Church. I will, Samuel, you know I will. There will be Christian kings hereafter." How long would it take her to fall pregnant, Anne wondered. Henry would not oppose her telling their children of the love of God, she was sure of it. He seldom denied her anything unless it meant confining himself somehow.

Anne opened her mouth to say what Henry had been saying all along: *Would you prefer a French king of England?* But something stopped her. She could see in Samuel's drawn face the difference between a foreigner and a heathen.

"We will have Archbishop Summerscales attend us," she said. It pained her to say the words. She could see the lines deepen on Samuel's face as she said them. Samuel would be Archbishop after Summerscales; she had always intended it. But he was not Archbishop now. The coronation would be performed by Summerscales, whatever Samuel had to say about it. And she remembered, all those years ago, hearing Samuel and Summerscales debate in frightened whispers whether her mother was right to burn the bastard of Cornwall. *Would you have us rock a broken throne?* Summerscales had said. Summerscales had let a child burn, to protect England. To have a queen protect the Church while the king left it alone and refused to turn up to Mass; that, she was sure, Summerscales would swallow. He was a man of the world.

Something inside Anne ached like a tired muscle. It was a heavy loss, to be glad that the Archbishop of Stour was a man of the world, not a man of Heaven. But they had come too far. A little change in the words of the ceremony, that was all it would take. Henry would swear not to oppose the Church; she could ask him for that. Maybe even to "protect" it, or something innocuous like that. His people would be a Christian people, and he would protect them.

Anne thought of something she had seen in Erzebet's letters, a letter she had not sent. It had been written to her sister, a letter which Anne's rusty Magyar had taken a moment to translate. *When I have grandsons to hold the throne of England,* Erzebet had written, *all shall be well.* Anne was beginning to understand the long game her mother had played, had stretched her every nerve to play. Given English grandsons from her English daughters, Erzebet could have relaxed, seeing the succession moored in safe waters. Till then, the question was to keep her daughters alive. Anne steeled herself. *When I have Christian sons,* she thought. *Claybrook snatched my mother out of the game before she could see it completed. But I will complete it, and the ending shall be good. We have only to hold out.*

She wondered whether she should discuss the issue with Henry, or simply draw him to bed and try again to ensure a son to carry the precious Church to safety. Perhaps both. But Summerscales must be dealt with first.

"I am sorry, Samuel," she said. "But all shall be better than you think. I shall speak to my husband, and you will see. All shall be well."

Samuel bowed. He did not look at her face.

~

Anne did speak to Summerscales. She set him to composing a new vow of kingship, one that glossed over the upholding of the Church. The old man's face was not pleased, but Anne held her head high and asked as calmly as she could, and he did not question her. Instead, he promised to study the matter. He did not say that he would do it, but he would consider it. Anne decided not to push, not yet; he could have a couple of days to compose his conscience. She would repay him in virtue when he did the right thing.

Anne thought of finding Henry to discuss it with him. But after a while, she sent instead for John Claybrook. The message was politely worded, in the way of a request; he would know it for the command it was. *We recall you told us once,* Anne said, *that you liked to row upon the river. We wish you to join us on an excursion and show us your oarsmanship.*

After that, it only remained to go down to the river and wait.

John appeared alone, tethering his horse beside Anne's. The boat awaited him, Anne already sitting in it. Her hand trailed in the water, feeling the lap and dip of the cold waves. She saw John glance quickly around, as if hoping she wouldn't notice.

"My lord husband is not with us," Anne said.

John looked up at her then, ducked his head. "Yes, your Majesty."

Anne smiled as well as she could. "I have often wished to travel the river in a small boat," she said. "Great excursions are a fine thing, but it would be pleasant to see the river from lower down. I am pleased you can join me, my lord."

John bowed his head again. All her life, Anne remembered his face being merry, amused, amiable. There was no smile on it now. He could hardly have aged in the short weeks since she last saw him, carrying his bottle of poison, but there was a slackness to his expression, like a hanging limb, as if, unable to smile, he didn't know what to do with his face.

"It is a great pleasure to see you again, my—your Majesty," John said.

Anne extended a hand as he walked towards the boat. John hesitated for a moment, then took it, making the boat jolt and sway as he set foot aboard. His hand was hotter than Henry's.

Anne sat in the boat and waited.

"Do you wish to go upstream or down, your Majesty?" John braced himself between the oars. Small though she was, Anne could have handled them, she reflected; if it came to a trial of strength between the two of them, she would have the deepsman's vigour on her side. But he was a subject, and could do the rowing. She would sit and watch him toil.

"Upstream," Anne said. "Let us have the current with you when we return. You will be tired then, I think. That takes us towards your father's land, I believe?"

"Indeed." John turned his head aside to study the oars, handles of wood he would have to negotiate by grip and heft, not by sight. He leaned back, and began to row. The oars split the surface cleanly, a flower of water exploding upwards with each dip. The boat moved, dragging through the water slowly for the first few moments, then settling into its momentum, moving forward with a steady flow. John's arms rotated, his body moving to and fro with each pull, as if he swam backwards through air.

"You row well," Anne said. Muddy banks and draggled grass slipped past them; overhanging trees dipped their frazzled heads in the water.

"Thank you, your Majesty." John's voice, though a little breathless now, sounded stronger, as if the effort of exercise gave him some cover for his nerves.

There were no listening ears; only the dark banks drifting away from them. Time enough, Anne thought, to speak openly.

"My husband misses your company, I think," she said.

John looked up. His face, a little flushed from rowing, was hesitant.

"He has spoken of you," Anne said, seeing his predicament. John didn't know how much Henry had said about his childhood. Married to him or not, Anne was still the Delamere that Henry's protectors had sought to overthrow; she might easily resent John's conspiracy. As far as John knew, this might even be an assassination, a lure away from prying eyes into some land of secretive punishment for his treason. Anne decided to leave him in uncertainty about her intentions for just a while longer. Just to see what he would do.

"Has he, your Majesty?" John trailed off, huffing as if the oars were heavy.

"He tells me you were playmates as boys," Anne continued. "He holds great love for you, I think. I would say he trusts you above any man."

An avenue of willows overhung them, drooping narrow branches into the water. There was nothing to see either side but long twigs bowing weak-stemmed under their own weight.

"He will regret that he could not join us," Anne said, as if John was not silent, emotion struggling on his face. "He has asked and asked that we should swim in the Thames together. He longs for it."

John stopped rowing, and the boat rocked in the water. "I did not know there was poison in the wine," he said. There was a raw edge to his voice, as if there was a hand around his throat.

Anne said nothing, raised an eyebrow. The suddenness with which John had broken out startled her; she sat very still, as if watching a deer she didn't want to alarm into flight.

John rocked the oars on the edge of the boat. Out of the water, the paddles beat in the air like flags. "My father gave me wine to take," he said hoarsely. "I wished to see Henry, to know if he was all right. And to know if he was going to name us. I did not think he would, but if he was tortured I did not want to end on the pyre. Henry—Henry and I watched the burning in Cornwall. I was so afraid I thought I would be sick, the whole time, but Henry just rode beside me, he insisted that he would go to it. He fears nothing, Henry. He just rides it down. I did not know what to do if he was captured. I just wished to see him. And—and my father gave me some wine to take. He told me to speak to Henry, to find out what was happening so that we could make plans. He always knew that—Henry cared for me more than for him. Henry hates my father, I think. I tried to tell him—I wished to tell him, he handled Henry all wrong, but what could I say? My father said Henry might speak to me, he would not speak to him."

The boat was turning in the current, its nose floating round towards the bank, but John did not put his oars in the water to check it.

"I went home and told my father that Bishop Westlake did not seem ready to turn Henry in, that we might have some time in hand. And he said—he told me . . ." John's face convulsed. "When he was counsellor to his Majesty Philip, my father felt sure he could direct the state. But when his Majesty turned more to the Bishop, my father was angry, he said things were slipping away from us. Then he said that

Henry was our best chance, that one iron in the fire was going cold and we should pull out the other one." John spoke faster and faster. "But Henry ran away before he could do anything, and then he turned up in Bishop Westlake's house, and—my lady, your Majesty, you must believe me, I had no hand in it. I never wished it. Henry has been my brother all my life. My father always told me, when I was a child, one day he and I might come out into the open, that Henry would be a greater king than—he told me about his Majesty Philip, too, but I did not—It did not seem . . ." The oars creaked on the sides of the boat as they turned in John's frantic hands. "My father is a subtle man," John said, drawing breath. "But when you are with Henry, subtlety does not seem to mean much. I never wished him harm, your Majesty. I will swear it on a Bible."

Anne sat in the stern of the boat, one hand sheltering the other. Her voice was quiet. "What harm did you wish to us?"

John looked at her again. There were frightened tears in the corners of his eyes. "None to you, your Majesty, I swear it. Henry—I did not know what would become of you, of you all. I—I feared for England with your royal father lost. It was only after that my father would meet him—but—I—I was a child, when Henry was found. I heard my father talk of him, talk of him for years before I met him. I only thought I would meet him, that he would be my brother. Your Majesty—I knew that if Henry rose, there would be war. But I always meant to speak for you. You have been kind to me, in the past. Henry listens to me. I always meant to ask him to spare you."

He had not mentioned Mary. Anne's heart was pounding through her chest, but her face felt a long way away from it, cool in the damp air of the river. She could not give way to feeling now, not when this man was pleading before her. "You have lived a long time with—incompatible ideas, I think," she said.

John blinked his eyes. "I swear to you, your Majesty, I only ever thought for the best. I prayed for the best, I prayed that God would see us through this. I—am no match for my father's subtlety. I have tried to be his loyal son and Henry's loyal friend, and I wished to be a loyal subject to England."

*To England,* Anne noted. Not *to you.* "I fear the time has come when you must choose between them," she said.

John had smiled at her, chatted with her, when she had been a sad, scared little girl. It cut at her heart, to think how many secrets there were behind those smiles. She thought of John, a child confronted with a strange new brother, a conspiring father, a freakish heir to the throne. What would she have wished him to do? What would she have done?

*God tell us to forgive,* Anne thought. But in her mind was Erzebet, screaming in a shroud of blood.

"I shall be loyal to you," John was saying. "Henry has always been first in my heart, your Majesty. I—I wish to serve you so that my loyalties may reconcile. But I miss Henry, I shall be his loyal servant. Please, let me see him so I may tell him so."

"What," asked Anne, "do you know of the death of my mother?"

Wood creaked on wood, and John looked at her, wet-eyed and white-faced. "Your Majesty . . ."

Anne clenched her teeth together. "Do not tell me you were out of your father's counsels," she said. "Or that he did not tell you what he had done, after the doing of it. I can have you racked. Henry will not like it, but he does not like liars either. Do you wish to place yourself between me and him? Tell me what you know of my mother."

The boat rocked. John looked away, dropped an oar in the water and gave a pull, turning the prow upstream again. His voice was very low. "He told me nothing," he said. "Only that she died of a fever. But he did not speak of it much, and that was uncommon. He speaks a great deal of the doings of court, and how they may play out, how we can best anticipate possible advantages. He did not speak much of his plans after her death. He said—he said before she died, that—that we could ill afford a queen who burned bastards and punished those who opposed the burnings. He said once, it was a mercy that she was no longer with us. And after that, he did not speak of it again."

Anne swallowed. "I do not believe you," she said.

"I will swear it on a Bible, your Majesty."

"If you would murder your queen, you would forswear yourself on a Bible."

"I did not know."

"You were no child then," Anne said. "You were almost a man. My lord Claybrook must wish for a son to follow in his ways."

"I was almost a man whose father did not trust him," John said. He spoke with desperate haste. "Henry trusted me. My father wanted me to follow him, yes. But he did not trust me not to tell Henry."

Anne sat silent for a moment. John sounded sincere. That didn't mean he was telling the truth, but if he was lying, he was lying too well to see through. His lies must have been weighing very heavily on his conscience if he would spit them out on such little provocation. Perhaps, under pressure, John lacked a talent for secrets.

"You have tried to please too many people," Anne said slowly. "I do not know if I can trust you not to tell your father of this conversation as soon as we reach land."

John shook his head. "I will not. I swear, your Majesty."

"You say so now." Anne looked into the water, the surface slick with reflections over the dark weeds below. "But you did not ask how I know of your father's hand in my mother's end. I had only guessed it before. Now I know for certain."

John shook his head again. He said nothing.

He had seemed so much older than her, only a few years ago, Anne thought. Time had passed by, too fast to grasp. "Your father will not survive this," Anne said. "We are not safe on the throne yet. There is more to do before England is secured. We cannot have such a man as your father, with all his irons in the fire. You will have to choose."

Here in the boat, she thought, it would not be a difficult choice. John would swear to them; he might even mean it. But if his father had hold of him again, could he be trusted?

"It would help," Anne said carefully, "if you would give us some earnest against your father. If you have information you can lay. Henry loves you; he wishes you to have your father's lands and waterways. I do not wish to confiscate them, not if you will be a loyal servant. But you are not to go home, my lord John. As of this moment, you are to consider yourself under guard. If you leave the court, if you go to your father, or speak to him alone, I shall know the choice you have made."

Anne's heart hurt. Too many men today that she'd had to set down. Samuel put aside for the Archbishop, John pulled apart from his father. Was it going to end, this restless division of side from side? Would there be a day when everyone could stand together?

John raised his hand to swear. "I am your man, your Majesty. Yours, and King Henry's." He looked her straight in the eye, but his hand shook in the air.

"Henry is not king yet," Anne said. "You must be his man before he is king, his man from this moment onwards, and no one else's. Do not equivocate, my lord John. We cannot afford it."

John's hand stayed in the air. His five fingers hung loose, like an autumn leaf curling up at the edges. "From this moment onwards, I am your Majesty's man, and my brother Henry's."

Anne drew a cold breath. This was winning, she thought. It was not as fine a sensation as she would have guessed, considering all the effort men put into gaining it.

"Your Majesty, I must plead for my father," John said. His voice cracked a little. "I am your loyal man, but I must ask you for mercy."

Anne didn't want to hear him beg, didn't want to see him cry. Erzebet had died skinless, Claybrook had raised a bastard to overthrow her. Too many people had bled. But how could she fault a son for loving his father?

There was nothing for it but the truth. "We have not yet decided what to do about your father," she said. Her tone was thin, the lapping of the water almost as loud as her voice. "We shall remember what you asked. We can make no promises. That is all I can give you today."

John bowed his head. "Yes, your Majesty."

There was a long silence. John did not look at her face; instead, he reached for the oars, pushed the little boat off from the bank where it had drifted. He glanced at her, but Anne was staring into the cloudy water, and gave him no directions. John hesitated, then he started rowing the boat back downstream.

"My lord husband will not swear to uphold the Church," Anne said after a while.

John looked up from his oars.

Anne shrugged with a lightness she did not feel. It was too painful to wrangle over a man's life, and there were pressing issues still to decide. She could not let this day go without more planning. "You are his brother," she said. "Perhaps you have some suggestions."

John pulled the oars, shaking his head. "Henry does not much concern himself with things he cannot see," he said.

"Did it ever trouble you, having a heathen for a brother?"

John frowned, his face anxious and puzzled. "We were boys together," he said. "We—we played together. There were other things to discuss."

John was not a holy man, Anne thought. If asked to choose between man and God, which way would he turn? But if it came to that, for all her prayers and her conviction, she herself did not know how to reconcile serving God and England. Too often, the two seemed to call for different things. How would God judge her now, sitting in a boat and telling a man his father was lost? She must have opinions about John if she was to make decisions, but she could not sit in judgement of him.

"It will go hard with the country if he will not swear to some form of it," she said. "Will you help me to persuade him, when the Archbishop comes back with a more acceptable ceremony?"

The look on John's face was of deep, passionate relief. Anne had said she would let him see Henry. The two brothers could talk to one another again. John could be their friend. It was going to be a longer struggle than she hoped, but if they were careful, they had at least that on their side. It was a blessing to be given thanks for. Anne was tired of enmity.

## THIRTY-FOUR

I T WAS GEORGE NARBRIDGE who brought the letter, and after that, all was thrown into confusion.

Anne had not written to Mary announcing her marriage. She had been waiting until after the coronation. In that time, she had thought often of her sister. Mary had understood things Anne had not, had put a sisterly hand inside Anne's. She had not been unkind; even for an older child, a pink-cheeked child with perfect health and a clear line to the succession, Mary had been as pleasant as could be expected. But by the time they had parted, it had been Mary who was the crier, Mary who trembled in public while Anne set her teeth and fixed her face and carried her head high. It had been hard having Mary around and keeping her self-control at the same time. There had been too many things Mary might have said, things that Anne could not afford to hear.

Anne was not prepared to see England break up over a French king, not when there was an Englishman on the shore who everyone would accept. It would cause havoc, the blood of thousands would weigh down her soul. But still, she thought of Mary.

What would have happened if Mary had been at home when Samuel found Henry? Anne had faced the court, heard men swearing loyalty to her, seen towering nobles holding out the reins of power and expecting her to grasp them. There was Henry. Even after so short a knowledge of him, already it was hard to picture the world without him: his certainty, his fierceness, his open demands, reshaped life around him so boldly that it was hard to believe he had not always been there. Mary was from another life. When Mary had been there, Edward had held the throne, and Anne had been the baby. She had been too frightened to speak to people. Now there was Henry, and Anne had come out of the shadows, out of the deeps. The new times demanded strength, and she was holding. Mary had kissed her when she was young and confused, had struggled to hold back tears before an audience. What would Anne be if faced again with her big sister?

So she had not written to Mary. Time enough when Henry was crowned. Edward lay dying, and his last day drew closer and closer, even as he held silently to life. There would be a funeral, and a coronation, and she could speak to Mary with silver and pearls on her head and the throne at her back. It was the politic thing to do, and it was also easier. Thinking of Mary right now shook up parts of her heart that she could not afford to disturb. Henry's prohibition against writing to her gave Anne a breathing space, time to pretend that, among all her other choices, she had not chosen to take the throne from her sister.

It was a long journey to France. Even a fast courier must ride to the coast, find a ship, carry his message along. It was for this reason that Anne was surprised when George Narbridge arrived at her door, bearing a letter.

"You do me honour to bring this yourself, Lord Tamar," Anne said, bewildered. She and Henry had been seated together indoors, debating when to meet with John. For a lord like Narbridge to act as courier was rare to the point of crisis; no man would come himself when he could send riders to do his work for him.

"I thought the letter should pass through as few hands as possible, your Majesty," Narbridge said with a low bow. Beside her, Henry stiffened. Bows did not usually antagonise him, not when someone was doing his job, and Anne suffered a momentary distraction, wondering what the problem was.

"Have you read it?" Anxiety prickled against Anne's skin.

"No, your Majesty. I only spoke to the messenger. He remains on my lands; I have bade him speak to no one."

"Has the messenger offended you?" Henry said. His voice was far sharper than it should have been; Anne shot a nervous look at his face. He was pale, angry.

Narbridge looked puzzled. "No, your Majesty," he said. "But this matter is one of secrecy."

Henry shook his head, as if shaking off a fly. Later, Anne told herself, she would ask him what was troubling him, but the arrival of the letter was too worrying. "We shall read it alone," she said, reaching out her hand. "What do you know of it?"

Narbridge made a careful bow. "Only," he said, "that it comes from your Majesty's sister."

The letter was short, written in a hasty hand. Mary had crossed and recrossed the page below her signature so no one could add anything, but there was no need for the precaution; Anne recognised her sister's script. The letters were almost comforting in their familiarity, but they stretched and straggled across the page and the seal was smudged. Mary had wasted no time before sending this missive.

*News has reached me that you are married, and to a bastard who has come out of the sea. I hear too that you intend to set this bastard on the throne and reign yourself as Queen of England. If this be not so, sister, you must write and deny the news at once, for I am troubled to the heart to think that England could be so easily usurped, and by the intervention of my own dear sister. What is the meaning of this message? I have heard nothing from you, Anne, but the message I received came from one who might be believed, and if you mean to take England from us, when I have not even heard news that our royal grandfather is dead, it is something I cannot understand. My royal husband . . .* (This last was scratched out.)

*I was to write to you before hearing this most grave rumour*

*to tell you that I am married, and that I was sorry to have missed
my dear sister from my wedding ceremony. But I did not reproach
you, for I knew you must remain in England and we must act
together to secure the throne, which my royal husband is ready to
do the moment we arrive in England. But if this rumour is true,
and you have impiously disobeyed the wishes of our royal
grandfather and turned aside from the laws of our land that doom
bastards to death should they attempt to usurp our soil—this, my
dear Anne, I am loath to believe.*

*Send me word as soon as this letter reaches you, sister, for I
am anxious to hear the truth of this matter. I hope I may be
misinformed, that I may not believe this of you.*

The letter was signed only "Mary." There were no greetings from
Louis-Philippe, no king's seal. Holding the letter in shaking hands,
Anne could only believe that Mary had not shown it to them before
sending it.

"What is the matter?" Henry tapped on her arm with a closed
fist. It was a hard push, the kind of blow a soldier might give to a
comrade, and Anne winced. Henry did not always know his own
strength.

Her throat was tight, and she passed the letter over without
speaking.

Henry studied it for a few seconds, the parchment held between
his fingertips. "I cannot read," he said. "What does it say?"

Even with her sister's words burning in her eyes, Anne blinked.
"You cannot read?"

Henry handed back the letter with an impatient air. "I refused to
learn when I was a child. Perhaps you should teach me, if you wish me
to know. But why does this letter have you so upset? What is in it?"

Anne swallowed, and laid the letter in her lap. Her hands rested
lightly upon it, as if she feared to damage it. "Someone has told my sister of our marriage," she said. "I do not know whether she has spies
here, or whether a spy was sent from England, but someone has told
my sister."

Anne's first thought was to speak to Samuel. Samuel would know what to do.

But Samuel thought she had married a heathen. He thought she was failing to protect the Church. If it really came to it, would he back them against a Christian Frenchman?

God was light, and in Him was no darkness, thought Anne. But she herself did not know what to do. Samuel did not like burning children, did not like death and war. He was a Christian man. But again, she thought of his grey, haggard face, all those years he walked on a damaged leg, surrounded by a court that murmured suspicion. Ambitious, they thought him. And now she was no longer a child looking somewhere, anywhere for reassurance, Anne accepted that it must have been so. No man would walk every step of his life in pain unless he had an iron will. Samuel directed that will towards gentleness, most of the time. But Henry was not a man of God; he was not even merciful, not by nature. If it went against his nature to accept a heathen king, Samuel would not lay his will aside.

"Perhaps we should consult with the court," Anne said, her voice quiet.

"Why?" Henry's body was thrumming, the walls closing in on him. There was some kind of attack coming, some predator circling them, passing words where they could not see. The idea of not telling Mary had seemed a simple one to him: everyone seemed to wish an English king, and keeping a secret from this woman he had never known could not be a bad idea if it would help that along. Now it appeared there was division somewhere. It was too close indoors, and he did not like it. He wished, intensely, to have his axe. It had been too long since he had held a weapon in his hands. But what good was an axe against a war of paper and ink? His skin felt dry, the seat beneath him hard and uncomfortable. He struggled to hold back a childish sense of horror at the strictures of land.

"I do not know why I expected otherwise," Anne said, as if to herself. "Any wise ruler will have spies. You cannot bottle news. We must have spies ourselves, we should look to it. I just did not think it would come this soon."

"What are you talking about?" Anne was speaking into the distance, to some invisible listener, and it made Henry nervous.

"Mary would have heard soon," Anne said. "But the distance—it would take some time. I thought we had more days in hand. Someone must have sent a courier, chartered a ship, rode fast all the way to France. I did not think the news would reach her this fast. Dear God, what shall we do?"

"Stop talking to God and talk to me," Henry snapped. "I am the one who is listening."

His wife blinked at him. The look of anguish on her face was, he thought, out of proportion to his remark. It was very tiresome of her to talk to some long-dead landsman when he was here and ready to listen to her. She had no business looking so wronged.

Anne drew a breath. "We must think who can have sent the message," she said. "And we must have as much news from France as possible ourselves. And we must decide what it will mean when Mary knows the truth."

"Claybrook probably sent it," Henry said. "He must know we are after him."

Anne rubbed her glowing face. "Very likely. But I wonder . . . Samuel looked at me so oddly when I told him you would not swear the oath to uphold the Church."

"Not that again," Henry said. "I will not stop anyone talking to your God idea if they wish to, I just will not pretend to be the subject of some foolish word. If people do as I say, they may think as they wish."

"It matters to landsmen." Anne swallowed. "If it were Claybrook— if it were him, Henry, we would have him. We could charge him with treason, there would be no question over it, we could hang him and the whole country would consider it justice. Oh, I pray it was Claybrook."

"I can ask John," Henry said.

"John will not betray his father, even if his father told him."

"John would not lie to me."

Anne shook her head. "This matters less than what we are to do. Henry, we should hold the coronation at once. I can delay writing to Mary for a day or two, if you will take the oath." Her face was blazing as she spoke, as if she were deep underwater where no light reached.

"You said I would not have to." Henry's voice rose. He had told her what his position was. She had accepted it. They had agreed, and that should be the end of the matter.

"Henry, I have spoken to Archbishop Summerscales, he has promised to study the matter. But if you could be baptised before the ceremony, or even during—it is a difficult point to strain, even at the best of times. I—I cannot command men against God, Henry. Nobody can. I would damn myself if I tried. I had hoped he could find some way around it, but now there is no time. If you will swear in the name of God to uphold the Church, I will do it for you, I will do all the upholding. I would like to, I would like to rule in the love of God." His wife put her hands on his arm, her voice going faster and faster. She sounded as if she was pleading. "Just accept the form of words, it will be no different from when we were married. I will take on the burden. God will protect us both then—I will do everything to do with the Church. But if we could just save this time before I have to write to my sister . . ."

Henry moved his arm away. "I will not subject myself to some landsman word," he said. His voice was angry; privately, his heart was pounding, torn between anxiety and hurt. He had thought she liked him. She had lain down obediently and wrapped her arms around him, she had saved his life, she had listened when he complained about all the stupid ceremonies and promised there would be an end to them. Now she was going back on her word. If there was another ceremony after the first, then there would be another, and another, and another. Either she meant her promise or she would bend it when new circumstances arose. "People either lie or they do not, and I will not lie. You should not lie either."

"I—" Now there were tears gathering in her eyes. Henry shivered with tension. You could not trust people who cried. You cried or you acted. Crying was defeat, surrender, a scream from the stake when nothing was left but the stupid hope that someone might save you—but here she was crying, and still trying to win the argument. It left him ensnared in confusion. "I do not lie to God, God sees into our hearts. I want only to secure what is best for the country."

Now she wasn't even listening to him at all. "You swore to be loyal to me."

"I am, Henry, I am trying to be . . ." She wiped her eyes, straightened her back. There was a taut look on her face that he did not like at all. "I do not mean to ask you to act against your conscience. But there are many questions at play." Her voice was hoarse, not as steady as she was trying to make it. "My sister is married to a man who was promised the throne of England. He will want it, whatever we may say. She will want it. It was promised her. We must decide what is necessary, and what we can do."

"If he wishes for the throne he may fight me for it," Henry said. It was appalling how easily landsmen overlooked the simplest solutions. "I am willing to chance it. I can hold my own against an inbred prince."

Anne clasped her hands in her lap. The gesture was a little too careful; the skin over her knuckles strained. "He will not do that, Henry. He will come with an army."

"Then he is a coward."

"He wishes to *win*. He will do what it takes to win. And my sister will act with him, she will have to." Anne blinked hard, her face gleaming.

"You talk to me as if I were an idiot," Henry said, angry. "People used to talk to me like that when I was a child, and I will not have you do it."

"Henry, we will have a battle on our shores. Ships of war will come, and the deepsmen who guard us will have to fight them, and so will our sailors. And if Louis-Philippe can bring a bigger family with him, he can try to turn our deepsmen against us. I would try it, were I in his position. They will bring ships and attack us. It will not be man to man, it will be many, many deaths. I do not want that blood on my hands. I do not want to war with my sister. She did not begin this conflict."

It sounded bad, but Henry was still angry. He changed to another thought, one that had been troubling him for some time. "If you do not want blood on your hands, why do you keep taking advice from George Narbridge? He is the one who burned a bastard like me. If he had caught me on his lands, I would not be here with you now."

Anne stared at him, wide-eyed. "Henry, please, let us keep to the point."

"It is a point that matters to me."

Anne spread her hands. "He obeyed the law. You were saved because someone broke it. Would you wish to have usurpers breeding against you when you are king?"

"I would not burn them," Henry snapped.

"What would you do, then?"

"I would take them in," Henry said. He was casting about a little, but he meant what he said. "They could be my children. My cousins. They could come with me into the sea, they could be useful."

"They would be threats to your throne."

"If I could only hold the throne because nobody else like me was alive, I would be a bad king," Henry said. A dreadful thought gripped him. "Would you burn bastards when you are queen?"

"No." His wife shook her head, quickly and wretchedly. "No, I do not wish to. But my mother—my mother . . ." She buried her face in her fingers for a moment, then shuddered. "We are forgetting what is important," she said. Her voice was a little muffled, and she lowered her hands. "We must decide what to do about this letter. Will you swear to uphold the Church?"

"I will not," said Henry. "I do not like this Church of yours that blesses burnings and talks nonsense."

Anne drew a breath. "Then I suppose I must speak to the Archbishop. I do not think I will prevail quickly enough, though. And I should see what intelligence I can learn about Louis-Philippe."

Henry shook his head. His wife was still crying, tears rolling silently down her face. But it made sense, now. She had given way.

Though he was still angry about Narbridge and God, her words cooled something inside him, quickly and thoroughly. He had said no, and she had listened. She was not betraying him after all.

"I can think of another solution," he said. "You make it too complicated. Leave it with me, and I can solve it."

## Thirty-Five

IT WAS GIVEN OUT that Henry had gone on retreat to prepare for the coronation. Anne spent the time learning what she could about Louis-Philippe. None of it was promising.

Louis-Philippe was the second son of King Louis. His elder brother, Louis the Dauphin, was clear in line to the throne, accepted as such. He was not a difficult choice of king. But God had seen fit to have him born with his fingers fused together, the smallest two on the outer edge of each hand. It did not stop him swimming or holding a weapon or giving court. But Louis-Philippe, Anne heard, was perfect. The royal blood had come out clean in him. How had it been, growing up under a brother who would hold the nation in crippled hands?

There had been no whispers of assassination. The remedy Erzebet's uncle had taken, the knife in the back to empty the throne, did not seem to have occurred to Louis-Philippe. But how must it have felt to see his older brother block his own perfection? If Mary had been the younger, how would she have felt seeing her blue-faced sister favoured for the succession? Louis the Dauphin might have all manner of virtues. But Louis-Philippe could not have been human for it not to rankle, at least a little.

So Louis-Philippe could have expected to make a good match. He was a prize, a pure-limbed prince of the royal blood, one of three sons, a strong and fertile line. His younger brother, François, had taken monastic vows suddenly a few years ago. Whisper had it that he had fathered a bastard himself with a landsman girl, appalling incontinence breeding a quarter-deep bastard, a weird-blooded threat to the succession. It was only a whisper. The child had never been found. But François was now a monk, a sharp example to any prince of what might happen if you didn't bide your time.

And the throne of England, an unguarded throne, a pretty wife you were doing a favour by marrying. All of this had been held out before Louis-Philippe.

Anne sighed, listening to the rumours. A healthy prince, a dynastic prize, a young man intelligent enough to wait for a good chance. To have all this held before him and then snatched away. He would fight. She could hardly blame him.

She wondered, in the secrecy of her own mind, whether he would be a good husband to her sister. They were at odds now; they had cast in their lots with men from opposite shores. Edward had chosen well for Mary, found her a choice close to perfect—in body, at least. A better choice than he could have found for Anne. Perhaps that had been love, holding out for an equally good husband for both girls, hoping it wasn't impossible. Anne had not envied Mary, even before Henry: the idea of marrying a stranger, however fine-figured, was not something either of them wished. Edward had arranged matters for Mary, and Anne had made shift for herself. She had to abide by her choice; to stop now would be fatal. By a prince's logic, if she were to be strong, there was no point in worrying whether her sister's husband was a kind man. But still, in her heart, she wished that he might be. It was a foolish thing, but none the less undeniable. She faced a possible war with her sister, but she did not wish her to be unhappy.

It had been too long since he had seen John, Henry thought as they met. The sparkle had gone out of him; though the day was blue and bright, John's skin had a dull look, as if the sky above him was overcast. He looked tired. Anne said she had been speaking to him, had had assurances; John's friendship with Henry was still a secret the court knew nothing of. "When we are crowned," Anne had said, "then whoever helped you will be a patriot, not a traitor. But before then, it will only put them at risk to make them known, in case we lose." Henry was not thrilled that she seemed to anticipate losing, but he wasn't about to risk John, just in case she was right.

John met him outside, under a tree, where Henry rested astride his horse—a new beast, faster and more docile than any he'd encountered before. The setting was familiar: they had spent so much of their childhood like this, Henry insisting on staying outside while John put up with the weather. As John rode up, Henry saw him anew: grown tall, strong-limbed, well-favoured. He had something of his father's good looks, but the cast of his face was different. Claybrook, when showing no feeling, looked smooth, impermeable. John just looked sad.

Henry studied him, unsure what to say. John sat, waiting. His posture was straight, but there was something a little worn about him nonetheless.

"My wife calls your father Lord Thames," Henry said in the end. "I did not know you had so many names."

"That is his title," John said. "He did not wish to tell you. He thought . . ." A small smile twisted the corner of his mouth; not his old bright grin, but an older-looking expression, wry. "He thought, if you knew London was so close, you might run away."

Henry sighed. "Do you wish me to say I am sorry?" he said. "I did not tell you so your father could not blame you when I was gone. I grew tired of waiting. I always meant to find you once I had succeeded."

John shook his head. "I could have helped you."

"No. I went for the sea, you could not have followed me in. I was caught, and arrested. They would only have killed you. I would not throw away your life."

"I am sorry about the poison," John said. His voice was raw. "I swear, I did not know. If I had known, I would never have given it to you."

Henry gritted his teeth. His brother had handed him a bottle of death. "You trusted your father too much. You should have thought."

"I do not trust him now," John said. "I am done with him. I swear, Henry."

Part of Henry wanted to knock John off his horse, wrestle him to the ground, make sure he had submitted. He could trust a man he had beaten, but this was a surrender of words. For a moment, the temptation overwhelmed him, but he held himself back. His wife had spent a lot of effort making peace with John, and it would only upset her if Henry started hitting him.

"Let us agree not to say sorry," he said. "I think there are better days ahead."

"I hope so." John stared at his horse's mane for a long moment. Henry waited. This conversation was uncomfortable, and he wished it to move to more enjoyable matters, but he was not sure how to accomplish it.

In the end, John looked up. His smile was a little strained, but he looked more like his old self. "How do you care for marriage?" he said.

"It is better than not," Henry said. "Women are pleasanter than I had thought."

John laughed. "That they are," he said. "I always wished I could smuggle some in for you. It would have caused trouble, but I did try to think of ways. I just never found a blind and mute whore."

"I have a wife," Henry said. He found he didn't want John laughing about Anne. "It is well enough."

"And how do you care for freedom?" John's tone was less joking; he looked at Henry, alert and serious.

Henry shook his head. "I do not call this freedom. Just more rooms. Do you know, they wish me to swear to all kinds of nonsense?"

"A king must learn to speak nonsense as though he means it," John said. "That is what makes a clever king."

Henry shrugged in disgust. "It is not so in the sea. A leader who speaks nonsense would soon be deposed."

"We are not in the sea now."

"No," Henry said. "We are not." The words weighed in his throat, as if he had lifted them above the surface and found them heavier than they'd seemed underwater.

After a moment, he swallowed. "You must go," he said. "I meet some other men soon." He almost added, *And where we go, you cannot know,* but he stopped himself. He was supposed to be off on a retreat. John, Anne had said, would assume he was on his way back there if he said nothing, but all of this was too much like lying. He did not wish to say any more: his tongue felt thick with untruth.

"Will I see you soon?" John said.

"Yes. I hope so."

John stroked his horse's neck before looking up. "Your wife said you wished to go to the Thames," he said. "Perhaps we could go when you are back."

"I would like that," Henry said. "Truly, I would. I grow tired on the land."

John nodded, turned his horse and cantered off. Henry sat under his tree, waiting for his men to come join him. The thought of the Thames cheered him, more than anything had for days. But he would do better than the Thames. While his wife was gathering intelligence, Henry would ride down to the coast.

~

Sneaking around unobserved was harder than he had expected last time, so this time they had brought someone with them: Thomas Hakebourne, lord of the north. Some of Hakebourne's men were following them, riding together in a party. Henry rode with his cloak up over his face, and horsemen on either side. They went by quiet roads, and they travelled as a band. Should anyone wish to trouble them, they would have more than just Henry to deal with.

After they reached the shore, Henry would go on alone.

"You have not asked me," Henry said to Hakebourne, "what I mean to do in the sea."

Hakebourne was a heavy man, but he sat astride his horse with a springing, muscular lightness. "I thought that if your Majesty wished me to know, you would tell me," he said.

Henry grinned. He was back outside, the air rushing past him, fresh scents on the wind and freedom of movement. Already he was feeling better. "Well done," he said.

"Thank you, your Majesty." Hakebourne looked at Henry for a moment; it was a studying gaze, thoughtful. He did not look mistrustful.

"My wife says you are loyal," Henry said, "and you have been good to me. But there are more spies than I thought. If I do not tell you, no one can overhear."

"As you say, your Majesty." It was a neutral phrase, but Hakebourne's tone was agreeable.

"Hakebourne?" Henry did not slacken his pace, but turned to look more closely at the man. The movement of their horses made Hakebourne bob a little in Henry's vision, but Henry focused his eyes, trying to see straight. Hakebourne seemed less rattled than the rest of them at being addressed by his real name. "Is it true that you would not have land if the Delameres had not given it to you? That your brother has the land you were born on?"

"Yes, your Majesty." Hakebourne answered without hesitation, plainly.

"So you needed my wife's mother." The thought of Erzebet rankled bitterly with Henry, but if he tried, he could push her into the past, not think of her too much. She was a fighter, Erzebet. It was his misfortune she had been fighting against him.

"I am grateful to your Majesties," Hakebourne said. It was the careful kind of phrase Henry associated with Claybrook, but there was no bow, no smile to disguise it. Henry was liking Hakebourne more as he spoke to him; it was a sensible man who weighed his words.

"So you were there during the war with Scotland," Henry said.

"It was a bloody battle," Hakebourne said. "I hope we shall not see such fighting again."

"Why did you go? You had no lands to protect." Henry was wondering whether Hakebourne saw advancement in such an opportunity, and if he had, whether he would admit it.

Hakebourne adjusted his reins, as if gathering something invisible between his hands. "England is my land, your Majesty," he said.

Henry thought about it for a moment. The word, *England,* was said over and over by these people. What did it mean? A line on a map between one place and another, a line you could step over and find yourself unchanged. Battles for territory were understandable, but Hakebourne had fought for a piece of land he was not using.

"Did you fight with him?" he asked the man to his right. "What is your name?"

"John Green, your Majesty. I fought." The man had a scar across his chin, a deep rivet that suggested a dented bone beneath.

"You gained no lands for it. Did you fight for England?"

"Yes, your Majesty. As I do now."

"You do not want a French king?"

"No, your Majesty." Green's face was firm, his *no* immediate.

"What do you want, Green? Kings aside," said Henry. "What would make you happy?"

Green's face was puzzled, momentarily.

"I would wish my people to be happy," Henry said. "How can they be happy if I do not know what to give them?"

"Most people want enough to eat," said Green. "And no oppression from landlords. They want to work the land in peace. But they do not want a foreign king bearing down his ways upon them."

"Do you agree, Hakebourne?" Henry said.

"Yes, your Majesty." Hakebourne nodded, and there was a general look of assent on the faces around him. "But that is the people. What courtiers want, if I may say, is often more complicated."

"Yes," Henry said. "It is easy to become complicated when you are not hungry."

He thought about it, working the land. He did not know what it involved, exactly, but he knew what it must mean. The black soil of England, so dense compared with sand under the sea. Burying tools in it, burying your hands in it, pushing aside heavy earth to pull out things to eat. Henry wondered how he would have liked life as a peasant. It would at least have been simple. And if it was hungry, he had been used to that, once. The deepsmen were not like these lords who spent so much time doing service to them.

*I should speak to more people,* Henry thought. *But if I did, would they say anything other than "Yes, your Majesty"? And if they wanted things, other than food, food that I do not know how to grow, that I could not hunt down for a whole country, how would I understand them? The* *people of England want an English king. They want me. And I do not even* *much care what England is.*

"We shall not have a war," he said aloud. "I shall see to it." He had seen the notch in Green's face, and he did not want to see more of them if he could help it. But as he rode, he could not help but look forward to the sea. Tense though he was, much though he was risking by this new dive into the Channel, it would be a release from conversation, from the burden of landsmen's words and ideas that he did not care for at all.

⤙

Too many solid walls had encased Henry within his life, but the sea was solid too. He saw that as he swam off into the cold. There was no seeing what was coming at you; instead of walls, there was a vibrant blank, beyond which, nothing was visible. The sea was a living fog. But you could hear. There was no hiding a sound behind a wall. Every sound in the world carried straight to you. There was little ambush. Few places to hide.

No chance of ambush, in fact, unless you were quiet.

It was a long journey he was on, and he was making it alone. As Henry swam off and the sea floor disappeared below him, the void enveloped him and he felt himself relax. His muscles strained at the effort of swimming, but the sensation wasn't entirely bad. It was more the feeling of scratching an itch, gulping down water when you were thirsty, a physical cry of relief at doing something you had put off too long. At the same time, his back was unbending. It was only as he stretched out in the water that he realised it. Since he had come out into the world and met all those landsmen, he had been unable to crawl. He had had to totter from place to place on his weak legs, leaning on what he could. His spine was beginning to curve. As he reached out, pulling stroke after stroke to drive himself forward, sharp pains crackled through his shoulder blades, but he kept swimming. He had been beginning to cripple up. He needed to move.

It was empty in the water, but it wasn't dull. There was no constriction, bound by gravity. When you were walking, you didn't think about air; you just passed through it. It was ground you thought about. But swimming, the ground held you, soaked into your hair, clotted in your ears, rushed into your mouth when you opened it. The bitter, metallic salt of home. It had been so long since he had swum like this, not just out to a bay, but beyond, far and far away, roaming like a nomad. He had been in England. When he was a child, he had swum past England, past France, up and down the cool currents that bound the world together, whatever the landsmen said about this patch of earth and its ways being so different from every other.

Tired and hungry after a while, Henry was enjoying himself. He floated, listening out. He needed to catch something, some crab or eel. He remembered how it had been, trawling the sea floor for crustaceans, creeping creatures that he could snatch up and crack open. He had seldom got his hands on a fish. But it hadn't been that he couldn't catch them, he thought. He had been quick enough with his hands. It was the other tribesmen. They were faster than him, stronger, and could knock him away from a fish he was just about to grab. That was because they didn't fear him. But he wasn't a child any more.

Henry hung in the water until he heard the clicking of fish. It was easy to lurk, hover close, until he saw it: a glittering shoal, every living body a vital handful of meat, enough to fill his stomach and strengthen his limbs. Mackerel, he thought; that was what the landsmen called them. There was another name for them in the sea.

Henry cruised beside them, and then dived. His hands shot out, grasped, and there it was: the prize in his grasp, a threshing, flexing meal, ready for his teeth. A victory he could swallow and digest. And when it was consumed, there could be other victories.

Why was it that life had been so straitened? He had been small and frightened before, but now he was meeting the world, and while it was big, he was less afraid of it. It wasn't the risk of death that was dimming his vision and bending his back. The words of the landsmen, their Gods and ceremonies and borders, their books and clothes and customs. They were all *things*. You had to know what they stood for, what they represented. There was so little in the landsmen's world that just *was*. As Henry floated on his back, swallowing cold mouthfuls of mackerel flesh, he felt his spirits lift. This world was real, chilly and flowing up against your skin, real enough to make you shiver.

It was a long swim. The light faded overhead, leaving nothing to see in the water, little to see when he surfaced for breath except a soft sky, clouded with stars like sand churned up by waves. Before he had come to the land, Henry thought, he could never have seen them. He had been too short-sighted; he had never needed to see more than a few feet before him. That was one thing he had taken from the land that he was glad of: his sight. It was far away, too far to touch, but still the sky was beautiful. He did not regret it when he dived back under again. He could see it next time he surfaced. It was real, of the world, and it didn't change when you took your eyes off it.

As the night wore on, Henry dozed for a while. It wasn't difficult; he had not lost the trick. You held a breath and you drifted, waking enough to surface and inhale when you needed to. No rough sheets to tangle with. No wife beside him, he thought, with a little regret. Anne's compliant flesh had become an enjoyable part of his life. But perhaps she could be persuaded to come swimming for a longer time with him, some day.

As grey skies dawned, Henry woke properly and swam further. The sun rose in the sky, sending shimmering fingers through the choppy surface. Henry caught another fish, feasted again, no less triumphant than he had been the first time. If this had been travelling by land, he would have felt lost by now, too many landmarks and hills, too many obstacles. But he knew where he was. He could hear the echo of the waves on the other side.

Drawn by the crash of water, Henry drew close to the shores of France. As he swam, he called out: *Challenge. I can beat you. I will lead you now.*

The tribesmen of France were many and loud-voiced, surrounding him like predators around a kill. *Stranger,* he heard. *Go away. Do not challenge us. This place is ours.*

Nobody liked a foreigner, Henry thought. There was never enough clanship to go around. And what were they, that they were so loyal to France?

*I come from the north,* Henry said. *From the tall cliffs.* There was no word for *England* in his mother-tongue, not as such. The deepsmen guarded their shores, but what happened on the land, they cared very little. His mother had never let him see a ship. It was not patriotism, he thought. His father must have come from one. Perhaps she wanted to keep him with her, then, and was afraid the landsmen would steal him. Perhaps the others doubted his loyalty. Well, they were right to. But that did not mean he was wrong.

*I am not a stranger,* Henry said. *Deal with me, not your landsmen.* There was a word for it, the treaties the deepsmen brokered with the men of the land. That was the word he used. *I am not a stranger. I am king.*

*We do not deal with you,* said a voice. From the bass tone, making the water all around them ring, Henry recognised a man of great strength. This would be the man to deal with, the man to challenge.

*Brother,* said Henry. *Your landsmen are stupid. They are weak, and fear dead men. Deal with me.*

*We have a landsman king,* said this leader. *We do not know you.*

Henry swam a little closer. What he saw on the deepsman's face struck him like a wave. He hung for a moment, his heart beating so hard it should have pulsed out through the water. There was a clench of fear, and then Henry remembered all those books, those courtiers, the endless negotiations. *England needs an English king.*

Henry dipped up to the surface for a breath, and as his head broke up into the air, he laughed, laughed aloud. He was still struggling to keep the laughter within his lungs as he swam back down.

The face of the leader was familiar to him. It had grown and changed, from a small child to a fine man, but he knew the features. He even remembered the man's name, a sequence of clatters no landsman's tongue could ever manage.

In the gloom, he thought he recognised another man, and a woman beside him. People sometimes swam off alone, joined other tribes. When he was little, his family had been almost entirely nomadic. There had been some changes of custom, perhaps, a few changes of side in the time he had been gone. But these were not strangers to him. Their dialect was familiar, and so were their faces. *Who would have thought it?* Henry thought. *After all this time, I am a Frenchman after all.*

The leader had not been too bad, he recalled. Older than him, ready as any to deal out a twisted ear or a pinch if someone became too tiresome, but not by nature a bully. Quick in a hunt, disinclined to steal food. A steady character. Very probably he was popular with his tribe.

Henry had come prepared to do battle. Remembering how a rope had defeated the English tribe, he had swum armed, even though the weapons dragged against his streamlined body a little: a rope around his waist, spurs on his heels. But now, recognising this man, he did not feel like a fight.

*I know you,* Henry said, naming his new-found friend. *I am no stranger. Your landsmen are strangers. You are my tribesman.*

The leader swam forwards, scanned Henry's face. *What is your name?* he asked. Around him, others were poised to fight. Henry could see the massive arms and tail, the mighty body he was trying to talk himself out of fighting. This was a splendid man indeed. He had thrived in the sea.

*Whistle,* he said. *I have been away a long time.*

# Thirty-Six

ANNE SAT in the church and lifted up her heart, or tried to. The news was not good. Intelligence returned fact after fact about the French: their strong navy, their popular king, their healthy sons. England's navy was not bad, but they would have to meet in the Channel to keep the French out. There were English deepsmen to protect their own shores, but they were not a guarantee, not if the French deepsmen came in support of their own ships. Country would fight against country, and tribe against tribe.

It could not be what God wanted. God could not create life and love killing, whatever politicians or theologians could argue about it.

She needed to talk to Mary. But what could she say to her? *Do not start a war to get what you want; let me have it instead?* She might as well send a letter saying *Surrender at once so that we can both be happy.*

Could God be against them? It was a hard question, but Anne was a prince, she told herself. Princes did not turn the hard questions aside. She had said to herself that she would protect the Church, that Henry might be a pagan but that God might exempt the deepsmen from such concerns. But by blood, Henry was as much a deepsman as she. If God could touch her heart, he could touch Henry's. Should she have tried harder to convert him? Should she have given way and handed the kingdom to the Christian French? She had begun this with no greater aim than keeping a strange boy from the stake. Now she was within a vow of the throne, ready to begin a war.

And, it could not be forgotten, very possibly pregnant as well.

It was hard to hear God when her mind was so troubled. And troubled it was. Samuel had not spoken to her since she had told him that she would ask Summerscales to rewrite the vows. He had looked at her, and backed away. There was something about his face. Angry with her, perhaps: he would have a right to be. Concerned for her soul. Betrayed, even; though she had never been the theologian he had, Anne knew full well that a heathen king in Christendom was, at best, a dispensation she did not have the spiritual authority to grant. But that wasn't what troubled her.

Samuel looked at her, and his face was frightened.

❧

"Tell me the truth," Anne said to John. "Did your father write to my sister?"

John had come before her, asked for an audience. His pleasant face was paler these days, and he smiled less. When he came into her presence, he brought with him a bag. Guards had tried to take it off him, but Anne intervened. Even if he had a weapon, she thought she could hold her own.

It was not a weapon he brought in his pack. John bowed before her, and drew out letters.

"I have letters here," he said. "They were to my father. He does not know I took them."

"Are they from France?" Anne's heart sounded in her ears, a faint echo of the surf.

John bit his lip for a moment, then handed them to her. "They are."

The letters sat in her lap, cold and brittle.

"So you have chosen your side," Anne said.

John lowered his head for a moment, then raised it. "I have," he said. "I do not want a war."

The letters were partial, referred to other letters, but their message was clear enough. There would be a force on the shores to sabotage the English fleet should it go out to meet the French. Ships were being built, small ships with harpooners aboard. There was no reference to their use, but Anne understood.

"You said that you went on a porpoise hunt when you were young," she said to John, looking up.

John did not need to ask which letter she was reading from. "Yes, your Majesty," he said. "There are older men enough who know how to spear from the water. And if you read the next one, you will see talk of nets."

The deepsmen had been a bane to her, but at the thought of them tangled in ropes, Anne shivered. With sailors battled on the shore and deepsmen hunted beyond it, France could sail across the Channel and step onto English soil unopposed.

"And what for us?" Anne said. Her voice was hoarse. "A bath of boiling water? A pyre and a stake?"

John shook his head. "I stole these letters," he said. "I know no more. But . . ."

"Speak," Anne said.

John did not answer for a moment. "Perhaps you should read the next one," he said. "Your Majesty."

Anne read. The handwriting was disguised, impossible to identify for sure. She did not think it was Samuel's. But there was no question that it was from a priest. A line stood out at her: *Better a battle now than the fires of Hell. I shall speak to the Bishop.*

There were other Bishops than Samuel. And even if he had been spoken to, Anne told herself, there was no proof that he supported it. But Samuel was a man who heard rumours. He had come to her with Henry. He had found Henry because he listened to whispers, and he had brought him to her.

He had not spoken to her of any of this.

Anne's eyes stung. "Bishop Westlake is a man of peace," she said. Her voice wavered, uncertain and childish. "He risked the pyre himself to save Henry from it. He would not wish for a war." The words cracked in her mouth and a tear ran down her face. She scrubbed at it, desperate and angry. She could not afford to cry now, she could not afford weakness.

"My lady, please do not cry." John was beside her, his hand on hers. "Please do not cry."

*My lady,* not *your Majesty.* Had she weakened so fast in his eyes? But John's hand on hers was warm, and she looked at his face. It was not contemptuous. He looked a little frantic, as if uncertain what to do, but there was honest distress there. He said again, "Please do not cry," and Anne swallowed.

"You have always wished to be a good friend," she said. Her voice was not steady yet; it came out small and tired. "Have you not?"

John gave a sigh, a little hiss of air like the sound of something falling. "I have," he said. "But we do not seem free to do as we wish in this world."

Anne blinked. "You said that once before," she said. "When I met you riding in the forest. Do you remember? Before the—the burning in Cornwall."

John nodded. His hand was still on hers. "I recall," he said. His mouth quirked, and he gave a sad little laugh. "You were always riding up to us in the forest and overhearing things. It made my father very nervous. You have good ears, my—your Majesty." As he said this, John looked down at his hand, still resting on hers, and pulled it away.

"Deepsmen do," Anne sighed.

John laughed again. It was a short sound, but good to hear. "I know. Henry could hear me from miles away. I warned my father about it. After that, he stopped saying anything out of doors. You should have been an intelligencer, your Majesty."

Anne leaned her head back against her chair. "Henry said he would adopt any bastards found. They might make good intelligencers."

John looked a little startled. "He means to adopt bastards?"

Anne shrugged. "Perhaps. He does not care for burnings, any more than any of us do, I think. He says they could carry messages up and down the shores, more detailed messages than the deepsmen could remember. He is full of ideas for them. I can well believe it would be a threat to the throne if there were too many people in line for it, though. You might as well have landsmen kings like the Switzers."

John gave a shadow of his old grin. "The Switzers do not have many civil wars, I think."

"That is true," Anne said. She thought about it. "They do not."

John didn't answer. The two of them sat side by side.

"What would have become of Mary," Anne said after a while, "if your father had raised an army and led Henry to the throne?"

The look of happiness left John's face. "Your Majesty, I have begged forgiveness, I will beg again if—"

"I only wish to know," Anne said. "I do not ask to trouble you, John. I have few enough friends in this world."

John blinked, then answered. "It would have depended how your royal family fought, I suppose. Perhaps he might have married her. Or imprisoned her. I—I intended to ask clemency for you. I, I liked you. I did not know your sister so well."

Anne checked herself. It had not happened, there was no cause to get upset. "A chancy business, this clemency."

"Your Majesty, I am sorry."

Anne looked down at the letters. "Do you expect clemency for your father?"

John did not look, looked away from her lap, into the distance. "Your Majesty has been merciful in the past," he said. "You married a bastard to save him from the pyre."

"I did," Anne said. "But . . ." There was no point in going on. Too much to be said, and too little to be gained by saying it. "I have heard there are great mountains in Switzerland," she said. "Black rocks and crags that no army can cross. Or almost none."

"I have heard that."

"I wish we had mountains," Anne said. "You do not need to treat with mountains to make them keep your borders secure."

"Your Majesty," said John. "Can we avoid a war?"

"Henry thinks so," Anne said. "I will—speak with my sister. We shall see."

"Your Majesty," John said. "I—have more news for you. More ill news. I am sorry."

Anne looked into John's face. His hands were twisting together, as if crushing an invisible letter between them. "What is it?"

"I—have spoken to Master Shingleton."

Anne's heart beat faster. Though the room was large and clear, there did not seem to be enough air to fill her chest. John's face was drawn, and one of his legs trembled a little, as if he was struggling not to get up and run.

He did not speak. Anne spoke for him. She could see it in his face. Now she could see it, she realised she must have known it for some time.

"How long has my grandfather been dead?" she said.

John's eyes went white around the centres, and Anne swallowed the burst of tears rising in her throat.

"It was—loyal of him to keep it quiet until the succession is clear," she said. Her voice dragged, but she could form the words. "But . . . it is time we buried his body."

She heard John's breath catch as he inhaled. "Did you hear this yourself, your Majesty?" he said.

Anne shook her head. "It needed no special ears. I . . . am not a fool, that is all." She closed her eyes for a second. Tears splashed out, and she pressed her fingertips to them. It would only upset John if she started crying again. "I wish I could have been with him. But his soul is free now. It was loyal of Master Shingleton, but we must be done now. He must have a Christian burial. It will take only one ship." Anne drew a long breath. She could get air enough to last her. "We shall have a funeral when my royal husband returns home. I shall write to my sister. It will be soon, and then you will see what follows."

## THIRTY-SEVEN

Henry had seen ships passing out in the open sea, but this was the first time he had been on one. He did not like it. A trip out of the bay had sounded good, but while the air was fresh and salt-sticky around them, the ship itself was horrendous: noise, noise everywhere, drummers banging away below, creaking wood and the slam of sail against caked sail, an unstable platform ready to tip him off his legs at any moment. The deck was crowded thick with pillars and crossbars, ropes and masts every way he looked; there was nowhere on board he could turn his eyes that wasn't oppressive. If it would not have upset his wife, he would have stripped and leaped off the side, swam his way forward. Henry stared over the side in frustration. When he had first gone back, to fight the English deepsmen, he had been fearful, but he found himself longing to dive now. He had made a place for himself among those deepsmen: he was no longer a weak little boy who could be pushed up a beach. He had shown strength. The deepsmen did not hold grudges against new leaders, not if they were reasonable after the conquest. He had had too little time to play, but he'd been starting to make friends.

Out here, the sea was as featureless from above as from below, stretching out grey in all directions. Beneath the surface, he knew, there would be an endless mesh of sounds, the chatter and roar of the ocean to guide his way. But as long as his ears were above it, that world was closed to him. Instead, it was landsmen's talk, as ceaseless as the seas, but no pattern of sounds to swim through, no echoes to guide your way. Landsmen's talk was a net that tangled you, in commitments and lies and promises half-understood. You could move through the sea. When you were in it, it did not hurl you about like this ugly boat.

Seated on the deck of the great ship as it creaked and pitched its way out to sea, he thought of the ships he had seen in his childhood, the ships he had been forbidden to encounter, some of them could have been funeral ships. Deepsmen had no word for *cannibal*. But they did not, on the whole, eat each other. They would eat the tongue of a dolphin, should they best it in a fight, and sometimes, perhaps, if an intertribal struggle between two great men came to killing, there might be a symbolic bite from the bleeding stump, torn out of a ripped-away jaw. But nothing more.

With landsmen, it seemed, they had no such scruples. But perhaps they had had scruples for him. Or maybe they had just not wished him to be seen.

It mattered little enough. They were going out to sea, to drop off the body of an old man who had held the throne for a long time. The king had balanced people and armies, had held off enemies. Anne seemed to have been fond of him; she sat beside Henry, grey-faced and close-mouthed, her eyes glinting with tears she would not release.

On board the ship were Samuel Westlake and Archbishop Summerscales, muttering about their God over the bundled body. So many garments to wrap a dead man; so many words said to a hulk that could not hear.

Anne had said that they should chant a funeral dirge. It was respect, the landsmen thought, but she had told him the words. They had nothing to do with respect: they were a call to the deepsmen to come and take the body, once the sound of the drums had summoned them close enough to hear. It was sensible to get rid of the corpse, but to call it respect was simply lying again. There were musicians surrounding them, piping out dismal-sounding creaks and groans, crashing their wooden batons out of sight below, and Henry's ears ached.

He had promised they would call the deepsmen, but not until there was a point to it. And until they were far enough out to sea, there was no point.

They had ridden the ship down the Thames. On board were men who owned land in England, great men, as Anne put it. John Claybrook stood there, and on the other side of the ship, looking out at the water, was his father.

Also on board was Philip. Philip was in a litter, kept far away from the body. At times he blinked bewildered eyes at the bundle, asking, "Father?" It was for this purpose that Henry had invited Allard, his scholar father, his first helper, to come and join them.

Allard had been shy of Henry when they met, standing before him in the great hall, his hands pressed together around a worn hat. He was smaller than Henry remembered; taller than Henry, yes, but an older man, thinner, than the master he had seemed all those years ago. It had been an effort to make conversation.

"Are you well?" Henry said.

"I am, I thank your Majesty," Allard said. Henry had frowned. Allard had given him his name. Now he was frightened to use it.

"And your wife?"

"Well. Well enough. She will thank you for asking."

She would do no such thing, Henry knew. She had always been terrified of him. Or perhaps just terrified to have him in the house, knowing what he could bring on them. She had thought him a wild animal, and a curse as well, a magnet to the anger of princes. She would be happier to have him away.

"And Markeley and his wife?" The man who had taught him all those weapons, weapons he had never come to use. He had been a part of his life, once. Henry doubted if he would ever see Markeley again.

"We—are all well, I thank your Majesty."

Allard had lost. That was how he seemed. His foundling was at the throne, ready to ascend, married to the princess; the whole of England seemed ready to take in the boy he had found picking shells on a long-lost shore. It should have been a triumph for him. But there was an air of defeat about the man. Henry wondered how grieved he had been to see his boy run away.

"You are a man of learning," Henry said. "I have a study for you. One that might interest you."

Allard looked at him with a quick bewilderment. "Your Majesty?"

"Enough of 'your Majesty,' my name is Henry to you. It should be. You were the one who chose it for me."

Allard blinked. "Yes . . . as you wish, Henry."

Henry paused for a moment. "I am sorry I ran without telling you," he said in the end. "I could bear no more of Claybrook's lies. I did not mean to hurt your feelings."

And Allard looked at him, his face white and his mouth open, as if he had heard an animal speak.

"I—You do not seem to me," Henry said, groping for words in the gaze of his astonished father, "like a man who cares for courts and politics. I think you took me in because you were—curious. And because you did not wish to see me die. I am right, am I not?"

"I—did not think it—I did not think I could leave you to die on the shore," Allard said in the end. "And yes. A wild deepsman. Such a thing I had never seen before. We bow before our kings and serve them, but we knew so little of the deeps. It could add so much to our knowledge of ourselves, if we could only study more."

"What did you learn from me?" Henry said. He was almost smiling. It was as good a reason as any to take someone in. And once Allard had taken him in, he supposed, it was the crown or nothing. What else could one do with a princeling body, with the laws as they were? And if the throne was the only place to send your curious child, what could a small landholder like Allard do if not seek shelter from a greater man like Claybrook? Allard had done what he could, over the years, and Henry had come too far to blame him if it had not worked quite the way they had anticipated.

Allard sighed. "Mostly, that we cannot easily bend others to our will."

At that, Henry laughed aloud. It was true. Allard had watched him all those years, and he had not made a landsman of him. But neither had he tried to force him beyond his endurance. Henry would not bear a beating, so Allard had not tried it again. He had foregone Latin and languages, reading and writing, all things, Henry saw now, that must have been dear to a scholar's heart. He had, as far as had been possible, tried to allow Henry to be his natural self.

"I have another study for you," Henry said. "It should interest you. And it will raise you in honour, if that idea appeals to you. I want you to take on the care of Philip."

"Philip?" For a moment Allard blinked again, as if not understanding.

"The prince. The sufferer. He cannot stay in court, he is too foolish. He has been too long out of the sea, he is bred out. He must be sent away, somewhere he can be cared for. A nuisance of a man, I think. But it might interest you, yes? To see one child just a day out of the sea, and compare him with a man too long on land? It would be a fine study, indeed. My wife is a lover of learning. I think your studies would find favour."

It took Allard a moment to recover himself. Henry was offering a proximity to the royal family many men would have killed for. That men had killed for, in the past. Allard had struggled to keep his captive royal alive all those years. He was not an unkind man, he would give Anne no cause to cry over her uncle being mistreated. If she was going to cry over him: Henry had seen how she shrank when Philip was in the room. Allard would take him far away, and Anne could forget about him; she wouldn't get that look she had when Philip came near. Allard could scratch in his books. It was not what Allard had planned for, but it was the best gift Henry could think to give him.

Allard bowed low. "Thank you, your—Henry. I shall be happy to."

"I shall send you some more staff, and guards," Henry said. "You will need help. Perhaps you may wish to dig a lake. Let us know what you need."

He hesitated.

"Allard," he said eventually, "they talk a lot here, of God and the Church. You did not talk of it so much. Why is that?"

Allard shook his head, as if in puzzlement. "I tried to tell you," he said. "But it seemed to upset you. You did not seem to understand. I thought that God would bring you to your own understanding, if He wished. But the Scriptures do not speak of the deepsmen. Perhaps they have another Christ. Or perhaps they do not need one; no scripture speaks of their fall. I thought, perhaps, that God might reveal Himself otherwise to you."

"There have been other bastards who became kings, have there not?" Henry asked. Allard studied. Allard would know. "What did they do?"

"A few. Very few, though. And I read all I could, everything I could find. What they thought in themselves, I do not know. But I could find no record of any of them being pious."

"These half-breed kings talk about God," Henry said. "My wife talks about it all the time."

Allard sighed. "God save the kings. But they have been out of the sea for many generations. I—you always seemed to me a deepsman, Henry. I did not dare to trifle with your soul."

So Allard stood beside Philip's litter, pouring water with his own hands, and watching the bewildered prince with alert, intelligent eyes. He did not soothe him quite as Westlake had, but Philip was submitting fairly quietly to Allard's ministrations. He made the occasional protest, and Allard listened with evident interest.

John came over to Henry's side. He hesitated for a moment before Henry gestured him to sit down.

"Are you all right?" John said.

"Something troubles me," Henry said.

"What?"

"My wife says that you and she were—friends?"

John's face reddened. Henry was a little surprised. The question he wanted to ask John was a difficult one, but he would have expected John to go white, if he was nervous.

John made no answer, only inclined his head, gesturing Henry to go on.

"If you were her friend," Henry said, "why did you not tell her about me?"

The colour faded from John's face, and he looked at Henry, shrugging. "You would have been burned. You did not want that, did you?"

"No," said Henry. "But she would have been in danger if we had marched on London. Did you not feel you should warn her?"

John raised his hands in the air, looking helpless. "I have spoken to her of this. I did intend to ask mercy for her, should we succeed."

"But she was in danger," Henry persisted. "And you did not warn her. She was your friend."

"You were my brother," John said. "I had to do my best."

Henry's face closed. He wanted to say more: that people either lied or they didn't, that politicking was something people did to keep secrets from those they were going to ask to take risks they wouldn't take themselves; that loyalty should be to people and should be firm, and that you could not be friends with people who were enemies. When it came to the clash between them, you would have to betray someone. There was no point to doing your best; you could do your best and lose, and you'd be every inch as dead as if you hadn't tried. Or someone else would be. John had been his friend. He had been his wife's friend, too, but it had been no doing of John's that Henry and Anne had come together. That, they had managed alone.

He wanted to say something to John, something of the absoluteness of action, how you did something or you didn't. Being loyal to *your best* was just another word-thing. But words were John's province, landsmen's province, and Henry could not find the right ones to speak. Nothing that would not hurt his friend too harshly.

They sat in silence. The musicians piped away, but nobody spoke. There was no royal chant. The ship was rolling out to sea, past the bay, out into the blue, further than a funeral ship should go, and Anne and Henry sat silent, making no call to the deepsmen.

It was Hakebourne who finally spoke up. "Your Majesty," he said, addressing Anne. His voice was low, his back turned to the others; wind from the keel was scattering locks of hair around his face. "Are you not going to call for the deepsmen to come?"

"In a while, Lord Tay," Anne said.

"Your Majesty—"

Anne raised her hand. Cool light shone through the thin webs between her fingers, the unadorned hand of a queen. She turned, facing down into the ship. Spray splashed up behind her, as if she stood with her back to a storm.

"My people," she said, "we have said nothing, for fear of spies. But as we bury the king my grandfather, we are also here on England's business." She stopped, but there was no murmur, no questioning, just a turning of faces in her direction. "I have heard word from my sister Mary. You will know, I think, if your intelligencers are as good as mine, the threat we face if she and her royal husband wish to bid for our throne. We would not have a war with France if we can avoid it; we will not spill English blood wantonly. My royal sister knows of this funeral. She is coming in her own ship, to witness our grandfather committed to the deep. I will speak to her then, and we shall parley. This is our decision."

There was a silence. When someone spoke, it was Claybrook, speaking finally to Anne, his face smoothly controlled, but his voice sharp with anger beneath. He spoke as to a child, a man utterly out of patience.

"Does it not occur to your Majesty," he said, "that we are only one ship? That if your royal sister wished to send a navy, she could sink us, unguarded as we are?"

Anne raised an eyebrow; keeping her face calm and hard to read would madden him more. It was the only aggression she could spare. She had hated this man for so long, it was hard to see his face without wanting to slash at it. A quick swing with her sharp nails and she could lay him open. God did not permit hatred, but Anne could only own herself a sinner when faced with this man. Though not, she thought, as great a sinner as he. Not nearly so great.

"Perhaps your Majesty might swim to shore," Claybrook said. "But your faithful subjects are not so lucky."

This was insolence, dangerous talk. Claybrook must never have expected a girl like Anne to come so far if he was having such difficulty reining his tongue. Anne's skin was cold in the wind, and she kept her hands at her sides.

Her voice was light, even as her body locked its joints. "I did not say we were unguarded," she said.

There was another silence. It was broken by, of all people, Samuel Westlake.

"Does your Majesty mean to attack your sister?" he said. In one hand he held an aspergillum, ready to sprinkle holy water on Edward's wrapped corpse; the other was on his cane. His hands were spread out, a lowered crucifix between them; his body looked thin and fragile. His voice was almost intimate, as if he were asking her a private question in the confessional. So much so that Anne felt a pang of conscience, as if she were again a child seeking comfort from the only man who had been kind to her. She swallowed.

"I do not," Anne said. "But arrangements have been made. There will be no battle."

She sat leaned against the prow. The ship rose and fell, lifted itself up and dashed itself back down into the scattering water, and Anne's horizon staggered.

As she looked over her shoulder, she saw the dark shape of a ship, sailing its way towards them.

"There comes my royal sister now," she said. "And look." There were white shapes flashing before the wake, breaking the surface, skimming along with the rushing water like hounds following a hunt. "She has brought her deepsmen with her. We must call our own."

She glanced at Henry, who was sitting silent on the deck. *Will we be safe?* she asked him in their own language.

For a moment, he did not respond. *Whistle,* said Anne. He turned his head and looked at her. *Will we be safe?*

Her husband stared at her, his face tense. He made a frustrated gesture, half a shrug, half a grab at the air, his hand closing on nothing. *Nothing is safe,* he said.

Anne swallowed. "I would seek spiritual counsel before this meeting," she said. "My lord Bishop, may I speak with you alone?"

Privacy was a difficult thing to manage on a boat. Anne had no desire to go below decks; she did not want to lose sight of the coming ship. In the end, the two of them retreated to the stern, Westlake tottering on the swaying deck, his cane slipping and sliding, Anne tugging herself hand-over-hand on the side. *Lame creatures, the pair of us,* Anne thought. *God made the lame walk. Christ blessed the weak. But I do not think we are weak.*

It was not very secure, or even very private back here. The wake spread out behind them like a foaming road. But it would have to do. There was nowhere on the ship, in any case, where Henry would not hear them.

Samuel Westlake leaned against a mast and looked at her. Anne balanced herself unsteadily against the side. It was not a secure position, but it hardly mattered. If she fell overboard, she could swim.

There was a silence.

"Do you wish to confess?" Samuel said in the end. His voice was almost entreating.

Anne spoke as quietly as she could, lowering her voice amid the creaks of wood and slap of the sea and the cries of gulls overhead. "I wish you to confess the truth to me, Samuel. I have seen letters. Was it you who told my sister of my marriage?"

The wind blew around Samuel, flapping his clothes like sails, and he stood against the mast like a martyr at the stake. There was a moment where she saw him brace, consider. Then he let his head drop.

"No," he said. "I did not reply to those letters. But I did not tell you either, when I could have."

Anne said nothing.

"I have loved you as my child, my lady Princess," Samuel said. "But I could not help a pagan king to the throne. God would have damned me for it."

Anne was too cold, too wind-blown for tears. Her skin pulsed in the coarse wind. "I thought you were helping a Christian queen," she said.

Samuel did not answer. "What is between you and Robert Claybrook?" he said.

So he had seen it, the look on her face. He had seen her knowl-edge. He had always been a perceptive man, Samuel Westlake. Though she was not prepared to abandon England, Anne felt, for a moment, frightened to her soul at the thought of turning away from the advice of so sharp-eyed a man.

"He is the one who killed my mother," Anne said. Quietly, so that no other landsman could hear.

"Have you proof of this?" Again, Samuel's manner was catechis-ing, as if he had not just confessed to keeping information treasonously from her. Even though he had betrayed her by doing so, Anne's heart could not help a little thump of admiration. It was a fine thing, courage. And the courage to keep doing what you must, even when fate might be closing in on you, was a bravery she had admired from her cradle.

"His son as good as confessed it," Anne said.

"You have parted son from father?"

"Robert Claybrook is a wicked man," Anne said. "He was the one keeping Henry hidden. He placed his son between his friend and his country. John shall be safe, we shall raise him up. He is safer away from such a father."

"My lady Princess," Samuel said. His voice was urgent. It was what he had always called her. Anne did not feel insulted that he did not say *your Majesty*. It was almost comforting to be addressed in the familiar way. "God commands against vengeance."

"But man must have justice," Anne said. "My mother would have said that."

The ship rolled, and Samuel grabbed at the mast behind his back for support. "Your mother's justice is not something you should fol-low," he said.

"I would not burn a child," Anne said. "Why else would I have married Henry?" Hearing herself say the words, she remembered that Henry could undoubtedly hear her say them too. It was not tactful. She cursed herself inwardly; now she would have to make amends.

"And what will you do with Claybrook?" Westlake said. "If you would follow your mother? Burn him? Poison him?"

"Poison him? My mother was no poisoner."

Gulls screamed overhead, and Westlake looked at her in desperate anger. "You know that is not so, my lady Princess."

"I know no such thing." Anne found she was gripping her skirt; embroidery pressed into her palms.

"I did not ask you to talk of it," Samuel said. His face was as grave as ever, but his voice, quiet enough for privacy, was as raw as Anne's. "You could not have stopped it. And you tried to make amends. I thought you were a good girl. But now you are striking for the throne any way you can. I have seen where that leads. I fear for England, my lady Princess, I truly do."

"What are you talking about?" Anne's voice began to rise, and she checked it. Across the deck came Henry's voice: *Are you all right? Do you need me?*

*Stay where you are, Whistle,* she said. "I want to hear this. What do you talk of, Samuel? I would have you tell me now."

Samuel glared at her, his face tinged red by the wind. "You cannot have known nothing of it," he said. "I cannot believe that."

"Samuel, tell me now, or I will call my husband," Anne said. Her voice was sharp, but underneath it she was frantic. Even if Henry came over, she had no idea what she would ask him to do, but she could not stand here another moment on her weak legs while Samuel talked of God only knew what sin on her conscience.

"You must have known it was your mother who poisoned me," Samuel said. "I survived, by the grace of God, and the care of Master Shingleton. And the medicine you sent me. But you must have known it was her."

Anne's lips cracked, dry as ash. All around her, the groaning timbers and whipping winds made a reckless commotion; there was no silence, no stillness to absorb the words she had heard. The horizon lurched, and the boat ploughed on its way towards her sister.

"You cannot be serious," Anne said in the end. Her voice came out papery, as if a dead wasp's nest rattled in her throat.

Samuel raised a thin hand. "Before God, I am."

"W-why?" It was all Anne could do to speak the syllable.

Samuel bent a look on her, frustration mixed with doubt. She had never seen his face so unguarded. "I wrote to her before the burning," he said. "I pleaded with her for the life of the child. And she sent me to bless the bonfire, myself, not the Archbishop or one of my brother clerics. She sent me. She said if I was so concerned for the child, I should be the one to bless his passage into Heaven. I thought that was enough for her, I thought that was how she had made her point. But it was not. There was poison in my food. Your mother decided she could not spare a man of God in England who would speak up against her authority."

Anne stood on the rocking deck, speechless.

"If you say it was my lord Claybrook who murdered your mother, that is a sin upon his soul," Samuel said. "But he saved my life by doing it, my lady Princess. Your mother died before she could make another attempt. If he was hiding a bastard, I can well believe that he would be frightened. Your mother was a fearsome woman."

Anne had never in her life minded the cold, had loved it as a memory of the sea on her skin, but now she was shivering. She grasped frantically at the remains of her thoughts, trying to see some way clear. "My mother was a Christian," she said. "Why should you fear a pagan king more than her?"

Samuel's eyes were pinched at the corners, as if holding back tears. "You were willing to overturn the Church to place him on the throne, to secure it," he said. "Against the laws of God. It was not him I feared, my lady Princess. It was you."

"Samuel, I love the Church. I would not have let any pagan king overset it."

"As long as a pagan king is on the land, we cannot have unity," Samuel said. "If the king himself does not honour God, what will become of us all? Frenchness breeds out in a generation, but heresy grows, my lady Princess. I did not want to see the Church fractured in a deepsman's hands."

"You—you are wrong," Anne said. She could think of no answer, but everything in her cried this out. "I would have preserved the Church. I will. God does not want us to make war. I have only ever acted to save lives, Samuel. Will you say that lives are of no account?"

Samuel leaned against the mast, hands behind his back. "Your mother would have said the same thing," he said. "I knew her. I do not say lives are of no account. But I do not think you have reckoned the price well."

*I should go in the water,* Henry's voice came across the deck. *It is time. Stop talking about dead landsmen and come and help me.*

Dead landsmen. That was how Henry spoke of Christ. Anne unclasped her hands from their wooden support, began the unsteady journey back to the prow. It seemed a long time before she reached the others. Samuel stood in the stern, watching her go. He made no attempt to follow her.

⟳

And Mary was in the water.

⟳

Anne and Henry stripped and prepared to dive off the end of the boat. This was not how a funeral was supposed to be conducted, but no one was going to argue with them. Henry's eyes lingered on Anne as she bared her skin to the air, but Anne could not feel any response. Samuel's news had struck her like a wave, and she was soaked in it. She could think only of her mother.

*I have always wanted this,* Anne told herself as she dived. *I have never been out past the bay. Now, for the first time, I am seeing the real ocean.*

But the sea was dark and obscure, a blank vista in every direction. Clouded light and shadows below, no different from a bay. Sounds carried, the shore of England quieter and France louder, the calls of deepsmen in the water and the bat-clicks of fish, but Anne looked at her own grey legs, light wavering over them from above, and saw nothing but her own flesh. No answers in the water.

*Mother,* she thought. Erzebet's face, tense and proud, raising her chin as the bruises on her body were laid open to all eyes. Erzebet sleeking forward through the water, hurling herself towards the deepsmen she had to appease, with only her own strength and endurance to do so. Erzebet cradling a child, Anne, her own daughter, sending maids out of the room and crooning, *Safe, my baby, safe.* Erzebet kissing Anne for asking whether or not princes should spare their enemies, and making no answer to the question.

Anne had waited all her life for her mother's love. She had had it all along, she thought now. But she had waited more for her mother's heart, to know what thoughts Erzebet was keeping behind that still face. As the deepsmen started to gather, as calls began to echo from the south in response to Henry's calls, Anne thought she knew.

It was fear.

It was so easy to say it: *This has to be done for the greater good. This has to be done to protect those I love.* To spend your life watching the faces around you, trying to anticipate, trying to protect, to conceal yourself and find out others, to compromise and bargain away pieces of yourself, waiting for the moment when the promise to the baby in your arms would one day be true. Erzebet had seen her uncle's skull crack under a blazing crown. Anne had seen her uncle thrash and bellow, helpless as a stunned bull, had seen her mother scream and bleed, had seen her sister, her only sister, sent away to a stranger. Always, always saying to herself: *One day I shall be secure. One day, we shall be safe.*

In the stillness of a chapel, Anne could feel God in her heart. But she never felt further from the light of Heaven than when she said to herself the same sentence she had been saying, heart-deep, since she could first remember: *One day, not today, but one day, I shall be safe.*

Anne had not been willing to see a man burned. But she had not been ruling very long. And there was a long time yet before she could reach that point. She was still only fourteen.

She had waited to be loved all her life. And in waiting, what would she become?

Somewhere, Mary was waiting. It had been months since she had seen her sister's face, but she would not see it here in the water. Diving down, Anne remembered the first years of her life: Erzebet's here-and-gone attention and Mary elsewhere, unmentioned by anyone. Why had Erzebet not told her that she had a sister?

The thought of being angry with her mother was terrifying, something she could not face; Anne fought down the thought as hard as she could: *My mother should have told me I had a sister.* It was not the thought for this moment, could do no good at all. But Anne remembered sitting at Erzebet's funeral, how Mary had reached for her hand while Anne sat rigid with her eyes straight ahead.

There was no turning back. It was the best chance England stood, to hazard a clean-blooded king, it was right for the country. But Anne swam through the dark water, thinking of how she had waited and waited for her mother's notice, had strained her eyes past Mary to find it, when all the time, Mary had been waiting for hers.

Henry's calls were being answered. The voices of the English deepsmen were drawing nearer. In the darkness of her own mind, Anne said to herself what she had said so many times before: *I must attend to business now, I have not time to think of this.* But would she ever have time?

*Whistle,* she said, *surface with me.* She could hardly see Henry in the black depths, but she heard, after a pause, the reply.

*All right. Surface.*

And the two of them pushed their heads above water.

"What do you want?" Henry said. "We have not much time."

Anne reached out, wrapped her hand around his shoulder. "Do not hurt my sister," she said. "Promise me."

Henry shook his head. He did not like having his ears out of the water like this; unable to listen properly, any predator might be closing in on him, and all his instincts jangled. "Why do you trouble me with this now?"

"Promise me." Anne's fingers clutched him, and her nails pressed against his skin. He reached up and took her wrist. It was small in his hand, narrow and delicate. She was floating up and down as the wind blew, and Henry reached out, laid his hand on her waist. In the privacy of darkness, intimacies were easy.

"If she fights me, I must defend myself," he said. He was trying not to sound angry. His wife seemed to be upset about something again. Henry felt some compunction about that; he did not like to see her unhappy—but she was unhappy a lot, quickly upset. It was no way to survive an active life, getting so distressed so easily.

"She will not, you—she is smaller than you, much smaller. Promise you will not hurt her."

Henry sighed. This was no time to wrangle, and if she wanted it, she could have his promise. He had committed himself to be loyal to her. "If you wish. Now we must get on."

His hand squeezed her waist, briefly, and then he was under the surface with a flick.

Anne hesitated. At the level of her eyes, the waves stretched out: great ripples, miles across, little swells that would rise and crash down on the beaches. She could see for miles, here in the daylight.

Then she plunged her head back into the darkness.

*Sister,* she called. *Come to me. Sister. Where are you?*

Mary's voice answered. *I am here.*

*Is your man here?* It was the answer she most needed to know. She did not want to hurt anyone, but the issue was Louis-Philippe. This man she had never met. She needed to know where he was.

A voice came ringing out of the depths. You could not say that it had a French accent; it spoke in their common mother tongue with the same ease that Anne and Mary had. But there was a cadence to it that was unfamiliar: not the English staccato chant, not Henry's hinterland bark; something was different about it. It was a strong voice, though. Fine lungs and a sound body behind it. *I am here,* it said.

The phrase, *I am here,* was spoken with a challenge. There were different inflections for certain statements, narrow and precise variations. Louis-Philippe was speaking with the lilt of a leader.

Anne could not, for a moment, answer. *Are you all right, sister?* she said.

There was a lull, and Mary's voice came back. The sound was thin. She sounded as if she was struggling for words to adequately express the foolishness of Anne's question. *I am more all right than you are.*

*Sister,* Anne said. *I do not wish to fight.*

There was another hush. Anne could not see her sister's face in the void, and Mary would not swim close enough to see her.

*Your man is bad,* Mary said. *You have made a mistake.*

*Not bad,* Anne said. *Not a stranger.*

*You have not backed me up,* Mary said. Her voice was rising shrill and pained, echoing across the miles. The deepsmen had no word for *betray.*

Louis-Philippe's voice cut in again, calling out a challenge. He called it to Henry, and Henry answered. Around them, a swirl of deepsmen rose, a spiralling army, circling the four of them in silent, grey-skinned ranks.

***

Deepsmen saw things tribally, Henry knew. But the deepsmen of France were his own tribe. So too, now, were the deepsmen of England. They recognised a victory by strength. You saw it sometimes: new faces joined, old faces left. There were no borders in the sea, no imaginary lines down solid earth. You could move with the tide.

It was not, therefore, a matter of landsmen's law that the deepsmen from the shores of France and England must be, now and for ever, rivals. It was a matter of habit, of custom.

And, given the right push, customs could change.

This was what the landsmen forgot: that while they thought so much of the deepsmen, of their salt-blooded kings and their guardians on the shores, most of the time the deepsmen were thinking of other things. They had no farms and crops to bring them food after they had schemed all day; it was hunt or die, all the time, continually. They paid loyalty to their visiting lords because they needed alliances and truces; they took an interest in their own territory because it was good to keep a place that was safe from your enemies.

But let them agree that another tribe was not the enemy, and a peace treaty could be sealed in the time it would take a landsmen to cut a pen.

His deepsmen had known Louis-Philippe since Louis-Philippe was a child, that much was clear. But he had not roamed with them. Henry's ties of blood, Whistle's ties, simply went deeper. Louis-Philippe was a good enough ally, but Whistle was one of their own.

So as Louis-Philippe called out a challenge, deepsmen rose. And Louis-Philippe bounced his voice in Whistle's direction, saying, *Enemy.*

Anne and Whistle had not called the deepsmen from England; there had been no need. They had known, because Whistle had told them, what to anticipate. They had followed the boat silently from beneath.

And as the deepsmen of France rose at Louis-Philippe's voice, they did not mass upon Whistle. They swam forward, past Louis-Philippe, going out to greet their new friends. Deepsmen whirled round each other, diving and dancing, following each other in twisting, joyous patterns; holding hands, embracing, play-chasing each other through the water. There were no calls of *Enemy, Fight, Challenge.* Instead, the water was filled with greetings. *Happy to see you again. We shall not fight. Would you like to be my friend?*

Great beams of light sliced through the choppy waves, glinting and flashing on grey skin as the deepsmen swam in and out, somersaulting and clasping hands. Deepsmen were fierce, but given a chance not to fight, to spare injuries and lives, given a chance to have peace instead of wasting blood, they were glad to take it. Deepsmen were fierce, but they weren't foolish.

Anne hovered in the water, watching the soldiers of the deep gambol around one another. She reached out, for a moment, and took Whistle's hand. He clasped it, feeling the narrow bones, the fine webs. She was emotional, his wife, but she could be pleased after all.

*Sister,* he heard her say, *we will not fight. The tribes will not fight, and I do not want to fight you.*

The sister was too far away for them to see her face clearly, but he heard a rising note in her voice. *What have you done? Have you taken away my tribe?*

*I love you,* Anne said. *I do not want to fight. I have made peace. Make peace with me.*

*I am a stranger,* came the girl's voice out of the dark. *I left my tribe. I wanted to come home. You have harmed me.*

Anne did not let go of his hand. *I know,* she said. *You need not be a stranger. Be my sister and I will be yours. I am sorry.*

The girl's voice came again, loud and high. *You have harmed me!*

*I have harmed you,* said Anne. *I have not been your friend. I want to be your friend now. I am sorry.*

What his wife was apologising for, Whistle didn't know; it had better not be for marrying him. He had counted on her to be happy about that. But her hand still gripped his in the silence.

Whistle spoke again, this time to Louis-Philippe. The man had no deepsman's name, nothing that could be pronounced underwater, and to even attempt his land name would be to swallow a lungful of brine, but he directed himself as well as he could in Louis-Philippe's direction. *Sister's man,* he said. *Do you want to be king?*

*What?* The reply came sharp and clear. The man had a fine voice, Whistle thought. He could deal with such a voice.

*Let us be friends,* Whistle said. *Make peace with us. Make peace, and my tribe will be better friends with you than with your brother. You will be king.*

*Do not fight.* That was Anne's voice, cutting across him. *Do not fight your brother, or we will not support you. But make peace with him and with us.*

That was a refinement Whistle had not thought about, and, considering how hysterical landsmen were about titles, would take a lot of talking in France to resolve: Louis-Philippe trying to take the kingship from his brother without fighting him for it. But then again, Louis-Philippe had lived on land all his life. Perhaps he could find a way. Whistle was not eager for more battles or enmities anyway; they only led to burnings, and hiding yourself away.

*Let us be friends, brother,* Whistle said to Louis-Philippe in the dark. *I am offering you something good. Take it.*

There was a long silence, filled only with the chirrups of fish. Then Louis-Philippe's voice came back. *I will take it,* he said. And Anne's hand relaxed in Whistle's grip, and she lay down upon the sea, stretching out her limbs in victory.

*Surface,* she said, swimming up to the top. Whistle did not need to breathe yet, so he let her go. There was a pause, the dark shape of her legs bobbing in the bright waves above. Then there was a crash: a shape falling through the water, long and wrapped. The tribe, both tribes, swam up to grab it.

Edward's body, Henry thought. The old king, now a victory feast, sealing a new treaty. His people could have it. They were dragging it down now, unravelling the bindings with their sharp nails; scraps of cloth floated all around them, like leaves in a gust, drifting slowly down.

The four of them. Whistle, Anne, Mary and Louis-Philippe, all stayed where they were. This was not a feast for any of them. They swam together, slower than the deepsmen had, but together nonetheless, reaching out in the murk to see the faces of their new allies.

BOOK EIGHT

❧

# DEPARTURE

## Thirty-Eight

It was a fine day when the court set out to hunt. Anne was glad of that; though nothing made her seasick, some of her courtiers' stomachs were not so steady, and finding porpoise to hunt would be a long journey out into the rough seas. She stood by the prow, watching as her deepsmen skimmed ahead, diving in and out of the wake like birds.

John came up and stood beside them. Henry was hunched over the side, chirruping down to the deepsmen. *Crabs are good to eat*, he was saying. *I will teach you how to open one.* There was a look on his face Anne had seen a lot lately. She had thought, at first, that it was anger, but she was coming to know him better. Now she thought she recognised it: yearning.

"I have not seen a hunt like this since I was small," John said.

"I know. You told me of it once, do you remember?" Anne said. Henry inclined his head a little, but did not join the conversation.

"I am glad to see the tradition revived." John smiled. The wind blowing the hair around his face made him look young and clean. "Do you mean to be blooded, your Majesty?"

Anne shook her head. "I hardly need to be baptised to the sea. And I do not wish to be baptised in blood."

"Baptised?" Henry said, turning his head a little.

"Received into the Holy Spirit," Anne said. "Holy water is poured, and you are cleansed of sin."

Henry shook his head and stared back down at the wake. "Holy water," he muttered, as if to himself.

"Are you resolved on the coronation tomorrow?" John said, ignoring Henry's mumbling with the air of one used to rising above what couldn't be helped. "That is, have you resolved the question of Henry protecting the Church? I do not believe the Archbishop is happy about it."

"How do you know of that?" Anne said.

John shrugged. "I have ears," he said. "And a tongue to speak with others that have ears."

Anne raised an eyebrow. "An intelligencer," she said. "We must find more uses for you."

There was something in her tone that made John look up, the happy expression suddenly gone from his face.

Anne hesitated for a moment, then nodded. "Send your father to us," she said. "We have something he must hear."

John paused, his face going ashen. Henry looked over his shoulder, seeing his friend stand mute on the deck.

"It is all right," he said. "We will be politicking." There was a look of displeasure on his face; Anne heard a lot of concessions in his tone. For a long time Henry had insisted that they do something about Narbridge, the man who had turned in the Cornwall bastard for burning. It had taken a lot of persuasion to get him to abandon that idea. Though he had survived Claybrook's attempt upon him, better than Erzebet had, he was not at all happy about Anne's new idea on Claybrook. For a moment, Anne wondered whether he was going to say something more, change his mind, but he only looked back out at the sea. In and out of the gleaming water dived the deepsmen, and he called down to them: *Swim well, brothers.*

John disappeared, picking his way across the rising and falling deck, to find his father. Anne laid her hand on Henry's shoulder. "Does it sit so very ill with you?" she said softly.

Henry shrugged. The gesture was an irritable one, but not hostile. "It sits ill. But this is landsman politicking. It is not how I would solve the problem. But if we were to solve it as I would, you would say I was a tyrant. I do not mean to be a tyrant."

"We can do good in the world," Anne said.

Henry shrugged again. "You think you will please your God."

She stroked his shoulder. "I do."

"That will never matter to me," Henry said.

Anne did not say anything, but she did not take away her hand.

John appeared with his father. The two of them stood side by side, but there was a distance between them; Anne could see the bright white sky, a slice of light keeping them apart.

"Please, your Majesty," said John, "do not send me away."

"We did not intend it," said Anne.

Henry turned at last. But even as he looked at Claybrook, his eyes wandered over the man's shoulder, out to the heaving sea.

"Claybrook," he said, "you are a murderer and a liar, and we will not have you on our shores."

Claybrook's face was white, but he tried for a careful smile. "Your Majesty—" he said.

"Do not talk." Henry's voice was level, and cut like a flint-edge. "You are a liar, and I am not interested in what you say. We know the truth of you."

Beside his father, John clasped his hands together, his knuckles paling as he gripped.

"I do not understand my wife," Henry said. "But she thinks her God wants her to be merciful. If it had been my mother you had killed, I would not have spared you."

Henry thought only for a moment as he said that sentence. Would he have spared a man who killed his mother? She had pushed him out of his home into this dry, word-twisted world, where people schemed and murdered behind closed doors, and cared about nonsense, and fettered him hand and mind. His mother had not been with the tribe of France; it had been a long time ago she drove him out. Very probably she was dead by now. He would never see her again, could never ask, even if he could have put it into deepsman's words. But he understood, nonetheless. She had pushed him away because he was a burden who would slow the tribe down. She had tried to keep him alive, and it had been growing impossible for her. In the sea, you did not bow to idiots, did not fetter yourself with words. That look he had seen on his wife's face when her uncle was present was not something he had ever seen in the sea. There was fear, yes, but there were no insane obligations. You did not deny your endless, passionate desire to live. You fought for life, and you lived the best you could, and you sloughed off burdens that would drown you. He was not a burden now. His mother had not abandoned him to a shark, after all, had not held him under. Maybe, when she chased him up that beach, she was hoping he could be cared for. He did not like the landsmen's care, did not want it. But really, why else was he angry with her, except that she had made him leave her?

"Your Majesty, I—"

"Be quiet," Henry said. "I do not love this God of my wife's, and if you try my patience, I will push you over the side. I have a job for you, Claybrook. You may take it, or you may face a trial."

"For murder?" That was John. He did not leave his father's side, but neither did he lean away as the ship rocked.

"For spying," Anne said. Her voice was not sharp, but it was firm. "My sister and I are allies now. She has given me the names of her intelligencers. It was from you, my lord Thames, that she heard of our marriage. And while you did not cause a war by the news, we have our own efforts to thank for that, not yours. The penalties for treason are severe, and we have seen too many burnings in this country already."

"We have a job," Henry said "We are not going to burn bastards. We still mean to stop sailors from fucking deepsmen women, but if a bastard is found, he will be under our protection. We will find means for him. If the deepsmen will not care for him while he is small, we shall. They shall be cousins of the king. All bastards. We will have an army. And you will spy for them."

"My—your Majesty, I—" Claybrook's face was still, but his hands were shaking; there were small twitches at the corners of his eyes and mouth, like a smooth pond with deep currents just rippling the surface.

Henry made an impatient gesture. "I do not expect you to go in the water. And I certainly do not expect you to fuck a deepsman girl and try to put yourself in power that way, Claybrook; the deepsmen will kill you if you try. You will stay out of the water. But you will remain on your ship, you will sail, and watch the water, and if you see a child with cloven legs, you will send word. The deepsmen will know your ship. If they wish to hand the child over, they will bring him up to you. Do not think you can hide him; the captain of the ship is a friend of ours." The young man was, in fact, Thomas Hakebourne's second son Robert: Hakebourne had approved the plan thoroughly and volunteered his boy. He was glad, he said, to see a good purpose for younger sons. He meant Robert, Henry supposed, but perhaps he meant deepsmen children as well.

"You will bring children to shore, and the captain will arrange passage for them. Your land contains the Thames; a ship will meet you where the Thames meets the sea, and the children will go up it. Your land joins my father Allard's, after all. He is to oversee the bastard children. Along with you, John," Henry said, turning to his friend. "You have stewardship of your father's estate while he is at sea. We take it all from him, now, for good. And Claybrook," turning back to the older man, who stood grey and frozen on the deck, "you will be at sea all your life."

A halloo rose from below the keel: the deepsmen had spotted prey. Henry turned, his expression animated for the first time that day. "Will you come?" he said to Anne.

Anne hesitated. "In a while," she said. Henry's face fell a little, and she laid her hand on his arm. "I will come," she said. "But you are the real hunter. John, oversee the small boats so the court can join the hunt. You are a man of fortune now. My lord Thames."

John looked for a long moment at his father. Then he bowed. "Yes, your Majesty," he said. "Thank you, your Majesty."

Was God pleased with her day's work? Anne wondered. Would Erzebet have been? She thought of her mother's fierce, still face, the terrible patience of a frightened woman. Even after Samuel's revelation, she could not, in her heart, let go of that longing for her mother: Erzebet's resolve, her courage, the bruised body she laid down in service to her country. God commanded forgiveness, but whether it was her right to forgive Erzebet for sins she had committed against others, Anne did not know. She could not, for all that, press the love out of her memory. Erzebet might have thought her weak, or taking too much of a chance, leaving Claybrook alive. But Erzebet's thoroughness had driven Claybrook himself to a bath of scalding water. That murder Anne could not, in her heart, forgive. But she could hold her hand. Fear led only to fear, and the frightened lashed out. Anne could only trust her heart to God, and pray that her mercy would not cause suffering later.

But then, she would be Queen, and could keep her eyes open all the time. Be merciful, and watch. That was the best she could plan for. It was time for a surcease of fear.

Samuel Westlake was not going into the boats; he had enough strength, apart from his leg, to handle a harpoon as well as any, but he was not by nature a huntsman. She went and sat beside him. He glanced up from his viewing of the departing boats as she did, and waited for her to speak.

"You heard what we promised Claybrook, I suppose," she said. He had sat a respectful distance away, but his ears were sharp for a landsman's. Very little escaped him.

Samuel nodded, slowly. "I heard, your Majesty."

"Do you forgive me, Samuel?" she said.

"For what, your Majesty?"

Anne shook her head, trying to resolve her thoughts. "For my ignorance of my mother, I suppose. Because I cannot stop feeling a daughter's love for her. For marrying a pagan and still believing I love God. Is that pride, Samuel?"

Samuel drew a long breath in. "Perhaps," he said. "But it is better to love God, even in pride or sin, than not to love God at all."

"A prince must act," Anne said. "We cannot always choose the best course. But I mean to try, Samuel. I will try to be merciful. If that leads to danger, I will face it. But I will not be the first to create danger in my kingdom. I will try to rule well."

Samuel sighed. "It is not my place to forgive you for ignorance," he said. "I believe you, now, that you tried to act for the best. But your husband, your Majesty. I—cannot sit with a pagan ruling the Church."

"Henry does not want the Church," Anne said. "I do not think he even wants the land."

"Your Majesty?"

Anne shook her head. "We shall see," she said. "All I can ask you is this: if I try to rule as God wills it, will you help me, Samuel?"

Samuel reached out and took her hand. "I am your man, your Majesty," he said. "I cannot act against my conscience, I cannot act against God. But I only desire your good, and England's. As far as God wills it."

Anne let her hand lie in his. "I cannot ask for more," she said. "I would not wish to."

~

Over the side of the boat, there were great plumes of spray rising. Porpoises were breaking the surface, great gleaming bodies rising out of the water, slick as metal in the light, diving in and out of the landsmen's harpoons as the deepsmen drove them up from below. It seemed a shame, Anne thought, to destroy such graceful creatures. Henry said that they and the deepsmen were enemies, that they would eat deepsmen children if they could catch them, but they were lovely nonetheless.

She had better join in the hunt. Stripping off privately, Anne dived over the side. The water closed around her, sharp and cold, deafening in its commotion as deepsmen called hunting cries from all sides, porpoises screeched, harpoons and bodies crashed through the surface with the sound of shattering glass. Anne could hear the calls: *Follow me! Go round eastwards! I am below! Forward!* And in amongst them, Henry's voice, calling as loud as any: *Drive them up, drive them up!*

Anne hung in the chaos of bubbles and white water, churned air fizzing upon her skin. Her husband dived and called with his people, ringing clear and strong amongst them.

She knew, in that moment, what she had known for some time in her heart. Henry, Whistle, her husband, was a deepsman. He had found his people, and he was not coming back.

Anne let out a great sigh of air, watching the bubbles rise to the surface above her. They shimmered in the water like scales, like silver, driving hard and beautiful towards the light.

## Thirty-Nine

WHISTLE COULD REMEMBER the arms of his mother, holding him up for his first lungful of air. The arms of his wife, around him in the cold, were soft, gentle, the kind arms of a woman who had never pushed him out. As the sea lapped around them, he clutched her to him, the pliable body of this strange girl who had, in the end, not forced him to act against himself. She had saved his life, and as for what she called his soul, she had left it alone.

Whistle was happy for that. He would miss her when he was away. But he knew, now, how to come back.

— 

The coronation was behind them, a dull ceremony that Whistle had sat through, knowing that this time, this final time, really was the last time he would have to sit in some grim cave of a building, bored by words he knew nothing about and cared for even less. John had been beside him. As the instruments had creaked out their weird music, Whistle had turned and whispered to him what they really meant, *Good eating, don't trifle with me,* and John had laughed behind his hand. But John was a client king now, a nominated regent, and had cleared his face quickly. John could understand the politicking, and he seemed to get on well with Anne. Whistle would just have to trust in their fidelity to him. But then, there would be deepsmen girls in the sea, the long months when he was away from his wife, and he was prepared to stay away from them; he had no desire for quarter-blood children. It was not a family arrangement, this deal between the three of them, but it would hold if they held to it. Whistle was determined to find that people could be trusted.

King in the water—that was what they were calling him now. Visiting his wife when the tides were right, speaking to passing ships, hailing sailors and courtiers who went out to fish, swimming out with his family. Perhaps he would not be king over the deepsmen, not in body: he was still small, always would be, for the sea. The deepsmen had no word for *negotiator*; they were, however, developing a verb: *whistle-talking*. Who would have thought it, Whistle reflected, finally amused. He had ended up a diplomat after all.

Anne embraced him a last time, and swam back to her people. For an instant, hanging empty-armed in the water, Whistle was lonely. He felt a catch of sorrow in his throat as the girl disappeared into the gloom. But she would be back.

Whistle drew a deep lungful of air and drove down, out to the sea where his own people were waiting for him. As the water stroked over his body, he felt it all shed away: words, books, straight-angled rooms and crosses of wood, of stone, of glass, the textures and weights and tastes of the land. He was coming clean, returning to the life he had lost.

It would not be safe in the sea. Nothing was safe. But if the sea was a life of movement and hunger, starvation and flight, so was life on the land, in its way. Whistle had lived skin-to-skin with danger all his life. It was nothing new. Nothing, in itself, he was afraid of. He would save his fear for real things, for sharks and poison fish and rocks in storms. He was going home.

He could hear the calls of his people, out in the dark water: *Come on. Welcome. We are waiting.* Whistle broke the surface one last time in an English bay, took a great breath of cold, sweet air, and dived.

ACKNOWLEDGEMENTS

I'm blessed to know and work with a lot of wonderful people, all of whom deserve thanks.

First, thanks to my wonderful agent Sophie Hicks and everyone at Ed Victor: I couldn't be more fortunate than to work with you. Without Philippa Harrison, I doubt the book would have been finished at all, and certainly it would have been much worse, so endless gratitude for riding in on a white horse at a critical juncture.

Everyone at Random House has been great, especially Dan Franklin, Betsy Mitchell, and Ellah Allfrey, whose superb suggestions went a long way towards improving the first draft. I'd also like to thank the sturdy proofreaders, Ellen Weider, and Maralee Youngs my fine designers and typesetters, whose skill and patience I can only admire.

The commenters on my blog have been a delight to me ever since I started it, and I much appreciate their thoughts and company. I'd particularly like to thank all those clever souls who gave generously of their time and effort to answer my call for nit-picks with an alarmingly well-informed array of suggestions and queries, which made the final polish much more useful than it otherwise would have been: Naomi Clark, James Donalbain Bremner, Jane Draycott, Jill Heather Flegg, Ursula L, Jos, Cowboy Diva, Robb, Joolya, Christopher Subich, hapax, Linda Coleman, Practicallyevil, Wesley Parish,

Margaret Yang, Sunlizzard, Lauren, Ecks, Michael Mock, Sheila O'Shea, Alfgifu, and everyone who falls into the category of "Anonymous."

At an important point, Tim and Joanna Harison recommended an essential book, *The Artist's Way* by Julia Cameron, which made a huge difference in getting over a pretty big crisis of confidence, so sincere thanks to them. Though I haven't met her in person, I'd like to thank Julia Cameron as well: it was good advice, I took it, and I'd recommend it.

My excellent friends have been great, so thanks to everyone: you're all fine people and a pleasure to know. I'd particularly like to thank Claire Bott, consultant on many things and stalwart ally; Peggy Vance, early reader and wellspring of confidence; and everyone else who encouraged me.

To my dear husband Gareth Thomas, for his suggestions, support, courage and faith, all my love.

And finally, I want to thank my family. When I wrote my first proper short story at eighteen, I showed it to my mother, knowing I could count on her for unqualified support. After that, I showed it to my father with some trepidation, knowing I could count on him to be frank. He read it, thought for a second, and said, "You could be a proper writer." For these things, and for so many others: love and thanks. I couldn't have done it without you.

## ABOUT THE AUTHOR

KIT WHITFIELD grew up in London. In her time, she has trained as a chef and a masseuse, as well as worked as a website editor, quote hunter, toy shop assistant and publisher. She is the author of two novels: *Benighted* and *In Great Waters*.

www.kitwhitfield.com/theauthor.html

ABOUT THE TYPE

This book was set in Granjon, a modern recutting of a typeface produced under the direction of George W. Jones, who based Granjon's design upon the letter forms of Claude Garamond (1480–1561). The name was given to the typeface as a tribute to the typographic designer Robert Granjon.

Whitfield, Kit.
In great waters

NOV - 2009